MW01118869

Never Forgotten

Kelly Risser

Clean Teen Publishing

PO Box 561326
The Colony, TX 75056

www.cleanteenpublishing.com

Content Disclosure

For more information about our content disclosure, please utilize the QR code above with your smart phone or visit us at

www.cleanteenpublishing.com.

Prologue

Meara, where are you?

I started to fall asleep when I heard Daddy's voice. At least, he told me he was my daddy. I'd never met him.

"Daddy?" I called in the dark. My throat felt funny, like when Mommy made me gargle with salt water when I had a cold. I held back a sneeze; a strange smell tickled my nose.

Meara, honey. I'm looking for you. Where are you?

He sounded far away. Why was Daddy sad? My stomach tightened, and my eyes welled with tears. "Where are you, Daddy?"

Silence. The pain vanished, quick as it came. He was gone. I jumped out of bed and ran to my mom's room.

"Daddy's so sad!"

I flung myself onto her bed and crawled up until I could wrap my arms around her. Burying my face in her neck, I breathed in the gardenia perfume she always wore. "He wants to see us, Mommy, but he can't find us," I mumbled against her skin.

My mom sat up, wrapping her arm around me. She whispered in my ear and stroked my hair. "It's okay, Meara. You just had a bad dream."

"I wasn't asleep." I raised my head and dared her to challenge me. She didn't say anything, but she looked funny. Was Mommy scared? My lip quivered. "Mommy, why isn't Daddy with us?"

"Oh, pumpkin." Mom sighed and leaned back against the headboard, her arm tight around me. "It's complicated. I love your father, and he loves us, but it just didn't work out. He can't be with us."

"Why not?" I searched her face, but she wouldn't meet my eyes.

"You won't understand, sweetie. I'll tell you when you're older."

All changes, even the most longed for, have their melancholy;
for what we leave behind us is a part of ourselves;
we must die to one life before we can enter another.
- Anatole France

Chapter 1

Present Day

"Meara, come visit the ranch. I'm sure Uncle Jake won't mind."

It was the second to last day of my junior year. I sat on the low, brick wall in front of Cedarburg High with my best friend, Kim. We were waiting for her boyfriend to pick her up. I didn't care for Mark. I kept my opinion to myself, so I wouldn't hurt Kim's feelings.

Kim would be working at her uncle's farm in Minnesota this summer. I was staying here. We wouldn't see much of each other, unless I visited her.

"I don't know, Kim," I said. "I'm scheduled to work most of the summer at the shop." My mom's friend owned a sewing and fabric store in downtown Cedarburg, Wisconsin. Mom and I both worked there. Rebecca and Mom taught classes, made quilts, and ran the store. I maintained the website and worked the cash register.

"You could get away for a week or two," Kim persisted. "Just ask your mom, Meara. You'll never know unless you ask."

"All right, I'll ask!" I laughed at her scolding tone. I said it to appease her, but the idea was interesting. Why couldn't Mom and Rebecca run the shop for a week or two without me? They did it during the school year.

"I'm heading home." I stood up and walked down the sidewalk. Mark pulled up to the curb in his crappy, old truck. There was no point exchanging words with him, so I avoided eye contact.

"Don't forget to ask!" Kim yelled after me.

I turned back and grinned. "Why do you think I'm leaving now?"

My smile slipped when I noticed Mark eyeing a group of freshmen girls. He exchanged meaningful looks with a tall blond. I wouldn't doubt if they hooked up at a party or something. Kim trusted him too much. When was she going to wake up and see him for the jerk he was?

"Mom? Hey, Mom, I'm home!" I yelled into the house as I always did, tossing my backpack on the bench in the front hall. When she didn't respond, I figured she wasn't home yet. Sometimes she stayed late to help Rebecca restock or change the window display. Heading to the kitchen to get a snack, I found Mom standing at the sink.

"What's for dinner?" I asked and kissed her cheek. Not waiting for an answer, I took a carrot off the cutting board and opened the refrigerator. I was so preoccupied in my search for something tastier than a carrot, that it took me a few minutes to realize she hadn't responded. I turned and looked at her. "Mom?"

She didn't respond. She washed the same dish over and over, staring out the window. What was going on? My mom was many things, but a daydreamer wasn't one of them. I walked over, placed my arm around her waist, and gave her a small squeeze.

"Meara!" She jumped and squealed. "You startled me. I didn't even hear you come in."

"Are you okay?" I asked. Her eyes were shadowed and sunken with dark circles. Mom never looked this exhausted. She was the most optimistic, dynamic person I knew. She exuded so much energy that she tired me out.

"Fine." She wouldn't meet my eyes. "Why do you ask?"

"Because I've been talking to you, and you didn't answer."

"Oh, sorry," she said. "I didn't hear you."

"Or notice when I kissed your cheek," I added.

She looked startled. "I guess I was lost in my own thoughts."

I touched her arm. "What's going on, Mom? You're not acting like yourself."

She smiled at me. My mom had a great smile, but this one worried rather than comforted me. It was fleeting, and it never reached her eyes. She touched my hair and motioned to a chair. "Honey, why don't you sit down? I need to talk to you about something."

Uh-oh. Whatever this was, it wasn't good. Mom sat first and waited until I was seated. She took my hands in hers, holding them tightly. It was painful. I resisted the urge to cry out or pull my hands away. She seemed to need the contact. We sat in silence while she clenched my hands, then she sighed and closed her eyes. Tears escaped in a trail down her cheeks.

"I saw Dr. Maxwell today." Her voice was so quiet that it took me a moment to understand what she said.

"Dr. Maxwell?" I was confused. Dr. Maxwell was my mom's oncologist; he treated her breast cancer five years ago. "Why didn't you tell me you had an appointment today?"

She sighed and touched my cheek, "I didn't want to scare you. I actually went in for some tests about a month ago, and he asked me to come back."

I couldn't believe that she kept this from me. "You're okay, right?"

When she tried to smile, her lips just quivered. She shook her head and began to cry in earnest. Big, wet tears slid down her pale cheeks. "Meara, he said the cancer is back. Only this time, he found it in my intestines, liver, and kidneys. This new growth is aggressive. 'Stage 4,' Dr. Maxwell called it."

I blinked back my own tears. While my mother, who was so strong, sobbed next to me, I thought about the first time she had cancer. I was in sixth grade, and the severity of her situation hadn't sunk into my twelve-year-old brain. Mom had been so strong, first going through a lumpectomy and then enduring months of chemotherapy and radiation treatments. She lost her hair and got so thin. I remember feeling each individual rib in her back when I hugged her. It was agonizing to watch the person I loved most in the world wither away in front of me. Thankfully, the treatments took effect, and she slowly got better. The doctor gave her a clean bill of health a year after her original diagnosis.

"You can fight it, right?" I asked.

"Dr. Maxwell recommends slowing the growth with chemotherapy and radiation." Mom composed herself a bit, wiping her eyes with the back of her hand. I followed her movements, and my eyes tracked the long, black streak her mascara left on her hand. After I handed her a napkin, she dabbed at her eyes and added, "He says surgery is not an option. It's too far spread."

"What does that mean?" I was angry now. Why would the doctor advise her not to operate?

Mom took a deep breath, and I sensed how much it pained her to say these next words. "If they open me up, I might never heal. My prognosis is six months to two years, perhaps a little longer with intense treatment."

It wasn't what I expected to hear. The horror of it made me jump from my chair and bolt into her arms with gut-wrenching sobs. "Oh, Mom. I don't want to lose you."

"Oh, baby, and I don't want to leave you." Mom held me tight, and we clung to each other and cried. Her body shook as she sobbed. I held her as tight as I could. I hoped to give her comfort and take my own in return. When we couldn't cry anymore, we simply sat together, each of us lost in our own miserable thoughts. After a while, Mom straightened up and pulled away. She wiped her face with another napkin.

"We'll make the most of our time together, okay?" Mom touched my cheek. "And, I'll do everything I can to fight this."

"Okay." Grabbing a napkin, I wiped my nose.

Mom patted my knee and stood up. "I'm turning in for the night."

I glanced at the clock. "It's not even six, Mom."

"I know," she said. "But I'm exhausted."

She looked at the vegetables on the cutting board and smiled apologetically at me. "I didn't get too far with the dinner preparations. If you are hungry, there are leftovers in the fridge or lunchmeat."

"I'll be okay, Mom," I said. "Thanks." I stood and kissed her on the cheek. "I love you."

"Love you too."

Once she left for her room, I put the vegetables away. I took out a container of leftover chicken salad and a Diet Coke, going in the living room to flop down on my favorite recliner. Aiming the remote control at the TV, I mindlessly grazed through the channels. I couldn't remember what was on that night. I barely noticed what I ate. I was seventeen years old, and my mom was all I had. What was I going to do?

I smelled the smokiness of bacon before my eyes even opened. Most weekday mornings were all about cereal and yogurt. We reserved hot breakfast for the weekend. Mom must have woken up early. I dressed fast and went downstairs.

I yawned as I came into the kitchen. "You're cooking?"

Mom smiled. Although her eyes were puffy, she seemed better. "I figured that I owed you one after bailing on dinner last night." She set a plate of scrambled eggs and bacon on the table. "Do you want some orange juice?"

"I can get it," I told her. "Go ahead and fix your own plate."

"All right. Pour me a glass, too, please."

We sat and ate in silence, but it wasn't uncomfortable. When we finished, Mom gave me a considering look. "I think it's time to introduce you to your grandparents."

"My grandparents?" I repeated. "Mom, I don't understand. You haven't talked to them in years."

"I thought about it last night," she continued. "Your grandparents are the only other family you have, Meara. When..." I gave her a look, and she corrected herself. "If I go, I don't want you to be alone."

"But don't they live in Canada?"

"Yes."

She looked at me expectantly, but I couldn't think of anything to say. Finally, I asked, "Are they coming here?"

"No," Mom said. "We're moving to Peggy's Cove."

"For the summer?" I'd never get to the ranch with Kim, and Peggy's Cove sounded boring. It was a fishing village in Nova Scotia. Super small and probably full of smelly, old people. I couldn't think of a worse place to spend my vacation.

Mom shook her head. "For good."

For good? My heart sank. "We can't move. All my friends are here! It's my senior year. I can't start over at a new school."

"Meara." Mom's voice took on that no-nonsense tone. "We're moving."

"But, Mom..." I whined, hating myself even as I did.

"No buts, Meara. I'm not giving you a choice. In two weeks, we'll be in Peggy's Cove." Her eyes filled with sympathy, but her voice remained firm.

"This is so unfair!" I was about to say more when I looked at my mom's pale face. Oh god. Unfair was the fact that she was dying. "Oh, Mom. I'm so sorry."

"I understand, Meara." Mom's voice softened. "I know this is hard for you. I wish there was another option."

Standing, I put my plate in the sink. I had to get out of here before I said something I'd regret. How could she move us to Canada and not even ask me first?

"I've got to leave for school," I said.

"Do you want a ride?" Mom asked.

"No thanks." I tried to keep my voice light. "I'd rather walk."

Slinging my backpack on my shoulder, I headed out the door. I barely noticed the walk to school. I was moving to Canada, where I knew no one. What kind of people were my grandparents? Would I like them? Would they like me?

My life was about to do a complete one-eighty, and I felt helplessly unprepared.

"Did you ask her?" Kim bounced up next to my locker before first period. When I stared blankly at her, she added in an exasperated tone, "About coming to my uncle's place?"

Instead of answering, I burst into tears. Kim's arm went around my shoulder. "Oh my God, Meara. What is it?"

"It's my mom," I sobbed. "Her cancer's back."

"How awful!" Kim hugged me.

"It's terminal." I closed my eyes as I said it.

"What?"

"She's dying, Kim." I bit my lip to hold back more tears. "She's dying." My voice shook as I repeated the words, bitter on my tongue.

Although Kim was a good five inches shorter than I was, she wrapped her arm around my shoulder. "I'm so sorry. Is there anything I can do?"

"That's not all," I whispered. Maybe if I said it quiet enough...it wouldn't happen. "We're moving."

"Where?" Kim looked bewildered. "When?"

"In a couple of weeks, I think," I said. "Mom wants us to move to Canada, so I can get to know my grandparents."

"You're moving to Canada for the summer?"

I met her eyes and felt miserable. "Not just for the summer, Kim. We're not coming back."

"What? No! What about our big plans for senior year?" Kim waved her hands in the air, and her curls bounced. The tears rolled down my face. I didn't know what to say. Kim slapped her hand over her mouth. "I'm such an ass! As if I should be worried about me with all you're dealing with. What can I do?"

"I don't know," I said truthfully. "I won't know anyone there. I'll be miserable."

"I'll come visit you," Kim said. "And, we're going to Europe, right?"

"Sure." I smiled weakly. Kim raised one blond eyebrow, her signature sign of skepticism, but then she linked her arm through mine and chatted about our European vacation plans to distract me. It worked. I listened to her, nodded occasionally, and felt myself relax. Everything was going to be okay. It had to be.

Chapter 2

Three days of sitting in a cramped car, counting semi-trucks until I lost count, eating greasy fast food, sleeping in uncomfortable beds in mediocre hotels, and we weren't even there yet. Not even close.

"Are you watching the exits, Meara?" Mom fiddled with the radio dial. She refused to let me play my music. Instead, I was stuck listening to whatever 80's station she found.

"I'm trying." Now that we were in Canada, most of the road signs just confused me. Why was everything listed in English and French? I smoothed the map across my lap. "Which one am I looking for again?"

"Meara." Mom sighed my name. "It's not that hard. Notre Dame du Lac, just think of the college or the church in France. Notre Dame, not that hard, right?"

Lucky for me, we were approaching a sign that listed the next four exits. I noted that the sought-after Notre Dame was only two away. "There, Mom." I pointed. "We should reach the exit in a couple minutes."

"Great," she said. "I'm starving."

A new song started, and Mom turned up the dial before I could stop her. It was Forever Live and Die—her favorite song by her favorite band. Unfortunately, I knew the song and didn't share the love. I remained quiet while she harmonized. She had a decent voice. I turned to watch her. The sun caught the copper highlights in her hair, and I saw the crinkles in the corner of her eye behind her tortoiseshell sunglasses. She looked happy. Content. I wanted to remember her that way forever.

While Mom registered us at the hotel and got the room key, I stayed in the car and thought about what I wanted to ask her at dinner tonight. I was less than thrilled about the big move to Canada. And I hadn't broached the subject of my grandparents. They scared me to death. What kind of people kicked out their only daughter because she got pregnant? Not the kind of people I wanted to know, let alone live with.

We had another day of solid driving left, and I needed to prepare myself for what was coming. Tonight was the night. I gave Mom some space the first couple of days on the road, but now it was time that I knew whatever there was to know. I wanted answers, and I was banking on the fact that she would be more open to talking about things now. Mentally, I prepared a list of questions—a long list.

The hotel was located in a nice, middle-class suburb, and there were several restaurants nearby to choose from. Mom liked Chinese food and noticed a restaurant near the hotel. When she suggested that we walk there, I agreed. Long legs and road trips were not friends. Plus, it was a balmy evening, and the sky was clear—the perfect night for walking.

Deep red, brocade tablecloths and shiny, ebony and gold accents filled the inside of the restaurant. A middle-aged Chinese couple smiled and greeted us. The woman led us to our table and introduced herself as Min. Mom asked for a glass of wine, and I ordered one as well. Mom shook her head at me. Can't blame a girl for trying, I thought, changing mine to a Diet Coke.

Mom read the menu, but I closed mine. I already knew what I wanted. Nothing said Chinese food like sweet and sour chicken and an egg roll. I ran through my mental checklist of questions again while I waited for her to decide, applauding myself for my patience. She finally set her menu down, and Min took our order. When she walked away, I fired off my first question. "Mom, why did your parents kick you out when you were pregnant with me?"

Her eyes widened. "They didn't kick me out. I left."

Seriously? This was news. So maybe not horrible, evil grandparents after all?

"Why would you do that?" I blurted, bewildered.

"I left when I married Phil." Phil was Mom's ex-husband. She married him when I was a few months old, and we lived with him in Chicago. We moved to Wisconsin when they divorced. Mom said Chicago wasn't big enough for both of them.

I shook my head. "I don't get it. That doesn't explain why we don't talk to them or visit them, or why they never came to see us…" I trailed off. Mom looked uncomfortable.

"Peggy's Cove is a small town, a simple fishing village," Mom said, and I sighed. Great, she just reinforced what I thought. How boring was my life going to be now? She continued, "My dad's a fisherman, and my mom stayed home and raised me. My pregnancy embarrassed them, especially since David left me—"

I interrupted. "Why did David leave?" My grandparents sounded like jerks, so I focused on my father. She never talked about him. I was surprised she mentioned him now.

I could tell she didn't like where this conversation was going. She paused to take a sip of wine, and then said, "He never planned to stay."

"Why'd you go out with him then?" I asked.

"Mmm," she murmured, eyes going soft. "I'm not sure I had a choice."

That was a funny answer. She seemed more open tonight. I could never get her to talk about him. Maybe she would now? "Mom, can you tell me about him? About David?"

She straightened in her chair. Looking at me for a minute, considering, she began. "I met your father the summer after I graduated, when I was eighteen. He was staying in town, helping at the docks for the summer, and I was working at the bed and breakfast where he happened to be staying. The first time I saw him, he took my breath away. He was so beautiful. I talked to him and found out that he was as smart and funny as he was good looking. He was so cultured and mature. I fell for him right away."

She paused to drink more wine, and I didn't want to interrupt her train of thought. I waited, and she continued. "Your grandparents didn't like him at all. They were leery of strangers. 'Outsiders' they called them. The fine citizens of Peggy's Cove see many people coming and going during the summer months. They're not fond of tourists."

She frowned and gulped the rest of her wine.

"You obviously loved him. Did he love you?"

Again, she seemed surprised by my question. "Meara, your father loved me. I know this for a fact. For a time, I think he loved me more than anything else in his life. But, David is not like other men. I couldn't hold him."

"What does that mean? Who leaves the woman he loves pregnant and alone?" A thought occurred to me, and I added before she could answer, "Did he even know about me?"

She worried her lip. "Of course your father knew about you. You weren't the reason he left." She squeezed my hand. It didn't reassure me. "Meara, your father stayed with me as long as he could. He picked your name, you know."

"No, I don't know. You never told me that before." I crossed my arms, and my foot twitched. Why had my mom kept all these things from me?

"I didn't?" Her brow creased.

"Mom," I said, "you never talk about him. Where did he go?"

Mom hesitated. "I don't know."

I couldn't tell if she was lying or not.

"Has he ever tried to contact you?" I pressed. "To come see us?"

"No. Never." Mom wouldn't meet my eyes. She was lying. She never lied to me. I decided not to call her on it, not wanting to fight with her tonight. Min brought our dinner. I pushed the food around on my plate, no longer hungry. I'd lost my appetite.

While I pretended to eat, Mom chatted happily, filling me with stories about her childhood and her best friend, Lydia. Her best friend she hadn't mentioned before today. I tapped my foot faster as I fought to stay calm. I nodded every now and then so she'd think I was listening, but my mind raced. Where was David, and why was Mom lying?

Chapter 3

"Meara? Meara, honey, wake up."

I opened my eyes to darkness. There were no streetlights, just the brilliant stars overhead. The car window was open, and a warm breeze caressed my face. I stared out, hoping to get a sense of where we were. I couldn't see far.

Though my vision floundered, my other senses sang. I smelled the salty tang in the air and felt a cool mist of water. The fragrant drops clung to my skin like a welcoming kiss. I breathed deeply, and my body absorbed the energy. It was a rush—better than a sugar high, better than caffeine—and unlike anything I'd ever experienced.

Home, I thought as a peace settled over me. I'm home. I shook myself and frowned. Where did that come from? The only "home" I'd ever known, or at least remembered, was thousands of miles away in another country.

My mom watched me. She started to frown. Before she could speak, I gave her a small smile and said, "So, we're here then?"

She relaxed and smiled back. "We're here. Welcome to Peggy's Cove, Meara."

It seemed surreal that we were in another country, even if the country was connected to our own.

"Sharon? Is that you?" A porch light backlit the silhouette of a woman. Floodlights followed, bathing the yard with brightness. The woman hurried closer, her crop of wavy, silver hair glinting in the light. This had to be my grandmother. She wore a nervous expression. There was no mistaking the resemblance between the three of us, although her face was wet with tears.

Next to me, Mom made a strangled noise. She jumped out of the car and ran over to her. "Mom!"

"Sweetheart," whispered my grandmother, her voice raspy from crying. "Welcome home." She squeezed Mom's hand, and they embraced. I got out of the car, staying by the door. After several teary minutes, both women wiped their eyes and blew their noses, almost simultaneously. Mom turned to introduce me. "Mother, I'd like for you to meet your granddaughter, Meara."

"Meara." She smiled warmly. "So nice to meet you."

"It's nice to meet you, too…uh, Grandmother." The last word felt strange on my tongue, formal and unfamiliar.

"Oh, none of that, child." She pulled me into a hug. "No formalities for me. Call me Grandma Mary. Everyone else does."

She was soft and smelled faintly of lilacs. I relaxed in her arms, finding it a pleasant place to be. She released me after one last squeeze.

"Sharon, pop the trunk. Let's get your bags inside."

When Mom opened the trunk, Grandma Mary pulled both bags out. As she walked away, she called over her shoulder. "Your father is at work. He should be home soon, but I made you dinner."

"Thanks, Mom." My mom took my hand. She didn't seem surprised that her mother carried both of our suitcases.

"I expected you'd be arriving late and, more than likely, hungry." Grandma Mary placed both bags on the porch and held the door open. "Come inside and make yourselves at home."

With the extra light, I could see that the house was modest, shingled in faded red cedar. The trim and shutters were white, while a screened-in porch faced the ocean. The flowerbeds along the front burst with color and fragrance.

Hurrying up the small step, I took the screen door from my grandmother. For an old lady, Grandma Mary sure moved fast. We crossed into the entryway, and my mouth watered. Something smelled savory and delicious. I licked my lips. Grandma Mary saw and laughed.

"Kitchen's right here," she called as she entered into a room just to the left of the front door. "Come in and have a seat." To my mom, she said, "I made your favorite."

Grandma Mary served up the food and placed it in front of us. I had no idea that chicken and dumplings was my mom's favorite meal.

After one bite though, I could see why. It was delicious, with chicken so tender that it melted in my mouth. Mom rolled her eyes and made funny noises as she ate. Grandma Mary watched us with an amused expression, her chin resting in her hands and her elbows propped on the table.

After dinner, we moved to the living room and talked about our trip. I was just about to ask if we could see our rooms when the front door banged open, and the fiercest man I'd ever seen walked in. His hair was steel gray, thick and windblown. It outlined a weathered, tan face. I wasn't a great judge of height, but he was easily six foot three. He frowned as he scanned the room. When his eyes settled on my mom, they softened. His mouth quivered slightly at the corners as he stood there.

My mom started crying again and biting her lip—a nervous habit of hers. Nobody moved. I looked back and forth between them. When I couldn't stand the tension any longer, my grandfather opened his arms. "Sharon," he choked.

"Dad!" Mom ran to him with a sob. He said nothing more, just held her close, bending his large frame to wrap her tightly in his embrace. I heard her muffled sobbing. When she stopped, he straightened up and fixed his piercing blue eyes on me.

"This is her?" he asked, nodding in my direction. "This is your Meara?"

I gulped. I couldn't help it; he was so intimidating. I felt myself blush under his gaze and struggled to meet his eyes. Mom wiped away her tears and smiled at me.

"This is my Meara," Mom said proudly. "Meara, meet your grandfather, Jamie."

I tried to smile, but I think it came out more like a grimace. "Hello," I managed to mumble. The expression on my face must have amused him, because he let loose a deep, rumbling laugh.

"Girl," he said, wiping his eyes. "You have nothing to fear from me."

He patted me firmly on the shoulder. I was sure he meant to be gentle, but the strength behind it made me wince. He turned his attention to my grandmother. "Mary, love, how about a big helping of whatever that is that I've smelled since I opened the door?"

Grandma Mary swatted my great beast of a grandfather on the arm. "Is your stomach all you can think about?" she chided. "Look at these girls; they're scarcely managing to stay awake."

Turning, she went into the kitchen, and we followed. She ladled a generous helping of chicken and dumplings onto a plate that could've been platter and set it before my grandfather. Once finished, she turned to us. "Come on, I'll show you to your room."

"Are we sharing?" I asked.

Grandma Mary laughed. "No. You get the porch. Sharon, you'll be sleeping in your old room."

"The porch?" I pictured lawn furniture and dying plants.

She patted my arm. "It's not so bad. We converted it to an all-season room a few years ago."

"I'll head off then. I remember where I'm going," Mom said. She kissed my cheek first, and then Grandma Mary's. "Goodnight."

Grandma Mary led me down the hall and pointed to the door on the right. "This is the bathroom. Only one in the house. I hope you don't dawdle."

One bathroom? Our house had two. Mom and I never shared. I thought about my morning routine—hair, makeup—and inwardly groaned. "I'll try not to."

When we reached the porch, she opened the door, stepping back to let me in. "I hope you like it. It's not much, but I imagine you'll enjoy the view."

The room was small, but airy. Large windows ran along the top half of all three outer walls. I approached the longest window, which faced the ocean. Although it was almost midnight, the moon reflected on the rocks and water below. By day, I would have an amazing view of the harbor. I turned toward my grandmother and smiled. "It's beautiful. Thank you."

Grandma Mary nodded. "Get your rest, child," she said. "I'm sure tomorrow you'll want to go exploring. It's a small town, but there's enough to see."

She closed the door behind her. Alone, I turned and took in my surroundings. My suitcase was already there, resting near the door. My grandmother must have brought it in while we were eating. The rest of our stuff was arriving by moving van. It would be another day or so before it got here. I had all my favorite things with me, so I didn't mind. Looking around, I wasn't sure all of my stuff would fit in this room anyway.

The lamp on the nightstand cast the room in a warm glow. The furnishings were sparse—a twin bed covered with a pale yellow quilt of faded daisies, a nightstand with the lamp, and a small dresser.

A framed picture on the dresser caught my eye. I walked over and picked it up. Why did my grandparents have a black and white picture of me? I looked closer and realized it was a photograph of my mom, probably taken when she was about my age. She laughed at the camera, looking young, happy, and ready to take on the world. I ran my finger lightly over her face.

I set the picture back down and bent to pick up my suitcase, grunting a bit from its weight. If I was going to travel to Europe someday, I needed to learn how to pack lighter. One week of lugging this bag around, and I was tired of it. I pulled out my pajamas and toiletries and went to use the only bathroom in the house.

I changed quickly, but took a few minutes to wash the travel grime from my face. It's good to be in a home and not another hotel, I thought as I climbed into bed. I was out almost as soon as my head hit the pillow. My last thought before drifting off to sleep was how clearly I could hear and smell the ocean from my room. It was almost like falling asleep outside on the beach.

I was walking along the shoreline. It was early dawn, and the sun barely skimmed the horizon. The world held in the silence, and I was alone. The stars twinkled in the fading night sky, and the pebbles caressed my feet, smooth and cold. I tasted brine and was tempted to lick the salt from my lips. A slight breeze teased along my skin, lifting strands of my hair.

It should have been peaceful, but I was restless. I moved as though an invisible force pulled me toward the ocean. The desire to dive in overwhelmed me. I quickened my pace toward the inviting waves.

My heart beat frantically in my chest. I needed to climb into the water, to feel the cool tide surrounding me, lifting me. Though I'd never swum in the ocean, I had no fear. The experience would bring me extraordinary joy.

I lowered myself onto one of the large boulders near the ocean's edge. The rock's surface was smooth and cool. Stretching out my leg until my toes touched the surf, I delighted when the water frothed around and over my bare foot. Millions of tiny bubbles ebbed and flowed over my toes. This was where I belonged.

Voices called to me. They were distant and faint. I scooted closer to hear them. Come in. Join us. When I tilted my head down and to the side to hear better, I noticed a person walking toward me. Who else was out at this time of the morning?

It was a man. He moved at a leisurely pace. His shirt was loosely buttoned and untucked, the sleeves rolled to his elbows. One hand held a leather jacket over his shoulder. He wore faded blue jeans, and his feet were bare. He was beautiful, with strong, distinct features and a lean build.

He continued to approach, his pace slow and unhurried. Stopping about three feet away, he smiled. I wasn't scared. He reached toward me, extending an open hand. I noticed that his fingers were slightly webbed, and—I looked down—his toes were webbed like mine. Curious about him as I was, I looked away toward the ocean, tempted to dive again. The pull was strong.

"Meara, you can't go in," he said. "It's too soon, and your mother needs you."

I heard his words, but I didn't understand them. His voice was a beautiful as his face, deep and melodic. I gazed at him in awe. The man appeared to be in his mid-twenties.

"Who are you?" I asked.

He didn't say anything at first, just stepped closer. I found myself comforted by his presence. When he reached out to touch my hair, I didn't move. He ran his hand gently along one side of my head and caressed my cheek in a gesture that was similar to my mom's. Letting his arm fall to his side, he smiled at me again.

"It's so good to see you," he said. "You look so much like your

mother." His voice was full of sadness. He watched me, his blue eyes holding mine.

"David?" I asked, and he nodded.

"Smart girl, you are your mother's daughter." He spoke with a bit of an accent, rolling his Rs. I couldn't place the gentle lilt. Irish, maybe? "Go back to sleep, Meara." He touched my arm, and my eyes grew heavy. "We will speak again soon."

I sat up in bed, fully awake, and glanced out the window. The dream was so real that I expected to see my father standing there in the flesh. The beach was empty. It was a dream, I thought, only a dream. And yet, I tasted salt on my lips and felt the dampness of early morning on my hair and clothes.

Shaking my head at my own fancifulness, I rolled onto my side. A quick glance at the clock on the nightstand told me it was only four, way too early to get up. But as I closed my eyes and tried to fall asleep, an image of a beautiful, barefoot man played in my mind and kept me awake.

Was it really David? And if so, was he here?

Chapter 4

I woke to the smell of coffee, cinnamon, and vanilla. My stomach growled in anticipation. What time was it? The last thing I remembered was tossing and turning. I sat up and looked out the window. The sky was clear, and the view unobstructed. The ocean looked wild, blue, and inviting this morning, the rocky beach deserted.

Just a dream, I told myself again. I stretched slow and deep. The bed was extremely comfortable. Overall, I loved my new room. Yeah, it sucked that I had to leave my friends, but it could be worse, a lot worse.

I picked up my phone and checked the time—8:05am. While I had it in my hand, I sent a quick text to Kim, letting her know we arrived. I could tell her the details later.

Throwing on jeans, my favorite t-shirt, and sandals, I headed to the kitchen. My mom and Grandma Mary were talking softly. Mom was updating her on the latest round of tests. Although I knew I shouldn't, I stopped out of sight a few feet away from the kitchen and listened. It didn't take long to realize I wasn't hearing anything I hadn't heard before. Still, why did Mom talk so freely to Grandma Mary when it took me the last three weeks to wring the information out of her? The answer was obvious. My mom saw me as a child. Sighing, I walked into the kitchen.

"Good morning!" Grandma Mary called cheerfully. She faced the hallway, leaning on the counter by the stove. She looked worried. Mom stopped talking.

"Please continue," I said, sitting down next to my mom and gesturing to them both. "Don't stop on account of me."

"It's all right," Mom said. "I've pretty much caught her up on everything."

"Did you sleep okay?" Grandma Mary asked as she rummaged in the refrigerator. She brought out bacon and orange juice. When I didn't answer right away, she looked at me. I shrugged, and Mom gave me the look. I couldn't tell them about my strange dream, so I came up with a non-answer that seemed to satisfy them both.

"The room is great," I said. "I like the waves."

"I've always liked that, too." Grandma Mary pulled out a frying pan. "I hope you're hungry."

"Starved," Mom and I said at the same time. We looked at each other, said, "Jinx," and then laughed. We had a habit of saying the same thing or finishing each other's sentences. Grandma Mary watched us, shaking her head with an amused expression.

"You're starved after that big dinner last night? Didn't you girls eat on the way here?" Grandma Mary laughed as she placed six thick slices of bacon in the pan. The cinnamon and vanilla I smelled earlier came from the huge, steaming stack of French toast already sitting on the table. Grandma Mary saw me eyeing it up and said, "Help yourself, Meara, before they get cold. The bacon will be done in a minute."

Mom slid the orange juice toward me, and I poured a tall glass.

"Sharon," Grandma Mary said, flipping the bacon. "Did you know that Lydia's oldest, Evan, is working with Jamie down at the docks this summer?" Her voice was nonchalant, but I smelled a setup. I raised an eyebrow at her, but she ignored me. Mom winked at me when Grandma Mary's back was turned, biting her cheek to keep from laughing. Very funny.

"Really?" My mom played along. "I had no idea. How old is Evan now?"

"Oh," Grandma Mary stalled. "I think he's only a year or two older than you, Meara."

I was being set up by my grandmother. The best approach when adults muddled was disinterest, so I did the shoulder shrug thing again and filled my mouth with syrupy goodness.

Grandma Mary took one look at my stuffed face and laughed, loud and merry. "Oh, I like her," she said to my mom, nodding at me. "She's a girl after my own heart. Food first, conversation later."

Mom smiled into her coffee and patted my knee. She knew all too well about my appetite. She picked at a piece of French toast and a slice of bacon. Grandma Mary watched her carefully. "I thought you were starving," she remarked dryly.

Mom shrugged off her concern. "My stomach is jumpy, that's all."

"Well, at least drink a little juice," Grandma Mary said, placing a glass of orange juice in front of her. I was about to ask her if she was going to sit and join us, when she grabbed a plate and loaded it up. We ate in silence, but it wasn't awkward. I was more relaxed than I'd been since Mom told me her news. I wasn't the only one looking out for my mom now. My grandparents would help. That knowledge lifted a huge burden from my shoulders. We could fight this together.

I finished my breakfast and took my plate to the sink. "Do you want me to clean up?"

"No," my grandmother scoffed. "I've got it. Why don't you and your mom go into town and check things out? I'm just going to clean up a bit in here, and then head out to the garden."

"Are you sure?" Mom hesitated. She hated leaving a mess.

"Yes, you girls go on." Grandma Mary practically pushed us out the door.

I was already dressed, so I followed Mom back to her room. Sitting on her bed, I talked to her while she got ready. "Where are we going?"

"I can tour you through town. You know, show you my old stomping grounds."

"Okay," I said. "Is there anywhere that we can wade in the ocean?"

Mom frowned. "I'm not sure. The Atlantic is cold and rough."

"It's almost July, Mom. Can we look into it anyway?"

"We'll see," Mom conceded. "Depends how much time is left after we've explored the town."

"Okay." I let it drop. The town held about fifty people. How long could the tour take? I figured we'd have plenty of time to play in the ocean.

"Are you ready to go?" Mom eyed my faded University of Wisconsin t-shirt. It used to be red, now it was a dusty pink. Didn't matter to me, it was super comfy. I wasn't dressed for a date, but who was I going to meet in this rinky-dink town?

"I'm ready," I said. She looked polished as usual. Her polo shirt was wrinkle free, and her khakis pressed. She even put on a bit of blush, although that may have been to give her some color. She was so pale with dark shadows beneath her eyes.

"Mom, are you feeling okay?" I asked. "We can always go another day."

"I'm fine," she said.

"Are you sure?"

"Meara...stop. I'm okay. Let's go out and have some fun."

Without another word, she grabbed her hat, sunglasses, and car keys, heading out the door. I had no choice but to follow.

Mom parked in front of a building. The engraved wood sign in front said it was The Cove Inn. The house was light blue with a brighter blue on the shutters. Pink flowers blossomed in white pots of various sizes scattered around the generous porch. A hanging swing made it look inviting, just the way a bed and breakfast should.

"Do you like it?" Mom asked.

"It's great," I said. "Is this the one your friend owns?"

"Lydia," Mom said, looking pleased that I remembered.

"Did you go to school together?" If she was Mom's best friend, why hadn't I heard about her until a few days ago?

"Lydia was four years older than me. We didn't see each other much at school. My mom worked for her mom, so we hung out on the weekends."

A middle-aged blond woman came around the house, carrying a watering can. She wore round, dark sunglasses, a large, straw hat, and gardening gloves. Her pace was unrushed and relaxed. When she noticed our car, she shaded her eyes with her hand to get a better look. Seconds later, she let out a joyful squeal, dropped the watering can, tore off her gloves, and came running toward our car, stopping outside of the driver's side window. "Sharon?" she shouted. "Is that you?"

Mom laughed and jumped out of the car. The two women hugged each other, hopping up and down like excited school girls before they pulled back to examine each other.

"Lydia," Mom said. "You look fantastic!"

Lydia struck a model's pose and grinned. "You know what they say about that fresh ocean air." She bent, lowering her sunglasses to look at me. "And this must be Meara."

"Yes," Mom said. "Meara, come out and meet Lydia."

I climbed out and went to stand by my mom. When Lydia extended her hand to me, I shook it, noticing that while she had fine wrinkles around her eyes and mouth, she was very pretty. Her eyes were a beautiful hazel, and she had a wide, full mouth.

"How is Darren?" Mom asked.

"After all these years, Darren's the same." Lydia laughed. I assumed Darren was her husband. "He's away right now on a business trip, but he returns on Wednesday. He'll be thrilled to see you."

"And the kids?" Mom inquired.

"Evan starts at the university in the fall. Can you believe it? He's working for your dad this summer, earning extra money for school." Lydia shook her head and added. "Somehow, he managed to finagle the morning off." Lydia turned her thoughtful gaze to me. "My daughter, Katie, is just a few months younger than you are. You'll both be seniors at Halifax West in the fall."

I nodded, mentally filing that away. It wouldn't hurt to have a friend before I started at a new school in a new country. I was already freaked out about the transfer. I'd gone to school with the same kids since kindergarten.

Lydia motioned toward the backyard, saying, "Evan's out back right now with his dogs if you want to say hi, Meara. I'm going to take your mother inside for a cup of coffee. We have a lot of catching up to do."

Mom and Lydia linked arms and walked up the front steps into the house, chatting away. I stood there, trying to decide if I should introduce myself to a stranger or follow my mom and her friend into the house, for what would probably be a boring conversation. I didn't make new friends easily. I met Kim in Kindergarten, and my few other friends I'd known just as long. I looked down at my faded t-shirt with regret. Why hadn't I worn something cuter today? On the other hand, what else was I going to do? Stand on the sidewalk and wait for my mom to return? Not only would that be pathetic, but also I had a feeling that she wasn't coming back any time soon.

You only live once, I thought with a shrug, walking in the direction Lydia had come from. Two colorful flowerbeds bordered the path. I wasn't a gardener, so I have no idea what kind of things were growing there, but they were pretty and smelled terrific. I wondered how well she knew my grandmother, who also loved gardening.

At the end of the path, I found a quaint, white picket gate. I opened it and walked into the backyard. It was larger than I imagined and overflowing with flowers and leafy ferns in large, glazed pots. A fountain gurgled happily in the corner, and several benches sat under shady trees. I was so busy taking in the landscaping that it took a moment before my eyes settled on Evan. When they did, I had to keep my mouth from dropping open. Wow. Hot. I patted my ponytail nervously and again regretted not taking a few more minutes to get ready. At least he was also wearing shorts, a t-shirt, and tennis shoes.

Evan didn't see me, so I leaned against the gate and watched him play with his dogs—some type of spaniel. One dog was brown and white, and the other was black and white. Their tongues hung out, and they jumped excitedly at his feet, waiting for him to throw a Frisbee.

He was about six foot tall with wavy, black hair that curled over his ears. Tanned skin, lean muscles, and strong hands that ended in long, graceful fingers. The only thing I couldn't see were his eyes, since he wore sunglasses.

Evan laughed as he threw one Frisbee after another. The dogs chased them down and brought them back. Each time they returned, he rewarded them with a vigorous ear scratching. After several rounds, the dogs begged for a bigger reward, flipping on their backs and presenting their bellies. Obligingly, he crouched down to pet them. Within minutes, the Frisbee throwing resumed.

"Ebb, come!" he commanded, and it was then that I noticed the black and white dog veering off toward one of his mother's beloved gardens. Obediently, Ebb turned and headed back.

"Let me guess, the other one is 'Flow'?" I called out, forgetting that I was trying to be invisible. He looked startled to see me. Then, that perfect mouth broke into a wide grin.

"Wow, great guess." He walked over, the dogs trailing behind him. "Most people think I'm saying 'Abe.'"

"Really?" I tilted my head. He stopped an arm's length away. His smile was amazing. When he flipped up his sunglasses, I saw that his eyes were blue. Not bright blue like mine, they were a deep, endless blue like the depths of the ocean, fringed in thick, dark lashes. I fought the urge to sigh. I had better be careful, or I was going to say something stupid. "It's the first thing that came to my mind."

He frowned. "I'm sorry, but should I know you?"

"Uh, no. Sorry," I stammered. "Your mom suggested that I just come back. I'm Meara."

"Ah." He nodded. "You're Jamie's granddaughter. I was wondering how I got lucky enough to have a pretty stranger end up in my backyard."

Did he just call me pretty? "You work for my grandfather, right?" I managed to sputter once I got over the pretty comment. I wasn't comfortable around guys my age, especially cute ones. The ones back home hadn't paid much attention to me, and here was Evan, totally hot, complimenting me.

"For the summer, I do. Earning some extra cash for college." He gestured toward the house. "I take it that my mom's holding your mom captive?"

I laughed and conceded, "Something like that."

Ebb and Flow, their bodies quivering with barely restrained excitement, sat at Evan's side. When I crouched down to pet them, they met me halfway, covering me with cold, wet noses and doggy kisses.

"Ebb! Flow!" Evan scolded.

"It's okay. I don't mind." I scratched them generously behind the ears, and then knelt to rub their bellies when they rolled over.

"What kind of dogs are they anyway?"

"Springer spaniels. They're littermates."

"They're beautiful," I said, petting them one last time before standing up. "How did you come up with their names?"

He shrugged. "I guess, living by the ocean and all...I was fourteen when I got them. I thought the names were kind of catchy."

"I think they're clever." He rewarded me with another crooked smile. Neither of us spoke. Heat built in my cheeks again. Lydia opened the back door, sparing me from further embarrassment.

"Are you ready for some lemonade?" she called.

Evan smiled at her. "No thanks, Mom. I need to go to the docks. I promised Jamie I'd help out for few hours today."

"I thought you had the morning off?"

"No rest for the wicked," he chimed, winking at me. I smiled weakly.

Lydia gestured to me. "Come inside, Meara. I'll pour you a glass and show you the house."

Was I relieved or disappointed? At least I hadn't said anything too stupid yet. "I'll see you later, Evan."

"Feel free to stop by any time." He even looked like he meant it. I watched as he walked toward the garage, Ebb and Flow following at his heels. He turned and sent them to the house, catching me watching him. I blushed, hurrying to the back door. Lydia held it open as I stepped into the hallway. The house was cool and inviting. It smelled spicy and floral. The dogs brushed against me, as they ran down the hall and turned left at the end.

"Their food and water bowls," Lydia said, by way of explanation.

As we walked from the hall into the living room, I paused to look around. The room was a deep purple and accented with an eclectic blend of antiques and comfortable furnishings. It was the kind of room that made a person long to grab a book and cozy into the oversized couch for a several hours. I spotted the source of the smell—a few candles flickered on the fireplace mantel. The effect was pleasant.

"If I were a tourist," I said, looking around, "I'd definitely stay here."

Lydia laughed, leading me out of the room. "That's quite an endorsement after seeing only one room, but thank you all the same."

The next room was the kitchen, painted creamy beige with warm cherry cabinets. My mom sat at one end of a wide, polished table with a large vase of fresh flowers at its center. Their fragrant blossoms filled the air with a light perfume, which mingled with the smell of coffee.

"Have a seat, Meara. Make yourself at home." A glass pitcher of lemonade sat on the table. Lemon slices even floated in it. Lydia handed me a glass before sitting down.

I pulled out a chair and took the seat next to my mom. "So, what were you two talking about?" Mom and Lydia exchanged looks and giggled. Actually giggled. It was weird to see my mom acting like a kid. I raised my eyebrow at her. She tried to look serious, but failed.

"Oh, a little of this and a little of that," said Mom.

"Reminiscing about the good ol' days," Lydia added. Somehow, that set them off on another fit of laughter.

I drained my glass and stood up. "Do you mind if I look around?"

"Go ahead. There aren't any guests here right now. Feel free to wander."

I left the women in the kitchen to continue their glory day's conversation, grateful that I didn't have to sit and listen. I walked back through the room with the candles and down the hallway where the dogs had gone. To the left, there was a small laundry room. The dogs stretched across the cool, tile floor, paws twitching as they slept. Across the hall, there was a dining room. The deep navy, burgundy, and gold color scheme complemented the colors in the spicy room.

Four doors remained. Three were guest rooms, and the last had to be the master bedroom. A wedding picture hung on the wall, the bride clearly Lydia. A picture of Evan sat on the dresser. It looked like his graduation picture. The other picture was of a pretty, blond girl.

I remembered passing a staircase near the kitchen. I went back and climbed up. Two more guestrooms were upstairs, one on each side of the hall. At the end, there was another door. It led to two more bedrooms that shared a bathroom. By the looks of the rooms, they belonged to Evan and his sister. I wanted to linger a bit, but it felt strange, and I certainly didn't want anyone catching me up there. Closing the door, I went back down to the kitchen.

"What'd you think?" Lydia asked.

"It's really nice," I said. She smiled at me.

"Are you ready to go, Meara?" Mom asked. She looked tired, her eyes tight with pain. She must have another migraine. She suffered from them frequently, and driving the majority of the trip could have triggered it. I should have pushed to drive more, but Mom insisted. Apparently, my driving scared her. Not sure why.

Lydia watched Mom with concern. "Are you okay?"

"Just a headache," Mom said.

When Lydia continued to frown, I felt compelled to reassure her. "I'll take her right home so she can rest."

Mom looked surprised. "What about the rest of the town?"

"I can see it later. Oh, and I'm driving us back." I took the keys from her.

She didn't protest as I led her outside and helped her into the passenger side seat. Lydia followed us to the door. I looked back to see her hugging herself, watching us. How hard would it be to lose your best friend after just rediscovering her again? I thought about Kim—moving here was like losing her. I returned Lydia's wave before we pulled away, my eyes drifting to the rearview mirror and scanning what I could see of the backyard. It was empty.

Mom closed her eyes and rested as I drove back to the house. Good thing I paid attention this morning when we left. It was no problem to find.

"We're back," I said. When she opened her eyes, at least she had a little color in her cheeks. "Feeling better?"

"Not really," she said. "I'm going to go lay down for a while."

Mom walked back to her room. The house appeared to be empty. I looked around, but Grandma Mary wasn't there. Eventually, I found the note that she left on the fridge that said she was running errands. Now what? I didn't want to read, had no interest in watching TV, and was too restless to just relax. I could go for a walk but, admittedly, I was lazy. I grabbed the car keys and headed out.

This time, I took the full tour of the town. It lasted about five minutes. There was a grocery store, a few small restaurants, and a couple of shops marketed toward tourists. No music store, no bookstore, no mall, no movie theater, not even a McDonalds—I didn't grow up in a booming metropolis, but this was ridiculous.

My stomach rumbled loudly, reminding me that it was lunchtime. A restaurant called Peggy's Place looked promising, so I parked and walked to it. The restaurant appeared to be a favorite with the locals. It was shortly after two o'clock in the afternoon, and the place was packed. Three older men sat at the far end of the counter, their empty plates in front of them. The man furthest away from me stroked his long, gray beard with one hand and held his coffee mug out for a refill with the other. He was exchanging niceties with the waitress, who looked about my age. The other two glanced at me curiously. After a moment, they turned back to continue their conversation.

"Can I help you?" the waitress asked me, not missing a beat on the coffee refills. She was pretty in a blond kind of way, with large blue eyes. She kept her hair pulled back into a long, straight ponytail.

Something about her had me asking, "Do I know you?"

"I don't think so." She frowned slightly. "Did you need help with something?"

"Oh, sorry," I apologized. "I just came in here for lunch."

"Well, you came to the right place." She gave me a friendly, open smile. A dimple appeared on her left cheek. "Welcome to Peggy's Place. I'm Katie."

"Katie," I repeated. Now I knew where I had seen her before—the picture on Lydia's dresser. "Are you Katie Mitchell?"

She looked at me curiously. "Yes. Who are you?"

I extended my hand. "I'm Meara."

"Should I know you?" She shook it, but looked confused.

I felt my face flame up. "I'm such an idiot. I met your mom and brother this morning. My mom is Sharon Quinn."

"Okay." Katie smiled, relaxing a bit. "I get the connection now."

"Sorry," I mumbled, hoping she didn't think I was a total nut job.

"Let me show you to your seat." She grabbed a menu and walked into the crowded dining area. "There's a table and a booth. What do you prefer?"

"The booth is great," I said. "Thanks."

She handed me the menu, saying, "Specials today are turkey chili and double bacon cheeseburgers. If you want my opinion, try the buffalo chicken club."

"Sounds great," I said. "Can I get a Diet Coke, too?"

"You bet."

As I waited for my food, Katie checked on the other customers. Sitting there, I started thinking about what I should do after lunch. A short distance off the main road, there was a lighthouse. I'd never been to one, so I figured it would be fun to see.

Fifteen minutes later, Katie set my plate in front of me. To my surprise, she slid into the other side of the booth instead of walking away. "Where is everyone?"

"Everyone?" I asked, confused.

"Your mom? Grandma Mary?"

"You know my grandmother?"

"Sure." Katie smiled. "Everyone knows Grandma Mary."

"My mom's got a migraine, so she's resting. Grandma Mary left a note about running errands."

Katie nodded and snuck a fry off my plate. "My shift ends in a half hour. Do you have plans for the afternoon?"

Was she serious? She looked like she was waiting for an answer, so I replied, "I thought about going to the lighthouse. I've never seen one before."

"If you wait," Katie said, "I'll take you to the lighthouse and show you around a bit. It'll be 'Katie's Famous Five-Minute Tour'."

"Famous?"

"Infamous," she added, and I laughed.

She stood and grabbed another fry. I had yet to try anything on my plate. "Okay, so it's a little longer than five minutes. Maybe ten, fifteen at most. I've got a few more tables to take care of, and then we'll be off."

"Sounds great," I said, finally lifting my sandwich to my mouth. The time passed quickly as I ate. Katie stopped by between tables to chat. By the time we headed out the door, I was completely at ease.

"You don't mind walking, do you?" Katie asked. "Peggy's Point is just a little south of town. It'll be a better tour if we walk."

"I don't mind," I said. "How far can it be?"

"It's not far." Katie nudged my arm, startling me. "Look, there's Evan. Hey, Evan!" She waved at her brother, and he raised his hand in reply. He was at a bait and hardware shop across the street, probably running an errand for my grandfather. Katie caught me staring at him.

"Not you, too," she groaned dramatically.

"What?" I asked.

"Okay," she said. "Play coy." She nodded toward Evan. "That guy?

My brother? Almost every girl at our high school has crushed on him. Disgusting."

It figured that I wouldn't be the only one to notice his hotness. I tried to be casual when I asked, "Is he with anyone now?"

"Nah." She stared walking, so I followed alongside. "He dated Jessica Alston, but they broke up in May."

Relief, pure and sweet, filled me. In demand was one thing, but available at least meant I had a slight chance. A slight chance in hell was better than none at all.

"Do you have a boyfriend?" I asked to change the subject.

"Not right now," she said. "I was dating this guy from Halifax, but we broke up about a month ago. It was dying a slow death anyway. Frankly, I'm relieved. This summer, I'm concentrating on earning some cash so I can get out of here after graduation."

"That bad?" I sympathized with her. I couldn't imagine living my whole life in a town this small.

Katie kicked a stone. "Yeah, that bad."

A town this small seemed like it could make you feel like you were slowly suffocating. Based on the local folk mingling about today, I figured the median age was around sixty. That didn't equate to good times.

"I'm thinking of heading to Europe, you know?" Katie continued. "Maybe take a year off and go backpacking."

"Really? My best friend and I were planning the same thing. This was going to be the year we started planning everything out, but then my mom got sick and…"

She touched my arm briefly. "Your mom is sick?"

"Yeah," I said, regretting that I brought it up. "Cancer."

She looked me in the eye. "Want to talk about it?"

I shook my head, and we continued to walk in silence. A few minutes later, Katie nudged me with her shoulder. "I'm sorry about your mom."

"Yeah," I said. I swallowed the lump that formed in my throat. Thankfully, she understood and didn't push me to talk. "Me too."

We came around a bend, and the lighthouse came into full view. Tourists mingled on the grounds in front, and the waves crashed against the surrounding rocky shore.

"Wow," I said. "Cool."

Katie stood next to me, covering her eyes with her hand to shade the sun. "The view's not too bad."

We walked around the grounds, and I took a few pictures with my phone. I'd send one to Kim later. The water churned below, and I moved to get a better look. Unlike the beaches I'd seen in photos, this shoreline was all rocks worn smooth by the rough waters. I stepped on some gravel and slipped.

"Careful." Katie caught my arm and pointed to one of the signs posted randomly throughout the area, warning tourists of high-wave dangers.

"Have people been hurt here?"

"It's been known to happen." She stood next to me and looked down. "Someone gets too close and, whoosh! They're dragged out to sea. Usually, they're rescued."

"Usually?"

"It pays to read the signs," she said solemnly.

Noted. This was not the place to go for a swim.

When I got back to my grandparents' house, it was almost six o'clock. After Katie finished showing me around, I offered to drop her off at home. I felt a little guilty about not calling, because I saw that the movers were there. They were in the process of unloading all of our stuff. Mom sat in a chair, an ice pack on her forehead, watching the progress. Grandma Mary walked beside one of the surlier-looking men, discussing where she wanted a particular piece of furniture placed in the house. She seemed a bit frazzled, and I thought she was worried about whether our possessions would fit. I kind of wondered the same thing myself.

I walked over to my mom and perched on the arm of her chair, leaning in and hugging her briefly. "The migraine is bothering you?" I asked as casually as I could.

She smiled up at me and patted my arm. "It's better. Thanks.

32

Where were you all afternoon?"

"I wandered into town, grabbed lunch, and then walked to the lighthouse with Katie."

She nodded, but I could tell she wasn't really listening when all she said was, "That's nice."

I watched the movers a little longer, growing bored. In the distance, a few dark clouds moved in, and the wind picked up. It looked like I was in for my first storm in the Cove. Hopefully, the movers would be done before it broke.

On her next trip in, Grandma Mary stopped in front of me. "You hungry?"

"Not really," I said. "I ate a late lunch. Sorry for not calling."

She waved her hand. "Don't worry about it. I was just going to tell you that I didn't make anything anyway. There are some leftovers in the fridge, if you do get hungry. Your mom already ate."

"Thanks, Grandma Mary," I said. She hurried toward the movers. Mom shivered a little, so I took her hand. It was ice cold. "C'mon, Mom. Let's head inside. The movers have this under control."

A little while later, I carried two mugs of hot chocolate into the living room and handed one to my mom, who was curled up on the couch. I sat down and snuggled up next to her, resting my head on her shoulder. She smelled like shampoo and her favorite perfume. The familiar scents relaxed me. "Can you tell me more about David?" I asked, closing my eyes and listening to the soft buzz of the television in the background.

She was quiet for so long that I didn't think she was going to answer. In fact, I wondered if she even heard me. Another minute passed, and then Mom kissed the top of my head and started talking. "I'll tell you about the first time I met him. I remember it was a Thursday morning. When I showed up for work at the Cove Inn, Lydia was positively glowing. She told me about a guest who had arrived the night before. She insisted that I had to meet him. I was curious, but I didn't think too much about it. Lydia was the beautiful one. If he were interested in either of us, it would definitely be her. It didn't even seem to matter that she was married. Guys hit on her all the time."

I could relate. Kim was flirty and outgoing. Whenever guys were around, she was the one who always got the attention. I never really minded though. It took the pressure off me. Mom took a sip of hot chocolate and then continued. "A few hours later, I was vacuuming the hallway when I met David for the first time. He smiled and told me good morning, but I was too stunned to speak. He chuckled then, amused at my awkwardness, and asked me if I had plans for dinner. He asked me on a date, just like that. I finally managed to shake my head no, that I didn't have plans. He smiled then, and said he would meet me out front at five."

"You had your first date that same night?"

She nodded. "Yes, and we were together the rest of the summer. In my wildest dreams, I never thought someone as beautiful as David would be interested in me, especially over Lydia. But, he was. To Lydia, he was cordial, but he only had eyes for me."

As my mom talked, I absentmindedly fingered the necklace that lightly rested on my collarbone. It was a gold sand dollar, and I never took it off. My mom gave it to me on my tenth birthday. She noticed and touched it with her finger, saying, "David gave that to me, you know. Besides you, it was the one thing I had to remember him by."

That was the first time I heard that, so I asked, "Why did you give it to me?"

She looked at the necklace again before responding. "I always knew that he meant it to be yours."

I thought maybe that was all she was going to say about David for the evening, but she seemed to have made up her mind that it was time for me to know more. She settled more comfortably into the couch. I got comfortable, too, and then she began to talk again.

"Even that first night, I knew there was something special about David. He consumed my thoughts. I wondered when I would see him next and where we could escape to be together. He didn't seem to have a real purpose for being in Peggy's Cove. Sure, he helped at the docks, but he would also disappear for days at a time. Whenever I asked him about it, he carefully evaded my questions. He never lied to me, but I knew there were things he wasn't telling me."

"Like what?" I asked.

"Well, he said he couldn't stay forever, and he was careful not to make any promises. It didn't concern me at the time. From the moment I met him, he was everything to me."

I wondered where she was heading with this story. When she first started talking, it sounded like your typical boy meets girl, boy asks girl out, boy and girl fall in love story, but it was heading in a new direction. I waited for her to say more, not wanting to break the spell.

"When he was around, we were inseparable. His passion about the sea, about history, about art, about so many things, was contagious. We talked late into the night, and I often felt like I knew him better than I knew myself. But there was something there; something that I couldn't put my finger on. I knew he was hiding it from me. He was mature beyond his years, had too many experiences for someone in his early twenties, and had a wilder, more primitive side than any boy I had known before."

She stopped and gave my shoulder a squeeze. I smiled at her in a way that I hoped was encouraging. It worked. She continued her story. "The logical side of me knew I should be careful, but my heart wouldn't let me. I was recklessly, wildly in love. By the end of summer, I realized I was pregnant with you."

"What did you do? Did you tell him?"

"Of course. He was surprised. Happy, I think, but reminded me that he couldn't make any promises."

"And then he left you?"

"Not right away. He stayed as long as he could."

"Why couldn't he stay?" I asked.

She looked at me, tears shining in her eyes. "I don't know."

I wanted her to say more. I knew the story was incomplete. She knew why my father left and chose not to tell me. I wasn't sure how I knew that. I just did. I couldn't push her. Not tonight, when I could see the migraine pained her and she looked so frail, so worn. Instead, I kissed her.

She touched my check and gave me a faltering smile. "I wouldn't change it, Meara. I want you to know that. If I had to do it all again, I wouldn't change a thing."

"I love you, Mom."

At that moment, my grandmother came in the front door. "Movers are all done and on their way. I'm amazed we—" She paused when she saw us. "Everything okay in here?"

"Fine," Mom and I said at the same time. Grandma Mary looked at us a moment, and then sighed. "Well, if you girls are okay, then I'm going to head back to my room do a bit of sewing."

"We're good, Mom," my mom said.

Mom and I continued to cuddle on the couch, eventually finding an old horror movie to watch. We loved the classics. This one was with Vincent Price. When the movie ended, I went to bed. I thought for sure I would dream of David that night, but I slept in peace.

Chapter 5

It was Friday, July 1. I powered up my laptop to work while the house was quiet. I promised Rebecca I'd maintain the Sew Beautiful website until she could find someone else. Sure, there were companies that would do it for her, but none as cheap as I was. Plus, after helping at the shop, I knew the business pretty well. The site looked good; I changed the main page to feature three fall projects and updated a broken link in the resource section. I e-mailed Rebecca a summary of my work and asked if anyone reported problems. Since online sales were far surpassing those at the store, I knew it was important to keep things easy to find and updated for her customers.

Once I finished work, I e-mailed Kim, attaching the picture of the lighthouse. She hadn't replied to my first one yet, but I wasn't surprised. She told me the internet connection was terrible at her uncle's ranch.

It was time to tackle the stack of boxes the movers left in the corner of my room. I could arrange the room to my liking. Not that I minded my grandmother's decorating, but it was always nice to be surrounded by your own things. Opening a box, I got started unpacking and decorating.

"Meara?" Mom popped her head in my room. "Did you want some lunch? It's just you and me, kiddo."

"Where are Grandma Mary and Grandpa Jamie?"

"At a barbecue."

"You didn't want to go?"

Mom made a face. "Head hurts."

Now that she said it, I noticed her pale face and bruised eyelids. "I can get lunch," I said.

"Are you sure?" When I nodded, she gave me a small, tired smile.

"Then I'm going to go and lay down again. Try to kick this thing once and for all."

"Do you want me to bring you something?"

"No thanks, hon. I'll eat later." She turned to leave, and then looked back. "By the way, your room looks nice."

"Thanks." I looked around, pleased with my progress. It was starting to feel like my room. It was a decent place to break, so I went to the kitchen and searched the fridge and cabinets. It was my first time in the kitchen without Grandma Mary there. I took advantage. The kitchen was well stocked, but I didn't feel like cooking. I settled on a turkey sandwich, chips, and a Diet Coke. I was rinsing off my plate when the doorbell rang. Who was here?

I ran to get the door. If Mom fell back asleep, I didn't want whoever it was to wake her. Opening the door, I found Katie and Evan. What was I wearing? Oh yeah, jean shorts and a tank top. Did I put on makeup this morning? Yep. Relax.

Evan looked as hot as I remembered. He wore cargo shorts and a polo shirt. He smelled good, too. It reminded me of fresh air and herbs. He leaned against the doorframe, keys in hand.

"Um, hi," I said. "What's up?"

"Mind if we come in?" Katie asked as she proceeded to walk around me. She looked around the room. "Did the movers come?"

"Yeah," I said, wondering why they were here. "Yesterday."

"Thought so. There's more furniture now. Looks nice."

"Um…thanks." I watched as Katie tried out the leather recliner from our old house. She leaned back in the chair and smiled at me.

"Katie," Evan drawled from the doorway, clearly amused at his sister. "Maybe you'd like to tell Meara why we're here…"

My face flared with heat. Would I ever be able to control that?

"Grandma Mary called this morning," Katie said from the chair. "Asked what we were doing. She said you were home unpacking and might need a break."

"I'm pretty much finished. What's up?"

"We're heading into Halifax for the festivities." Katie stood and smoothed the hem of her sundress. "Do you want to come with us?"

"Sorry for just dropping in," Evan added. "I thought Katie called first."

"Whatever, Evan." Katie rolled her eyes at him before she winked at me. "You might want to grab a jacket or something. It'll probably cool off a bit later tonight."

"Um," I mumbled. "I'm not sure…I don't know if I should leave my mom alone…"

Katie peered across the empty living room. "Where is she?"

"Sleeping. The migraine's bothering her."

"Still?" Katie asked.

I nodded. "Sometimes they last a few days."

"It's okay if you don't want to go," Evan said.

The problem was that I really wanted to go. Should I leave Mom alone? What if she got worse? On the other hand, Grandma Mary did tell Katie and Evan to come over and get me.

"No, I'll go." I would leave a note for Mom in the kitchen. She could call my cell phone if she needed me. She might even be awake. "Be right back."

"We'll wait for you in the car," Evan said as I went to grab a coat. I was going to have to keep a close eye on my grandmother. She seemed to like to meddle. She could have given me some notice. I would have spent more time getting ready and less time unpacking. On the other hand, I was going to hang out with Evan. Right, Evan. Definitely called for more makeup. I stopped by the bathroom and added a bit of shadow and lip gloss, tossing the tube of gloss in my purse. On my way back down the hall, I checked on Mom.

"Mom?" I whispered. She didn't respond. Her back was to me, but she appeared to be asleep. I jotted a quick note in the kitchen and left it in the middle of the table.

"What took you so long?" Katie teased as I climbed in the backseat.

Before I could answer, Evan spoke. "What are you talking about, Katie? She was ready way sooner then you ever are."

Katie stuck out her tongue. Evan ignored her.

"I hope you don't mind," Evan addressed me through the rearview mirror as he started out of the driveway, "but we're meeting up with some other kids."

"It's kind of a tradition," Katie added. "Just some friends from school."

"No problem," I said, although I wondered how many others would be there. I didn't do well with crowds.

The drive to Halifax took about twenty minutes. Along the way, Katie peppered me with questions. I wanted to hear more about Evan, but in the end, all I could do was answer Katie. Where did I grow up? What was it like back home? What were my friends like? What did we do for fun? She went on and on.

"Katie," Evan said after about the fifteenth question. "Give the girl a break!"

Katie pouted. "What else are we going to talk about?" She crossed her arms and turned to stare out the window.

When the silence ensued, Evan glanced in the mirror at me. "Thank you," I mouthed when I caught his eye.

"Welcome," he mouthed back.

We circled the parking lot a few times to find a spot. Beyond the building, which looked like a police station, I could see a Ferris wheel and a few other carnival rides. When I opened the car door, I smelled cotton candy and French fries. From the sound of things, at least two bands were playing. Rock n' roll and country battled for volume, but they mingled pretty well together.

Katie hooked her arm through mine and pulled me along. "We're meeting everyone by the midway." Evan trailed behind us.

Katie started waving as soon as she spotted her friends. A few waved back, so I knew where we were headed. There were four girls and three guys. It was a pretty big group, but I'd manage. Katie gave my arm a quick squeeze before letting go.

"Hi everyone," she said. "This is my new friend, Meara. She just moved here."

A couple of kids muttered "hi" and a few waved. Katie introduced each of them, not that I would remember their names. The two girls standing closest to Katie—Val and Jen—seemed nice enough. From the way the three of them talked, I guessed they were best friends.

"So, where should we start?" Jen asked.

The general consensus was food first, so we hit the concessions. Evan walked next me and leaned toward my ear. "Sorry about my sister in the car," he apologized. "She can be a little overpowering."

"It's okay," I said. "I'm sure I'll get used to it."

He laughed. "Really? When you learn the secret, let me know. I've been trying to figure her out for seventeen years."

I thought maybe he would walk up next to his friends, who were leading the way, but he stayed at my side. One of the two other girls, I couldn't remember her name, but she was a tall, skinny redhead, tried to get Evan's attention. She asked him about hockey, and if he was playing in the fall.

"You play hockey?" I asked him. I realized I knew very little about him yet.

"He was the captain of the team last year," the girl said as she smiled up at him and batted her eyelashes. *Try a little harder*, I couldn't help thinking.

"I play," he said. "I'm not sure if I'll play in the fall or not."

"You have too!" Flirty girl actually stomped her foot. I bit my lip to keep from laughing. She was too much. Evan caught my eye, and I knew he was thinking the same thing.

"How about pizza, guys?" Katie called back. Based on the murmurs of consent, we walked toward a pizza vendor.

"I want fries first," Evan said. "How about you, Meara? Do you like fries?"

"Of course. Who doesn't?" I was waiting for the redhead to gush about her love of fries, but she had already lost interest in Evan, flirting with one of his friends instead.

"You go ahead," Evan said to Katie. "Meara and I will meet up with you all."

Katie raised her eyebrow, but didn't say anything. The group walked off, leaving us alone. He took my hand and pulled me in the opposite direction from their friends. "I saw fries back this way."

There was a long line, but we got in it anyway. Next to the booth was a lemonade stand. One of those that advertised it was made with real lemons and fresh squeezed. That was always the first stop for Mom and me at the State Fair. Although, over time, the fresh squeezed gave way to freshly tapped. The last time we went, we joked that the only squeezed part was the lemon garnish that they added at the end to make it seem authentic. I hoped Mom was feeling better. I should have left her a sandwich or something.

"Are you okay?" Evan asked. I realized that I must have been frowning.

I smiled at him. "Sure. Why?"

"You just looked upset." He studied my face, and I wanted to squirm.

"Do you want lemonade?" I changed the subject. I didn't want to talk about Mom.

"Okay."

"I'll get it while you wait for the fries," I said.

Evan reached for his wallet.

"I got it," I said.

He shook his head. "Let me pay."

"Thanks." My cheeks burned as I took his money. Was this a date? I wasn't used to guys paying for me either. On the other hand, I might not have been able to use my money. I only had American bills. I needed to get it converted to Canadian money.

The lemonade line was much shorter. When I returned with a cup in each hand, Evan had five more people in front of him. "Do you want to find us a place to sit?" he asked, motioning to the area behind the vendor's trailer. I could see tables and chairs under a large tent.

"Good idea."

The seating area was crowded and, at first, I didn't think I would find an open table, but an older couple looked like they were cleaning up empty plates.

"Is this table available?" I asked them.

The woman smiled sweetly at me. "Yes, dear. It's all yours."

I thanked them and set the lemonades down. Before I sat, I turned my chair to watch for Evan, so I could stand and wave if he didn't see me. There was no need; he spotted me right away.

"I didn't think I'd ever get through that line," he said as he sat down. I looked at the plate he set on the table.

"What's that?"

"Fries." He gave me a strange look. "You did want fries, right?"

"What's on top?" The fries were covered with globs of cheese and some kind of brown sauce. I'd never seen anything like it.

"It's Poutine," he said, as if that explained everything.

"The 'poo' I get. Looks like the diapers I changed babysitting."

He laughed and nudged the plate at me. "Try it."

"How do you eat these things?" I didn't see how I could pick up a fry without getting covered in messy goo.

"With a fork." He handed me one. I could tell he was trying not to laugh.

"Thank you." I delicately stabbed a fry with cheese. They were both covered in the sauce. With reluctance, I tasted it. Salty, cheesy, and crispy. "Not bad."

"Not bad?" He took a huge bite. "These are great."

I ate another one. It wasn't as good as the sour cream and chive fries back home. How could anything compete with sour cream and chives? The lemonade tasted fresh squeezed. It wasn't the watered-down version most fairs sold.

"What do you think of Canada so far?" Evan asked between mouthfuls.

I had just popped a fry in my mouth, so I chewed thoughtfully before answering. "It's better than I thought, but I miss my friends."

"I bet. Senior year in a new school. That's gotta suck."

I tried to think of something else to talk about. "Where are you going in the fall?" I asked. I hoped it was somewhere close.

"University of King's College, do you know it?" When I shook my head, he added. "It's in Halifax. They have a great Marine Biology program."

"That's what you want to do?"

"Since I was a kid," he said. "I love the ocean. How about you?"

"I don't know," I said. "I have a year to decide, right?" I tried to make a joke out of it, but it came out sounding dumb. Evan didn't seem to think anything of it.

"You'll figure it out," he said.

"Hi Evan." I looked up to see a girl standing by our table with her arms crossed. Great. Another fan. Only this one could give Barbie some competition. Her long, brown hair was a mass of stylish curls, but her dark eyes blazed. She did not look happy to see Evan with me.

"Jessica." Evan nodded at her, but didn't move from his chair.

"Who's this?" Jessica jerked her head in my direction.

"I'm Meara," I said, emphasizing the I'm. Who talked in front of someone like they weren't even there?

"Nice to meet you," she said, although her expression clearly told me she did not find anything nice about it. "Evan, can I talk to you privately?"

"Not now," Evan said. "Meara and I are going on the Ferris wheel."

Evan stood and offered me his hand. As I took it, he squeezed mine. Jessica didn't see it, but I got the message—play along. I nodded and smiled. "Oh, yeah. I love Ferris wheels."

In reality, my stomach flipped as I said it. I hated Ferris wheels.

Evan led me away from Jessica, who looked ready to scream. She apparently doesn't get turned down much.

"Old girlfriend?" I guessed.

"Sorry," Evan said. He dropped my hand once we were out of Jessica's sight, and I fought the urge to grab his back. "We don't have to go on the Ferris wheel if you don't want to."

"Good."

He laughed. "Don't like the Ferris wheel?"

"I hate heights," I admitted. "But, I like the Tilt-A-Whirl."

"Me, too."

The Tilt-A-Whirl turned out to be the perfect ride. Thanks to gravity, I spent the entire time pressed against Evan's side, both of us laughing. He took my hand to help me down and didn't let go.

"Want to try some games?" he asked.

"Sure."

We played three games, and neither of us won. The next game was one where you threw darts to pop balloons. Evan was good at it. It took him two tries, but he won a pink teddy bear and gave it to me.

I hugged it to my chest. It was silly, but I liked it anyway. "Thanks."

We shared cotton candy and rode the Tilt-A-Whirl again. "Should we find Katie and your friends?" I asked. I felt bad, like I was keeping him from them.

He pointed to the Ferris wheel. "I spotted them already. They're in line."

"Oh." I was not going on the Ferris wheel, but Katie saw us and motioned to come over. We joined them.

"Want to ride with us?" she asked.

Evan answered for me. "Meara doesn't like Ferris wheels."

Katie scowled at him, but then her face brightened. "That's okay. You ride in my place. I saw a fortune teller. C'mon, Meara. Let's get our fortunes read."

It was better than the Ferris wheel, though maybe not much. "We'll meet you back here," I told Evan as Katie pulled me away.

"Your friends don't want to come?" I asked her.

"Nah," she said. "They teased me and said it's a bunch of hooey."

I agreed with her friends, but I didn't say anything. I could play along. She led us to a small, purple tent. A hand-painted sandwich board sat near the entrance: Madam Tresola—Palm Reading, Tarot Cards, and Psychic Energies...Fortunes Foretold!

Katie stopped outside the entrance and linked her arm through mine. "Let's go in together."

"Gurlz," a heavily accented voice called to us from the dark tent. When my eyes adjusted, an ancient woman of skin and bones stood before us. Her magnified eyes peered at us behind thick glasses. I'd never seen so many folds and wrinkles in a face. A scarlet scarf covered her head, with a few white ringlets of hair escaping near her bejeweled ears. Bracelets jangled on both wrists, and richly toned scarves of sapphire, emerald, and ruby draped every surface in the tent, including Madam Tresola herself. For someone so tiny, she was an imposing figure. I fought the urge to flee.

"Pleeze, seet." She gestured to the chairs across from her. We sat, and she nodded her approval. She reached across the table to Katie.

"Do you want my hand?" Katie asked.

"Pay first," Madam Tresola ordered. Although her voice was low and gritty, it held power. Katie obeyed and handed her some bills.

"I paid for you, too," she told me. "My treat."

"Thanks."

"Now, hand," Madam Tresola barked. Katie held out her hand, palm up. Madam Tresola gripped it between both of hers, turning it over and back, then tracing the lines in Katie's palm.

"You are strong gurl. You get vhat you vant. You marry handsome man. Raise strong cheeldren. Is good." She patted Katie's hand. "You have good life."

"That's it?" Katie asked.

"Vhat you vant? Eez good fortune!" Madam Tresola huffed out a breath, and then gestured impatiently for my hand. I held it out, and she wrapped it in her own. Her hands were surprisingly firm and warm. My hand tingled in her grip. I wondered if Katie felt the same thing. If so, she didn't say anything. My entire hand pulsed as a strange energy flowed up my arm and across my chest. My ears filled with a loud pounding, and I tasted salt.

"Very unusual," Madam Tresola murmured. "I not seen palm like yours een long time." She traced the line that ran from the side of my hand down past my wrist. "You vill live long life, but not easy von."

That didn't sound promising.

"There is beeg change in your future...sadness."

"My mom? Will she be okay?"

Madam Tresola's eyes softened with sympathy. "I not see fortunes of others. Only you. Understand?"

I nodded. She angled my hand back and forth. Her face solemn. "I see joy, too. You are greatly loved."

She touched a mark near my ring finger. It looked like a star. "Your destiny." She looked at me expectantly. I waited for her to say more, but she released my hand. The absence of her touch was like a slap of cold.

"It vas a pleasure to meet you." She stood and bowed to us. Katie, who was clearly bored and not impressed by Madam's performance, now sported a French braid.

"Thanks," she said as she left the tent.

I stood for a moment and looked at Madam Tresola. Was it my imagination, or did she seem like she wanted to tell me something else?

"Good luck, Meara."

"Thanks? Uh...goodbye, Madam Tresola."

Katie pounced on me as soon as I stepped out of the tent. "Wow, is she a crackpot or what?" I shrugged, so she continued. "I bet she tells everyone that mumbo jumbo."

"I dunno—could be." I thought about the feeling of energy that flowed from her. "What did you feel when she held your hand?"

"Wrinkles and bones. She's so old."

"Anything else?"

"No. Why?"

"Nothing."

We found Evan and the rest of the group hanging out in the middle of the midway. It was getting late, so we said goodbye. Evan and Katie dropped me off at home, and I thanked them for taking me. It wasn't until much later that I realized I never gave Madam Tresola my name.

Chapter 6

That night, I dreamed of David again, but instead of standing near the shore, we were by the lighthouse. He sat next to me on the cold, stone steps, our backs against the weathered, oak door. We didn't talk above the thunderous waves breaking on the rocks. A light, salty spray misted my skin, and I tasted the brine on my lips. I was content to sit and listen. My ears pounded with the tidal beat, and I began to hear voices speaking in the rhythm—jump in, go now, come to us, we're waiting.

Was I losing my mind? Panicked, I looked at David. He watched me carefully. "You hear them." He nodded to the sea.

"Yes," I said. Then, "Who are they?"

"They are us. We are them. You will meet them in time, but it's best that you try to ignore them for now." He reached for my hand. "They will grow more persistent."

His hand felt warm and calloused, not uncomfortable, but certainly not welcomed. What kind of response was that? Irritated, I tried to pull my hand out of his. He squeezed mine once, and then released it. I waited for more explanation, but he was silent.

"That was cryptic," I muttered. "What does it mean?"

"When you're ready to know, I'll tell you." He raised his hand to brush some stray hairs off my forehead. I leaned back sharply, my agitation growing. What right did he have to talk to me in riddles, and then try to play the affectionate father? In pulling away, I noticed the angry red gash on his hand.

"What happened to you?" I asked, momentarily forgetting my anger and reaching for his hand. He pulled it out of my grasp and hid it at his side.

"It's nothing," he said. "I was careless. That's all."

Was this man going to tell me anything of value? I let it go, for the time being, and switched topics. "Why are you here?" I asked instead.

"For you," he said simply. "For your mom."

"Does Mom know that you're here?"

"Not yet," he said, giving me a wry smile. "Though I imagine you'll tell her."

"Why would I do that? This is just a dream."

He raised an eyebrow at me, but didn't say anything. I was dreaming, right?

After a moment, he shrugged. "Whatever you say. You can tell your mom when you're ready. I'm not going anywhere for the time being." He offered his uninjured hand and, this time, I took it. He pulled me to my feet. "Walk with me?"

We walked along the shore, the voices softened to a murmur, the words indistinguishable. David pointed out various constellations in the sky and told me stories about them. I relaxed and listened to his rich, melodic voice. He was in the middle of a tale about Cassiopeia when I interrupted.

"Why did you leave?"

"I had to," he said. Why wouldn't he meet my eyes?

"That's not a good enough reason," I pushed, asking again. "Why?"

After more silence, he finally looked down at me. His eyes were sad and ancient. "It's my nature, Meara. It's who I am. I cannot stay here long."

"What do you mean—your nature?"

"I can't tell you that," he said.

"Why not?"

"You'll find out soon enough."

I screamed in frustration. "Why do you even bother talking at all? Nothing you say means anything or makes sense."

"It will," he said. "I promise."

"Yeah, well, I don't know what that means." I crossed my arms and glared at him. I wished the dream would end. I pinched my arm and tried to wake myself up. The pain shocked me.

David saw and laughed. I was about to tell him to get the heck out of my dreams when a barking commotion near the shore caught my attention. I turned from David to see three seals on the rocks. Two were small with reddish-brown fur, and one was large and light gray. They appeared to be playing. There were seals in Canada? I had only seen them at the zoo.

"Do you see that?" I whispered to David, not wanting to scare them. The seals weren't too far away from us. David didn't answer. I looked back to find him scowling at the seals.

"They are not supposed to be here," he muttered.

"No doubt," I agreed. "I didn't know seals lived here."

"They do," he said. "In abundance, too."

"Oh...cool." It was dark and hard to see, so I took a step toward them to get a better look. David grabbed my arm and turned me to him. He kissed my forehead and said, "Sleep well, Meara."

I woke to the sun beaming in my eyes. I felt great, and it actually took a few minutes before my dreams or vision, or whatever it was, came back to me. It wasn't until I was standing in the bathroom and brushing my hair that I thought of my dad—um, David. In my dream, he seemed so fatherly, like he cared about me. It didn't make sense. Where had he been all these years?

I found Grandpa Jamie alone in the kitchen, reading his paper at the table. He didn't look up as I came into the room, opening the refrigerator to find a drink. He must have realized I was there, however, because when I sat across from him, he cracked the paper and wished me a good morning.

"Morning," I said. "Where are Grandma Mary and Mom?"

"They're in the garage," he answered from behind his wall of newspaper. "I think they're bartering on the rest of your things. What stays and what goes."

"Where would it go?" I asked.

"Donated, I s'pose," he said, unconcerned. "We certainly can't keep it all here. I can barely walk through the house right now."

I didn't have plans for the day. Taking a long drag from my Diet Coke, I stood up. "I'm going out to help them."

Grandpa Jamie peered at me over the top of the paper, raising one bushy, white eyebrow. "Suit yourself," he said. "But I'm staying far away."

"Why?"

"You didn't live in the same house with those two women for nineteen years." He shook his head and went back to reading his paper. I sat back down and watched him read. It was my first real opportunity to sit with him since the night we arrived. He worked long hours, leaving before sunrise and returning late at night. Though his skin was tan and weathered, smile lines softened his face. Today, he wore a pair of silver-rimmed reading glasses. At some point, they must have slipped to the bridge of his nose. He hadn't bothered to push them back up.

"What are you doing today?" I asked.

He folded the paper, set it to the side, and took off his glasses. "Why? Aren't you going outside now? Did I change your mind?" His eyes twinkled, so I knew he was teasing. I shrugged and he laughed, adding, "I'm going to the docks."

"On your day off?" Didn't he want a break?

"I'm a fisherman," he explained. "I don't get a day off. At any rate, the DFO was questioning my team yesterday, and we didn't get a lot done."

"DFO?"

"Department of Fisheries and Oceans...uh, I think maybe you call it the Department of Natural Resources?"

"Okay," I said. "Why was the DFO questioning you?"

"Some drunken tourists were playing around near the boats late Thursday night. They managed to make a mess of the nets and traps. They also tormented some poor seal with a harpoon."

"Is it okay?"

"Don't know." When I just looked at him, confused, he explained. "There was a lot of blood, but when we tried to get close to it, it dove into the water."

"Does this happen a lot?"

"No, but it's not the first time," he grumbled. "Damn tourists.

Think they own the town. At least the DFO nailed them. Found 'em passed out in their car a little ways down the beach. Stupid fools."

"If the DFO found them, why did they talk to you?"

"They asked if we were going to press charges, too."

"Will you?" I asked.

"No." He rubbed his forehead. "Nothing was damaged beyond repair. Those boys will be in enough trouble without me adding to it."

I liked my grandfather. He worked hard, and he was fair minded. "Can I come with you?" I asked. I realized I wanted to get to know him better.

He looked at me thoughtfully. "If you want to, you can. I'll put you to work. Ask my team, I put anyone to work who has a pulse and is standing on my pier." I thought of Evan, and my heart skipped. It was Saturday, so he might not be there, but I was betting he was. "You'll want to change," Grandpa Jamie continued. "Put on something you don't mind getting dirty. And tennis shoes. No sandals."

"When are we leaving?"

"Can you be ready in fifteen minutes?"

I grabbed an apple from the bowl on the counter and ran from the room, calling back, "You bet!"

I changed in about ten minutes, but Grandpa Jamie was already waiting in his pickup truck with the engine running when I came out. My mom and grandmother were standing in the front yard, our old vacuum between them. Mom turned and looked at me. Her hair was mussed from running her fingers through it, something she did when she was irritated. Grandma Mary was counting off on one hand all the reasons why our vacuum, which was clearly more modern that hers, was not worth keeping. Stupid as it sounded, Mom loved that vacuum. She spent months researching the perfect model to buy. Grandpa Jamie was right. It was time to get going.

I kissed my mom on the cheek. "Bye, Mom. I'm going to help Grandpa Jamie for a few hours today."

"Dad?" my mom called, ignoring me for a moment. "Is it safe?"

"It'll be fine, Sharon," he called. "You worry too much."

"Hmph." Grandpa Jamie's response did not help her irritation level. She managed a smile for me. "Have fun. Be safe."

"I will." I hugged her. She looked like she needed it. "See you later."

I walked over and started climbing in the cab when mom called my name. "Yes?" I said, half turning.

"I want to hear about your new friends later," she said. "I tried to stay up and wait for you, but I was just too tired."

"We'll talk tonight," I said. Mom and I talked about everything. The few times I did go on dates, I always came home and talked to her about it. For some reason, I wanted to keep Evan to myself. I smiled at her in reassurance.

"I'll hold you to it," she teased and waved me off before turning back to Grandma Mary. I climbed in the truck, and we drove away.

It was a short drive. The buildings near the docks—they were more like shacks—stood crookedly, their weathered, gray wood sagging from Mother Nature's brutal torment. In contrast, most of the boats gleamed in bright whites and brilliant primary colors, clearly the pride of their owners. Two or three boats were tethered to each pier, and a few appeared empty this Saturday morning. I didn't know which boats belonged to Grandpa Jamie, so I followed him closely, quickening my pace to keep up with his long stride. He didn't say anything to me as we walked, and I was about to ask him which was his when he stopped in front of the longest pier. It had two boats on the left side, one on the right, and one tied on the end.

Grandpa Jamie strode down the pier and stopped at the last boat. I pulled up right behind him, peering around his right side. He was broad enough that I didn't feel safe standing next to him; the pier was narrow. There was one man kneeling on the deck of the boat, his back to us as he tore out a broken board. He wore a baseball cap on his head, his white t-shirt tucked in the back pocket of his cargo pants. His muscles rippled, and his skin glistened from the heat and the labor.

"What's the status?" Grandpa Jamie demanded, and the man jerked. Clearly, he did not hear us approach. When he turned and stood, I swallowed in surprise. Evan.

Evan relaxed against the sideboard and smiled at me before addressing Grandpa Jamie. "Good morning to you, too. Thanks for the heart attack."

"You're young," Grandpa Jamie grunted. "You'll get over it." He nodded at the boat. "How is she?"

"Damage is minimal." Evan pointed to the board he was replacing, and three others he had clearly just nailed down. "This deck got the worst of it. I'm about ready to sand and paint."

Grandpa Jamie pulled me forward. I think he meant to be gentle, but I almost tumbled into the boat. I caught myself just in time. He didn't seem to notice. "That sounds like the perfect job for you," he said. "Evan, can you show Meara what's needed?"

Evan grinned. "Absolutely."

Grandpa Jamie scratched his head, his eyes already scanning the other three boats and the rest of his team. As an afterthought, he asked, "You've met each other before, right?"

Evan's grin widened. "Briefly." I took a sudden interest in the anchor as my cheeks burned. Once again, Grandpa Jamie didn't notice.

"Good...good," he said absentmindedly. He was already walking away.

Evan held out his hand to help me into the boat. I took it and climbed in carefully. My sea legs were far from developed. I'd only been on a boat twice, and both times were with Kim's family. The summer before eighth grade, they invited me to their cabin in Minocqua, Wisconsin. They vacationed there every summer. That week I got violently sick both times I was on the boat. I was miserable. Kim and her family were sympathetic, but they never invited me back.

"You just couldn't stay away from all this, could you?" Evan teased, gesturing to himself. I rolled my eyes and laughed. He rewarded me with a dimpled grin before turning to pick something up from his pile of tools. It looked like a small, wooden block.

"How are your sanding skills?" he asked.

"Nonexistent?" I answered, adding, "I've never done it, but how hard can it be?"

"It's not," he said, handing me the tool, "but there is a definite technique. Here, I'll show you." He wrapped his fingers around my wrist and guided me down until we were kneeling side by side in front of the board he just installed. He covered my hand with his and said, "You want to maintain an even pressure and move with the grain, not against it."

I moved the block back and forth a few times, my hand under his. My blood pounded in my ear, so loud he could probably hear it. His hand was warm and firm on mine. Stay cool, I told myself. I looked over at him and asked, "Like this?"

His eyes fixed on mine. He didn't move his hand. "Perfect," he said, as his gaze moved to my lips. I swallowed.

"How's she doing?" Grandpa Jamie called from the boat next to ours. We jerked apart.

"Fine," Evan called back, getting to his feet. To me, he said, "I'll go and get the paint."

Sanding was kind of relaxing. I took comfort in the repetitive nature of it. The sun was hot on my back, but it felt good. I always soaked it up in the summer, knowing that I would be wishing for some of its warmth in the dead of winter.

Icy cold water dripped on my shoulder and made me jump. I looked up to the source and saw Evan holding out a water bottle. "Sorry for startling you," he said. "I thought you might be thirsty."

"Thanks." I opened the cap and downed half the bottle. I didn't realize how thirsty I had gotten. "Did you get the paint?"

Evan held up one gallon of paint and two brushes in response. "Is the sanding done?"

"Almost." I pointed to the last board. "I just have that one to finish."

"Okay." Evan set the paint supplies down near the boards I'd already sanded. "I'll get started then, and you can join me when you're done."

I finished sanding as fast as I could, and then went over by Evan. He smiled and handed me a paintbrush. "You've painted before, right?"

"A little." Mom and I had painted the kitchen in our old house. I didn't tell him about the mess we made in the process. We were covered in paint, but laughing when we were done.

"Why'd you come here today?" Evan asked.

I shrugged and dipped my brush in the paint.

"Just a little," Evan cautioned as he watched me.

"I just wanted to hang with my grandfather a bit, I guess."

"Is it hard?"

"What?"

"Getting to know them?"

"No…yes…I don't know. It's weird. I don't understand why we never visited them or why they didn't come see us."

"Yeah. That's a little strange, although I can guess why they didn't come see you."

I looked at Evan and waited for his answer. His eyes took in the boats surrounding us before he gestured with his paintbrush. "This takes year round dedication. Your grandfather can't leave."

"Sounds hard," I said. Evan returned his brush to the paint bucket. In his haste, droplets of paint flew, and one landed on my nose. Evan started laughing before brushing it off with the sleeve of his shirt.

"Sorry about that." He grinned at me, but it soon faltered. Once again, I was locked in his gaze. We leaned toward each other. He brushed a strand of hair back from my face and tucked it behind me ear. "Meara?"

"Yes?"

"Do you want to go to dinner?"

"Tonight?"

"Yeah."

"With you?" I asked, realizing that was an incredibly stupid thing to ask.

Evan grinned again. "Yeah. That would be the general idea."

"Okay."

Chapter 7

I took my time getting ready, applying makeup and a bit of my favorite perfume. I brushed my hair, contemplating putting it up, but decided to leave it down. When I finished getting ready, I sat back on my bed and tried to concentrate on the latest mystery I was reading. It didn't work. I stared outside instead. It was pitch black and rain pelted the long wall of windows in my room. About an hour after we got home, the skies went from overcast to ominous gray to pitch black before the clouds broke. It down poured for over twenty minutes, and I wondered how bad the driving conditions were.

The doorbell rang. I waited, holding my breath, until Grandma Mary called, "Meara! Evan's here to see you!"

I stood, smoothed my shirt, and tucked my hair behind my ear. I didn't want to seem too anxious. When I came around the corner, he was standing in the living room talking to my mom. He looked fantastic in dark jeans and a bright red polo.

"Hi," I said. I hated the way my voice sounded all breathy and weak, but Evan didn't seem to mind.

His smile just widened. "Hi yourself."

It was about then that I realized we had three sets of eyes on us, observing our every move and every word. They were wearing identical "I-told-you-she'd-go-for-him" expressions, too.

"Do you have a raincoat?" Evan asked.

"Um, no." I thought of my windbreaker. It would be drenched in two minutes in this weather.

Evan held out a purple and turquoise raincoat. "It's Katie's, so I'm sure it'll fit."

I slipped my arms in. "Where's yours?" I asked.

"By the door. I didn't want to get the floor wet."

"How thoughtful," Grandma Mary said, and I bit my cheek to keep from laughing. Evan went to put his raincoat on. He was right, of course, as there was a puddle of rainwater on the hallway tile beneath it.

"Do you have a mop I can use?" Evan asked.

Grandma Mary waved us off. "I'll clean it up. You kids have fun. Be safe."

"I'll have Meara back at a decent hour," Evan said.

If anyone replied, I didn't hear it.

The rain was pouring down in sheets, and I was glad he had my hand. I had no idea how we were going to see to drive anywhere. When we got to the car, Evan dropped my hand, shouting, "Sorry, this is an exception I make to the door opening rule. Get in as fast as you can!"

I maneuvered fast and shut the door, slipping off the hood of the raincoat. The car smelled a bit like salami. "What's that smell?" I asked.

"Sandwiches," Evan said and grinned. "It's too crappy outside to drive anywhere far, so I thought I'd bring the date to you. Let's drive to the lighthouse. It's close, and we'll get a little privacy."

My heartbeat picked up considerably when he mentioned privacy. What did he have planned for the evening? He was cute and all, but I barely knew him. If Evan sensed my nervousness, he didn't say anything. Music played softly, but otherwise the drive was quiet. Visibility was poor. I didn't want to distract him.

When we reached the small parking lot of the lighthouse, Evan shut off the car. The rain pelted the roof of the car. The parking lot lights revealed we were the only car there. Go figure.

"You're right about the privacy part," I commented. Evan grinned and reached into the backseat, pulling out a bag of chips, two subs, and a couple of Cokes. He handed them to me, then he leaned behind my seat and picked up a small, black case. Evan winked as he unzipped it, and I realized what it was. "We're going to watch a movie in your car?"

Evan frowned. "That's okay, right?"

"Sure," I said. "What are we seeing?"

"Goonies. I hope you don't mind. I have a thing for old movies."

"I love that one!" It was one of mom's favorites, so we watched it often when I was growing up. The food was in my lap. Evan took one of the sandwiches and nodded to the other.

"They're the same. I didn't know what you like, so I just got ham and turkey."

"Sounds good to me," I said. "Thanks." I unwrapped my sandwich and bit in. Evan did the same. He opened the bag of chips and laid it on the seat between us. We watched the movie and laughed at the same parts. The windows steamed up, and the rain pelted down. It was the most crazy, romantic date ever.

The rain began to let up just as the movie ended. Evan drove back to my grandparents' house and parked. With the dome light on, I helped him gather all the empty wrappers. Between us, we had polished off the chips.

"It's nice to see a girl with an appetite," he teased.

I rolled my eyes. "You ate most of them."

He reached for a strand of my hair, twirling it on his finger. "I had a good time."

"Me, too." My voice sounded quiet and a bit shaky. Was he going to kiss me? Should I say something else? Just as I was about to spout something stupid out of nervousness, Evan leaned across the seat and kissed me. It was light and fast. His lips tasted salty, like the chips.

"Is it too much to ask to see you again tomorrow? I know it's Sunday, and I have to work, but only a half day. I can come by after, if that's okay."

I nodded, unable to speak for a moment. "I'd like that," I finally managed to croak.

He slid his hand along my hair once last time, and then he reached over me to open my door. "Goodnight, Meara."

"Night, Evan."

The rain continued to fall, though softer now. I was about to shut the door, when I remembered Katie's raincoat. I went to shrug it off, but Evan shook his head.

"Keep it. She's got about three more. You'll need it. Rains a lot in these parts."

"Then I'll look forward to more movie nights."

I heard his laughter as I shut the door. I couldn't believe I just said that! But he did already ask me out on another date. Living in Canada

---

wasn't turning out to be such a bad thing. Nope, not at all.

Mom was curled up on the couch when I came in. She opened her eyes, blinked twice, and stretched. "Did you have fun?"

"Yeah. We did." Hanging the coat in the hall, I joined her on the couch. I snuggled up and rested my head on her shoulder. She smelled like her usual shampoo and gardenias. It reminded me of so many similar moments that I felt myself relax.

"So?"

"We drove to the lighthouse and watched a movie in the car."

Mom sat up a bit and looked at me. "Really?"

"Yeah."

"That's interesting."

"It was fun."

She gave me a quick hug. "Do you like it here?"

"It's not bad."

"I'm not a horrible mother for bringing you here?"

I laughed at the voice she used. It was the voice she used for the Big Bad Wolf and all the other villains in my childhood books. "No, you're not a bad mother."

She gently pushed me up and turned to face me on the couch. She looked almost sad, certainly serious

"I start my cancer treatments on Monday," she said. "In Halifax. Would you mind driving me?"

"Of course, Mom."

"We'll be there for a few hours."

"No problem. I'll bring a book and my laptop."

"Thanks, honey." She gave me a kiss on the cheek and stood up. "I'm going to bed. It's pretty late."

"What time?" I asked. When she looked at me blankly, I added. "Monday. What time do we need to leave?"

"Probably about nine."

"Ok. Night, Mom."

Chapter 8

"Sharon Quinn?" An elderly nurse with brassy red hair stood in the doorway, a clipboard in hand.

"Should I come in with you?" I asked.

Mom patted my knee. "No, honey, I'll be okay. Just wait for me here."

I leaned forward and sifted through a stack of magazines on the table. Most were from last year and looked rather sad with soft, torn covers.

"That your mum?" I looked up to find a girl sitting across from me. I hadn't noticed her before. Her coppery curls fell past her shoulders, and her nose was splattered with freckles of the same shade. She eyed me with wide, green eyes. She looked about my age, but she wore bell-bottom jeans and a Bob Marley t-shirt.

"Yeah," I said and sat back. None of the magazines interested me.

"First time here?" she asked. Her voice lilted. Was she Irish? When I nodded in reply, she said, "That's rough."

"What about you?" I asked. "Why are you here?"

"Me mum," she said. "Like you." She inclined her head toward the door where my mom had gone. "She's in there now."

I didn't know what to say to that, so I changed the subject. "I'm Meara," I said as I extended my hand. She looked at it briefly before she shook it.

"Nice to meet you. I'm Ula." She gave me a tentative smile. Her name was so unique. She pronounced it Oo-la. "Do you want to see something?"

Curious, I asked, "What?"

"Er, rather, somewhere." When I hesitated, her eyes filled with understanding. "It will be hours before she's done. Trust me. We'll be back here in plenty of time."

She stood up and threw her brown leather backpack over one shoulder. Her jacket was army green and frayed on the edges. Her entire outfit looked like something from 1970.

"Where you'd find such vintage clothes?" I asked as I hitched my own backpack on my own shoulder and followed her to the exit.

She looked down at her outfit. A look of surprise crossed her face before her checks tinged pink. "Oh, you know. Shopping."

"Are there good resale shops nearby?"

"Um. Yes? Uh. No?" She sighed. "I don't know actually. I got this in Ireland."

I should have figured good vintage clothes would be from somewhere else. I loved old t-shirts. Hers rocked. "Are you from there then?"

"Around there, yes." She beamed at me. "Have you ever been?"

"No," I said. "This is my first time out of the United States."

"Is that where you were...um, from?" she asked. We were crossing the parking lot now, walking to the park next door.

"Yes. Wisconsin," I said. "Have you been there?"

"No," she said. "I've never been there. Is it nice?"

"I liked it," I answered distractedly. A rhythmic beat pounded in my ear, and my mouth filled with a brackish taste. My senses sharpened as my nerves were soothed.

"Meara?" Ula was watching me closely, a worried look on her face.

"Did you ask me something?" I focused on her face. The noise subsided slightly.

"Do you like it here?" she asked.

"I do," I said. "Where are we going?"

She grinned at me and skipped a little. "I found this spot here. You won't believe it. We can sit near the ocean."

"The hospital is that close?"

"I was surprised too." She took my hand and squeezed it. "I like to come here. I hope you do. It's nice to have a friend."

"It's been lonely, huh?" I felt bad for her. I couldn't imagine just sitting in that waiting room, day after day. That would have happened to me, too, if Ula hadn't come along.

"It has," she said. "But not anymore, right?"

A narrow path led us down to the coastline. We sat on flat rocks about five feet above the water. Close enough that a slight mist filled the air when the waves broke, but high enough not to get wet.

Ula used her backpack as a backrest. She leaned back and crossed her legs at the ankles. Her face was serene. "I love it here. It calms me."

She stared up at me as if wondering what I thought. I looked at the water. It was wild and frothy, nothing calming about it. I couldn't see anything but whitecaps on the horizon. "Is it always this rough?" I asked.

"Usually," she said. "If you want peaceful, try the Pacific. The Atlantic? She's all feisty and fierce."

I laughed. "You talk about the ocean like a person."

Ula quirked a red eyebrow at me. "In many ways, she is."

"I suppose." I dropped down onto the rock next to her, crossed my legs, and rested my arms on my knees. "It's all new to me."

"You've never been in the water before?" Ula asked.

I shrugged my shoulder. "Lakes, but never the ocean."

Ula leaned close. "And, I've never been in a lake."

"No?"

"No," she confirmed. She leaned back against her pack again. "We're quite a pair then, aren't we?"

"Do you go to school here?" I asked. I liked her, and it would be nice to have another friend at school.

"I'm homeschooled," she said, almost as though she was apologizing. "We move a lot."

"I bet that's rough."

Ula studied me for a minute. "It's okay. After all, I get to meet all kinds of interesting people. Like you."

I shook my head. "I'm not that interesting."

Ula looked surprised. "Yes, you are."

She said it with such conviction that I almost asked her what she knew that I didn't. In the end, I just laughed. "You apparently don't get out much."

She looked like she was going to argue with me, but she laughed instead. "Maybe you're right."

We stayed at the park for several hours. The path down to the water was nearly impossible to spot. Wispy vegetation and leafy trees camouflaged the opening. I was surprised Ula ever found it, but then again, she had plenty of time to explore while her mom received treatment. No one joined us all morning, and the seclusion was calming.

"Do you want a sandwich?" Ula held something wrapped in wax paper out to me. "I brought two."

"Why two?"

"I never know how long I'll be here."

"Oh." I hadn't thought to bring anything with me this morning. I took the package from her. "Thanks."

"It's vegetarian," she said. "I hope you don't mind. I don't eat meat."

"No problem. Thank you."

It was good. Cucumbers, sprouts, tomatoes, and shredded carrots with a hummus spread.

"Water?" Ula handed me a bottle.

"Thanks," I said. "I forgot that, too."

"It was your first time," she said. "You'll remember next time."

"Let's hope so!"

We both laughed. Ula stuffed all the wrappers back in her bag and then stood.

"I'm sure me mum's almost done," she said.

"Of course," I said. "Thank you again, Ula. You made what could have been a long, boring day fun."

Ula looked pleased. "My pleasure."

We returned to the hospital, and I excused myself to use the restroom. When I got back to the waiting room, Ula was already gone. Her mom must have been waiting for her. Hopefully she wasn't waiting too long, and Ula didn't get in trouble.

Resuming my previous spot, I pulled out my book and waited for my mom. I was in a much better mood. I had a new friend and a secret hangout spot.

"You'll be okay?" Mom asked. She tried to sound calm, but I heard the anxiety in her voice. Sitting on her bed, I watched her pack. It was hard to believe that yesterday I waited for her at the clinic and, today, in a few hours, she would fly to Toronto for the rest of the week. Dr. Stahlman was sending her to a cancer research institute. Some of Mom's test results concerned him.

"I'll be fine," I said. "Will you?" She worried about me, but I had my grandparents, Katie, and Evan. She was the one who would be alone.

She managed a wry smile. "I'll survive, I think, under the constant attention of medical staff. Don't worry about me." She finished packing and sat next to me, a slight frown on her face. I knew the look. It meant she wanted to tell me something serious—something that had been bothering her.

"Talk to your grandparents, okay?" she asked. It was not what I expected her to say. "I know you're just getting to know Evan, and you like him. And, I like him, too, but it would mean a lot to your grandparents if you spent time with them."

"Okay, Mom," I promised. "I will."

"Good." She looked at her watch, kissed my cheek, and stood. "I better get going. You never know how long it will take to get through security."

I stood and walked her to her car, carrying the suitcase. She kissed me again and promised to call daily with updates. I held back the tears as I watched her drive away.

Chapter 9

The first night without Mom, I ate dinner with my grandparents. Grandma Mary made us fried chicken, mashed potatoes, and corn on the cob. The food tasted delicious. I could tell that my grandparents tried hard to make things comfortable. Grandpa Jamie was rarely even home for dinner. He usually got back after sunset.

"So, Meara," Grandma Mary asked. "What do you like to do for fun?"

"I read, shop, listen to music, you know, the usual things. Oh, and I like emailing and texting friends, blogging, and posting pictures. "

"Oh?" Grandma Mary's eyes widened a bit. I think she was searching for something to say. She finally settled for, "That's interesting."

I bit my cheek to keep from laughing. I hadn't seen my grandmother use the computer yet. I think it was a bit out of her comfort zone.

"I see that you and Even seem to be getting along." She said this nonchalantly, but I knew she was fishing for information.

"Yes, he's nice," I answered blandly, taking a bite of my chicken so I didn't have to say more. I chewed slowly.

"You should have seen the repairs they made to my boat. She hasn't looked that good in years." Grandpa Jamie winked at me as he took another bite of potato.

"Have there been any more problems with tourists?" I asked.

"Not since that last group," he said. "And they got a hefty fine. I don't think they'll be making trouble again soon."

Thankfully, Grandma Mary did not bring up Evan again. She asked about my friends, school, and life in Wisconsin. I answered these 'safe' questions happily, probably going into more detail than necessary... my grandfather stifled a yawn one or two times. After dinner, I was so relieved to be excused that I offered to do all the dishes. Grandma Mary looked pleased. They both settled in the den—Grandpa Jamie to read the paper and watch television, and Grandma Mary to work on crossword puzzles.

When I finished the dishes, I told my grandparents I was going out to get some fresh air. My coat hung in the front hall. I was putting it on and backing out the door when I ran into something solid.

"Oomph," it said.

I turned; it was Evan.

"What are you doing here?" I asked.

"Hi, Meara. How are you?" he asked in a teasing voice. He leaned in and whispered. "It's customary to say 'hi' before you ask people questions."

"Hi, Evan. How are you?" I mimicked the singsong tune he used, adding. "Why are you lurking on my grandparents' porch?"

"I'm not lurking!" He held up a bucket of tools. "I brought these back for Jamie. I won't be at work tomorrow, and he'll need them."

"Oh," I said, stepping to the side. "Come inside then."

"Thank you." Evan stepped past me and went into the den. "Hi, Jamie. Where would you like the tools?"

"Hall's good," Grandpa Jamie said. "You could have brought those back on Thursday."

Evan gave me a quick look. I smirked at him. Too late, I realized that my grandparents watched our exchange with interest.

"Where are you off to?" Evan asked.

"Just going for a walk," I said. "Want to come?"

"Sure." He turned back to my grandparents. "Have a nice evening."

"You too, Evan!" Grandma Mary called. She smiled at us sweetly. "Have a nice walk."

The sun was setting, and the air had cooled from earlier in the day. So far, summer in Nova Scotia was colder than Wisconsin. I was glad I wore my coat.

"Do you have a destination in mind?" Evan asked.

"No," I said. "I just wanted to go out. What do you think?"

"We could take the path down to the water."

"Okay. Lead the way."

Evan took my hand, and we walked down to the water's edge. The water was almost calm. The waves lapped, rather than beat, against the rocks. The almost-black water shimmered in the golds and reds of the setting sun.

Evan released my hand and wrapped his arm around my shoulder.

"Where are you going tomorrow?" I asked.

"Halifax," he said. "Hockey practice with the new team."

"You start already? I thought hockey was a winter sport."

"We play inside," he said. "So, we can pretty much play all year."

"I've never seen a hockey game."

"You're joking, right?"

I shook my head, and Evan's jaw dropped. "You're coming to my next game then," he said.

"Okay," I said. "When is it?"

"Third Saturday in August. I can't remember the date off hand."

"That's a few weeks away," I said. "Just let me know."

The vibrant colors of the setting sun dulled to a deep maroon. The blackness of the water took over, and gulls cried overhead.

"Do you want to head back to the house?" Evan asked.

"I'm good," I said. "Do you need to get going?"

"No hurry."

We sat on the rocks, our hips touching. I found small stones and tossed them into the water, listening to the soft plop. I was amazed by the stillness. Soon the stars appeared above, and a sliver of moon. It was dark and quiet.

"I'm glad you stopped by," I told Evan shyly.

He nudged me with his shoulder. "Me, too. Even if you scolded me at first."

"I didn't scold you."

His fingertips grazed along my jaw as he leaned in to kiss me. I snuggled against his side. When the kiss ended, I rested my head on his shoulder, shivering slightly.

"C'mon," he said. "Let's head back. It's getting cold."

Just like she promised, Mom called every day that week. The appointments were going well. The doctors seemed to think they could slow the cancer with aggressive treatment. They worked with the clinic in Halifax and set Mom up with a treatment plan. She would go to the clinic three days a week for several hours each day. In the fall, she'd commute with Katie and me—we'd drop her off on our way to school and pick her up on our way home.

"I think it's going to work, Meara!"

"That's great, Mom," I said. Her optimism was infectious.

Chapter 10

"Meara, you don't have to do this," Mom said for about the fifteenth time that morning.

"I know, Mom. I want to. Honest." I was driving her to her first chemotherapy appointment. I didn't know how she'd feel afterwards, and I didn't want her driving home by herself. My grandmother offered to drive her, but she had her monthly garden club meeting. She would have missed it and all the fresh gossip. I insisted that I drive. I didn't have anything going on, and she was my mother.

"Maybe Ula will be there," I added. I told Mom about Ula after the last appointment. I had so much fun the last time when I met her. I was looking forward to hanging out and getting to know her better. I was nice to have someone my age to talk to that understood what I was going through.

"That would be nice," Mom said. "I'm glad you met a friend."

When we got out to the car, I opened the driver's door and Mom gave me a strange look. "I can drive there, Meara."

"It's okay, Mom," I said. "I'll drive."

When my mom drove to the clinic last time, I paid attention. I knew the way there. Within a few minutes, we were out of Peggy's Cove and on our way to Halifax. I decided to tell my mom about my dreams. I was thinking about them often. I had never seen a picture of David and that was bothering me. Did he look like the man in my dreams? They were so real. I'd never had dreams like that before, the kind that gave me goose bumps. I took a deep breath.

"Mom, I dreamed about David."

She patted my knee. "That's natural, honey. Peggy's Cove is where I met your father, and you know that. I'm sure it's stirred your imagination. Besides, you used to dream about him when you were little."

"I did?" I only remembered the one time when I was about seven.

"Oh sure. All the time." She smiled at me briefly, and then turned to look out the window. Was she nervous?

"What did he look like?" I asked. "Do you have any pictures of him?"

She bit her thumbnail, proving that she was either nervous, worried, or both. "No, I never took any. I didn't have a camera, and when we were together, I wasn't thinking about capturing memories or anything like that."

"Can you describe him?" I asked. "How tall was he?"

"Over six foot. My head only came to his shoulder."

"And his eyes?"

"Blue."

"His hair?"

"The same color as yours. He wore it a little longer than most men, and it curled slightly." She smiled at the memory.

"How old was he?"

"A few years older than me. Maybe twenty-three?"

Everything she described sounded like the man from my dreams. The man who called himself David. How could I dream about my father exactly as he looked when Mom dated him? How would I know that?

"Well? Does that match your dream man?" She tried to make a joke, but her voice shook a little.

"It does. In my dream, David looks about twenty-five. How can I dream about a man I never met?"

"They're just dreams, Meara," Mom said. I could tell that she didn't believe that by the way she worried her lip. That left me with another question, one that I wasn't ready to ask her. Why did my dreams bother her? "But, you'll tell me if you dream of him again, right?"

"Sure, Mom," I obliged, although not sure at all. "Of course."

We arrived at the clinic, and I found a parking spot near the entrance. We walked in together, dropping the subject of David. The waiting room was full, but I didn't see Ula.

"Is your friend here?" Mom asked.

"I don't see her," I said.

Mom looked disappointed. She wanted to meet her and had hoped to see her here today. "You brought some things along?"

"Of course. I'll be fine." I had my backpack slung over my shoulder. This time, I packed snacks, a drink, a book, and my laptop. I wasn't worried about being bored.

The same nurse called Mom back a few minutes later. Not wanting to stay in the waiting room, I walked outside. It was sunny and not too hot. A light breeze blew my hair. I headed straight for the park, my destination was the secluded spot Ula had shown me.

As I was walking down the path, I noticed someone wearing a baseball cap already sitting there. I thought about turning around and heading back up, but then I noticed the curly ponytail sticking out of the back of the hat. Ula.

She turned at that moment and smiled at me, gesturing for me to come down.

"Hi Meara!"

"Hi!"

When I reached the ledge, I sat down next to her and dangled my feet over the side. "I didn't think you were coming today."

"I've been here for about an hour already," she said. "You weren't here last week."

"No," I said. "Mom had to go to Toronto for some tests."

"Everything okay?"

"Yeah," I said. "How's your mom?"

She shrugged. "Eh. I'd rather not talk about it."

"Sorry."

She tapped my arm lightly. "No need to apologize."

We stared out at the ocean for a while, not saying anything. There were several sailboats, fishing boats, and other watercrafts. It seemed everyone was enjoying this gorgeous day.

"Do you always come with your mom?" I asked.

"Usually."

"Do you have any brothers and sisters?"

"I do," she said. "But I'm the youngest. They're much older than I am. How about you?"

I shook my head. "It's just me. It's always been just Mom and me."

She looked at me and frowned. "That must make this that much harder then."

"Yeah."

"I hope you don't find this too forward of me, but where's your dad?"

"I don't know," I said. "I never met him."

She looked like she might say something else, but she ended up hugging me instead, which seemed to surprise both of us. "Let's talk about something happier," she suggested.

"Okay. Like what?"

She got a twinkle in her eye. "How about boys?"

I laughed. "What about them?"

She crossed her legs and turned to face me. "Do you have a boyfriend?"

I thought about Evan. Was he my boyfriend? We'd seen each other several times the last couple of weeks. We kissed with an increasing frequency, which was fine by me, but we never talked about our relationship.

Ula watched me, her green eyes narrowing. "Well, come on then. I want details."

I laughed again. "What gave it away?"

She smiled at me. "You're blushing. So, who is he?"

"His name is Evan."

"And?"

"And he's smart and cute. He plays hockey, too."

She tilted her head, as if she was going to ask another question. Before she could, I jumped in with one of my own. "How about you? Do you have a boyfriend?"

"Me? No." Her curls swung as she shook her head. "It's hard to meet boys when you're homeschooled." She frowned and twirled a strand of her hair. "People in general, actually."

"Evan invited me to one of his games. You should come, too."

"I don't know..."

"C'mon. It'll be fun."

"When?" Ula asked.

"August 17. It's right here in Halifax. Will you come?"

"I'll think about it."

Chapter 11

July passed too quickly. I became Mom's regular driver when she had to go for chemo. She seemed to take the treatments okay, although they made her tired and gave her an upset stomach. We didn't talk about David on those drives. I hadn't dreamed of him again, and Mom never brought him up. On the days Mom didn't have treatments, I hung out with either Katie, Evan, or both of them.

I tried to avoid thinking about school, but my enrollment materials came in the mail, along with a supply list and class schedule. I was comfortable with every class they placed me in. Katie called that night, and we compared notes. We had lunch together, as well as first period Literature.

"You're not worried, are you, Meara?" Katie asked.

"A little," I admitted.

"Don't be," she said. "I'll show you around, especially since we have first period together. How cool is that?"

"It's great," I said, and I meant it. Katie and I had grown close over the last month. At first she came across kind of strong, but once I got used her personality, she was a lot of fun.

"Are you ready for our shopping trip tomorrow?"

Katie convinced me that the best time to shop for new school clothes was the beginning of August when the stores had the best selection. I hadn't been to the mall yet. As soon as she heard that, she arranged the trip.

"All set," I confirmed. "You'll give my mom a lift to the clinic, right?"

"No problem," Katie said. "I'll pick you up at nine o'clock, okay? See you tomorrow."

"Bye." I hung up the phone and flopped back on my bed. I was excited about tomorrow. Sure, it was just shopping, but I hadn't been to a mall in forever. I missed Kim, and I was getting apprehensive about starting at a new school, in a new country. There was nothing like a new outfit or two to boost your confidence.

I'd asked Ula on Wednesday if she wanted to go with us, but she declined. She gestured to her outfit, a bright paisley swirled dress reminiscent of the 60s, and told me that the mall didn't sell the type of clothes she liked to wear. I couldn't disagree with her. I told her she could just hang out and not buy anything, but she politely declined.

I eventually fell asleep and dreamed I was on the beach again, where I first saw the man who said he was David. This time was different from my previous two dreams about him. Rather than participate in the dream, I was a bystander.

My mother stood in front of me. Young and beautiful, she looked like she did in the black and white photo on my dresser. Her glossy, chestnut-brown hair waved down her back and ended at her waist. She wore a bright yellow sundress that swirled at her ankles. Her feet were bare, as was her face. She looked fresh and vibrant, a rosy hue blooming on her cheeks. She was locked in the arms of a handsome man. The man from my dreams. David.

He held her close, resting his chin on her head with his arms wrapped around her waist. Their eyes were closed, and they appeared to be swaying to a song I couldn't hear.

"You'll leave," she said.

He nodded without opening his eyes and tightened his grip on her. "I have to."

"Will you return?"

He paused for a moment, and then sighed before replying. "I don't know."

I watched my mom's face tighten as if struggling with some internal war. For a moment, she looked desperate, and then her face relaxed. She opened her eyes and stared up at him.

"I don't care!" she cried. "If we only have this summer together, it's more than I've ever had with anyone else. I love you!"

He took her chin in his hand and leaned close, whispering. "If

I hurt you, it's never what I intended. I love you, Sharon, more than I have ever loved another woman."

With that, he kissed her deeply. I shuffled my feet, embarrassed. Jeez, these people were my parents. If this was a glimpse of what had been between them, then I had no doubt that David had loved my mom. Very much.

After dropping mom off at the clinic, it was a short ride to the mall. Katie circled to find a spot. Apparently, we weren't the only ones who thought this was a good day to shop. I spotted a small car backing out in the next aisle over, and Katie maneuvered into the spot like a pro. She jumped out of the car and, once I was by her side, pulled me along, not stopping until we stood at the center of the mall.

"What do you think?" Katie turned to me. "Where should we start?"

"It doesn't matter to me," I said. "You pick."

Apparently, that was the right thing to say. Katie took me to her favorite store, and she started to pick out outfits for both of us. She held up a pair of designer jeans. The pockets were embellished and sparkly. "What do you think?" she asked.

"For who?" I eyed the jeans cautiously. The price tag told me that they'd eat up almost the whole clothing budget I'd allotted myself.

"I guess either of us, but I was thinking me. You don't strike me as the sparkly type."

Relieved, I nodded. "Yes, for you, they're cute. You're right. My tastes run a little more plain."

Katie shook her head. "Simple, maybe, but not plain." She handed me a pumpkin orange, V-neck sweater. It was fuzzy and soft. "How about this?"

"I love it." It was on sale, too—40% off.

She nodded absentmindedly, already moving on to another rack. "I knew it. That's a great color for you with your dark hair. It would look horrendous on me."

We took armfuls of clothes into the dressing room. The wildest thing I tried on was a faux fur vest in a spotted leopard print. I thought it looked ridiculous, but Katie kind of liked it. I didn't get it, but I found plenty of things to buy. Within a couple of hours, we were laden with shopping bags.

"Do you want to get some lunch?" Katie asked.

"Sure," I said. "Can we put the bags in the car first?"

"Good idea."

We took the bags out and placed them in the truck. I felt so much lighter and freer without them, which made me realize how hungry I was. Katie wanted tacos, and I wanted a turkey wrap and fries, so we split up to order. When I turned to find a table, Katie waved at me from one by the window.

In between bites, we talked about school. The volleyball team started practice on Monday. Katie wanted me to try out, but I wasn't into sports. She tried to convince me, so I told her I wanted to limit my extracurricular activity so I could spend more time with my mom. Once I said that, she dropped the subject. I felt a little guilty using my mom as an excuse, but it worked.

I sipped my shake, nodding while Katie described the recent team drama. I was only half listening. My mind kept wandering to the dream I had last night.

"Are you okay?" Katie asked. "You seem distracted."

"It's...ah." I struggled, fidgeting with my straw. Could I tell Katie about David? I looked up to find Katie watching me, waiting. Her blue eyes filled with concern, and she reached for my hand.

"Meara, what is it?" she asked. "You know that we're friends, right? That you can talk to me? Tell me anything. Even if Evan is being a pig-head, you can tell me."

Her concern touched me. "It's not about Evan."

"Then, what it is?"

I debated, ultimately deciding that I needed to tell someone. It was killing me not talking about my dreams. Once I started, it all poured out. I told her about all three dreams. She listened, a myriad of emotions crossing her face from disbelief to awe.

"Holy crap!" she exclaimed when I finished. "Have you told anyone else?"

"Just my mom," I said. "But only about the first two."

"Why didn't you tell her about the last one?"

Once again I debated how much to tell Katie. I had my reasons for not telling my mom. Katie was one of my only friends here, what could it hurt to tell her? "I...I think she was scared."

"Scared of what?" Katie asked, her blue eyes wide.

"I don't know."

"Wow." Katie took a sip of her soda. She looked deep in thought and had a strange expression on her face.

"Do you believe me?" I asked.

Katie paused. "I want to show you something." She reached in her purse and dug around, eventually producing a small, worn, black and white photo. She held it out so I could see, pointing at the figures. "Here's my dad. You haven't met him yet. Next to Dad is Mom. Your mom is beside her. On the end? That's David."

"Can I see?" I reached for the photo.

"Sure." Katie handed it to me. "I've been meaning to show it to you. That's why it's in my purse. I'm not some weirdo who carries around pictures of my parents and their friends."

Katie laughed at her own joke, but I was too distracted. I stared at the photo, recognizing a younger, prettier version of Lydia and an image of my mom similar to the photograph in my room. On the end, with his arm around my mother, was David. Goose bumps covered my arms when my suspicions were confirmed. This was the David of my dreams, and seventeen years later, he looked almost exactly the same.

"That's him." I handed the picture back.

"Keep it." She pushed my hand away. "Have you told Evan?"

"No."

"Okay, I'm sure you have a good reason, and it's none of my business, but you know I'm going to ask anyway...why not?"

I sighed and finished my shake before answering. "I guess I'm worried. What if he doesn't believe me? What if he thinks I'm crazy? We've only been going out for a few weeks."

"Meara," Katie said. "Evan is really into you. I've never seen him so head over heels before. He's spent all his free time with you. You're not giving him enough credit."

"You're right."

"You'll tell him?" she persisted.

"Yes."

"Soon?"

"Yes."

She nodded. "Good. Well, now that we're refueled, we're ready to tackle part two—school supplies."

"Ugh," I said.

"Right," she agreed.

Chapter 12

*I*t was close to dinnertime when we returned to Peggy's Cove. Katie drove me home, but didn't stay. Her parents were having some friends over that night. They expected her to be there for the dinner. She promised to catch up with me on Tuesday, her day off that week.

I went in and headed for the kitchen, since I heard my mom and grandmother talking. My grandma was at the stove making dinner. Mom stood at the counter chopping vegetables. They turned and smiled when I came in.

"How was shopping?" Mom asked.

"Great," I said. "We had fun."

"Did you get some new clothes for school?"

"Yes." She looked at me expectantly, so I added. "Three shirts, two pairs of jeans, and a sweater. I'll show you later. I left the bags by the door."

"Do you need money?"

"No," I said. "I've got it." I'd saved up quite a bit from work. I rarely spent anything back home, so I had a nice savings account. Mom wanted me to save it all for college. I disagreed. It wouldn't hurt to spend a little.

"Well, let me know when you want to go and get your supplies."

"We bought those, too." I hoped she wasn't disappointed that I didn't wait for her. She didn't seem to mind, although she insisted on paying me back for the supplies.

"Evan called while you were out," Grandma Mary said. She tried to sound casual. Her curiosity dripped from every word.

"I'll go and call him back."

"Go?" she asked with a frown.

I bit my tongue to keep from smiling. This would kill her. "To my room. I'll be back in a few minutes." I kissed Mom's cheek, and she winked at me when Grandma Mary's head was turned. She knew what I was up to. She probably did the same thing when she was my age. Grandma Mary was sweet, and she loved juicy gossip.

I decided to use my cell phone, since both of my grandparents' phones were tethered to the wall. One was in the kitchen, probably the one Grandma Mary had hoped I would use, and the other was in the family room. Honestly, had they never heard of cordless phones?

"Hello?"

I didn't recognize the voice on the other end of the line. It was a deep baritone.

"Hi. This is Meara. Is Evan there?"

"Oh, Meara. I finally get to talk to you. This is Darren, Evan's dad. One minute, I'll get him."

"How was shopping?" Evan asked without saying hello, adding. "Katie sure brought back a haul."

"Yes, well, she bought more than me."

"Doesn't surprise me."

"She also has a job." I felt the need to defend Katie.

"I thought you did, too." Evan knew that I worked on Sew Beautiful's website.

"I guess, but I'm kind of phasing out of it," I said. "It doesn't pay much, that's for sure."

"Not compared to those big diner tips, I suppose."

I knew he was teasing, and I chose to ignore it. "You called earlier?"

"Yeah," he said. "Do you want to go to a museum tomorrow?"

"Sure. Where?"

"It's in Halifax. The Museum of Natural History. I'll pick you up at ten."

"I'll be ready." I heard Evan's name being called in the background. It sounded like Lydia. "I think you're wanted."

"We have company."

"I know. Katie told me. It's okay. I'll see you tomorrow."

"Goodnight, Meara."

"Night."

I went back to the kitchen and ate dinner with my grandmother and my mom. Grandpa Jamie was working late as usual. After I helped clean up, I took my shopping bags back to my room and put away my new clothes. Then, I sat on my bed and wrote an email to Kim. In her last email, she begged me to tell her more about Evan, Katie, and Ula.

Details, Meara, she wrote. You know those little words called adjectives? Use them. Oh, and send pictures too.

So I described my friends with as much detail as I could, and I even wrote about Katie giving me the picture of my mom with my dad in it. The picture! It was in my purse tucked behind my driver's license in my wallet. I pulled it out and studied it again. How was it that David only looked a few years older? Mom, though still pretty, was obviously much older now than when the picture was taken. Same with Lydia. I couldn't speak for Darren, since I hadn't met him in person yet, but I imagined he had aged too. Everyone aged. Everyone, apparently, but my father. What was going on? I hoped he planned to visit me in dreamland tonight, because I had questions.

I decided to put the picture in the same frame on my dresser that held the picture of just my mom. She wore the same yellow dress in that photo; it must have been taken around the same time. Picking up the frame, I carried it to my bed. The back was the kind that slid off, but it was tight. I pressed hard. Eventually, it slid down. A stack of photographs fell out. I expected the typical foam padding or some cardboard, but there was none. Curious, I picked them up and flipped them over. The first one was my mom; the one I had seen in the frame. When I looked at the picture under it, I almost dropped the whole stack. It was a picture of me when I was three. With shaking hands, I flipped it over and read the inscription.

Dear Mom and Dad,

Here is Meara at age three. She's getting big so fast. I wish you could see what a smart, beautiful child she is. Mom, she has your curiosity and Dad, your persistence. She keeps me on my toes!

I hope you are well. Not a day goes by that I don't miss you. Hopefully, we will be able to come for a visit soon.

Love Always,
Sharon

I quickly went through the rest. There was a picture of me for every year, including my junior picture from last year. Each one was inscribed with a similar message, hoping to visit, but not finding the time. Mom said she never talked to her parents, that they were estranged. If that was true, why did she send pictures of me with loving notes on the back? What was Mom not telling me?

I left the frame on my bed and went to find her. She was in her room, reading.

"Mom? Can you come to my room for a minute? I want to show you something." I kept my voice even and calm, although I was seething inside.

"Sure, sweetie." Mom put her book down and stood up. "Do you want to show me what you bought today?"

"No, something I found in my room."

"Oh, okay." She sounded surprised, but she followed me. I picked up the pictures and held them out to her. She was smiling until she saw my grinning toddler face. She clutched at the collar of her shirt and didn't make any attempt to take the pictures. "Where did you find those?"

"In the frame behind the picture of you." Since she was clearly not going to take the photographs, I fanned them out for her to see. "They're me, Mom. They're all me. If you weren't talking to your parents, why'd you send pictures?"

"They're your grandparents," Mom said, as if that explained everything.

"But you weren't speaking to them. Or were you?"

"I wasn't." Mom didn't move from the doorway or let go of her shirt. I didn't even think she was aware she was holding her collar in a death grip.

"Were you fighting with them?"

"What kind of a question is that? Do you think I was lying to you?"

"I don't know, Mom. The evidence is pretty strong." I flung the pictures across the bed. "I sure wasn't expecting to find these in a frame in my room!"

"Everything okay in here?" Grandma Mary stood behind my mom in the doorway, peering over her shoulder. She saw the pictures splayed across the bed and sighed. "Oh, I see."

"Grandma," I said. I left off Mary, hoping to soften her up. "Have you been keeping in touch with my mom all these years? She told me that you were estranged. That she didn't talk to you anymore."

"That's true, Meara." My grandmother said it quietly, placing her arm around my mom's shoulder. Mom's eyes were shiny like she was about to cry. Well, let her, I thought, swallowing a lump in my throat.

"Then why do you have all these pictures of me?"

"Your mom mailed them to us, one letter every year with a picture of you. No return address. Always sent from a different location."

"Why?" I asked. We looked to my mom for an answer.

Mom was crying in earnest now. She walked past me and sat on the edge of my bed. "I'm so sorry!" she cried. "When your father left, I was heartbroken. I couldn't take the chance that he would try to take you from me. So, when the opportunity came, I moved as far away as I could."

Grandma Mary sighed. She sat next to Mom and patted her knee. "That's why the letters were unmarked and from all over."

"I didn't want him to find us," my mom whispered.

"You didn't trust us?" Grandma Mary's voice filled with hurt. Mom hugged her fiercely.

"No, Mom. I didn't trust him."

"Why?" I asked. "Is he dangerous?" I wondered if I should be worried.

My mom shook her head. "He would never hurt you, Meara. He loves you."

"But he would take me away?" I asked, which made her frown.

"I don't know."

I reached behind them and sifted through the pictures on the bed. I found the small one I was looking for. I gave it to my mom.

"Is that him?" I asked, pointing to David in the picture Katie gave me.

"Yes," Mom said. She traced his face with her finger, and then looked up at me with wide eyes. "Where did you get this?"

"Katie gave it to me."

Mom nodded. "Lydia. I forgot she had this picture."

"You said you don't have any pictures of David. Is that true?" I asked. She gave me an assessing look, and then shook her head. She'd lied, another one to add to the recent list.

"May I see them?" I placed equal emphasis on each word. Calm, Meara. Stay calm, I told myself.

"Mom, do you mind if I talk to Meara alone?"

My grandmother looked surprised, but she nodded. "Of course. I'll see you in the morning, girls."

"Come with me, Meara."

Once we were in her room, Mom went to her dresser and sifted through the contents in the top drawer. "Have a seat on the bed."

I sat and waited. She returned with two photographs. Both were about the same size as the one Katie had given me. She handed me the one on top.

"Lydia took this one, too. On the same day."

My mom and David laughed into the camera, their arms wrapped around each other.

"You look happy."

"We were."

"David looked like this in my dreams," I said.

Mom frowned at me. "And you're sure you never saw his picture before?"

"Where would I have seen it?" I asked. "You never showed me."

She lowered the other picture so I could see. This one was just David. He looked at the camera the way he gazed at my mom in the dream.

"You took this one."

She looked at me, surprised. "How'd you know?"

I took the picture and studied it. "Because I can tell he's looking at you."

"I loved him so much." Mom spoke in barely a whisper, but I heard it. My anger dissolved in her sorrow. How hard had this all been for her? To be pregnant so young, and then raise a daughter all alone. The father of your child, the man that you loved, gone.

"Why did he leave?" That was the real question. I had yet to find a satisfactory answer.

"He had to," she said. The same thing she always said.

"But why?"

She shook her head. "Only he can tell you that."

"Why does he look only a few years older in my dreams?"

She took the photographs back and stood. "I don't know, Meara. It's only a dream." She crossed to the dresser and put them away.

Why did she insist that it was just a dream? How could I possibly dream of a man I'd never met and have him look exactly the way he did seventeen years ago? Goose bumps rose on my arms. What was going on?

"I'm sorry, Meara." When she turned back, she was crying again. "For keeping secrets. For keeping you from your grandparents. I did what I thought I had to do."

"It's okay, Mom." I decided to keep my fear to myself for now. Mom was upset enough.

"It's not," she said. "But I hope you'll forgive me."

I stood and gave her a hug. She kissed my forehead.

"I love you, Meara."

"Love you too, Mom." I hadn't said I forgive her, but she didn't push. I wasn't sure yet. There was too much I didn't understand.

Chapter 13

About an hour after it opened, Evan and I arrived at the museum. I sulked a little after we left my grandparent's house, stinging from my conversation with Mom. Evan listened to my recount. He didn't understand my mom's actions either, agreeing it was strange.

"Can you ask your mom what she remembers about David?" I asked him.

"Sure. I'll see what I can find out."

"Thanks."

We parked in the attached structure and entered the museum through a side door. There were large posters hanging in the hall featuring sharks, whales, and giant squids, as well as mythical creatures such as mermaids and sea serpents.

"Wow, I can see why you like this museum," I said. They had a huge maritime collection.

Evan nodded. "That's why I wanted to bring you here today. And this exhibit." He pointed to a Monsters of the Deep poster featuring a giant squid called a kraken. "I haven't seen it yet."

"It's about sea monsters, and you haven't seen it? How long has it been here?"

"It just opened." He took my hand and pulled me forward. "So, do you want to start with my favorite exhibits or should we start with the Monsters of the Deep?"

"To be honest," I said, "I've only visited two museums in my life. I'm a little out of my league here, so I'll let you pick."

He grinned. I got the suspicious feeling that he was hoping I would let him pick. "We'll start with some local history," he said.

We spent the rest of the morning exploring the museum. Evan's favorites were the archaeology and marine biology exhibits. He explained everything to me and answered my questions with great patience.

We ate cheeseburgers and fries in the museum cafeteria. He teased me when I went through the museum brochure at lunch, checking off all the exhibits that we had already seen. I didn't want to miss anything. To my surprise, we had seen almost all the regular exhibits. That left the Monsters of the Deep display.

The special exhibit section of the museum was cavernous; the walls draped in blue fabric. The lighting made the room glow with a bluish tint. It felt like we were underwater. Suspended from the ceiling was a skeleton. The creature was snakelike and easily twenty feet long. The room was divided into vignettes—one side showcased real or extinct creatures, the other featured those that were legendary.

I was drawn to the mythical side, fascinated by the lore surrounding these creatures. The exhibits ranged from the fierce—fire-breathing sea serpents, giant squids, and octopus-like monsters called Kraken, to the beautiful—mermaids, Selkies, and Sirens.

Evan, too, seemed engrossed. We stood side by side, reading the captions and stories interspersed with beautiful pieces of artwork inspired by man's hopes and fears of these beings. Several monsters were depicted in life-sized statues or in carvings and tapestries. One tapestry caught my eye. It portrayed Odysseus's encounter with the sirens. The women were beautiful and appeared to be seducing Odysseus. The colors and detail were amazing.

"Did you see this?" I asked Evan, thinking he was next to me. He wasn't. I spotted him two exhibits over, staring at a mermaid statue. I walked up behind him and placed my hand on my hips in mock anger.

"Leave it to a guy to find the half-naked female in the room."

He laughed and turned to me with raised eyebrows. "Jealous?"

"Of a fish woman? Never."

He leaned down and kissed me. "You're cuter than her anyway."

"Thank you."

"What did you want to show me?"

"Just a tapestry. It's no big deal. I just didn't realize you weren't next to me."

"Are you having a good time?"

I nodded. "It's great. Thanks for bringing me."

"I knew you'd like it." He looked at his watch. "Do you want to stay or are you ready to go?"

I shrugged. "It's up to you."

"Let's look in the gift shop, and then we can get going."

"Okay."

The gift shop was filled with unique, fun items. Many were maritime themed. The back corner was filled with limited-edition items from the Monsters' exhibit. I found a small mermaid statue and bought it for Evan as a joke. He laughed when I gave it him.

"What's this for?"

"Now you have your own personal mermaid."

"To remind me that you're cuter?" he teased.

"Exactly," I said, surprising myself by giving him a quick kiss. He didn't seem to mind. He pulled me closer and kissed me again.

"Thank you," he said.

Chapter 14

"This is where he plays?" I glanced in awe at the long building in front of us. Families were pouring in, tickets in hand. My experience with sporting events was limited to the handful of times that Mom took me to Milwaukee for a basketball game. That arena was big, but I'd never been to one like this before.

"Yep," Katie said. "Hockey's pretty popular here."

"That's an understatement," said Jen, one of Katie's best friends, who joined us for the game.

"Is your friend Ula coming, Meara?" Katie asked. "Or should we just get our tickets?"

I frowned at her. "I think she's coming. Didn't Evan say he got us the tickets?"

"He did." She pointed to the ticket windows. "We need to go to Will Call and pick them up."

"Oh, okay. Well, I guess she's not coming. Otherwise, she'd be here by now. I asked her to meet me by the ticket counter."

"We can walk closer and look," Jen suggested.

As we neared the ticket area, I saw a girl who looked like Ula, although her back was to us. She appeared to be having an intense conversation with a tall man. I couldn't see his face that clearly, since he was wearing a baseball cap pulled low over his eyes, but his arms and chest were well defined under his snug Mooseheads t-shirt. He raised his head and nodded in our direction, and the girl turned. It was Ula. She smiled and waved before turning back to the guy and giving him a firm push on the chest that clearly said go away. He shook his head and laughed at her. He was easily a foot taller, so her push had no impact on him. He gave a short wave in our direction before turning and walking away. Ula watched him leave and then ran over.

"Meara! Good to see you!"

She gave me quick hug. When she pulled back, I introduced her to Katie and Jen. Katie seemed amused by Ula's outfit, which today consisted of bell-bottom jeans and a Beetles t-shirt.

"She has great vintage clothes, don'tcha think?" I asked.

"Absolutely!" Jen gushed. "Where did you find that t-shirt?"

Katie and I left Ula and Jen chatting clothes while we went to the Will-Call window to get our tickets. Katie whistled when she saw them.

"What?" I asked.

"Evan got us front row center, near the penalty box."

"Is that good?"

"It's great," she said. "We'll be able to see everything."

I hoped the tickets weren't too expensive. I asked Katie as much on our way back to Jen and Ula.

"It's fine, Meara," she said. "Evan can get free tickets to give to family and friends. I'm sure he's just happy that you're here."

We passed through the turnstiles. The smell of freshly popped corn, hot dogs, and pizza assaulted me. My stomach rumbled.

Ula laughed. "Should we get snacks before we find our seats?"

I ordered nachos and a large Diet Coke. Katie got a soft pretzel, and Jen bought cotton candy. Ula didn't buy anything.

"I ate just before I got here," she told us.

We walked around the arena until we found the right section. Then we headed down to the front row. By the time we took our seats, I was impressed with how close we were. The guys were on the ice, warming up. I figured out which team was Evan's, but with all the padding layers and helmets, I had no idea which player he was. Katie nudged me with her elbow and pointed.

"That's Evan, number 14."

As she was talking, he skated over and along the glass, winking as he passed. He had a patch on his uniform that set him apart from his teammates.

"Why does Evan's uniform have a patch?" I asked.

"He's the captain," Katie said.

"He's the captain?" Why didn't he ever mention it to me?

Jen nodded enthusiastically. "Oh yeah. Evan's great at hockey."

Ula was quiet. I looked over and saw her scanning the crowd. Her eyes settled on someone, and she scowled. I followed her gaze.

"Who's that?" I asked. It looked like it might be the tall guy from earlier. At least, I could make out similar baseball cap and t-shirt, but he was too far away to see any real details.

"Someone annoying," Ula said. "He's not important."

"Is that the guy you were talking to outside? Is he your boyfriend or something?" Jen asked. By now, all of us were staring at him.

"Ex," she stressed, "but yes. Something like that."

He waved at us again. He obviously knew we were watching.

"Just ignore him," Ula muttered. She looked annoyed. I wondered what happened between them.

The buzzer sounded, announcing the start of the first period. Evan squared off against the captain of the other team, the hockey puck dropped, and the game began.

The game was fast paced, and yet, by the first break, I had a good idea of what was going on. The crowd, loud and boisterous, chanted and jeered in a way that seemed almost choreographed. "Sieve, Sieve!" Katie and Jen yelled.

Once we learned the common phrases, Ula and I joined them. At the end of the second period, we all yelled, "How much time is left?"

We cracked up when the announcer replied, "One minute left in the period."

Evan scored three goals that period and assisted with four others. It was a high-scoring game and, by the middle of the third period, Evan's team was ahead of the other team by two. He scored again, and I whistled and cheered. My friends joined me.

"He's really good," Ula said.

"He's great!" Jen shouted. "Go Evan!"

Katie put her fingers to her mouth and whistled shrilly. "That's my brother," she said and grinned. "I told you, Meara. He's pretty amazing at hockey."

I was stunned, proud, and flabbergasted as to why someone as talented as Evan was interested in me.

The buzzer sounded the end of the game, and we jumped up.

The teams lined up on the ice and shook hands. Katie gathered our wrappers and stuff.

"C'mon, let's go," she said.

"Why the rush?" I asked.

"The team's signing autographs. I thought you'd like to meet some of the players."

"Do you know them all?" Ula asked.

"Not all," Katie said, "but most. Evan's had a few over to the house for dinner or whatever." She smiled at Jen and Ula. "They're pretty cute."

By the time we reached the lobby, long lines had formed for the signing. I noticed the teenage girls and again wondered why Evan chose me. I must have frowned at them, because Katie patted my arm.

"Don't you worry, girlfriend," she said. "Evan only has eyes for you. Trust me."

Evan signed pictures and interacted with his fans, ruffling little boys' hair and shaking people's hands. I noticed the other players doing similar things. Some flirted a bit with the teenage girls, but Evan never did. He smiled politely and moved them on.

It didn't take too long to reach the front of the line. Evan grinned at me. "What would you like me to write, young lady?"

"Hmm..." I played along, pretending to contemplate. "How about 'to my biggest fan'?"

"That's a pretty big role to fill," he teased.

"I think I'm up for the challenge."

Evan nudged his teammate next to him. "Phil," he said, "this is my girlfriend, Meara."

Phil looked at me and grinned. "Nice to meet cha."

Katie cleared her throat behind me, so Evan added, "And of course, you've already met my sister, Katie, and this is her friend, Jen." Evan paused when he got to Ula. He hadn't met her yet.

"This is my friend, Ula," I told him. "From the clinic?"

"A pleasure to meet you," Ula said and shook his hand.

"Hello, ladies." Phil tipped his baseball cap.

"You bringing 'em to the party later, Mitchell?" This came from the guy sitting on the other side of Phil.

"Do you want to go?" Evan asked us, and I looked at Katie.

"Sure!" she said.

Evan looked pleased. "We've got about fifteen more minutes of signing, Coach will want to run through a few things, then we can change and get going."

"Where should we meet you?" Katie asked. "I don't want to sit in my car for forty-five minutes."

"How about The Goal Post?" Evan suggested. I had no idea what it was, but it sounded like a sports bar or restaurant.

"Okay," Katie said. "We'll just order an appetizer or something."

"I'll be there as soon as I can," Evan promised. "An hour or less."

"Hey...are you girls almost done yet? My kid wants an autograph." This came from a grumpy-looking man behind us. His son was a chubby middle schooler who looked more interested in us than the hockey players.

I smiled apologetically. "We're leaving now. See you soon, Evan."

The Goal Post was a restaurant. One of those sports-themed ones that catered to the fans. It was crowded, but we managed to get a high table in the bar area. We ordered a pitcher of root beer, breaded mushrooms, and poutine, which was starting to grow on me. Sure, it looked disgusting, but the combination of cheese and gravy with the crispy fries—mmmm, yum.

"What did you think of the game?" Jen asked.

"I liked it," I said. "Seems simple enough to follow."

"It was a pretty mellow night," Katie said. "No fights."

"Right," Jen said. "Kind of boring actually. So if you liked this one, you'd like one of those."

"Does Evan get in fights?" I'd seen a few guys slammed up against the Plexiglas during the game. Katie told me it was called checking. It looked painful. At least Evan did more of the checking and got checked less often. He was quick on his skates.

Katie laughed. "What do you think? I'm not sure his opponents like getting slammed into the glass."

"Does he get hurt?" I couldn't bear it if he was getting black eyes or losing teeth. Jen told me it was pretty common for hockey players to have fake teeth.

"Nah," Katie said. "They have all that padding, and he's a pretty good fighter."

Ula was picking at the fries. She hadn't said anything since we got here, and she kept glancing at the door.

"Are you okay?" I asked her.

"Sure," she said. She gave me a half-hearted smile.

"Is it that guy that was with you at the game? Did he bother you?"

"Him?" She shook her head. "No. I can handle him. It's nothing. I'm okay. I'm sorry I can't go with you."

"It's okay," I said. We all called our parents on the way over to the restaurant. Katie suggested I just stay over at her house, and her mom said it was okay. My mom was fine with it if Lydia was, so getting permission was easy. Ula didn't even try to call home. "Your parents are protective, huh?"

"You could say that." She looked out the window again, and then hopped off the barstool. "Looks like my ride's here. Goodnight, ladies."

I gave her a quick hug. "See you next week?" I asked, referring to the clinic.

"See you then," she confirmed.

Jen waved, and Katie called, "Nice meeting you!" After Ula was out of earshot, she added. "She seems nice. Dresses a bit odd, but nice."

"She likes vintage." It didn't bother me. I thought her style was kind of cool. Jen echoed my thoughts aloud.

"Her clothes are wicked. Wish I had the courage to wear whatever I wanted."

"Why don't you?" I asked.

"Are you kidding? They'd laugh me out of school," Jen said. She took a sip of her root beer.

"You should've seen the Bob Marley shirt she was wearing the first time I met her," I said. "If I could get my hands on that one, I'd wear it." Katie and Jen exchanged a look that said "yeah right," which I chose to ignore. I would wear it. I wasn't much of a slave to fashion, so I had a tendency to wear what I wanted regardless.

Evan entered the bar. His hair was damp and curling around his ears. He wore dark jeans and a gray, button-down shirt. Three of his teammates followed him. He smiled when he spotted me, crossed the room, and gave me a quick kiss.

"Hi," I said. "That didn't take too long."

"Coach's lecture was short since we won tonight." Evan turned to the guys who were with him. "This is Joe, Peter, and Brian."

The bar had cleared out a bit, so the guys pulled over some barstools and joined us at the table. It didn't take them long to notice our barely eaten appetizers.

"You gonna finish those?" Brian asked.

"Help yourself," Katie said.

They demolished the two baskets in a few minutes, and Evan finished my root beer. They still seemed hungry.

"Do you guys want to order something else?" I asked.

"Ah, there will be food at the party," Peter said. "Kevin eats more than the rest of us."

"Ready?" Evan asked.

"Let's go," Brian said.

Katie glanced at Brian. Her expression was calculating, although I was the only one that saw it. "Can one of your friends ride with us? Then Meara can go with you, and if we get lost, he can get us to Kevin's."

"Good idea," Evan said.

"How about you, Brian?" Katie asked.

"Sure." He nodded to his friends. "See you at Kev's."

I followed Evan, Peter, and Joe out to the car. They recapped the game, Evan glancing at me periodically. I smiled, reassuring him that I was fine. It was kind of interesting to hear the recount from their point of view.

Peter wasn't much taller than I was. He talked a mile a minute and seemed to have an endless supply of energy. Joe spoke slowly and thoughtfully. He was lanky, lean, and the opposite of Peter.

When we reached the car, Peter made for the front seat. Joe blocked him and asked me pointedly, "Would you like to sit in front, Meara?"

Peter seemed surprised to see me there. Apparently, in providing his play-by-play of the game, he forgot that I was with them.

"Oh, yeah, right," he stuttered. "Sorry, Meara. The front's all yours."

"Thanks, Peter." As I walked around them, Joe winked at me. I grinned in reply.

The ride to Kevin's house was pretty short. He lived about fifteen minutes from the arena in an apartment he shared with two other teammates. The guys told me more about the team on the ride over. I learned that the players ranged from mid-teens to early twenties. Kevin and his roommates were on the older end.

"They're hoping to get picked soon," Peter said.

"Picked?" I repeated. I wasn't familiar with the term.

"They want to go professional," Joe explained. "The Sea Dogs are like a farm team for a farm team."

"Oh," I said. I didn't understand.

"Farm teams are where the professional teams get their players," Evan said. "Are you familiar with the National Hockey League?"

"I don't think so."

"Where are you from again?" Joe asked.

"Wisconsin."

"Milwaukee Admirals," Peter said. "AHL."

I stared at him blankly. Joe shook his head at Peter. "American Hockey League provides the players for the professional teams. That's where we'll play next."

"Okay," I said.

"Are you familiar with the Chicago Blackhawks?" Joe asked.

"I've heard of them," I admitted.

Joe nodded. "They're a professional team. National Hockey League or NHL."

I looked at Evan. He was silent during this conversation.

"Why American teams?" I asked.

"That's where the money is, baby!" Peter gave me an exaggerated wink. "I'm hoping for Texas. Love those Lone Stars!"

"Do you all want to play professionally?" I asked.

"Hell, yeah!" Peter yelled and fist bumped with Joe. Evan didn't respond.

"Evan?"

"I'm not sure," he admitted.

"What?" Peter leaned forward and clasped Evan on the shoulder. "Mitchell, you're the best on the team. You could probably go pro now if you wanted to."

"I don't," Evan said. "I'm not ready."

"Why not, man?" Peter pursued. Evan kept his eyes on the road, but his jaw tightened. He clearly didn't want to have this conversation.

"I'm finishing school first," he said finally.

Joe leaned forward and patted his shoulder. "That's cool." He gave Peter a warning look. "Don't you agree, Pete?"

"Yeah. Cool," Peter said, although from the look on his face, he clearly didn't mean it.

"Can I get you something?" Evan shouted so I could hear him above the thumping music. The house was filled with the players, their friends, and random acquaintances. We were in the living room, sitting on the couch.

"What are you having?" So far, Evan had only drunk a Coke, although there was plenty of beer and bottles of liquor.

"I'll probably get a beer."

I didn't know what I wanted, but I knew I didn't like beer. "I'll come with you," I said, following him to the kitchen.

Katie and Jen sat at the table with Brian and Peter. They were playing some kind of drinking game with cards. They both looked happy already.

"Is she going to be okay to drive?" I asked Evan.

He frowned at his sister. "I'd say 'no' if she continues at her current pace."

"I'll just have a Diet Coke then," I told him. "I can drive Katie's car back to your house."

"You sure?"

"Yeah. I'll follow you, if that's all right. My mom okay'd me staying over." I felt strange telling him this, since it was his house, too. Until the words came out of my mouth, I hadn't considered the implication. I felt my cheeks warming.

If Evan noticed my discomfort, he didn't say anything. He reached into the cooler for the Diet Coke and handed me the can. Taking a cup, he filled it at the beer keg. "Do you want to go outside for a bit?" He motioned to the patio door. "At least it will be quieter."

"Sure." Once again, I let him lead the way. We had to go by the table. As we passed, Katie grabbed my hand and pulled me closer.

"Isn't Brian cute?" I'm sure she meant to whisper it in my ear, but it came out as more of a slurred shout. He was not as drunk as she was, and it was obvious he heard her, too. He grinned at us.

Katie opened her eyes wider and pouted at me. "I'm sorry, Meara. I don't think I should drive us home. Maybe we can leave my car here and ride with Evan? Mom won't be happy…"

I patted her shoulder. "It's okay, Katie. Evan and I talked about this already. I'll drive your car home."

"You sure?"

"Yes."

She jumped up, knocking her chair over in the process, and threw her arms around me. "You're the best! Jen, isn't she the best?"

Jen raised her glass at us and nodded enthusiastically. "The best!" She polished off whatever was in there, and Peter quickly refilled it.

"Are you okay?" I asked Jen. Her eyes were glassy, and her face flushed.

She waved off my concern. "I'm good. I'm…I'm great!"

She took another big gulp. At this rate, they would be throwing up within the hour. I looked at Evan, unsure of what to do. He was talking to Brian and Peter, but when I caught his eye, he nodded. He must have been listening to our conversation, too. He excused himself, went around the table, and grabbed a bowl of pretzels from the counter. He placed it between Katie and Jen.

"Have something to eat," I told them. "And maybe slow down a little."

Jen pouted. "We're fine, Party Pooper."

"Listen to her," Evan said. "You are both going to be hurting tomorrow."

"Hey, Mitchell, can we please get back to our game?" This came from Peter, who was pretty wasted himself. He threw a pretzel at Evan.

Evan took my hand and led me outside. The apartment had a small patio, but their unit faced a courtyard with a path that circled an in-ground pool. The few chairs on the patio were already taken, and by the looks of things, the couples sitting in them paid us no attention.

"Should we go for a walk?" Evan asked.

"I'd like that," I said. Anything was better than hanging with the make-out couples. They appeared to be on the verge of moving beyond, and I didn't want to stick around for that. Apparently, you lost your inhibitions with alcohol. I wasn't the world's most experienced partier, but the events at Kevin's house sure opened my eyes.

Evan took my hand again, and we walked to the pool.

"Some party, huh?" He looked back at the apartment and shook his head.

"Do you usually have parties like this after your games?" I wondered if this was something he did a lot. Did he crash at the party house? Did he meet girls? What would happen if he was drunk, and I wasn't around? There were lots of pretty girls in the house.

"Someone usually has something, but Kev's house is always a big one. Sometimes, we just hang out and order pizza. Just the guys. It's not always so many people." He stopped talking and scratched his head.

"Oh," I said.

"I don't always go either," he went on to add. "With school starting, I'll probably just head back to the dorm. Or if it's a weekend, come see you."

He smiled at me, and I returned it. I was happy that he would choose to see me over partying with his friends. On the other hand, I planned to go to more of his games, so maybe we could do both sometimes.

"What happened to your friend that was with you at the game? Ula?" He said it like you-lah, so I felt the need to correct him.

"Ula? Oh, she had to go home."

"She's the one you met at the clinic, right?"

"Yeah. She's homeschooled. I don't think she gets out much."

"She seemed nice." Evan opened the gate by the pool. I thought we were going to continue on the path around it.

"Where are you going?" I asked.

He turned back and raised an eyebrow. "Don't you trust me?"

"It's a little late for a swim, and I don't have a suit."

He laughed. "We're not going to swim. I just thought we could sit and put our feet in the water." He held up his hand. "Scout's honor. I promise not to push you in."

"You were a Boy Scout?"

"Of course. Weren't you in Girl Scouts?"

"Not so much," I said. "Didn't care for the uniforms."

I could tell Evan didn't know whether to take me seriously or not, but I didn't expand. I sat by the water's edge and debated about showing Evan my feet. Reluctantly, I pulled off my socks and tennis shoes. I tried to put my feet in before Evan sat down, but it was too late.

"Your toes," he said as he sat next to me.

I looked away, embarrassed. "I know. They're so ugly."

"Let me see." He wrapped his hand around my calf and lifted my foot out of the water. "I don't think they're ugly. They're fascinating."

I turned at looked at him then. Was he crazy? "They're disgusting. I always tried to get out of swimming lessons, but my mom insisted. The kids laughed."

"Kids are mean," Evan said. "Webbed toes aren't common, but people have them. They're like flippers."

"Very funny," I muttered.

He lowered my leg into the water and removed his hand. My calf tingled from where he had touched me. He took my hand in his and looked into my eyes.

"I'm sorry that kids made fun of you, Meara. You shouldn't be ashamed of anything about you. You're beautiful from head to toe, inside and out."

I didn't know what to say, but my heart responded by leaping in my chest. He took off his shoes and socks, rolled his jeans up a few times, and placed his feet in the water next to mine. He entwined his right foot with my left, and somewhere, inside of me, some of the hurt from all those years ago began to fade.

Chapter 15

It was easy enough to follow Evan's car back to his house, even with Katie and Jen talking, laughing, and singing the entire way. Loudly. Evan waited by the garage door, and he warned us to be quiet. "Mom'll have a fit if we wake the guests."

I'm sure Katie and Jen thought they were being quiet, but between stumbling into furniture, cursing, and loudly whispered shushes, they didn't fool anyone. On the other hand, no one came out of their rooms, so I took that as a good sign.

Evan and I pursued them up into Katie's room. Katie wanted to play music, but we convinced her it was too late and, after much cajoling, she and Jen climbed into bed. I was stunned at how quickly they were out. It was like their heads hit the pillow and nighty-night.

Evan whistled softly. "They are going to be hurting tomorrow."

"No doubt."

I wasn't sure where I was going to sleep. Katie and Jen took up her double bed. I wasn't above crashing on the floor, though, if I had a blanket and pillow.

Evan inclined his head toward the door. "Want to come to my room?"

I hesitated. I wasn't sure that I should.

"C'mon," he said. "We'll just watch a movie."

"Okay."

The first time I came to the house, Evan's room was messy with clothes strewn about. It looked a little better this time. There was a mound of discarded shirts in the corner, and the comforter was lumpy. I guessed that he hastily cleaned up.

"Where's Ebb and Flow?" I hadn't seen or heard the dogs. They must have heard all the commotion that Jen and Katie made.

"They sleep in my parents' room when I'm not home." He took off his shoes, picked up the remote, and sat on the bed. Leaning back against the headboard, he turned on the TV. I stood in the doorway, and he looked at me curiously. "Are you going to come in and sit?"

I took off my shoes and sat next to him.

"What do you want to watch?" he asked.

"Honestly? I'm not usually up this late." I felt like a loser admitting it, but it was after one. The only time I stayed up that late was New Year's Eve.

"Old music videos or classic horror movies?"

"Classic horror." I loved Vincent Price and Bela Lugosi. Those movies were so much better than the computer-generated blood and gore. They had class.

"Good choice." Evan flipped the channel. Apparently, House of Usher was the featured film tonight. I'd seen it enough times to know it was halfway done.

"One of my favorites," I said.

"You've seen it before?" Evan seemed surprised.

"Like twenty times. You?"

"Maybe ten. I guess I'm not as big a fan as you, but I love old horror movies."

I couldn't believe it. I'd never met anyone around my age before who liked them. Most of my friends didn't even know these movies existed. Kim tried to sit through one every once in a while when she came over for a sleepover. She usually fell asleep. I would stay up to the end and finish it every time.

Evan sat up. He had a mischievous expression on his face. "Let me see your feet again."

"No!" I crossed my legs, tucking my feet away before I faced him.

"Why not?"

"You have some kind of foot fetish?" I challenged.

He raised an eyebrow before responding slowly, "Maybe I do."

He reached for my foot. I tried to scramble away, but he was too quick. I thought he was going to take my sock off but, instead, he tickled the bottom of my foot through my sock. I was extremely ticklish, much

to his delight, and before long, I was breathlessly urging him to stop. I couldn't breathe.

Evan leaned down over me and wiggled his eyebrows dramatically. "Now I know your secret."

"No fair. I know none of yours." I pretended to pout, which made him smile even wider.

He bent forward and kissed me. "You're cute when you pout."

He lifted his head and looked at me. Self-consciously, I remembered that I was lying on his bed. I cleared my throat. "I should, ah, probably go to bed. I'm going to be exhausted tomorrow."

"Probably," he said. His leg covered mine, and he didn't make any attempt to move. He slowly lowered his head, and his eyes never left mine. This time he kissed me slow and deep, and I found myself breathless again.

"Evan, I really…"

"I know, I know." With a sigh, he rolled onto his back, turned his head, and looked at me. "You probably need a pillow and blanket, right?"

"Yeah. That'd be great."

He stood and motioned for me to follow. There was a linen closet in the hall. From the topmost shelf, which I never would have been able to reach, he pulled down a pillow and a fleece blanket.

"Thanks." I was having trouble meeting his eyes. He pulled me into his arms again and kissed me. It was light and quick.

"Goodnight, Meara."

I couldn't sleep. For about the fifteenth time, I looked at Katie's alarm clock. Four-thirty. Great. Ten minutes had passed since the last time I checked.

A throat cleared, and I whipped my head toward the sound, straining in the dark until my eyes grew accustomed. I almost screamed until I recognized the man.

"David?" My father stood by the window, leaning against the wall. "What are you doing here? How'd you get in?"

"I wanted to see you," he said. He ignored my second question. He pulled out the chair by Katie's desk and sat down. "How are you doing? How's your mom?"

"I'm fine. Mom's, well...she's okay. Wait. Are you here? I'm not sleeping?"

I pinched my arm. It hurt.

"I'm real," David said. "Not a figment of your imagination."

I thought I'd be afraid, but I wasn't. This was my father. He wouldn't hurt me. I stood and walked to him. My fingers itched to reach out.

"Go ahead," he said as though he knew what I was thinking. Maybe he did.

I touched the hand that was resting on his knee. He didn't move. His hand was warm. "I thought I was dreaming you," I said in a daze.

"I know." He stood up, and I took a step back. "I'm here, Meara."

"Does Mom know?" He shook his head, and I remembered I'd asked him that before in my dream.

"The previous times I saw you, was I sleeping?"

"Yes and no," he said. "I suppose it was like you were sleepwalking."

"Were we at the lighthouse?"

"Yes."

"And the beach? The first time?" I tried to control the fear in my voice.

"Yes." His voice was quiet. Calm. Like he knew I was getting scared, and he was treading carefully.

"How?"

He shook his head. "I can't tell you. You wouldn't understand."

"Why do you look so young? What are you?" I wanted to know, and I was afraid at the same time. Had I asked this before, too? I couldn't remember.

"You'll find out. Soon."

"Why won't you tell me?" I didn't understand his obscure responses. He was about as open as a bank safe. I had so many questions, and so far, he only had mediocre answers. I studied him, wondering what I could ask that might get a real answer.

"Are you human?"

He paused and searched my face, as if measuring how I would react. Finally, he said, "No, I am not."

I swallowed. "And you won't tell me what you are? What I am?"

"Not yet. The timing's not right."

"What's timing got to do with it?" After all these years, he was worried about timing?

"Everything."

Well, that helped.

"You're dating your friend's brother, aren't you?" he asked. I wasn't sure if he was trying to change the subject or if he wanted to know.

"Maybe," I said. What was it to him? If he could be cryptic, so could I.

"Be careful, Meara," he said. "Take things slowly."

He was a fine one to talk. "Oh, like you and Mom?" Angry, I sat up and crossed my arms. "Please!"

"Exactly." He continued to speak in a frustratingly calm voice. "Learn from us."

"Dad," I said in my most sarcastic voice. "Is that right? Should I call you Dad?"

He winced, but recovered quickly. "I'd like it if you would."

"I'm not sure that I can. You suck as one. You come back into my life after seventeen years, tell me I'm not entirely human, but don't disclose what I am. And then, of all things, you give me dating advice?" My hands shook, and I was on the verge of yelling. I closed my mouth and took a deep breath.

"Relax," David said. "Your friends can't hear you."

"Why not?" What did he do to them? Cast a spell or something?

"They're drunk. Passed out cold."

Oh yeah. There was that.

He stood. "I have to go."

"Go? You just got here!"

He chuckled and leaned forward to kiss my cheek. "You need your sleep. I'll see you again soon."

"When?" I asked. I wanted answers. He needed to give me something.

"Take care of your mother."

Those were his last words before he disappeared. Literally. Not like walking out of the room or jumping out the window, he just vanished. Poof. Gone. I shivered. What in the world was he? What was I?

I lay back on the floor and wrapped the blanket tight around me. My head pounded, but my mind raced. I needed sleep. I couldn't have gotten more than twenty minutes so far. Taking deep breaths, counting sheep, and even meditating didn't help. I gave up and stared at the ceiling. Sleep was not coming.

Chapter 16

"Oh my God, please shoot me now," Katie mumbled from beneath her pillow. Jen moaned next to her.

"I warned you," I said. Katie lifted her pillow long enough to shoot daggers at me. Then she winced and dropped it back on her face again.

"Where's the aspirin?" I asked. "I'll get some for you."

"Bathroom medicine cabinet. Across the hall. Disposable cups on the sink."

I chuckled to myself, pleased that I had shown restraint last night. I did not want to be feeling what they were right now. When I opened Katie's door, the bathroom door opened at the same time. Evan wore his pajama bottoms, but his chest was bare, a towel slung over his shoulder. I raised my eyes to his, and he grinned.

"Mornin'." He crossed the hall, wrapped his arms around my waist, and gave me a hug. He whispered in my ear, "You look good."

I hugged him back. Unwelcomed, David's voice whispered in my head. I mentally pushed him away, and then stepped out of Evan's arms. His smile faltered.

"What if your parents come upstairs?" I didn't want him to think I was rejecting him.

"I'm just giving you a hug."

"They wouldn't know that."

"Fine." He huffed out a breath. I'd won that argument. "What are you doing anyway? Did you need the bathroom?"

"I'm getting them some aspirin. Katie said it's in here?" I motioned to the bathroom.

"Yeah, I'll get it for you." He went back in and pulled a bottle

109

from the medicine cabinet. "I'll let you fill the water cups."

"Thanks."

"Give my sister my best. I'm sure she's in a sorry state." Evan squeezed my waist as he passed me, which made me jump. He turned and winked at me before closing his bedroom door. I filled the cups halfway with water, knowing that I'd spill them otherwise.

Why did David visit here last night? What did he want? Why, after seventeen years, was he making an appearance in my life?

"Meara? Meara!"

I shook myself from my reverie. Katie screeched like nails on a chalkboard—so much for her pounding head. I walked in the room, handing her one of the Dixie cups and two pills. She swallowed them eagerly.

"What took you so long?" she whined.

"Sorry. I thought you fell back asleep."

"Ha! Like I could sleep through this misery."

"Some of us are trying to!" Jen snapped from under the covers. Apparently, she didn't appreciate Katie's volume in the morning.

"Sorry." Katie apologized in a quieter voice. She scooted back against her headboard. "So, Brian asked me out."

"That's great!" I liked Brian and Joe. I wasn't so sure about Peter.

"Peter asked Jen out, but she turned him down." Katie patted the covers where Jen's head would be. "Broke his heart."

"Did not!" Jen's voice rose from beneath the blanket again. Katie and I giggled. "You two are so annoying when I'm hungover," Jen added. She sighed and threw back the covers. "Meara, you have some of those magic pills for me?"

"I don't know how magic they are, but they should help." I handed her the other cup and pills. She thanked me and tossed them back. I settled back onto the floor where I'd slept, or attempted to sleep. It hadn't been too uncomfortable.

There was a knock at the door, and then Evan called, "Is everyone decent?"

Katie rolled her eyes before answering, "Yes, come in."

"Good morning." Evan carried a tray of muffins and doughnuts. In his other hand, he held a carafe of orange juice.

"A man who brings you breakfast?" Jen looked wistful. "Do you have a twin?"

"Thankfully, no," Katie said as she rose from the bed and took the orange juice. She did kiss him on the cheek and thank him. He set the tray down at the end of the bed, and then sat on the floor next to me, crossing his long legs at the ankles.

"I wasn't sure what you would want to eat, but grease is always good with a hangover."

"And nothing beats sugar," Katie added before she took a huge bite of a chocolate doughnut.

Chapter 17

I spent the last week of summer with my mom and Grandma Mary. I rarely saw my grandfather. He left early in the morning and returned late at night. I thought the life of a fisherman looked hard, but he seemed to enjoy what he did. He told me that he found solace by the water.

Evan's classes started already and, apparently, there was no honeymoon period in college. He told me he needed to spend almost every moment of his free time in the lab or the library just to stay afloat. I missed him, but he called every night. Mostly, he told me about his classes. I listened with growing enthusiasm. The more I learned about the ocean, the more fascinated I was. He offered to bring me some books. I told him I preferred to learn from him. "You're a natural teacher," I teased.

It was Thursday night, and I was listening to Evan talk about his classes again. I closed my eyes. He had the best voice. It was smooth, with just the right amount of depth. Every time he laughed, my heart skipped.

"Tell me something that would surprise me," I said.

"About me?" he asked after a moment.

I laughed. "Well, you could do that, too, but I meant about the ocean. Something few people would know."

By his silence, I presumed he was thinking. "You know the exhibit on sea monsters that we saw at the museum?"

"Yeah?"

"Some of them exist."

"What? Like mermaids?" I joked.

No," he said, not rising to the bait. "Like the giant squid. They've already found them washed ashore in Asia."

"Really? That's amazing."

"I know. It's hard to believe that something that large lives on this planet, and only a handful of people can claim to have ever seen one."

"Makes you wonder what else is out there," I said.

"Exactly," he agreed. "It's getting late, Meara. I better go. We're on for Saturday night, right?"

"Yes, but are you going to tell me what we're doing?"

"Not a chance. Good night."

"Night."

I hung up the phone and glanced at the clock. It was almost eleven. Definitely time to get some sleep. Mom and I were heading into Halifax in the morning. She had her usual appointment at the clinic but afterwards, she wanted to spend some time getting pampered. We were both in need of a haircut—the real fun, though, was splurging on manicures and pedicures. We were staying over at a hotel, returning home Saturday afternoon. I was excited to spend the time with her. I felt a stab of guilt for how much Evan consumed my thoughts. My mom needed me. She was struggling with her health. I made a promise to myself to be there for her going forward.

I more or less confessed as much to her on our drive to Halifax the next day. Mom patted my knee. "Meara, you're a teenager, and Evan is your first real boyfriend. I'm happy for you."

"But, Mom…"

"No buts. Why do you think I brought you here? If something happens to me…"

"Mom!"

"Let me finish." She gave me one of her mom looks. "If something happens, you will be surrounded by people who love you." She looked at me over the top of her sunglasses. "You are happy, right?"

I nodded and smiled at her. "I am."

When we got to the clinic, a quick glance around the waiting room told me Ula wasn't here. I wished she were. Hearing my mom's contingency plan made me feel weepy. I wanted a friend to talk to, someone who was going through almost the same thing. Flopping down next to Mom, I picked up the latest copy of People magazine. I quickly buried my nose in it, not wanting my mom to see my tears. Too late.

"Meara, are you okay?"

I looked up at her. "You're asking me? Shouldn't I ask you that?"

Her hair was falling out. I noticed a few days ago. She kept it pulled back under a wide headband, but it was thin and wispy, not thick and wavy like usual. That was part of the reason for the haircuts. Mom was getting hers cut short.

"I'm fine," Mom said. "I'm going to beat this. I did it once, and I can do it again."

She smiled at me. I knew she was trying to be brave. I returned the gesture, wanting to be brave, too. Deep inside, though, I worried. She was getting so thin. This morning when I hugged her, I could feel all the bones in her back.

The nurse called her, and she stood. I jumped up and hugged her, afraid to let go. "I love you, Mom."

She kissed my cheek. "Love you, too, kiddo. I'll be back soon."

As I watched her follow the nurse, my only thought was that I wanted things to be as they always had been between us. Everything was changing. Our relationship, our family, was something different, something new. There were my grandparents, Lydia, Katie, and most importantly, Evan. They had changed my life, in more ways than one. Thinking about all of them, I appreciated all that my mom had done for me, moving us here. I was determined that the rest of the afternoon would be just about Mom and me. With all that she was going through, I was determined to make it a happy memory.

"Meara, are you awake?"

I opened my eyes. Mom stood in front of me. My neck hurt, and my foot fell asleep. The last thing I remembered was putting down a magazine after I read every article in it and closing my eyes for a minute to rest. I guess I rested a bit too much. A quick mental calculation told me that I napped in the waiting room for about an hour and a half.

I stretched and yawned before asking, "Are you done?"

"For today," she said. "Are you ready to get pampered?"

Her grin was infectious, so I smiled back. The circles under her eyes looked darker, but otherwise, she seemed okay.

"Yeah," I said. "Let's go." The clinic waiting room depressed me.

Lydia had recommended the salon, à La Mode. It was small—it only contained four styling stations—but what it lacked in space it made up for in style. Crystal chandeliers hung from the ornately tiled ceiling. The walls were painted in black, white, and hot pink. The effect could have been gaudy. They pulled it off. I'd never been to Paris, yet this is what I imagined it looked like.

Mom's stylist gave her a pixie cut, which diminished the effects of her treatments. The cut flattered her delicate features. She chose a soft, neutral pink for her fingernails and toenails.

"Mom, you look great!" I said, and I meant it. The pampering was good for her; she looked more relaxed and happy than she had in weeks.

"I love your hairstyle," Mom said. "It's so bouncy."

I didn't get much length cut off, but I agreed when the hairdresser suggested layers. My hair hung past my shoulders, but the layers provided movement and framed my face. For my fingernails, I chose a color called Vampire Vixen, a glossy, burgundy shade. I picked bright silver for my toes. Mom raised her eyebrows, but didn't comment. She liked neutral colors, and matching worked for her. I thought it was boring.

"Mom, are you sure you got this?" I asked when we got to the counter. It was more expensive than I thought it would be.

"I've got it, Meara. Don't worry."

When we left the salon, Mom wanted to shop. We were in a shopping district. Stores lined both sides of the street for blocks.

"Are you sure?" I asked. "You're not too tired?"

She brushed off my concern. "I'm fine."

Mom bought a new dress, two sweaters, and a pair of dress pants. The dress was for Thanksgiving, a coppery wrap dress that floated around her calves. It came with a braided belt of copper, silver, and gold. The clasp was a cluster of metal leaves. It was beautiful, and I told her so when she twirled to model it for me.

She insisted that I find a dress for Thanksgiving, too. We were going to go to the Mitchell's house. They hosted a big dinner every year.

The dress I found was much simpler, a deep green sweater dress. It was fitted and fell a little past mid-thigh.

"That's too short," Mom protested, but when I agreed to wear tights and boots with it, she bought it for me.

Originally, we planned to go out to dinner but, after shopping, Mom was pale and tired. I drove us to the hotel, checked us in, and carried the bags to our room. Mom followed me up the stairs, took off her coat, and laid down to rest. While she napped, I turned on the TV to channel surf. I ended up watching the last half hour of a spy movie, and the entire romantic comedy that followed. Mom barely stirred on the bed next to me.

When the movie ended, I ordered a pizza. I brought money with me, so I paid for it. Mom stirred and sat up.

"Smells good," she said. "What did you order?"

"Cheese, sausage, and mushroom. Is that okay?"

"Perfect." Mom came over and sat next to me. "What do I owe you?"

"I got it."

"You don't have to, but thank you."

The guy who delivered the pizza forgot plates and napkins. So, we just opened the box and dug in. I was on my third piece before I noticed that Mom barely touched hers. She was picking at the mushrooms on top.

"Not hungry?" I asked.

Mom sighed. "I guess not. My stomach's a little queasy."

"The medicine?"

"Yes."

"Do you want me to get you something else? I could see if they have crackers or bread downstairs."

Mom shook her head. "That's okay. I'm not that hungry." She stood up. "I'll go downstairs and get some tea. Do you want anything?"

"I can come with you."

"It's okay, Meara. I'll be fine. Do you want a Diet Coke?"

"Yes, please, if they have one."

When Mom left the room, I put the rest of the pizza on the dresser next to the TV. I didn't have much of an appetite anymore. I was worried about her. She was so thin, and she barely ate.

I put on my pajamas, which were yoga pants and a T-shirt. We weren't going out tonight, so I might as well get comfy. As I lay in bed worrying about my mom and waiting for her to return, I wondered, when did our roles reverse?

Chapter 18

The alarm blared, jarring me from a pleasant dream about Evan and our date last Saturday. He'd surprised me by taking me to a fancy restaurant. Our table overlooked the water. It was wonderfully romantic. I wished I was back there now.

Blurry eyed, I reached out to hit snooze, cursed, and sat up. I might as well get going. It was the first day of school after all. I hated the process of figuring out where my classes were and who was in them. Today was no exception. In fact, it was worse. A new school in a new country—how much more nerve-wracking could you get?

Over the weekend, Katie had combed through my closet and helped me pick out the perfect outfit for the first day. I dressed, turning in front of the mirror and admitting she had a good eye. The dark green blouse complemented my eyes, turning them almost aqua. My waist looked tiny in the black pants, and my new boots, well, they were sexy as hell. I loved them. My hair wasn't quite as bouncy as it had been when it was first cut, but it would do

I glanced at my bedroom clock—fifteen minutes until Katie picked me up. Enough time for breakfast at least.

I was pleased to see that Grandma Mary made waffles and bacon, and a steaming plate of both was set out for me.

"Thanks, Grandma Mary!" When I smiled at her, I realized she really did feel like my grandmother now.

"Syrup, Meara?" My mom passed me the bottle before I replied. I forgot about the name dilemma and focused on my breakfast instead. Mom watched me eat and sipped her coffee.

"Are you nervous?" she asked.

"A little."

"First day jitters." Mom smiled. "You'll be fine."

"Are you nervous?" Katie asked when I met her on the porch. "You look nervous."

"I am," I admitted. "A little."

"It'll be okay," she said. "I can't imagine high school here is all that different than anywhere else. Besides, you met several of my friends over the summer. I'll introduce you to the rest. I'm sure you'll get along just famously. We love you."

She gave me a hug, and I felt a little better.

When we arrived at school, the parking lot was almost full. I could see kids hanging out in groups across the campus. Katie waved at one or two people and honked at a few more. I was getting the impression she was popular, not that it surprised me.

When I received my class list about three weeks ago, Katie compared it to hers. We shared the same lunch hour, and we had first period together. At least I could follow her to our class, and then I would be on my own until lunchtime. I had studied the campus map they mailed out with the paperwork. It didn't look too complicated.

As soon as we entered the building, Jen ran over to us. Her black hair, which had been past her shoulders this summer, was freshly cut into a chin-length bob.

"Katie!" She hugged Katie enthusiastically and then turned to me, smiling warmly. "Good to see you again, Meara. Welcome to Halifax High."

"Thanks," I said. "Great haircut."

Jen patted her hair self-consciously. "You like it?"

"Super cute," Katie confirmed.

Jen started to fill us in on the latest gossip. Since I didn't know anyone, it didn't matter too much to me. I trailed slightly behind them as we walked, half listening and half taking in my surroundings. Jen stopped, and I caught myself just before I plowed into her back.

"I'm so rude," she said. "I'm sorry, Meara. I don't mean to ignore you. This must be hard for you, being new and all."

I shook my head. "It's okay. I'm just trying to get my bearings, you know?"

"Right." She nodded. A look of disgust crossed her face, and I wondered what I had done when she added, "I wouldn't know anything about that since I've been here my whole life."

"Before I came to Canada, I spent my whole life in Wisconsin. Let me tell you, it's not any more exciting."

"I guess," she said. "I wouldn't mind hearing about somewhere else..."

"Maybe later," I said quickly. Or, maybe never, I thought. As if I wanted my new friends to realize how absolutely, terribly boring my life had been before I came here.

"I better go," Jen said. "I've got science first period. It's down the other hall."

We said goodbye to Jen, and Katie led me further down the hall. When we reached the end, she gestured to a door on the right side.

"Here's our class. Do you want to go first or should I?"

"You," I said. I felt like a coward, but she was the one who knew people here.

What if I sat by the most annoying kid in school? Or the one who tried to cheat? No, better that she found a seat first. She'd know where to go.

Katie waved to a few boys in the back before walking to the far side of the room and sitting about halfway. She motioned to the seat in front of her. I quickly took it.

Mr. Murphy started as soon as the bell rang. He introduced himself and provided a high-level outline of what we would cover this year. One of the Shakespeare plays we were going to read, Hamlet, I had already covered my sophomore year. Everything else would be new. Perfect. I liked to read, but I didn't care to re-read.

I made it through my morning classes with no major mishaps. Valerie, another friend of Katie's that I had met at the Canada Day festival, was in my Biology class. It helped to have a friendly face nearby, and I was feeling more confident by the time lunch rolled around.

Katie was partially standing and waving to me when I came into the cafeteria. I was glad she had been looking out—most of the tables were already full. I would've been lost if I hadn't seen her. She scooted over to make room for me, and I sat down next to her.

"How's it going?" she said, handing me a Diet Coke and a bag of chips. "I stopped at the vending machine for you. I forgot to mention that you do not want to eat the hot lunch here. If you can, avoid it at all costs. Oh…" She dug in her backpack and pulled out an apple. "This is for you, too."

"Thanks, Mom." I grinned at her, and she laughed.

"How're things going?" Jen asked as she took a seat across from me.

"Good," I said. "Val's in my Biology class."

Jen nodded at the lunch line. "She's coming. She's getting hot lunch."

"I can't believe she likes that stuff," Katie said.

"I know," Jen replied. They both shuddered, which made me laugh.

"C'mon," I said. "It can't be that bad."

"Just you wait," Jen whispered, leaning across the table. "Here she comes now."

Valerie sat down next to Jen. I had to admit, the lunch didn't look too appetizing.

"What's for lunch today?" Jen asked.

"Can't you tell?" Val frowned at her before digging her fork into her food and taking a bite. "Mmmm. It's meatloaf. Yummy." She looked at my chips and apple. "That's all you're eating?"

"I'm not hungry," I said, and it was true. I bit the apple and avoided looking at Val's meal while I chewed.

Jen, Katie, and Val launched into a fresh batch of school gossip. Not knowing anyone yet, I wasn't really interested and studied the lunchroom instead. It was funny how you could be in a totally different country and be reminded so much of home. The faces were all different, but other than that, it could have been a high school anywhere. From what I could tell, there were the same cliques and groups here that were at my high school back in Cedarburg. Actually, I found that comforting. At least I knew what I was getting into.

"Meara?" Katie was looking at me funny. Great. How long had she been calling my name? "Are you okay?"

"Sure," I said. "Just thinking about how similar Halifax is to Cedarburg."

Katie's expression turned smug, and I remembered her words in the car this morning. "Told you so. See, Meara, you'll fit in fine here."

"Uh huh." I was not entirely convinced. I threw away what was left of my lunch. Nerves usually worked as an excellent appetite suppressant for me. It was the only time I couldn't eat.

"What do you have now?" Katie asked.

I glanced at my schedule, since I had already forgotten. After I looked, I wished I hadn't. "Ugh. Gym class."

"Me, too!" Val said, coming over to stand next to me. "I'll walk with you."

"Great. See you later, Katie. Jen."

They waved and walked away. Val and I started toward the gymnasium.

"Do you play sports?" she asked. She walked with a natural grace. No wonder she was on Katie's volleyball team.

"Not really," I said. "I played a bit in grade school, but I wasn't good."

She frowned. "That's too bad. We could've used another strong setter on our team."

"Katie already tried to recruit me."

She flashed me a grin. "Figures."

After gym, I had history and psychology. The rest of the day passed quickly. As far as first days of school went, I chalked this one up as a success. Katie was right. Her friends were great, and I was confident that I would soon be calling at least some of them my friends, too.

Chapter 19

"Ms. Quinn, what is your answer?"

I felt my face go hot. Busted. I'd just sent Evan a text, and I had no idea what Mr. Hersh asked me. Thankfully, I'd managed to slide my phone into the pocket of my jeans before he caught me.

"Could you repeat the question?"

Mr. Hersh looked at me over the top of his glasses. "Pay attention, young lady." His eyes scanned the room before landing on the brunette in the front row. "Simone, did you hear the question?"

"Yes, Mr. Hersh." Simone turned and gave me a smug smile before answering. "World War II ended in 1945."

I slid lower in my chair, grateful that the class had turned their attention away from me. My phone vibrated in my pocket, but I didn't dare look at it.

The bell rang. Finally! School was over.

I walked back to my locker and threw my books in, grateful that I finished my homework in study hall. At least I didn't have to worry about that this weekend. I was a little sad that Evan wasn't coming home. I hadn't seen him for over a week.

My phone vibrated. I pulled it out, only then remembering the text I received during History class. The first was Katie. *TGIF!* She was probably already in the gym since she had volleyball practice tonight. There was a big volleyball tournament tomorrow. "It's last-minute prep," Katie told me on the way into school. "Coach insists, although we're totally ready."

My heart sped up when I read the second text, which was from Evan. *I'm out front.*

I grabbed my jacket and bag, slamming my locker closed. He was here! I hurried to the main door, but made myself slow down as I pushed it open. I didn't want to appear too eager. He leaned on his car, surrounded by a group of people. I recognized a guy from my science class, but the rest were strangers. I saw the moment that he noticed me—his eyes lit up, and his attention focused entirely on me. The rest of the group turned to look where he was staring. Embarrassed again, I felt my face heat up.

"Hi Meara," the guy said as I approached. I waved and hoped it wasn't obvious that I couldn't remember his name. He turned to Evan. "Catch you later."

"Sounds good, Max," Evan said. Ah, right. Max Spencer. Max left, and the others followed. He was on the hockey team, if I remembered correctly.

"I didn't mean to scare off your friends," I said. Evan laughed and pulled me into his arms.

"I'm glad you did. Now I have you all to myself." He kissed me. I shivered slightly and leaned into him. Breathing in his cologne, I rested my head on his shoulder. I hadn't realized how much I'd missed him.

"How was the first week?" he asked.

"Not bad," I admitted, stepping back to give us some room. I didn't want to make a scene. "It exceeded my expectations."

"Meara," he said, shaking his head. "You could have tripped in the lunchroom on Monday, dropped all of your books in front of everyone on Wednesday, and slammed your fingers in your locker today, and that would have exceeded your expectations. When they're that low, there is nowhere to go but up."

"True," I said. "But I didn't trip or drop my books or slam my fingers."

He took my left hand and kissed the tips of my fingers, then pretended to inspect them. "You're right. They look fine to me."

"I'm thrilled you're here, but where's my mom?" Mom told me this morning she was planning to pick me up after her appointment. She knew Katie wouldn't be done with practice until much later.

"I think her appointment ended early. She called and asked if I could pick you up."

"That's weird. She's never done early."

"Maybe she's getting better?"

"Maybe." I didn't believe it. This morning, her face was ridiculously pale, and her hair seemed to thin before my eyes. Just two days ago, she'd started covering her head with a scarf when she went out.

Evan opened the car door. "You ready?"

"Are you sure this is okay? I know you're busy with school..."

"Get in, Meara. I wouldn't pass up an opportunity to see you. I'll study first thing tomorrow. I promise."

The car was warm and smelled like Evan's cologne—clean and sporty. I loved that smell.

"Are you hungry?" he asked as he pulled out and merged into the "get me the hell out of here, it's Friday" traffic.

"Antonio's?" I suggested. A few weeks ago, he took me to his favorite pizza restaurant in Halifax. It was near campus and super yummy. I'd been craving it ever since.

"Antonio's it is."

Twenty minutes later, a hot, steaming pizza was placed between us. It smelled amazing, but I knew better than to try and bite into a slice right away. I burnt my mouth the first time. I slid a piece onto my plate to cool and sipped my Diet Coke instead.

"Can you show me around after?" I asked. "You know, since we're so close to campus?"

"Sure. We can take a walk. You can see my dorm room, too." I raised my eyebrow at him, and he lifted his hands in defense. "What? I have a roommate. Chances are that he'll be there."

I laughed. "I'm just teasing you."

"Just for that..." He reached over and took my cooled slice, taking a huge bite.

"Evan!"

"What? It's good. Why don't you have some?"

I rolled my eyes, but couldn't help smiling. The pizza had cooled a bit, and I was able to eat the first slice I took. The cheesy tomato perfection melted in my mouth. It didn't take long for us to finish the whole thing.

Our waitress brought the check and placed it on the table. I reached out, but Evan covered my hand before I could take it.

"I've got it."

"You don't have to—you're not working anymore."

"Meara, I can pay for it. Let me treat you."

Okay." I relented, looking into his puppy dog eyes. "Thank you."

"Anytime." He pulled out his wallet and paid before sliding out of the booth to stand next to me. When I stood, he took my hand. "We'll just leave the car here. Campus is literally two blocks away."

As we walked, Evan pointed out the coffee shop where he got breakfast, the bookstore, which carried university sweatshirts, and even the Laundromat, although he admitted that he rarely used it. He brought his clothes home.

"You make your mom wash your clothes?"

"She likes to do it. She insists."

"Yeah, right." I gave him a little nudge, and he laughed.

"Okay, so maybe she doesn't like it," he admitted.

"I'm sure she's got enough laundry with the inn and all..."

"You're right." He sighed dramatically. "I suppose I could do my own laundry." He stopped and motioned in front of us. "We're here."

If I hadn't been caught up in teasing Evan, I would have noticed that the rows of neat shops had ended at the start of a beautiful, green space. Neatly trimmed hedges and tall trees lined several paths, which led up to classic, brick buildings.

"It's beautiful," I said.

"It's not bad." He tugged my hand. "C'mon, I'll show you the science building."

We took the path on the right and passed several buildings. The air was cooling, but comfortable, and many windows were open. Between the movie posters I could see on the walls, and the various songs I could hear blaring from within, I knew these had to be dorms.

"Do you live in one of these?" I asked.

Evan didn't even glance up at them. "No, I live on the other side of campus. These are for upperclassmen."

"Oh."

Evan stopped in front of a long building. It looked more modern that the others we passed. I guessed it was built at least fifty years later.

"Is this the science building?"

"This is it," he said. "Want to go inside?"

"It's open?"

"Night classes. It will be open until nine or so."

I stared at the building. I wasn't sure I was comfortable going inside. "Will we get in trouble?"

"Why would we get in trouble?" He tugged at my hand. "C'mon, Meara. We won't stay long."

As we walked up the stairs, I felt a prickle on the back of my neck. It was the most curious feeling, like someone was watching me. On one hand, I wanted to turn around and see who it was. On the other, I was scared. I'd never had that feeling before. It creeped me out. Curiosity won. I turned around.

A man stood near a tree in the middle of the green space. I couldn't make out his features. He was tall, and his hair was light. He nodded his head, turned, and walked away. The feeling vanished.

"Do you know him?" Evan asked, and I startled. For a moment, I forgot he was there.

"No, I thought maybe you did." I looked up at Evan, and he shook his head.

"Never seen him before." Evan opened the door. "I'll show you the lab first."

Evan was like a kid in a candy shop. He was so excited about everything in the building. Science was not my favorite subject, but it was hard not to get caught in his enthusiasm. He was so focused, so passionate about what he believed in. I thought about how it felt when he turned that same focus on me. My face grew hot.

"Are you okay?" Evan asked.

"Fine," I blurted. "Where are we going next?"

"Do you want to see the animals?"

"Animals? Like classroom pets?"

He grinned at me. "Kind of. We keep them for observation. Most are retired zoo or circus performers."

"What kind of animals?"

"You'll see..."

We walked down an empty corridor and through the door at

the end. It was a staircase, and Evan led me down. The air took on an unusual smell, and I heard splashing.

"Is there a pool in here?"

"Of sorts." Evan opened the door. "Ta da! Our pets."

The lights were dimmed, but I could clearly make out the large tank of water and the animals swimming inside. "Seals?"

"And sea lions. We have some pretty cool aquariums, too. In the room back there." He pointed to the back corner. "Do you want to get closer? We can climb on the platform."

The door Evan had just pointed at burst open. "Excuse me, but no one is allowed in here after hours." A nervous-looking man approached us. When he saw Evan, he relaxed. "Oh, Mr. Mitchell. It's just you."

"Hi, Professor Nolan. Sorry, I was just showing my girlfriend, Meara, the animals. We'll go now."

"No problem. Take your time." He smiled at me and nodded at Evan before going back the way he came. I was impressed. A teacher had never given me that kind of respect.

"Wow. Mister Mitchell. Very impressive," I whispered to him.

"Very funny," he whispered back. He put his hands on my lower back and guided me to the stairs.

"I have a part-time job here, you know, caring for the animals." He spoke quietly next to my ear. "Professor Nolan heads the research program. He's a pretty cool guy. Nervous, but he knows his stuff."

The stairs that lead to the top of the tank were covered in wide strips of non-slip material.

"Are we going to get wet?" I asked.

"I don't think so," Evan said.

Great, I thought. I didn't feel like spending the night in wet clothes.

The platform was sturdy and dry. It was actually much higher than the surface of the tank. A ladder led down about three feet to another platform below, where the seals and sea lions could come out and rest.

"Do you want to go down?" Evan asked.

I looked down. Pools of water scattered across the platform. "Looks kinda wet."

Evan laughed. "We can stay here."

We sat on the edge of the platform. It didn't take long for the animals to notice us. They started to jump and spin as if they were performing. Then, one by one, they came onto the platform below us. Soon, they were barking.

"They like you," Evan said.

"Why...What...?" Then I remembered that he said he worked here. I shoved his arm playfully. "Right. You feed them, don't you?"

He laughed. "Yes, I do. It's past their dinnertime, but we can give them a snack."

"Do we have to go down there?"

"No, we'll just toss it over." He walked to a cooler at the back of the platform, picked up a bucket near it, and filled it. He brought it back over. "Frozen fish. They love it."

I looked in the bucket. The fish looked disgusting, and smelled, well, fishy. Evan looked at me, so I picked one up. I fought the urge to drop it or gag. It was slimy.

"Now what?" I asked. The tail was pinched between my fingers.

"Toss it down." He threw a few fish down to the animals. The group nearest dove for them, the rest looked at me expectantly.

"You're going to need more than one," Evan said.

I took a handful and dropped them down. Then another. It was kind of fun. When the fish were all gone, Evan showed me where the women's bathroom was so I could wash my hands.

We went back to the stairwell. When we reached the main floor, I turned and wrapped my arms around his neck. "Thank you for the tour. I'm impressed. You've made a name for yourself."

"I like it here." His arms went around my waist. "But I miss you."

Evan leaned down and kissed me. A quick glance confirmed the hall was empty. Apparently, night classes were not held in this corridor. I thought about the last time he kissed me like this. The night of his hockey game. I remembered what else happened that night, and I broke the kiss, looking down. I couldn't meet his eyes.

That was the same night of David's last visit. When I confirmed he was real, and he told me he wasn't human. I hadn't said anything to Evan yet.

"Is something wrong?" he asked.

I cleared my throat, and finally looked up at him. "I need to tell you something. I'm not sure where to begin."

"There's always the beginning," he joked. His expression grew serious when I didn't laugh. "What is it, Meara?"

"I saw David again."

"Your father?" he asked. "When?"

"I had a dream about him my first night here, and I had a few more after that," I said. "I thought they were just dreams, but then he showed up in Katie's room..."

"What do you mean 'he showed up'?"

I shrugged. Under Evan's gaze, this was even harder than I imagined. "I woke up and looked at the clock. I heard someone clear their throat, and David was standing by the window."

"When did this happen?"

"The night we came to your game..."

"Why was he there?"

"To talk to me, I guess, although he never tells me anything useful. He just spouts obscure garbage and then disappears."

"What does he say?"

"Stuff like, 'he had to leave, I'll understand someday...he's not human...'" The last part was barely a whisper.

"Wait. What?"

I looked up at Evan, and then glanced down the hall. It was still empty. I didn't need anyone else listening and thinking I was crazy. "He says he's not human."

"What is he?"

"I don't know!" I ran my hand through my hair. "He wouldn't tell me."

"And you're sure he was there? You weren't dreaming him?" I could tell Evan was trying to be understanding, even if he didn't believe me.

"I was awake. I know it. I'm not even sure the dreams were dreams. I mean, the first time I saw him, he looked exactly as he did in that picture Katie gave me."

"What picture?"

"The one of the four of them together. The one on the beach."

"Katie took it from my mom's room?" Evan seemed mad about this.

"I don't know," I said. "She gave it to me a few weeks ago while we were shopping."

"Do you have it with you?"

"No, it's at home on my dresser. Why?"

Evan shook his head. "I'm not sure. I don't understand how he can look the same as he did then. That was seventeen years ago..."

"He said he's not human. Maybe he doesn't age."

"Meara." Evan sounded a little exasperated when he said my name. "You don't believe that, do you? What would he be? He's probably just referring to his behavior. You know, how it was inhumane to leave you and your mom."

"I suppose." I frowned and considered what Evan said. It didn't sound right, yet I had no evidence to argue otherwise. David gave me no clues as to what he was, if not human. He sure looked human.

"So, is he living here now?"

"I guess," I said. "He told me he was back."

"But not where he's living?"

"No."

"Did you ask your mom?"

I shook my head. "No, I just told her about my dreams."

"And?"

I chewed my lower lip. I was ready for this conversation to be done. "She didn't say much except that it's natural for me to dream about him since we're here now, where she met him, and I never had. As far as I know, she hasn't seen him."

"I'm surprised he wouldn't talk to her first. Do you think he's here to take you?"

A chill ran down my back, and I gave an involuntary gasp. "I hadn't even considered that. But, I'm seventeen years old. In a few months, I'll be eighteen. Why would he come now if he wanted to take me? Why not when I was little?"

"No idea," Evan said. "It was just a guess." He took my hand and squeezed. "Let's go back to my dorm. It's more comfortable than a deserted hallway."

I followed Evan out of the building and across the green space. His dormitory was almost directly across from the science building.

"Convenient to be so close," I said.

Evan gave me a lopsided grin before opening the door for me. As we walked to his room, we passed several people in the hall. Everyone smiled, waved, or said hi. I wondered if Evan was friends with them or people were just friendly here. Outside his room, he slid the key card and opened the door. It was dark.

"Okay, so my roommate's not here."

"Apparently."

"I'll be on my best behavior." He held his hands up in a gesture of innocence, but his wink ruined it.

I laughed. "Uh huh."

The room was relatively clean, considering two guys lived here. Evan's bed wasn't neatly made, but the comforter at least covered the sheet. On the dresser was a framed picture of his family, one of me, and a bottle of cologne. That great cool, spicy smell that was Evan wafted lightly from the bottle when I picked it up. He cleared his throat, and I turned to find him sitting on the bed watching me.

"I saw your dad once," Evan said. "At least, I think it was him."

"How'd you know it was him?"

He shrugged. "That picture Mom has in her room of the four of them. She keeps it on her dresser."

I knew what he was talking about. It was the picture Katie showed me. I turned and looked at him. "When?"

"About ten years ago. I was covering the neighbor kid's paper route. He was on the rocks. Near the lighthouse."

The lighthouse? That was where I saw him, too, twice before in my dreams. "Did he see you?"

"I don't think so. If he did, he didn't say anything. I was on my bike, and it was early. I didn't know what he was doing there. It spooked me."

"Do you remember when you saw him? The time of year?"

"Yeah. Because it was freezing. February."

What was my father doing in Peggy's Cove the month of my seventh birthday?

Chapter 20

The next day, I found Mom in the yard, facing the sea. She wore her pink robe over jeans and a sweater. She had gotten so thin that she was constantly cold. It wasn't unusual to find her dressed in layers, while the rest of us wore only t-shirts. I approached her slowly, not wanting to surprise her. She turned as I neared her chair and motioned for me to sit on the end. I leaned over and hugged her, kissing her cheek. Her skin felt soft, her body frail.

I knew I looked tense. I couldn't seem to put on pretenses any longer. I was so worried about her that I bordered on being physically sick. "Hi, Mom. How are you?"

I'm okay," she said. I rarely heard, I'm well or I'm good anymore. I suppose okay was a neutral word, but it didn't tell me how she was really feeling. As always, she changed the subject. "How are you, Meara? How are things with Evan?"

"Everything's fine," I said. "I told him about David."

She watched my face closely. "What did you say?"

"I just told him how I dreamed about David. Or, I thought they were dreams. The last time, he was there."

"What?" Mom sat upright and stared at me. "When? You didn't tell me about this."

Her reaction surprised me. She almost seemed scared. "It was the night I stayed over at Katie's house."

"What did your father say?"

"Not much." I paused and took a deep breath. "Mom, he told me that he wasn't human."

At first, Mom seemed like she was about to say something. Then the look passed. She bent her head and took a sip of her coffee, not meeting my eyes.

"Mom?" I said. "Do you know why he might say that?"

"I don't know," she murmured. "That's an odd thing to say." There was something my mom wasn't telling me. I could always tell when she was holding something back.

"I asked him why he left us," I said, watching her closely. As I suspected, there was something there. She was trying hard to remain neutral. It wasn't working. "He said he couldn't see us, not that he wouldn't see us. He also said that he hadn't expected you to take me inland."

I paused and then added, "Does that mean anything to you?"

She fluttered her hands near the opening of her robe, clearly struggling. A light pink flush spread up her neck and across her cheeks. I waited. She didn't say anything.

"Mom?"

Her eyes glittered with tears, and she took a deep breath. "Oh, Meara, I'm so sorry!" she cried. "When you're father left, I was heartbroken. I couldn't take the chance that he would try to take you from me too. So, when the opportunity came, I took you and moved to the States."

"Why would he take me away?"

"I didn't know if he would. I didn't know if it was something he could control..." She trailed off, staring out at the sea.

"I don't understand." This wasn't making any sense. If my parents loved each other, why would my dad take me away? "You took me to Wisconsin to keep me from my father?"

She looked at me with remorse. "I never wanted to keep you from your father. I had no way of knowing whether he would come back or not. And, I..."

I interrupted her. It was rude, but I wanted answers. "Why wouldn't he come back for us? Why is everything such a mystery?"

She paused and stared in her cup, purposefully avoiding my eyes. "Your father has secrets," she said in barely a whisper.

"What are they?" I demanded.

She shook her head. "You have to ask him, Meara. They're not mine to tell."

Frustrated, I stood and began to pace. "I've tried. He won't tell me."

She leaned back and looked at me then. "Well, then the timing's not right."

"You sound like him!"

She shrugged. Her face was once again neutral.

"You won't tell me." It was a statement, not a question. My voice quivered as I tried to control my anger.

Mom held her ground. "No, not about this."

"Fine!" I said. I turned to stalk back to the house. I heard my mom call my name, quiet at first, and then more insistent. I paused, not looking back. "Yes?"

"I know it's hard, Meara. Please have some patience. I'm sure your father has his reasons for not telling you. When the time is right, you'll know."

I went inside. I didn't feel her request warranted a response.

I didn't mean to let the door bang into the wall when I came in. I was so angry. Why wouldn't my parents talk to me? How awful was this big secret? What could my father be? Was he an alien? I couldn't imagine any other kind of non-human being. Werewolves and vampires didn't exist, and nor did mermaids or pixies. Evan had to be right. It had to be a figure of speech. I could agree with that. He was an inhuman jerk for leaving us.

I ran down the hall, kicked off my shoes, and flopped on my bed. I heard pans rattling in the kitchen as I passed. I didn't stop to talk to my grandmother. I was feeling sorry for myself. Today, misery did not want company.

I put my hands behind my head and stared at the ceiling, not thinking about anything in particular. Eventually, my eyes wandered to the pictures on my dresser. I rose, grabbed the frame, and went back to the bed. I stared at my parents and Evan's parents. They all looked so happy. My mom was so pretty, and David was good looking. They made a nice couple. What happened? What was the reason why he couldn't stay?

My phone rang. I didn't feel like talking. Kim's name appeared on the display. I missed her. We'd been exchanging texts and emails, but we hadn't talked in weeks. She was busy having fun, and I was busy... well, busy.

"Hi Kim," I said. I tried to keep my voice cheerful so she wouldn't hear how I felt. I shouldn't have bothered—she was crying.

"H-he, he dumped me," she managed to get out between her sobs. I didn't have to ask who she was talking about. I'd hoped they would break up, because I figured Mike was cheating on her anyway. I didn't like to see her sad.

"What happened?" I asked her.

"He left me for Sally Paulson."

I knew Sally. She was rich—beautiful and a cheerleader—not nice though. When we were in eighth grade and she was in seventh, she got in trouble for bullying another girl. I was sure that Sally was making the breakup even harder on Kim, and I wished that I could be there to help her through it.

"I'm sorry, Kim," I said. "Mike's totally slumming it."

"No kidding," Kim said. "I think she got a boob job over the summer. That's totally got to be it."

"I'm sure you're right," I said, although I didn't think so. It wouldn't surprise me if Mike had been seeing Sally on the side for a while, at least for the past summer while Kim was gone. I couldn't tell her that.

"You're terrible at emailing." She sniffed, but the drama was over. That was the great thing about Kim. She vented and moved on. I didn't answer her; I knew she was right. I wasn't one for including a lot of details. "So, spill, Quinn. What's going on in your life?"

"Besides what I sent you in my last email?" I asked sweetly. She snorted in reply, and I laughed. "What would you like to know?"

"Come on, Meara! Do I have to beg? Dish on that hot boyfriend of yours. You're together, right?"

"Right." I recounted almost the entire last month. By the time I was done, Kim sounded happier. And, she perked up considerably when she told me she had a date tonight. I was happy that she wasn't going to be sitting home and moping.

"So...." Kim said. "I have news."

"Besides your date?"

"Better than my date."

I waited, but she didn't say anything. "Well?" I asked.

"I'm coming to see you!" she squealed.

"What? When?" I asked.

"The second weekend in October. I'm flying in on Friday," she said. "We don't have school that day, so my parents said okay. I called your mom, and she helped me arrange everything. I was going to surprise you, but I—"

"Can't keep a secret," we said at the same time, and then laughed.

"That's the best news," I told her. "I wonder if Mom will let me skip out of school early on Friday?"

"Uh huh," Kim said. "That's what she told me."

"Sweet!" I'd be able to meet her at the airport. "How long can you stay?"

"That's the best part," Kim said. "My parents are letting me skip two days of school. My flight home isn't until Tuesday."

"Then you get to celebrate Thanksgiving with us," I said.

"I'm coming in Oct-o-ber..."

"I know. Canadians celebrate Thanksgiving in October."

"That's weird," Kim said. "Do they eat a big turkey dinner with the fixings?"

"I think so."

"I'm good with that. I get to have Thanksgiving twice this year then."

"Lucky you," I told her. Kim promised to email me her flight information, and after I helped her decide between a blue sweater and purple blouse for tonight's date—which was not easy to determine over the phone—we said goodbye so she could get ready.

I flopped back down on my bed, considerably happier. My best friend was coming to visit!

Sunday morning I sat on my bed, staring out my window and contemplating what to do. I had the whole day to myself, and the house was empty. My grandparents and Mom had gone over to Lydia's for brunch. Yesterday, after I talked to Kim, I finished my homework. Not exciting, but it had to be done. Last night, Katie and I went to Evan's game. It was a close call. Evan's team won. Afterwards, I only saw him for a few minutes. He needed to go back to the dorm and finish a big project. So, Brian took us to his favorite diner for burgers. Afterwards, we went home.

I told Katie that Kim was coming to visit. I was excited to introduce her to everyone. I planned to tell Kim about David, too. I hadn't mentioned anything yet, wanting to see her face when I told her.

The house was so quiet. I read for a while and tried to watch TV. Nothing held my attention. I was finally desperate enough to clean my room. Turning my music on loud, the way I always cleaned, I got busy. An hour later, my room was spotless. It was time I got out of the house. Walking outside, I was surprised to see my grandmother raking in the yard. "You're back?"

She looked up at me. "Sure, sweetie. We got back about an hour ago. You looked so busy in your room, so we didn't want to disturb you."

"Where's Mom?" I asked. Since she went out this morning, I hoped that meant her migraine was gone.

The smile vanished from Grandma Mary's face. "She's sleeping in her room. Her head started bothering her again about an hour ago."

I dug my toe into a small mound of upturned earth, swallowing the heavy lump in my throat. "I'm going to check on her," I said, without looking up. I knew if I met my grandmother's eyes, I would cry.

"Okay, honey. Let me know if she needs anything."

Heading toward my mom's room, I was lost in my own thoughts. As I neared her door, I paused and listened. How odd. I heard two voices coming from her room—hers, of course, and a deeper, male voice. It sounded familiar. I couldn't quite place it. I knew it wasn't my grandfather. I stepped closer, taking care to avoid the squeaky board in the middle of the hall, and came up short just outside of her room where I wouldn't be seen.

"…Sharon, love, I would have come sooner, but I wasn't sure how you were going to react…"

"How I was going to react? You've been gone for seventeen years, David. You left me with our infant daughter. I knew, of course I knew, the possibility was there that you were going to leave me. I'd hoped that my love for you, our love for each other, was enough to keep you here."

"I never promised you anything, Sharon. In fact, if you recall, I warned you before we ever got involved."

Silence ensued. As I waited for my mom's response, I realized I was holding my breath, so I let it out in a quiet gush. The mysterious male voice was David. He was here, in our house, in broad daylight, visiting my mother. I wasn't sure what to do, but something told me this was not the time to pop in and say 'hello'. Curiosity got the better of me, and I waited silently, my back against the wall, to see what would be revealed.

Finally, my mom spoke. "You were right, of course."

"Do you think that I don't know my own nature?" His voice sounded sad. "If I could change things, change who I am, you know that I would. I would have liked to have been there for you both." I heard something hit a wall with force, and I cringed. "Damn it, Sharon! Why did you have to take her to the mainland? Why did you hide her from me?"

"Do you have to ask?" Mom's reply was so quiet that I barely heard it.

"Am I that much of a beast?" David asked. Hearing the tone of his voice, I pictured a sneer marring his face. "Do you think I would steal our daughter from you?"

"I didn't think you would intentionally, but what about her? What would her choice have been?" I had to strain to hear my mom now. Without thinking, I had moved so close that I was within the doorframe and able to see my mom sitting on her bed, her back to David. He stared at her with a dark expression on his face.

"What if she had left me as you did?" Mom's voice was little more than a whisper. I made out the words, but didn't understand what she was saying. I was only a baby. Why would I have left her? How could I have left her?

Whatever I missed, David understood. His face softened and he dropped to her side, placing his hands on her face. "Oh, Sharon, is that what has worried you all these years? That she would come with me of her own free will?"

Mom nodded, closing her eyes tight. It didn't stop the tears from escaping. "I couldn't bear it, David. I couldn't lose her, too."

He kissed her, and she clung to him as if her life depended on it. I turned away. It was a private moment. Why did Mom worry that I would leave her? I would never leave her. She was everything to me. I walked back outside. I'd heard enough for one day.

Grandma Mary looked up as I came out. "How is she?"

"Resting peacefully," I lied. I worried that something on my face or in my posture would give me away. My grandmother merely nodded and turned back to clearing the dead stems out of her flowerbed. I started past her, down the driveway.

"Wherever you're headed, Meara, be back in about two hours for dinner."

"I will," I called back, although that was a good question. Where was I headed? I didn't know where to go. This was turning out to be a strange day. I wanted to think more about my mom and David's conversation. I had no idea where to start. I was trying to put together a puzzle that was missing all the center pieces. Sure, I had the border more or less figured out, but the whole picture, the main part of it, was a mystery.

Evan wasn't coming over tonight, and Katie was either at work or hanging out with Brian. I was on my own.

I realized that I was heading down the path to the shoreline. Apparently, some part of my brain knew where I wanted to go. When I realized it, I quickened my pace. The brush cleared and I stood before a mile or two of rocky shore, the large stones smoothed by water over time. The sun, low on the horizon, bathed the ocean in fiery shades of red and orange. The scene staggered me—the rough, natural beauty of it. There was no one else in sight.

I sat on a large, flat boulder. Leaning back, I rested on my elbows, staring off at the roughest waves. That was when I saw it—a large, grey seal sitting on the edge of the shore. It looked at me with its enormous, wise eyes. As I watched, it nodded as if in greeting. Had I not been alone, I would have felt silly. Seeing as no one else was here to witness, I nodded back. It stretched its neck out and barked. Was it talking to me? No, I was being ridiculous. As we watched each other, I couldn't help feeling a connection to the magnificent animal.

I rose and approached. It watched me cautiously. When I got within five feet, it turned and slid into the sea. I stood for a moment, feeling a profound sense of loss. I didn't understand the feeling, but it was there nonetheless. I watched until the sky darkened to a brilliant pink purple. The seal didn't return. With a sigh, I headed home.

Chapter 21

The next few weeks of school passed quickly as I anticipated Kim's visit. Before I knew it, Evan and I were waiting for her in the airport lobby. It was the Friday afternoon before Thanksgiving—the one that fell on a Monday, that was. Would I ever get used to Canadian holidays? I bounced on my toes, straining to see Kim coming out of the gate before she spotted us. Evan leaned down and whispered in my ear, "A bit excited, aren't you?"

I didn't turn to him for fear of missing that first glimpse of her, and the expression on her face when she saw me. "She's my best friend, Evan. And, it's been almost six months since I saw her last."

"I know, I know. I'm just teasing."

"There she is!" I began to wave when I spotted Kim's strawberry-blond curls. She was walking next to a man in a business suit. He was pretty good looking for someone who had to be in his forties. She was talking animatedly, and he nodded in reply, a bemused expression on his face. Leave it to Kim to have made friends on the plane. I pointed to her. "She's the one in the green sweater."

"Oh? You mean the one running at us?" Evan asked. When I looked back, Kim was indeed running at us. Within seconds, she tackled me, wrapping me in a big bear hug. Well, as big of a bear hug as my barely five-foot-tall friend could give.

"Meara, you look fabulous!"

"Thanks. You do, too. Single life is treating you well."

She shrugged. "I'm not single anymore, but we can discuss that later. Oh, I can't wait to hear all about everything. Let's grab my bags and get out of here. I'm ready for a good meal and lots of juicy gossip, I hope." She linked her arm through mine, then looked up and saw Evan.

Her jaw dropped slightly. She recovered fast, snapping it closed. She raised one eyebrow—speculating, I'm sure—and then tapped me on the arm lightly. "Were you planning on introducing me, Meara?"

"Maybe if you stop talking for a minute," I teased. "Kim, this is Evan. Evan, my best friend, Kim Greeley."

Kim extended her hand and gave Evan one of her widest, dimpled smiles. "Nice to meet you, Evan. Meara's told me a bit about you." She scowled at me. "Not as much as I'd like to hear, of course."

"Of course." Evan nodded in agreement. His eyes lit with laughter. "It's nice to meet you, too, Kim."

Kim linked her arm through mine and talked nonstop as we walked to baggage claim. Evan grinned at me when she wasn't looking. I just rolled my eyes. It was so Kim, and to be honest, I found it comforting to know she hadn't changed.

From the moment we picked her up until we said goodnight to Evan, Kim kept the conversation flowing nonstop. We went out for pizza, and then headed back home. When Evan dropped us off, he and Kim were well on their way to becoming friends. I shouldn't have been surprised, knowing Kim and her outgoing personality, but a part of me just couldn't believe how easily my oldest friend fit into my new life.

We all got out of the car and started walking toward the door. Kim stopped us, patting Evan on the arm and giving me a quick squeeze. "I'm just going to run up, say hi to your mom, and introduce myself to your grandparents."

"What? No. I'll come in with you and introduce you to them."

"Your mom can introduce me, Meara."

"True, but..."

"Give the poor boy a break. He put up with your pesky best friend all evening and was on his best behavior. Doesn't that deserve some kind of reward?" She stressed the last word and wiggled her eyebrows suggestively. Evan was pretending not to listen, taking a keen interest in Grandma Mary's flower garden, but I saw his lips twitch. She gave me a meaningful glance. "No rush, Meara."

"You're exasperating," I muttered. Kim laughed at me, winked once, and then ran up the steps and knocked on the door. Mom opened it and let her in. She waved at Evan and me, closing it again. Wasn't everyone accommodating tonight?

"Sorry about that," I said, turning to wrap my arms around Evan's waist.

His arms circled my waist and pulled me closer. "I like her. She's a lot of fun, and she cares about you. She's a good friend."

"Yeah," I said. "She's the best."

I leaned forward and brushed my lips against his. He raised one arm to run his hand down the length of my hair, and then down my back, which sent a shiver up my spine. I would think that by now that I would be getting used to his touch. Instead, I seemed to be reacting stronger each time.

"Are you cold?" he whispered, nuzzling my ear and then kissing my neck.

"No," I said, tilting my head to give him better access.

"Mmm...too bad," he murmured against my neck. "If you were cold, I'd have to warm you up."

"Oh?" Intriguing thought. "In that case, I'm freezing."

He laughed and kissed me one last time before reluctantly pulling back. "I better let you go. I'm sure Kim is anxiously awaiting details."

"As if she'll get them," I said. "One more goodnight kiss?"

I closed the distance between us, wrapped my arms around his neck, and kissed him. When I pulled back, Evan asked breathlessly, "What was that for?"

I grinned. "If she wants details, I might as well give her something to talk about."

"I'll see you on Monday?"

"Yes." He was driving back to campus tonight. At least I would see him at his house on Thanksgiving. One last kiss on my cheek, then he went to his car. He waved once before starting the engine. I waved back, and then went inside.

Kim was waiting for me. She sat on the couch next to my mom, talking to her and my grandparents. When she saw me come in, she feigned a big yawn. "Oh my, it's been a long day traveling. I think I better get some rest." She stood. "Meara, would you mind showing me to your room?"

My mom lowered her head and bit her cheek to keep from

laughing; she was used to Kim's antics. My grandparents, however, were easily fooled by the charade. Grandma Mary jumped up and went to grab some extra blankets for my "travel-weary" friend. Grandpa Jamie said goodnight to us both and seemed relieved to turn his attention back to the television.

Mom rose from the couch and walked over to me. "I think I'll head to my room, too," she said. "We have a lot of cooking to do tomorrow and Sunday."

When Mom said 'we', she meant Grandma Mary, Lydia, and herself. I had been told that there were enough cooks in the kitchen, and Kim and I would not be needed. It wasn't that I was a bad cook. Scratch that. I was a bad cook, and the three of them were outstanding. Plus, Mom wanted me to have as much time as possible with Kim. Who knew when I'd see her again after this visit?

Hugging me tight, my mom kissed my cheek. "Have fun catching up."

"Night, Mom," I said. "I love you."

Kim grabbed her bag and followed me down the hall into my room. As soon as we were there, she dropped it, shut the door, and pulled me over to the bed.

"Spill, Quinn," she ordered. "Where in the world did you find that gorgeous man, and what have you done to him? He is putty in your hands."

"Mind if I change first?" I picked up my pajamas. "I'll be back in a second. I have a feeling you're going to keep me talking for a while. I might as well get comfortable."

She growled at me, but didn't say anything else. I took it as consent and continued to the bathroom, stalling. The curiosity would eat her alive. A special part of our friendship was how much we enjoyed pushing each other's buttons. It was almost a contest between us. I went through the usual nightly ritual—brushing my teeth, combing my hair, and washing my face. It didn't take long, but I waited an extra five minutes for good measure before heading back to the room. I couldn't help myself; I loved to torment her.

"What'd you do?" she asked dryly. "Fall in?"

"Funny," I said. I took an extra minute to fluff the pillows and pull back the covers before sitting down again. Kim ground her teeth, barely containing herself.

"Meara!" she yelled. I raised my finger to my lip to quiet her, and she lowered her voice—just barely. "Will you please tell me something?"

"What would you like to know?"

She rolled her eyes. "I haven't seen you since June. Why don't you start at the beginning or wherever you think will be most interesting. It's not like your emails were descriptive. In fact, you suck at writing, Meara...At least when it comes to keeping your best friend up to date on your life."

Where some people might take offense, I just laughed. "Okay, okay. The trip here was rather uneventful, but our first day here, my mom and I went into town. We stopped to visit Mom's friend, Lydia, at her bed and breakfast. I met Evan there," I added, "He's Lydia's son and my friend Katie's brother."

"Convenient," she said. I ignored her.

"I went out with Evan, Katie, and some of their friends to a carnival, and after that, Evan asked me out."

"And the good parts?" she asked.

"What good parts?"

She sighed. "You know, the first kiss, when you discovered you were in madly in love...that kind of good stuff."

"Oh, that." I cleared my throat. I wasn't used to sharing details about my love life, mainly because Kim was always the one dating, not me.

"Our first kiss was the night of the carnival. Katie stayed in town at a friend's house, and Evan brought me home."

"Has he said the 'L' word?"

"Not yet."

"Have you?" I shook my head. "You will. It's coming. The way he looks at you? Wow. Hot."

"Really?" It was weird to hear Kim's perspective. Katie would never say something like that. Evan was her brother after all.

"Definitely." She relaxed back against the headboard. "All right, Meara, I'll stop interrogating you. I know how uncomfortable you probably are right now." She leaned forward again and looked in my eyes. "Seriously, I'm happy for you. Evan is great."

"Thanks," I said, more than anything relieved to be changing the subject. "What about you? You said you're no longer single. What's that about?"

"Do you remember Ryan Johnson?"

"Sure." I'd known Ryan almost as long as I'd known Kim. I remembered he was a bit of a class clown.

"He's the one who asked me out last week. One date turned into several dates in a row. He is so fun! We have a blast together."

I hugged her. "I'm so happy for you, Kim. I always liked Ryan."

"And you never cared for Mike."

I shrugged. "I'm happy as long as you're happy." She looked at me with one brow raised; I squirmed a little. "But, since you are no longer with him, I guess it's safe to say that no, I never liked Mike."

She laughed and shrugged her shoulders. "I suppose I should have dumped him a long time ago and saved myself some heartache." She leaned in and looked at me intensely. I squirmed again, wondering what was coming next. "Now that the boys are out of the way, why don't you tell me what you've really been holding back?"

"I haven't," I said defensively.

Kim stared at me in silence, crossing her arms and waiting for me to continue. "I've got all night, all day tomorrow, all day Sunday, most of the day Monday, and the drive to back to the airport. It's just a matter of time, Meara. We can do this the easy way or my way. I've known you too long, and I know that there is a much bigger story than Evan Mitchell, cute though he may be."

I sighed, resigned. Under my breath, I muttered, "I met my father, David."

"You what?" She jumped off the bed and stared at me. "How? When?"

My face flamed under the intensity of her gaze. She huffed out a breath and sat back down. "You better start at the beginning and don't skimp on the details. I can't believe you kept this from me."

"It wasn't intentional, Kim," I apologized. "I just had no idea how to tell you. You know I hate phone calls and email. Forget about me writing you a letter. This was better left for in person."

147

I told her about my dream the first night at my grandparents' house and all the occurrences since then, up until the afternoon last weekend when I eavesdropped on David and my mom. For a change, she didn't interrupt. I could tell she was hanging on every word, every detail.

When I finished, she asked. "That was the last time you saw him?" I nodded. "That is quite a story, Meara." She leaned back against the headboard and studied my face. "I don't know what to make of it." I must have looked shocked, because she quickly added, "It's not that I don't believe you. It's just that…you know me…I have never believed much in fairy tales or ghosts or whatever."

"I know," I said. "Me either. I've been racking my brain for months, and I can't come up with a plausible explanation. If it was just dreams, fine, I could explain that. And that's what I thought at first, that moving here where my mom met David triggered the dreams."

"But you don't think they're just dreams anymore?"

"No. First, my mom confirmed my description of him, and she had never told me what he looked like before I saw him in my dreams. And second, when Katie gave me that picture, well, I knew it was no dream. How could I dream up the man exactly as he looks without ever seeing him before? The only logical explanation is that they weren't dreams. Maybe some kind of vision."

"Do you have the picture?"

"Sure." Getting off the bed, I went to my dresser and removed it from the corner of the frame. "Here it is."

Kim took it. After a moment, she let out a low whistle. "Wow, Meara, congratulations on winning with the gene pool. He's gorgeous." She looked closer, and then looked up at me. "You look a lot like him. Same hair, right?"

"Yes," I said. "Eyes, too."

She was studying the picture again. "Your mom looks so happy and in love. And, I'm guessing the blond woman is Lydia, and the tall guy her husband."

"Right."

She sat back on the bed, looking at the picture, a puzzled expression on her face. "Wait, didn't you say David looked just like the picture?"

"Yes."

"Just like?"

"Barely legal," I said.

She looked up at me. "How could that be? This was taken years ago."

"Sixteen or seventeen, give or take."

"And he hasn't aged?" Her mouth hung slightly open in disbelief.

"Not that I could tell."

She handed the photo back to me, and I placed it back in the frame.

"You've certainly given me a mystery to solve." Kim cracked a wide smile. "This is so fun! I always wanted to be Nancy Drew."

"If you find any clues during your visit, Nancy," I said, "be sure to let me know. I haven't put one piece of the puzzle together yet."

"Evan knows about David?"

I nodded. "Mom and Katie do, too."

"I'll meet Katie on Monday?"

"Of course. The whole gang will be there."

"Good." Kim gave me a tight hug. "I'm glad I'm here, Meara. I missed you."

"Missed you more, and I am sorry for not telling you about David."

"Don't worry about it. After hearing the story, I completely understand. Even with my gift of gab, I think I would have waited, too, if had I been in your shoes."

"Thanks, Kim." I yawned, unable to help myself. "Do you want to get ready for bed? I know I was just playing around before, but I really did get ready."

"Good idea." Kim stood and placed her bag on the bed, pulling out her pajamas and cosmetic bag. "The bathroom's right next door, right?"

"Yes."

Kim stepped into the hall, closing the door. A moment later, it opened again and Kim stuck her head in. "You don't think David will come while I'm here, do you?"

"I don't think so."

"Damn."

Chapter 22

I woke at nine. Kim was still sound asleep. I went to the kitchen and was halfway through my second bowl of cereal before she stumbled in.

"Mornin'," she mumbled.

"Hi, sunshine," I teased. She had never been a morning person. "What can I get you? Orange juice? Cereal? Eggs?"

"Coffee?" The hopeful expression on her face was priceless. I checked the pot that my mom brewed. It was half full. Mom must have started it around six-thirty—she was an early riser—but it brewed into a thermos that kept it warm. I poured a cup and handed it to Kim.

"Let me know if you need it heated up."

"Should be fine," she said. "Still not drinking this stuff?"

"Can't stand it," I said. "I'll take my Diet Coke any day."

"In the morning?"

"Any time of day. Is that so wrong?" I placed a clean bowl and spoon on the table, figuring Kim would get around to the cereal soon enough. "We've got the rest of the morning and early afternoon to ourselves," I said. "What do you want to do?"

She shrugged. "You live here. You tell me."

"Do you want to see the lighthouse?"

"That's one of the places you spotted your dad, right? So, it's like the scene of the crime?" Her eyes lit up. She was getting into her detective role.

An hour later, we were bundled up and walking to the lighthouse. I would have driven us in Mom's car, but Kim was all about the fresh air and nature. When we rounded the corner and it came into view, I heard Kim suck in her breath.

"Oh my god." She put her hands to her mouth. "It's beautiful. This is fantastic! I can't wait to get a closer look."

I followed Kim to the rocky shore, trying to see the lighthouse again with new eyes. The way it looked the first time I came here with Katie. The sky was muted gray and the wind bit our cheeks, but the lighthouse remained a pristine white monument—the calm against the wildness of the sea.

"Look!" Kim grabbed my arm and pointed to a jagged ledge. "Is that what I think it is?" I followed her gaze and saw a lone seal watching us from the rocks. I couldn't be sure if it was the same one from my last visit, but it watched us with a combination of curiosity and caution.

"Yep. It's a seal," I said. "According to Evan, there is a small population of them living around Peggy's Cove."

"So you've seen one before?"

"Sure. I've seen one or two here or there. I'm never sure if it's the same ones or not."

"Have you ever gotten close to one?" She stepped toward the seal. I followed since she pulled my windbreaker in her deathlike grip.

"I've tried, but they dive into the ocean before I can get too close."

"Oh." She stopped. We were about ten yards away. While we watched, the seal nodded. I had the strangest feeling that it was listening and understood what we were saying. But that didn't make sense. For one thing, it was an animal, and second, we were whispering.

Kim grabbed my sleeve again, tighter this time. "Can you see that? Is it nodding at us?"

"Nah," I whispered back. "That's not possible. It's just nodding its head; it probably does that all the time."

I didn't take my eyes off the seal, and a second later, it winked at me, as if to say, "I'll prove to you that I'm paying attention." Then, it barked once and dove into the water. I stared at the vacant spot on the rocks. The seal winked at me. Was I losing my mind?

"Meara!" Kim squealed. "That seal just winked!"

Okay, so if I was losing my mind, then Kim was losing hers, too.

"You're right," I said slowly. "I think it did."

"Why are seals winking at us?"

"Honestly, Kim, I haven't the slightest idea."

Chapter 23

Sunday morning, we woke up to a terrible storm. The sky was so dark that it looked like night outside.

"Ugh," Kim muttered, pulling the pillow over her head. "What's with Canadian weather?"

I laughed. "I don't think it's all of Canada, but we are on the ocean. Besides, you live in Wisconsin, remember?"

"Right. Snow." She shuddered delicately before sitting up and smoothing out her curls. "What's on the agenda for today? Hopefully, you weren't planning a picnic."

"Nope. No picnic." I didn't want to tell her that I hadn't planned anything. "We could start with breakfast, and I'm guessing Grandma Mary made coffee."

Mom was sitting at the table when we came in, looking exceptionally pale. I crouched in front of her and grabbed her hands. They felt clammy. "Mom? Are you feeling okay?"

She started to say 'yes', but quickly closed her mouth and shook her head. I watched her turn green before she jumped up and ran to the bathroom. Motioning for Kim to stay in the kitchen, I ran after my mom and knocked on the closed bathroom door.

"Mom?" I called. "Can I help?"

"Just a minute," she said. A moment later, she opened the door.

"Do you need anything?" I asked.

"No." Turning back to the sink, she ran a washcloth under the cold water and pressed it lightly to her forehead and then to her neck. Looking at me through the mirror, she said, "I think I've come down with the stomach flu. It's probably best if I go back to bed. Your grandfather headed into town early this morning to play cards with a few of his friends. On his way, he dropped your grandmother off at Lydia's house. I was supposed to follow and be there in about twenty minutes. Can you call and let them know I won't be coming?"

"Of course," I said, walking with her to her room. "Can I get you anything?"

She squeezed my hand. "No, I'll be fine. I just need some rest."

When I returned to the kitchen, Kim was sitting at the table with a mug of coffee. She had made toast, but hadn't eaten it yet. She looked at me with concern. "How is she?"

"Stomach flu," I said, adding, "nothing too serious."

She relaxed. "That's a relief. How do you handle all of this, Meara? I mean, it's a lot to deal with."

"I just do, I guess, although I never know if I'm doing the right thing." Kim nodded and took a bite of her toast. While she chewed, I added, "I try not to think about it too much."

Kim slid the plate to me. "Toast?"

"Thanks, but I need to call Lydia first and let her know Mom's not coming today. Looks like you and I will be hanging out here, taking care of Mom."

"That's fine. I don't mind."

I called, and Evan answered.

"I thought you went back to the dorms?" I asked.

"Study group was cancelled," he said. "I came back here to catch up on homework."

He didn't say it, but I knew he was also giving me some space to just hang out with Kim. I told him my mom wasn't coming and asked him to relay the message.

"I'll tell my mom right away," he promised. "Call me if you need anything, okay?"

"I will," I said. "I'll see you tomorrow."

Every thirty minutes or so, I checked on my mom. Once or twice, she appeared to be sleeping, but mostly she just laid there, looking miserable. I brought her dry toast and white soda at lunchtime, something that I remembered her doing for me when I was sick. When I checked on her after Kim and I finished our sandwiches, she hadn't touched the food.

"Liquids, Mom," I reminded. "You need liquids." She took a small sip from the glass, and I nodded. "Keep it up. I'll take the toast back to the kitchen."

"Thank you," she said in little more than a croak.

After lunch, Kim and I watched one of my favorite movies, The Goonies. She humored me; she wasn't into any movie that was more than one or two years old. By her standards, this was ancient. My mom and I always watched this one together, and today, when I was worried about her, this managed to comfort me.

When the movie ended, I checked on Mom again. As soon as I stepped into her room, I sensed something was wrong. Her breathing was labored, coming out in short gasps. As I approached her bed, I noticed her eyes were closed and moving furiously back and forth under her eyelids. I pressed my wrist to her forehead; she was burning up. I called her name, and then shook her shoulder. She didn't respond. I tried a little harder. No response.

"Kim!" I shouted. "Come quick."

She was at the door within seconds, looking alarmed. "What is it?"

"She's burning up, and I can't wake her. We have to get her to the hospital in Halifax. Can you call Lydia and let them know where we're heading?"

"Wouldn't it be better to call 911?"

"Does that work here?" I asked.

Kim pulled out her cell phone. "One way to find out." While she dialed, I wiped my mom's forehead with the washcloth lying on her nightstand. She moaned, but otherwise didn't respond.

"I need assistance," Kim said suddenly. "I'm staying with a friend. Her mom is feverish and unresponsive. She has cancer. We think she needs to go to the hospital."

Kim looked at me. "Address?" she mouthed.

I grabbed a pen and paper from the bedside and wrote it down. Kim read it to the dispatcher.

"Okay, thank you," Kim said. Then, a minute later, "We will. Goodbye."

She hung up and put the phone back in her pocket. "They're on the way. We're not supposed to try to move her. The paramedics will take care of everything when they get here. He mentioned that we could try a cool washcloth, but you're already doing that."

I nodded, and then remembered. "Kim, can you take over for a minute? I need to call over to Evan's house."

Kim took the washcloth from me and placed it gently on my mom's forehead. I went to the kitchen to call.

Lydia answered the phone, so I quickly explained the situation to her. I told her that Kim and I called the paramedics, and they were on their way. I thought they would take Mom to the hospital, and I planned to follow in our car. Lydia said that she would tell the others, and they would meet us there.

Before returning to my mom's room, I went to the bathroom and ran a fresh washcloth under the cold water, wrung it out, and then headed back to the room. Kim lifted the old washcloth so I could place the new one.

"Anything?" I asked. Kim shook her head.

"I'll rinse out this washcloth," she said, jumping up suddenly. While she was gone, I straightened my mom's nightgown and smoothed her hair. *How much longer?* I thought. Someone must have heard me, because the doorbell rang. I ran to get it.

There were two paramedics at the door—one male and one female. Each held a medical bag.

"Where is she?" the woman asked.

"Follow me," I said, leading them back. The paramedics placed their bags on the bed, opened them, and began checking my mom's vitals. She called the results to the man, who held a chart and was recording them. The whole process was unbelievably fast.

While this was happening, another medic came in with a stretcher. The two men loaded her onto it and strapped her in. The female medic asked me, "What is your relationship to the patient?"

"I'm her daughter," I said.

"Are you coming with us?"

Kim stood in the doorway. She looked pale and scared. I looked back to the woman. "We'll drive separately."

I followed behind the medics as they took her out of the house and placed her in the back of the ambulance. Standing just inside the front door, I watched until they were out of sight. The cold air raised goose bumps on my arms. I barely noticed. Kim came and stood beside me.

"Should we get going?" she asked.

"Yes." I grabbed my coat from the hook in the hallway and began to walk to the door.

"Your purse?" Kim reminded me.

"Oh yeah." I ran back to my room to get it.

I didn't know where my mom would be, so we went to the emergency room entrance. I approached the attendant at the admittance desk.

"Hello. My name is Meara Quinn. My mother, Sharon, was just brought in by ambulance."

"Do you have ID and an insurance card?" she asked with no trace of warmth in her voice.

I pulled the two cards out and handed them to her. She picked up a clipboard in front of her and handed it to me. It was full of forms. "While I make a copy of these, please fill out as much information as you can on these forms." She motioned to a group of uncomfortable-looking orange plastic chairs, one of which was occupied by a coughing old man. "You can have a seat over there in the waiting room."

Kim and I looked at each other, and then we both sat as far as we could from Mr. Hack-My-Lungs-Out. I quickly flipped through the pages. This is going to take a while, I thought. I turned back to the first page, balanced the clipboard in my lap, and started filling it out. Pulling out her phone, Kim slouched in the chair and began playing a game.

I finally finished the last page, and then carried the clipboard back to the desk.

"Thank you," the attendant said. She attempted a smile. It was a small one, and I didn't smile back. She thrust her hand out at me, holding my license and the insurance card. "Here are your cards."

"Thank you," I said. "Will I be able to see my mom soon?"

She frowned at me, and I couldn't tell if she was impatient or sympathetic. "I can't answer that. Once the doctors have a chance to look at her, they'll come out here and give you an update."

I walked back over by Kim and sat down. The waiting room was quiet. The man with the cough was called back when I was about halfway through the packet of forms. I grabbed one of the dog-eared magazines and started flipping through it. I wasn't retaining anything.

"Meara!"

I looked up just before Grandma Mary smothered me in a hug. She smelled like cinnamon and cloves. I squeezed her back, and my eyes welled up with tears.

"Have you heard anything?" she asked. I noticed my grandfather, Lydia, and Evan standing behind her. I tried to smile at Evan, but couldn't quite make it.

"Not yet," I said to all of them. I motioned to the chairs. "Have a seat."

Evan sat on the other side of me. My grandparents sat and faced us. Their fear made them look older. Lydia continued to stand, her arms wrapped around herself. "I need a coffee," she said. "Can I get anyone anything?"

"A can of Coke?" I asked. No diet for me today—I needed sugar and lots of it.

Lydia nodded at me. "Anyone else?"

"Can I go with you?" Kim stood. "I need to walk."

"Of course," Lydia said. "You must be Kim."

Kim's cheeks flushed. "I am. Sorry. I should've introduced myself first."

"No worries," Lydia said. "I'm Lydia, although I'm guessing Meara told you that?"

"Kim's the one who thought to call 911," I said.

Everyone looked at her, and Kim blushed deeper. "Then we owe you our gratitude," Grandpa Jamie said.

"It was nothing," Kim replied, looking uncomfortable.

Lydia took pity on her and grabbed her hand. "Let's go find that cafeteria."

After they left, I leaned my head on Evan's shoulder, and he wrapped his arms around me. I closed my eyes, listening to the steady beat of his heart and the calming pattern of his breathing. My tears poured down. Was she okay? Why was it taking so long? Someone handed me a Kleenex—I didn't look to see who—and I wiped my eyes and nose. Evan squeezed my shoulder every so often. Otherwise, he said nothing. We all waited.

"Meara Quinn?" A middle-aged doctor stood at the edge of the waiting area, holding a clipboard in his hand. He was tall, with kind blue eyes behind wire-rimmed glasses. When I stood up, he smiled warmly at me and stepped forward, his hand extended. "I'm Dr. Riley. I have just finished visiting with your mother, and she asked to see you."

Relief washed through me. "She's okay, then."

He nodded. "She's quite weary and more than a bit dehydrated, but she's alert and stable. You did the right thing. Her body wasn't successfully fighting the fever and stomach bug on its own."

"When can I see her?"

"I'll take you back now, if you like."

"What about them?" I asked, motioning to my grandparents and Evan.

"I apologize," Dr. Riley said, "but Sharon should have no more than one or two visitors at a time."

Everyone nodded. Grandma Mary said, "You go first, Meara. She asked for you."

I followed the doctor through a set of doors behind the reception desk. We turned down a couple of hallways before coming to Room 132. Dr. Riley opened the door and gestured for me to enter first. "Here she is," he said.

Mom was propped up in her bed, an IV in her arm. She had a bit of color in her normally pale cheeks, and she was sipping something out of a Styrofoam cup.

"How are you doing, Sharon?" Dr. Riley asked.

Mom smiled. "Better, thank you."

He nodded. "If you can keep the liquids down for another hour, we'll try you on some broth."

"I can hardly wait," Mom joked.

Dr. Riley laughed. It was a pleasant sound. "Have a nice visit, you two."

He closed the door as he left. Mom motioned for me to come closer. I walked to her bed and leaned over to hug her cautiously. She

159

laughed and hugged me tighter. "I'm not going to break, Meara." She let me go and patted the side of her bed. "Have a seat." When I did, she added, "Thanks for taking care of me."

"You don't have to thank me, Mom," I said.

"All the same. I should be the one taking care of you, and now I can't." Her voice faltered. I tried to see her face, but she turned away to look out the window.

"Mom," I said quietly. "It's okay. I'm almost eighteen years old. You're sick. I think it's time you let me take care of you."

"Oh, Meara." She turned back, her eyes full of tears. She touched my hair, saying, "I love you, honey."

"I love you, too, Mom."

Chapter 24

I awoke completely disoriented, with no idea what day it was. When I realized it was Monday, Thanksgiving Day, I had two thoughts almost simultaneously. Please let my mom come home from the hospital today, and where in the world is Kim? She wasn't in my room.

I got up and went to look for her. It didn't take me long. I found her in my mom's room, fast asleep. Confused, I stood there for a minute and vaguely remembered. When we got back last night, Grandma Mary changed the sheets in Mom's room and insisted that Kim sleep in there so she could have more space. Mary promised we'd both sleep better. As usual, she was right. I might have slept too deeply.

I decided to take a shower and clear my head. Yesterday felt like a blur, and I swear I could smell the hospital chemicals on my skin. I stood under the hot stream of water for the longest time, not thinking about anything until I heard an impatient knock at the door. I shut the faucet off.

"Yes?"

"Meara!" came Kim's frustrated voice. "Are you going to be in there all day? Some of us need to pee out here."

Oops. Only bathroom in the house.

"Be right out!" I grabbed my towel and wrapped it tightly around myself.

Kim sprinted in the minute I opened the door.

"Sorry," I said, closing it behind me. The house was cool, bordering on chilly, so I hurried to my room and got dressed. I was combing the knots out of my hair when Kim came back to the room. Her hair hung in damp curls. "You showered already?"

161

"Some of us know how to shower quickly." She gave me a sweet smile. I stuck out my tongue in reply. She threw on her clothes, a pair of jeans and a light blue sweater.

"Are you hungry?" I asked.

"Starved."

"I'm sure my grandma made breakfast." We went to the kitchen. Sure enough, pancakes and sausages waited on the table for us with a fresh pot of coffee. My grandpa was reading the paper.

"Good morning," I said. Grandma Mary tried to smile. The effect was lost since her eyes were bloodshot from crying. My grandfather's greeting came from the other side of the paper; he didn't lower it to look at us. Were his eyes puffy too? I couldn't imagine it.

"Can I take the car in a bit to pick up Mom?" I asked.

Grandpa Jamie lowered the paper. His eyes were red. He looked at me for a long moment. "I'll bring her home."

"You don't have to do that."

"Your grandmother needs to finish the cooking for tonight, and you have your friend visiting. I am perfectly capable of picking up my daughter, Meara."

"I know that, but…"

"It's settled then," he said, snapping the paper straight and disappearing behind it once again. I was a little irritated at his response. Okay, so I was a lot irritated, but what was I going to do? He did have a point. Kim didn't come all this way to visit me only to spend half of her time in the hospital.

Since we were standing just inside the kitchen, Grandma Mary gestured to the table. "C'mon girls, sit down and eat your breakfast before it gets cold."

I sat and let out a sigh. Kim reached for the coffee, pouring a full mug before sitting down and turning to me. "What are we going to do this morning, Meara?"

I wasn't sure. It was her last day here, and I knew we were going to Evan's house around three o'clock for Thanksgiving. I turned and asked Grandma Mary, "Do you and Lydia need any help?"

"Not really," she said. "We're pretty much ready to go. I'm going to help her get the table set, and the food's all ready to go in the oven."

"Oh." I had no idea what to do for the next few hours.

"For the love of the Lord," Grandpa Jamie muttered, folding his paper and putting it to the side. "If you two are that bored, you're welcome to come along with me."

I looked at Kim. Her mouth was full, but she shrugged at me as if to say "your call". I thought about it for a minute, and then told him we'd go.

I ate quickly, and so did Kim. I guessed that, like me, she had a plan. I wanted to discuss it with her before we got in my grandfather's truck. When she was almost done, I said, "Kim, we should probably finish getting ready." I looked at Grandpa Jamie, who was reading the paper again. This time it was flat on the table. "What time are you planning on leaving?"

He glanced at the clock above the stove. "Oh, probably in about a half hour."

"Okay, we'll be ready." With that, Kim and I left the kitchen and raced back to my bedroom.

"What do you have planned?" she asked as I closed the door.

I frowned a bit. "I haven't talked to my grandfather that much. He works long days and gets home late. You saw what he was like at breakfast. Anyway, I want to see if he'll tell me anything about David or that summer."

"Could be a touchy subject," she mused, wrinkling her nose before saying, "He seems a bit crabby, too."

"He's not." I waved it off. "He's all bark and no bite. I can handle that."

She grinned. "This could turn out to be an interesting ride after all."

Grandpa Jamie was true to his word. Exactly a half hour later, he was ready to go, standing at the door with his coat on and a worn tweed hat on his head. "You girls ready?"

We hurried out the door after him. The first ten miles or so we drove in silence. Kim and I looked out the window while Grandpa Jamie watched the road. He didn't have the radio on. The silence wasn't uncomfortable. In a way, after yesterday's excitement, it was a welcomed bit of peace.

Kim kicked my ankle, hard enough that I knew it was deliberate, but not enough for my grandfather to notice. I sighed. The peaceful moment was over.

"Grandpa," I began tentatively, "do you remember much about my father?"

"Your father." He snorted. "As if he even deserves to be called that—the man did little more than provide half of your genetics." He paused a moment, and then added. "I try hard not to think of him."

"Did you and grandma know him well?"

He looked at me suspiciously. "Why the sudden interest?"

"He is my father." I tried not to make it sound defensive. "And, Mom met him here, right?"

My grandfather sighed. It was a long-suffering sigh. He picked up his coffee and took a deep drink. He looked at me; I tried to keep my face innocent and inquisitive. It must have worked. He sighed again, and then said, "The first time your mom told us about David was the day she brought him home to meet us. She'd been seeing him for about a month."

"What'd you think of him?"

"He surprised me."

"How?" Kim blurted it out before I could. It was an unusual thing to say about someone. Kim's cheeks reddened, but my grandpa just laughed.

"He had old eyes." He shook his head. "What I mean is, he looked like he was in his early twenties, but he was too mature. Too worldly..." He took another sip from his travel mug and adjusted the heat. I think he was stalling. "There was something odd about him. I can't explain it. I just didn't trust him."

"And then Mom got pregnant," I said. "With me."

He looked at me and nodded. "It was about five weeks later when we found out she was with child." He turned his attention back the road, squinting a bit as he remembered. "David was with her, holding her hand, when she told us. Your grandmother and I were shocked by the news, even more so when there was no talk of marriage."

"Did you ask Mom about it?"

"Your grandmother tried. Your mom wouldn't talk about it. She said David couldn't stay here. Sure enough, he lived here until you were born, and then about a week later, he disappeared."

"He left us when I was a week old?" If he loved my mom, why couldn't he stay? Didn't he want me to know who he was? And why was he back now, after all these years?

"He did." I waited. He paused for a few moments, and then added, "I'll never forgive him for hurting my daughter."

Kim leaned closer, and I appreciated the comfort of knowing she was there. This was hard, but it helped to know my best friend was hearing everything, too. I knew she would share her impressions with me later.

"Why did Mom leave with me?" I asked quietly.

A hurt expression crossed his face. He quickly recovered. "I imagine it was a combination of things. The tension at home was thick. We weren't used to a new baby, your mom was crying all the time, and then there was the small-town scandal. She couldn't leave the house without people clucking their tongues and giving her dirty looks. I guess it got to be too much. Then, that businessman Phil came into town..."

His voice trailed off. I already knew the story about Mom's ex-husband, Phil. "Why didn't she come back to visit?"

Grandpa Jamie sighed and shook his head. "I honestly don't know. You'll have to ask your mom about that one. She wrote us often and sent pictures of you."

"If Mom sent letters, why didn't you visit us?"

"Every letter was postmarked from a different location. No return address. We didn't know where to find you." He confirmed what my grandmother already told me. At least one story added up. Reaching over, he squeezed my hand. "You've always been so smart and beautiful. The things your mom wrote of you, we were just as proud as she was. You look so much like her, but your father is there, too. That's the hard part."

"How am I like David?" I didn't see any similarities between us, besides our hair and eye color and webbed toes.

He looked at me briefly, assessing. "Your hair is the same and your smile, but sometimes, where I see the strongest resemblance, is when I look in your eyes. I see the same depth as his."

"What do you mean?"

He frowned at me. "I can't explain it."

I looked at Kim, and she raised her eyebrows. It was obvious she thought his comment was weird, too.

When we arrived at the hospital, Mom was waiting in the lobby in a wheelchair, looking healthier than she had in weeks. She blushed prettily at Dr. Riley, and I wondered if she wasn't developing a bit of a crush.

I ran forward and hugged her, kissing her cheek. "Hi, Mom."

"Meara! Kim!" she exclaimed, delighted. "I didn't know you were going to come! I feel so popular. Here I was just expecting Dad, and instead I get an entourage."

Dr. Riley squeezed Mom's shoulder. "I would expect nothing less than a regal send-off for my favorite patient. Take care of yourself, get plenty of rest and fluids, and have an extra helping of stuffing today, okay? You are too thin, Sharon."

Her blush deepened. "I'll do that."

Dr. Riley shook hands with each of us, wishing us a Happy Thanksgiving. I picked up Mom's bag. "Can you walk?" I asked, uncertain.

"Of course." She laughed and stood. "Dr. Riley is the one who insisted on the wheelchair."

"Hospital protocol," he said, winking at me.

"Thank you for taking care of her." I sincerely meant it.

"It was my pleasure," he said, and I think he sincerely meant it, too.

Kim and I climbed into the back of the truck so Mom could sit up front. I leaned forward to tease her. "What was that, Mom? Dr. Riley's favorite patient?"

Mom blushed. "He's a nice man, that's all."

I laughed. It wasn't every day that Mom was embarrassed. I let it drop. The ride back was rather quiet. Mom closed her eyes and fell asleep. Grandpa Jamie put on an oldies radio station, a definite signal that he didn't feel like talking. I was dying to compare notes with Kim, but we had to wait until we were alone. Unfortunately, by the time we got home, we only had enough time to get ready and head over to Evan's house for dinner.

When we arrived, Evan and his dad, Darren, were watching a hockey game on TV. I liked Darren, even if I didn't know him well. Evan didn't look like his dad, who was tall and wiry with thinning blond hair, but he had a lot of his dad's personality. They were both hockey fanatics, and they shared the same sense of humor.

Darren was in sales, so he was often away on business. When he was home though, it was clear that he and Lydia were in love. They stood close enough to touch. It was sweet, and I hoped that someday I would have a similar relationship with my husband.

Katie was in the kitchen, helping Grandma Mary and Lydia get the table set. Kim and I tried to help, only to be shooed back to the living room by Lydia. "Go, relax. We're almost done. We'll be eating in about fifteen minutes."

When they called us in, I was amazed at the amount and variety of food. Growing up, it had been only Mom and me celebrating Thanksgiving together. We always had the staples—turkey, stuffing, pumpkin pie— but nowhere near the feast that lay before me now. Evan squeezed my arm and whispered in my ear, "You okay? You look like you're in shock."

"This is amazing."

"This is what happens when my mom and Grandma Mary get together and cook." He pulled back a chair for me. "Please, have a seat."

"Thank you."

Kim sat next to me, and Katie sat on the other side of Kim. Katie asked Kim a million questions about what I was like when I was younger. Kim seemed amused by her. She told her a few funny stories. Being my best friend, she left out all the embarrassing ones. I'd thank her later.

I ate so much I thought I was going to explode. The conversation flowed comfortably. At times, everyone chimed in on one topic, at other points of the meal, several smaller conversations erupted.

After dinner, Kim, Katie, Evan and I stayed in the kitchen to clean up. The adults retired to the living room, after some coaxing from us. Once we were alone, Kim and I brought up the car ride today and told Evan and Katie what my grandfather said.

Evan shrugged. "It's kind of interesting, but I don't see that it tells you anything."

Katie looked thoughtful. "You know, I could always ask my mom about that summer. She might have more information, or at least a different perspective."

"Could you?" What did Lydia know? Would she share?

"Sure," she said. "Don't get too excited, though. I'm not sure that my mom will tell me much, if anything."

"It's worth a shot, anyway," Kim added.

We were almost done with the dishes when my grandma and Lydia came back into the kitchen for the desserts—pumpkin pie, pecan pie, and chocolate torte.

"Do we get to do this again next month for the American Thanksgiving?" I asked.

Lydia laughed. "I don't know about that, Meara."

"Maybe on a smaller scale." Grandma Mary winked at me.

Evan rolled his eyes. "Do you always think about food?"

"Almost always," I said.

"I can vouch for that," Kim said, grinning at me.

"Speaking of food," Grandma Mary added. "These desserts aren't serving themselves."

We helped plate the desserts and took them and coffee into the living room. It was so nice to sit around with everyone and just relax. I imagined that this was what life would have been like if I had grown up here. It made me think about how different things might have been, how different I might have been, had my mom stayed. Then I looked at Kim, and I realized that I never would have known her. She was such a wonderful friend—I couldn't imagine my life without her. It just proved that everything happened for a reason. As my grandma would say, there was no use thinking about the might-have-beens.

Mom sat in the chair closest to the fireplace. Her eyelids were heavy, and her head lulled to the side. I hadn't considered what a long day this must be after her last two days. My grandparents were deep in conversation with Darren, but I caught my grandfather's eye and nodded toward Mom. He nodded back, and quickly wrapped up his conversation.

I was leaning against Evan, warm and comfortable. Turning my head, I kissed his cheek. I felt the slightest bit of stubble. "I think we're going to get going. Mom is exhausted."

He tightened his arms around my shoulder before I could stand and whispered, "I'll walk you out."

I shivered slightly. When I caught Kim's eye, she smiled knowingly and mouthed, "Go." She went to help my mom. Evan stood and pulled me up, walking me to the door and holding out my coat. Throwing on his own jacket, he stepped out behind me. Once the door was closed, he pulled me close for a kiss. I felt a quick thrill course through my body. It had been too long since Evan and I were alone. He pulled away and left me wanting more.

He smiled wickedly. "Pleasant dreams, Meara."

Kim and I stayed up most of the night talking. I was sad that she was leaving tomorrow. While I managed to make it this long without her, I forgot how much I enjoyed having her around. Her cheerfulness and high energy always managed to lift me, too. She brought a fresh perspective to my life, since she was the only person, besides my mom, who knew me before.

When I asked her what she thought, she said. "I'll miss you, Meara, but this was the best thing your mom ever did for you."

"How can you say that?"

"You are thriving here. You have family, you have a seriously gorgeous and wonderful boyfriend, and you have friends who love you."

"But I miss you."

"I miss you, too, and you'll always be my best friend. I'd love for us to live closer." She took a deep breath. "That said, this is where you need to be right now."

She was right, of course. I knew it. We hugged each other, crying a bit. We talked about love, about the future—next summer, college and beyond. Kim planned to apply to the University of Wisconsin—Madison. She wanted to be a veterinarian. I admitted that I hadn't been giving much thought to college and would probably start at a community college nearby to be close to my mom. It was past midnight when we fell asleep, and we were both disoriented when the alarm went off.

This time, I drove Kim to the airport by myself. I watched as she went through security. She turned and waved. I waved back until she was swallowed by the crowd of fellow travelers. My heart ached. I would miss her. I thought back to that day in first grade, when she had insisted I use her red crayon after I broke mine. We'd been inseparable ever since.

In many ways, Kim was a sister to me. I didn't know when I would see her again.

Chapter 25

I hurried home. Mom had an appointment at the clinic, and I offered to take her.

"You don't have to do this," Mom said once again. "I can drive myself."

"Mom," I said. "Why do you argue with me every time I drive you?"

"You're out of school today, Kim just left, don't you want to do something other than drive your mom?"

"All the more reason for me to drive you," I said as I opened her door. Once I walked around and got in, Mom sighed.

"You already miss her, don't you?"

"I do."

"I'm sorry, Meara."

Mom looked like she was going to cry. I wanted to cry, too, but instead I gave her a wide smile. "I'm okay, Mom. I like it here."

"Do you?"

"Yes."

This time when I looked at her, she was biting her lip. Never a good sign. "What now, Mom?"

"Have you seen your father lately?"

"You mean dreamed about him?" I hadn't told her about seeing David in Katie's room or seeing the two of them talking together.

She caught herself, and her checks grew red. "That's what I meant. Have you dreamed about him?"

"Not lately."

"Oh." She looked out the window so I couldn't see her face. "That's good."

Why did it sound like she didn't think it was good at all?

"Meara!"

Ula was in the waiting area at the clinic, reading what looked like a science book. I waved at her, and Mom raised her eyebrow at me. "Is that your friend? I forgot her name."

"Yes," I said. "That's Ula. We usually hang out while you're in treatment."

"Is she here often?"

"When her mom has an appointment," I said.

"Oh." Mom gave me a quick hug. "Why don't you go and catch up with your friend while I check in."

"Hi, Ula," I said. She looked up from her book. Her hair looked especially red against the bright turquoise sweater that she wore. The tattered leather backpack sat on chair next to her. She moved it so I could sit down.

"Don't you have school today?" she asked.

"No. My mom called me in," I said. "I just dropped my best friend off at the airport."

"That's rough. You okay?"

"Yeah, except my mom was in the hospital over the weekend."

"Oh no." Ula glanced over at my mom, who was now reading a magazine and waiting to be called. "She looks good today."

"Yes," I said. "I think she's better."

When the same grumpy nurse as usual called Mom back, Ula gave me an expectant look. "So what should we do today? It's a bit cold to go to the ocean."

"I don't know. You come here more than I do. Is there any cool place in the clinic?"

Ula wrinkled her nose. "Not likely, although there is a coffee shop around the corner."

"That'll work. I can always get hot chocolate."

"Don't like coffee?"

"Uh, no."

Ula laughed. "Me neither."

We bundled up and walked outside. I wasn't worried about leaving the building. I knew Mom would call if she got done early.

It didn't take us long to walk there. The warm and delicious smells inside were welcoming. October was colder here than Wisconsin, because the wind had more bite. My cheeks froze, and my eyes welled up. I was about to comment on the weather to Ula, but one look at her and I knew the cold didn't bother her. Her cheeks were a lovely pink, and her smile was wide.

"Don't you love that fresh air?" She bounced a little on her toes.

"Um, yeah. It's great."

"So, can I get you a hot chocolate?" She walked to the register. "Do you want anything else?"

"You don't have to get it, Ula." I didn't expect her to pay for me.

She waved me off. "It's my treat. You're having a rough couple of days. It's the least I can do."

When our drinks were ready, we settled into two plush chairs near an electric fireplace. The heat felt wonderful against my chilled skin. Ula turned her chair so the heat wasn't blowing directly on her.

"I don't like to get too warm," she said. "So, how was your visit with your friend? And, what is her name anyway? I can't keep calling her 'friend'."

"Kim," I said. "It was great. I told her about my dad, and she was trying to help me figure out what it meant."

Ula leaned forward, the smile vanishing from her face. "What about your dad?"

I felt my face grow hot. No wonder Ula was confused. I hadn't told her about David's visits yet.

"Remember when I told you that I'd never met my dad?" Ula nodded, but didn't say anything. "Well, I've met him now. At first, I thought it was just dreams, but now..."

"Now?" She leaned back in her chair, her eyes never leaving my face.

"Now I know that he's real, and that he's here."

"So, you've talked to him?"

"Yes, several times." I couldn't figure out Ula's expression. She looked leery. Why would my meeting my father bother her? Maybe she had a bad relationship with her dad. "Is this bothering you? We can talk about something else..."

"No," Ula said quickly. "You just surprised me."

"Tell me about it," I said. "He surprised me. Popping in and telling me I'm not..." Crap! I almost told her that he told me I wasn't human. She would think I was crazy. What was I doing?

"You're not..." Ula prompted me to continue. When I remained silent, taking a drink of my hot chocolate instead, she continued. "What is it, Meara? You can tell me. I promise not to laugh or anything."

I searched her face. She looked earnest. I trusted Ula. She was there for me when no one else was, and she understood what I was going through. I took a deep breath and then told her.

"He told you that?" Her eyes had gone wide, but her face betrayed no other emotions.

"Yes, weird, huh?"

Ula didn't say anything. She was staring into the fire. When she turned to me, her eyes were teary. "Meara, I have something to tell you..."

My phone rang. It was my mom. It was a quick appointment, and she was ready to leave. When I hung up, Ula was already standing and zipping her coat. "I'll walk you back."

"What were you going to tell me?" I asked.

"It's nothing," she said. "I can tell you next time when we have more time to talk."

"Are you sure?" I asked.

"Absolutely." She smiled at me, but her eyes looked incredibly sad.

October passed in a blurry rush. Between mid-term tests and research papers, texting Kim theories of what David could be, and seeing Evan's hockey games, I had little free time. When I did have a few minutes, Katie and I spent it planning a surprise birthday party for my mom. Her birthday was October 31, and Mom loved Halloween as much as I did. It had always been our favorite holiday. In past years, we spent weeks planning our costumes and decorating the house. The trick-or-treaters used to flock to our door, the most decorated house in the neighborhood. It helped that we always gave out the best candy, too.

"Does your mom know?" Katie asked. Again. She was paranoid that my mom would find out early.

"She doesn't have a clue," I said. I wasn't worried. Since Katie was my closest friend here, and Evan was my boyfriend, my mom had no reason to question why I was spending time at their house. Plus, I made a point of being home for dinner, and spending at least an hour with her every night to keep her informed of things—friends, school, and stuff. I enjoyed that time with her. I was amazed at how much better she seemed to be feeling. I guess the visit to the hospital helped her.

The party was tomorrow, and we were almost ready. Grandma Mary and Lydia had made most of the food. Katie designed the invitations and sent them out. She even sent one to Mom and me, inviting us to a costume party at the Mitchell residence. For all Mom knew, we were just going to Lydia's annual party.

We were just putting the last touches on the decorations in the common room.

"Hand me another bat?" I asked. Katie gave me a rubber bat, and I threaded the fishing line and suspended it from the ceiling. "How does it look?"

She smiled. "Creepy."

I came down the ladder and stood next to her, eyeing the room critically. Then I smiled, too. It looked amazing. Giant spiderwebs draped in the corner, a flock of bats flew along the ceiling, and black rats with glowing red eyes crouched under the table.

"We do awesome work," I said.

"We do," Katie agreed. "But the real question is—what are you and Evan going as?"

"I'm not telling," I said. "Unless you tell me what you and Brian are wearing."

"It's a surprise."

"Well, then ditto."

Katie pouted. "You're no fun."

I laughed. This party was going to be great.

"Bride of Frankenstein!"

Katie stood in the doorway, watching me put the final touches on my makeup.

"Good guess," I smiled at her from the mirror.

"I love your green skin, and how in the world did you get your hair like that?" My hair was standing straight up in the air—about two feet tall.

"Don't ask," I muttered, concentrating on attaching a false eyelash. Man, these things were trickier than they looked. I looked at Katie again and noticed that she was in her jeans and sweatshirt. The party was starting in fifteen minutes. "Are you planning on changing any time soon?"

"When Brian gets here."

"Why the big secret?"

She smirked at me. "You'll see."

The doorbell rang. Neither of us jumped. People had been coming and going all morning. This was turning out to be the biggest party that Peggy's Cove had seen in a long time; it seemed like everyone was contributing something.

Brian's voice rang in the hallway. "Has anyone seen the love of my life?"

Katie grinned at me. "It's showtime. See you soon, Meara!"

I had no idea what their costumes were going to be, but with all this secrecy, I was dying to find out.

"How's my bride?"

Evan stood in the doorway. His hair and eyebrows were darkened to jet-black, and his skin tinted green like mine. He had thimbles on the sides of his neck to mimic bolts. He wore a gray suit and big, black shoes.

"Glad I don't wear false eyelashes every day," I said. "How's my monster?"

He came and stood behind me, so I looked at him through the mirror.

"Wow, Meara, you look stunning...and frightening all at once. I'm impressed." He eyed my hair skeptically. "Where's your white stripe?"

"That's where you come in," I said, handing him the can of white hair paint. "I can't spray my hair and cover my eyes."

"True," he said, holding up the can in his right hand and shielding my face with his left. "Hold your breath."

When he finished, I looked in the mirror. Perfect. The two of us looked like we stepped right off a movie set. I grinned at his reflection. "I think this is my best costume ever."

"Mine, too."

"What time is it?"

"Ten minutes until party time. Does that mean I get to kiss you?"

I laughed and stepped back away from him. "Not on your life. You'll ruin my makeup. This took me twenty minutes."

He sighed. "Ah, the joys of dating a high-maintenance monster."

As we headed down the stairs, I took in the view. The Inn was transformed. It was like stepping into a haunted house. Decorations draped every corner and available space.

The buffet featured green punch, steaming with dry ice, "eyeball" meatballs, monster fingers, broomsticks, "bat-wing" buffalo chicken wings, and every other kind of spooky or gross-looking food item Grandma Mary and Lydia could create. The cake looked like a witch's cauldron, with gummy worms and bugs floating inside.

"I don't think I've ever been to a party this lavish."

Evan laughed. "It's something else all right. I hope your mom likes it."

"She'll love it."

"You guys look great!" Brian called from behind us.

I turned around and laughed. "This was your big secret?"

"Do you like it?" Katie asked, twirling around. She was dressed as the Statue of Liberty, and Brian was Uncle Sam.

"It's patriotic," I said.

"We wanted to remind you of home."

"That's sweet," I said. "Although, I don't recall Uncle Sam and Lady Liberty strolling around my neighborhood growing up."

"No?" Evan asked. "Well, that's because you didn't have Katie there. She probably would have latched onto this costume idea a long time ago. Any excuse to wear a toga."

Katie stuck out her tongue just as Lydia ran into the room. She was dressed as a lion tamer, and Darren was a lion.

"Shhh…everyone. Sharon's here. She just pulled up."

There were too many people to hide. Darren dimmed the lights, and everyone moved to the corners or against the wall. I felt the anticipation in the air, and my heart thumped in my chest. I prayed that she would be surprised, that she hadn't somehow already figured it out. Katie picked me up earlier in the day, and I told my mom I was coming over to get my costume ready. She didn't seem to think anything strange was going on.

We heard the knock at the door and Lydia opened it, stepping back to let Mom in. At that moment, we all yelled, "Surprise!"

She jumped, but quickly recovered. "Holy cow! This is for me?"

We all broke into an off-key Happy Birthday. Darren placed a glass of punch in Mom's hand, and she started to work her way around the room. I ran up and kissed her, noting how radiant she looked tonight. She was Red Riding Hood. Her cheeks flushed, and her eyes brightened with excitement.

"Happy Birthday, Mom!"

"Were you in on this?"

"Uh huh." I smiled and hugged her tight. It was easy to do these days, because she was so incredibly thin. "Surprised you, didn't we?"

"Almost gave me a heart attack then and there," she agreed. "I think this was the biggest surprise I've ever had."

"Besides me, of course."

Her brow crinkled until she realized I was teasing. Then, she relaxed into a grin. "Yes, besides you."

Guests continued to arrive, and soon the house was swimming with people. I didn't know a lot of the guests. They were people from town or mom's childhood friends. It was even harder to recognize anyone with costumes. We could have had a bus full of party crashers, and I didn't think anyone would know the difference.

"Do you want to step outside?" Evan whispered. "It's getting unbelievably hot in here." He grinned down at me. "And, I'm not just talking about you."

I shook my head. He just couldn't resist those cheesy one-liners. "Sure. Let's just grab some punch, and we can head out."

My mom stood in the corner of the dining room, talking animatedly to a masked pirate. Strange, I thought, he looks familiar. She seemed to know him well. They stood close, and he touched her often—on the arm, the hand, and the shoulder. Once, he even brushed back her hair and tucked it behind her ear. I was about to go over by them when I heard my grandfather behind me.

"You!" he growled. "What are you doing here?"

Mom whipped around to face my grandfather. She looked... guilty. "Dad, please. Don't make a scene."

Grandpa Jamie gestured to the masked man. "Who invited him? Where'd he come from?"

Gasping, I knew exactly who the masked stranger was.

David touched my mom's arm, which had my grandfather snarling in response. "Keep your hands off her."

Ignoring him, David addressed my mom. "It's okay, Sharon. I'll leave."

"No!" Mom shook her head. Tears glistened in her eyes, but she looked determined. She lifted her chin and faced my grandfather. "I invited him, Dad. David is my guest."

Now it was my grandfather's turn to look surprised. Her confession seemed to knock the wind right out of him, and I watched as he sank into a chair, his eyes never leaving my mom's face. "Why on earth did you do that?"

"I love him, Dad," she said. "I always have."

By now, the doorway to the room was crowded shoulder to shoulder with curious onlookers. No one seemed sure of what was going to happen next. I wished there was something I could do...like hide. This was so embarrassing!

Lydia stepped through and waved everyone away with a sweep of her hands. "Okay, nothing more to see here. Let's give the birthday girl a moment of privacy, shall we? Who would like some coffee and dessert? I made the most fabulous apple tart..." She kept up the social prattle as she led the onlookers back into the living room.

David stepped forward and offered my grandfather his hand. "I'm sorry, Jamie, for all the pain I have caused you and your family. I don't expect you to forgive me. Just know that I do love Sharon and Meara."

I perked up at my name. He loved me? How could he love me when he barely knew me? I didn't love him. He was practically a stranger.

My grandfather looked at David's outstretched hand. He stood and, at his full height, he was a good three inches taller than David was. His voice boomed. "Leave them again, and I'll find you and deal with you myself."

With that, he turned and left the room.

David lowered his hand. He looked humbled; Mom looked mad.

"He shouldn't talk to you that way," she said. "I'm going to go find him…"

"Sharon," David said. "It's okay. I'd say the same thing in his shoes."

David put his arm around my mom's shoulder and whispered something in her ear. She relaxed and smiled at him. I didn't think she even realized I was in the room. Evan came up beside me, took my hand, and squeezed it. "Are you okay?"

Was I okay? "I think so," I said.

When I spoke, Mom realized that I was in the room. She ran over and placed her hands on either side of my face. Her eyes were full of concern. "Meara, I'm so sorry. I didn't mean for things to happen this way."

David stepped behind her. He placed one hand on Mom's shoulder and reached out to touch my hair with the other. "Hello, Meara."

"Hello, David." I was not about to call him Dad or even Father. Evan squeezed my hand again, so I introduced him. "David, I'd like for you to meet my boyfriend, Evan Mitchell. Evan, this is my father, David."

David's eyes appraised Evan as he shook his hand. "You don't look surprised, Evan."

"Well, Meara's told me quite a bit about you."

"The little I know…" I grumbled under my breath.

David chuckled, a delighted expression on his face. "Sharon, Meara has absolutely no patience."

"No patience!" I sputtered. "You first appeared to me almost four months ago, and I've barely learned a thing about you."

Mom looked up at him. "Perhaps it's time you tell her more."

David shook his head. "Not yet. Not here. We have time."

"I'm standing right here," I mumbled. "Why don't you try talking to me?" I wasn't some small child they could pat on the head. David exchanged another meaningful look with my mom. Great—now they were all lovey-dovey and keeping secrets from me—me of all people! The one who needed to know! I turned angrily and took Evan's arm. "I can see I'm not going to learn anything new tonight. Come on, Evan, let's go."

Evan gave my parents an apologetic look, which had me fuming even more, and then followed me out the patio door and into the yard. He listened while I ranted, offering an "uh-huh" or "of course" at regular intervals. It didn't take me long to get it out of my system, and when I calmed down, I realized how ridiculous I was acting. It didn't stop me from telling Evan, "If you say 'uh-huh' one more time, I'm going to punch you."

"Uh-huh."

"You asked for it." I went to punch him in the arm, and his hand wrapped around my wrist. He lifted my arm until it was around his neck, then wrapped his other arm around my waist and pulled me closer.

"Don't you know?" He breathed in my ear. "I'm a lover, not a fighter."

Any remaining anger and irritation disappeared as I lost myself in his kiss.

Chapter 26

It was almost unnatural the way that David folded into the fabric of our lives. He was frequently at dinner. Tonight was no exception. There was only one wrinkle in this fabric. My grandfather, Jamie.

"Jamie, can you pass the potatoes?" David asked my grandfather, who continued to eat his food and act as though no one spoke. I bit my lip to keep from smiling and exchanged a glance with Evan. It was his first dinner with us as a family. I couldn't wait to get his thoughts about it later.

"Dad?" My mom—the peacemaker. "The potatoes?"

"Oh? Did you want some, Sharon?" Grandpa Jamie passed her the bowl. Irritation flashed on Mom's face, but she took the bowl and handed it to David.

I considered my grandfather's current behavior an improvement. When David first started coming to dinner, Grandpa Jamie wouldn't stop talking about how David was bound to leave us again. They argued about anything and everything. The outright confrontation eventually settled into Grandpa Jamie just ignoring him. I sided with my grandfather. I didn't trust David.

"The food is delicious, Mary, as usual." David knew the way to Grandma Mary's heart. With his frequent compliments on her meals and even bigger appetite, she seemed almost as charmed by David as my mom did.

She beamed in reply. "Can I get you anything else, David?"

David swallowed his last bite of potatoes, smiled, and patted his stomach. "No, thank you. I'm quite full."

Grandma Mary laughed and stood up. "I hope not too full for

dessert."

David stood as well. "Let me help you, Mary."

I watched as David and my grandmother walked to the kitchen. With his thick, dark hair and youthful appearance, David looked closer to my age than Mom's. He only looked a few years older than Evan did. Why did he look so young? Why wasn't it strange to everyone else? So far, no one had commented on it, not even Grandpa Jamie.

"Are you okay?" Evan asked. "You seem distracted."

"I'm fine." I smiled at him and hoped it was convincing. I was saved from saying anything else, because my grandma and David returned from the kitchen.

"I made apple pie," Grandma Mary announced. "And we have vanilla ice cream, too."

She winked at me, and I was touched. Grandma Mary made this meal just for me. She even invited Evan to surprise me. She cooked turkey and all the fixings. Technically, it wasn't American Thanksgiving, since it was a Saturday night, but it was close enough. And I was grateful to have my family and my boyfriend with me. I was even okay with David being here. This time.

The pie was delicious, with the ice cream on top melting to perfection. Grandpa Jamie smile as he bit in. "One of my favorite desserts," he said.

Mom laughed at something David said, and I looked at her. Ever since her trip to the hospital, I found myself watching her closely. In the morning, she was stiff and slow. Pain darkened her eyes and pulled at her features. When David appeared, she changed. It was as if his mere presence eased her pain and discomfort. At those moments, she was at her happiest, almost carefree. Her skin flushed prettily, and her eyes glowed.

While I appreciated the effect David had on my mom, I was suspicious. As far as I was concerned, he had a motive and I needed to find out what it was. Poisonous thoughts filled my head, and suspicion clung to me like a well-woven cloak. Why was he here? When would he leave again? I practically choked on these questions, swallowing them bitterly as I watched my mom thrive in his company.

"David found an apartment in Halifax," Mom announced to no

one in particular. "He moves in next week."

"So, David," I said casually, toying with my pie. "How long are you planning on staying this time?"

Grandpa Jamie had asked Mom this question numerous times. I felt him watching me, but my eyes were on David and my mom. Mom's eyes flashed in anger, and she scolded me. "Meara, what kind of question is that?"

David covered her hand to stop her from saying more. "It's okay, Sharon. It's a reasonable question." His gaze was measuring while he gave me a small smile. "To be honest, I'm a bit amazed it's taken Meara this long to ask."

What did he know about me? He knew me mere months, not years. I glared and waited. Finally, he answered, "I'm not going anywhere. I'll stay as long as your mother wants me to stay."

"Convenient, then, isn't it?" I responded curtly.

He seemed confused by my words. "How so?"

"Well," I paused. "You shouldn't have to wait too long. Her days being limited and all."

I regretted the words the second they left my mouth. But there they were, and I couldn't take them back. Mom gasped, visibly paling as though someone had slapped her. Essentially, I had. David's mouth set in a thin line. Disappointment. My grandparents stared at me, mouths gaping. I hated myself at that moment. It was by far my lowest point. I couldn't even look at Evan.

"Excuse me," I murmured, pushing back my chair and running from the room.

I knew someone followed me, but I didn't turn to see who it was. I could have headed to my room, but that would have meant staying in the house, hearing the ramifications of my outburst, and seeing the hurt on my mom's face. I went to the front door, yanking my coat off the hook on the way out. Then, I ran toward the shore. I didn't stop until I was a foot away from the rocks. A sob shook my body, and I dropped to the ground.

I felt myself pulled backwards into a lap while arms wrapped around me. In my despair, it took me a minute to register who held me. It was David.

"Meara." His voice was quiet. Soothing. He smelled like the ocean. It was comforting. I stiffened, because I wanted to relax into him. He didn't seem to notice. Instead, he continued. "Don't hate yourself. I'm the one to blame. If I hadn't abandoned you and your mother all those years ago, you would have no reason to doubt me now."

I didn't turn to look at him. Why was he being kind now? My eyes welled up, and the tears streamed down. "I di-didn't mm-mean w-what I s-said!"

He stroked my hair and rocked back and forth, as if he were comforting a small child. "Of course you didn't, honey, of course you didn't. Everyone knows that. You're under a tremendous amount of pressure. Your mother is worried sick about you."

I sniffled and turned to look at him. "That's exactly why I'm such a horrible person. She is dying, and she worries about me. Who do I worry about? Myself!"

"Is that true?" By the tone of his voice, I knew he didn't believe it. He pulled me back again, resting my head against his chest and stroking my hair. "Were your words tonight for you or for your mom?"

When I didn't answer, he answered for me. "You worry about her. For all those years, you just had each other. It's natural that you have such a strong bond. Your mother loves you. I love you, too, Meara."

I pulled away to look at him. His pained eyes searched my face. "I'm so sorry for what I did to you both. It's unforgivable, and unfortunately, there is no way for me to explain why I did it."

"Can't you try?"

He shook his head. "Not tonight, although you, out of everyone, may get the closest to understanding me."

"Why not tonight? When is this perfect time you're waiting for?"

"You're not ready. I'll tell you soon. Then, it will all be clear to you."

"See?" I stood and pointed at him. "This is what I don't get. You speak to me in rhymes or phrases that don't even make sense. Why the secrecy? Why can't you just tell me everything, so I can understand?"

He stood and turned away from me as if to head back to the house.

"David? Are you going to answer me?"

He looked back at me. His eyes were sad. "You're not ready yet."

"You keep saying that. What do I have to be ready for? Does insanity run in your family? Is it that bad?" The way he was acting, the way I was feeling, mental illness didn't sound that far off.

"I can't answer that for you. That's something you'll have to decide for yourself." He turned to leave again. When he was about halfway to the house, he called back, "Take your time out here. I'll let everyone know you're okay."

"David?" I asked. He paused again. "Can you send Evan out?"

"Of course," he said.

I turned back to the sea, lost in my thoughts. I didn't have to wait long before I heard Evan approach. He stopped just behind me, but didn't touch me. I wondered how repulsed he was by my obnoxious behavior.

"Meara." He sounded quiet. "Are you okay?"

I nodded, not turning, wrapping my arms around myself. Evan placed his arms over mine and rested his chin on my head. He didn't say a word, so I broke the silence. "Do you think less of me now?"

"Why on earth would you think that?" He spun me around and stared into my eyes. I felt myself tearing up again, so I broke his gaze and started to pace.

"Because I was horrible in there," I said. "I shouldn't have said that. Did you see my mom's face? I broke her heart."

"Meara, stop it!" Evan held my arms to stop my pacing. He waited, forcing me to look at him before he continued. "What you said was no worse than what everyone else has thought since your mom's birthday party. Of course you surprised your mom, surprised us all, but no one blames you."

"I shouldn't have said her days are limited. It just slipped out."

"I know that, and your mom knows that, too," he said. "Give yourself a break. Your mom is dying. A few months ago, she was all the family you knew. You've been thrown into this new place, and then, from out of the blue, comes your father who abandoned you at birth. How differently do you think anyone else would react in your shoes?"

I paused. He had a point. Evan continued. "Obviously, even David feels he should shoulder the responsibility, since he followed you out here. What did he say to you, anyway?"

I smiled. It was a bitter smile. "He started by saying practically the same thing you did, and then he lost me."

"What do you mean?"

"He started talking about how someday I may understand why he did what he did. That I share traits with him…" I trailed off. For the life of me, I couldn't remember the rest of our conversation.

"What kind of traits?"

"I don't know. He wouldn't say."

"Odd." Evan shook his head. "So, when's he planning to enlighten you on all of his secrets?"

"I don't know that either. He told me I'm not ready."

"Ready for what?"

"I have no idea.

Evan laughed. It wasn't a happy sound. "Geez, Meara. No wonder you're frustrated. The guy talks in circles."

"Exactly."

"Do you feel better now?" Evan stepped closer.

"Yes, thank you." I watched as his face drew near. He lifted my chin in his hand.

"I love you, Meara," he said. My heart beat erratically, and my face flushed. Did he just say he loved me?

"You love me?"

He smiled. "I do. Never doubt that."

"I love you, too," I whispered.

"I'll never get tired of hearing that," he murmured, just before his warm lips covered my own.

Chapter 27

*I*t was the week before Christmas, and I was getting desperate. In between going to school, cramming for exams, writing to Kim, and talking to Evan, I spent all of my free time online, desperately searching for his gift. Nothing seemed right. I wanted something unique. I tried not to let it show when I was around him how much trouble I was having finding his present. It didn't help that he gloated about how he found me the perfect present. How could I compete with perfect?

Everyone else was easy. I bought a new cookbook from some up-and-coming American chef for Grandma Mary, a thick, flannel coat for Grandpa Jamie, and a pair of silver hoop earrings for Katie. I sent Kim a sweater from Gap, the one that she had hinted more than once that she liked. I bought my mom a new robe. It was lavender and plush. I tried it on in the store, and it was like wrapping up in a cloud. She was going to love it.

I made another present for my mom, something more personal. It was a scrapbook. To be honest, it was a gift for both of us—something for her to enjoy now, and for me to have to remember all the good times when she was gone. I equally laughed and cried as I created it.

I bought David a sweater. I shouldn't have bothered. The day after I bought it, he practically ordered me not to get him anything. He claimed that he traveled light and would probably have to leave it behind anyway. Whatever. He could be so weird sometimes. It ticked me off that he hadn't told me anything. Apparently, soon in his world meant a lot longer than mine.

"Earth to Meara...Are you there?"

Katie stood in front of me, holding a red sweater in her left hand and a black sweater in her right. I was thinking about something that David said the night before, so I had no idea what she asked me. I assumed it had to do with the two sweaters she held up.

"They're great," I said, glancing at them but not seeing. They looked like every other sweater Katie had shown me over the last hour.

Katie raised one blond eyebrow at me. "You're right," she said slowly. "They are. Except—what I asked you—was which one you liked better, the red or the black?"

"Remind me again," I said. "Who is this for?"

"Brian! I've been shopping for Brian for the past twenty minutes!"

"Then the red," I said. "Definitely the red."

"Are you sure?" she asked, biting her lip.

I grew tired of Katie's indecisiveness. "Buy it. It's great."

"Okay," she said. "Come stand in line with me."

The line was six-people deep. Why didn't they bring in extra cashiers around the holidays? It was worse than waiting in line at an amusement park. At least there, you went on a ride when you go to the end. Here, you gave some stranger your money and were lucky if they thanked you for it.

My phone rang. I didn't recognize the number, but I answered anyway.

"Hello?"

"Meara? It's Ula. How are you?"

"Ula!" I didn't even know she had a cell phone or knew my number. I missed her. She hadn't been at the clinic the last few times I went with Mom. "I'm great. How are you?"

"Good. Listen, I hope you don't mind that I called you. I was hoping we could get together? Finish our conversation?"

I remembered that she was trying to tell me something the last time we hung out.

"Uh, sure. I'm at the mall with Katie."

"You are? Are you going to be there a while?"

I glanced in front of me. The line hadn't moved. The cashier was paging a manager. Inwardly, I sighed. To Ula, I said, "Yeah, I think so."

"How about if I meet you there?"

"One sec," I said, turning to Katie. "Ula wants to meet us. Do you mind?"

"No," she said. "That's fine."

"When will you get here?" I asked Ula.

"In about fifteen minutes. Should we meet by the food?"

"The food court? Sure. We'll see you there."

I hung up and realized that the difficult customer was gone. The line began to move, and soon, there was only one person in front of us.

"What are you getting Evan?" Katie asked.

"I have no idea."

"You better decide quickly. Christmas is only a week away."

"I know. Don't remind me!"

Katie seemed to hesitate, and then she asked, "Are you getting anything for David?"

"I got him a sweater," I said. "But maybe I should have bought him a compass, so he can find his way back to us if he gets lost."

"Ouch. That's a bit harsh, isn't it?"

"It's a joke," I muttered. Katie obviously didn't think it was funny. She fiddled with the neck of the sweater and seemed uncomfortable. Great. Now I was alienating my friends. I mentally sighed, and then pasted a smile on my face.

"I know!" I said. "You can help me think of something for Evan. You must have some great ideas. What did you get him?"

Relief flickered across her face. This was safe territory.

"I got him a book he wanted about Scottish legends or something." She shook her head. "It's not the type of book he normally reads, but he wanted this one. He has a whole bunch of books on his list."

"What's different about it?" I asked. Evan liked anything to do with the ocean, so I didn't see why this was unusual.

"He likes nonfiction. His favorite ones read like textbooks. Boring." Katie wrinkled her nose in distaste. "This one is a fantasy book with a mermaid and a sea monster on the cover. More fiction than fact."

"Interesting."

"You could get him one of the others." Katie unzipped her purse and began to search around it. "

I have his list. It's in here somewhere...aha! Here it is."

Katie handed me half of a torn sheet of loose-leaf paper. On it, in Evan's handwriting, were about ten things that he wanted. Katie had crossed most items off and written names next to them stating who was giving the gift. Boring things like socks and t-shirts were left on the list, but then I saw the books he wanted. As I read the titles, a shiver ran down my spine. What was Evan up to?

"After we meet up with Ula, can we go to the bookstore?"

"Sure," Katie said. "I'm done after this anyway."

Katie paid for the sweater, and we walked to the food court. I spotted Ula right away. She wore another pair of vintage jeans and a black sweater. We were out of earshot when Katie asked, "Why does she always have that ratty old backpack with her?"

"I don't know," I said. "Maybe it's like her purse. I actually think it's kind of cool, her whole vintage look."

"It's different. I'll give you that."

Ula grinned when she spotted us and started walking over. I hugged her when she reached us. "You remember my friend, Katie?"

"Yes," Ula said. "Hello, Katie."

"Hi, Ula. So, do you have shopping to do, too?"

"Not really. I was just bored and hoping to hang out for a bit." She eyed Katie's shopping bags. "Looks like you've had luck."

Katie smiled. "A bit. We were just about to go to the bookstore. Meara's going to buy Evan some books he wants for Christmas."

"Sounds fun. Let's go," Ula said.

I walked between my friends and tried to keep the conversation going. Katie got along well with Kim when she visited, but she didn't seem to like Ula. I got the impression she thought Ula was weird. Ula did not seem to mind or have much interest in Katie either. So, why did I feel obligated to make sure everyone got along?

When we reached the bookstore, Katie handed me the list. "Here are the books he asked for. You may have to ask where to find them."

I read the list. "The Mythical Creatures Bible, Monsters of the Deep, Ocean Lore and Legend...What kind of books are these?"

Katie shrugged. "Who knows? Maybe Evan's doing some kind of research project at school. You know how crazy he is about anything related to the ocean. Find him a mermaid, and he'd probably marry it."

Ula looked pale. "Those are books Evan requested?"

I showed her the list. "Guess so. It's in his handwriting."

I asked the bored-looking man at Customer Service if he could help me find them. He perked up when he saw this list, confessing his love of fantasy and folklore.

"It's for my boyfriend's Christmas present," I told him, before he gave me a play by play of the last fantasy con he attended. He stopped smiling, but he showed me the section where I could find them. As luck would have it, they had all three books in stock.

I thumbed through the pages and shivered as image after image of giant squids, shape-shifting creatures, and merpeople caught my eye.

"Are you going to be here a while?" Katie asked. She was clearly bored, never mind that I already spent hours helping her shop.

"Probably a little longer. Why?"

"I'm going to get a cappuccino in the café downstairs. Come get me when you're ready to go?"

"Sure," I said, not looking up.

"'Kay. See you soon," Katie said.

Ula picked up the book on top and nodded toward a table in the corner. "We can sit over there if you like."

We sat down, and I set aside the first book and opened the larger one. It contained detailed illustrations, known facts, and retellings of legends. I lost myself in its contents, forgetting Ula was there until she cleared her throat and I looked up.

"About our last conversation…" she started. Her voice wavered. Was she nervous?

"Yes?"

"I…uh…I just wanted to tell you…" She looked down. "Well, I haven't told you the whole truth."

"What do you mean?"

Her cheeks reddened. "The big one, to start with…Me mum is not being treated at the clinic."

"What?"

"She's dead."

I gasped. "Oh no, I'm so sorry!"

Ula shook her head, her eyes filling with tears. "No, you don't understand. She's been dead. For many years."

My throat constricted painfully. What was she saying? I cocked my head to the side and looked at her. "Why were you at the clinic then?"

"For you."

I found it difficult to swallow. My heartbeat thrummed in my ears. She wasn't making any sense. "I didn't even know you."

"No." Ula's voice grew stronger. "You didn't, but I knew you."

"What? How?" My questions came out in a whisper.

"I'm your aunt, Meara. David's sister."

I looked around. Was this a joke? Was she crazy? "You're kidding, right?"

She shook her head. "I wanted to tell you sooner. Believe me, I did."

"Why should I believe you? I talked to you about David. How do I know you're not making this up?"

"I'm not," she said. Her voice was firm.

I started to cry, but brushed the tears away. "You lied to me."

"I misled you. Yes. For that, I am sorry."

"You're sorry," I repeated. How did one apology make this all better? "You're not the person I thought you were. You're not my friend." I stood. "I think...I think I need to go now."

Ula watched me with sad eyes. She didn't try to stop me. I picked up the books to leave. I was several steps toward the escalator when I heard her.

"I can give you answers, Meara. I can tell you what he won't."

I stopped. It would be easy to go back and sit down. I wanted answers so badly that I could taste it. The taste was bittersweet. She lied to me. Could I trust her? Would she tell me the truth? I didn't know, and for that reason, I didn't turn around. As I started to walk again, she spoke once last time.

"Find me when you're ready to know."

Her voice sounded strange. Distant. My own curiosity made me turn back.

The table was empty.

Chapter 28

Why didn't Evan tell me he wanted these books? I flipped through the thickest one as I sat on my bed. I planned to wrap them, but the illustrations caught my eye. Many of these creatures I had never even heard of before. Then again, I'd never been to the ocean until we moved here.

I stopped at picture of a fierce-looking man. Well, I guess you could call him a man. He looked human, except for the fact that his skin was blue and his teeth were sharp and pointy—a shark in a human's body. I read the caption,

The Blue Men of the Minch live in underwater caves in the Minch, a straight between Lewis, Long Island and the Shiant Islands near Scotland. They attempt to wreck ships unfortunate enough to pass into their territory by conjuring storms and luring sailors into the water. The captain will save his ship only if he can finish their rhymes and solve their riddles.

My eyes traveled back to the image. The artist did an amazing job. The sharp-toothed monster seemed to smile right at me. It was super creepy. I gave an involuntary shudder and turned the page. I saw serpent-like creatures, underwater horses—real horses, not sea horses—and giant squids. Most were more like animals and less like humans. Some could be real, like the giant squid, and some might be other animals mistaken for a monster, like a manatee or stingray. The book did a good job providing the myth and the facts to support or debunk it.

I came across another human-like monster. It was creepier than the blue man was. It was small and green, and even in the drawing, it looked evil. Grindylow, I read.

These water demons were first mentioned in British folktales

in the county of Yorkshire. British parents told their children stories of Grindylows to prevent them from going into ponds and lakes alone. Grindylows are water demons with long fingers that drag children into the deep.

Were all sea monsters evil? If I believed the stories, most sunk sinking ships or lured humans to their death. The author theorized that these legends explained drowning and shipwrecks, and of course, stories of scary monsters would keep kids who couldn't swim from going into the water. I suppose it was like saying, "Don't take candy from strangers". It gave me the chills. Why did Evan want these books? I wanted to call him and ask, but I couldn't ruin the surprise. Christmas was only a couple of days away. Although I didn't want to wait, I had to.

I wish I could find the courage to ask David. I never seemed to get the question out when we were alone. Even if I did, I didn't know that he'd tell me. He seemed to be following his own schedule to reveal information to me, and it was excruciating. Of course, now that I knew Ula was my aunt, I could get answers. She told me so. If only she were here.

I felt bad about the way I reacted yesterday. Once I got over my initial shock, I was less angry, more bewildered. And, I was hurt. How could she lie to me? How could she pretend to be in the same situation as me with a sick mother, when her mother wasn't even alive anymore? Her mother. My grandmother. Did I have other relatives I didn't know about?

"Hullo."

Ula popped into existence on the end of my bed, sitting cross-legged in her faded blue jeans. I screamed and jumped back, hitting my head on the headboard in the process. Her shocked expression must have mirrored my own. Her mouth dropped open just before she disappeared.

"Meara! Are you okay?" Mom slammed my door open and ran over to my bed.

"It was a spider." I tried to look sheepish.

She sighed and shook her head. "For crying out loud, you almost gave me a heart attack. Where is it?"

Lucky that Mom knew I was afraid of spiders. She had no reason not to buy my story. I pointed to the floor. "It crawled under my bed."

She raised her eyebrow. "And you're not going to kill it?"

"I'm not crawling under there after it!"

Mom lifted the bed skirt and glanced along the length of the bed. "Well, I don't see anything now." She straightened and ruffled my hair. "Next time, honey, just hit it with a rolled-up magazine."

"Okay, Mom." I smiled at her while leave, leave, leave played in my mind. I wondered if Ula would come back.

Mom started to the door, then turned and gave me a strange look. "You sure you're okay?"

"Yeah, why?"

She shrugged. "I don't know. You seem edgy or something."

I laughed. It sounded fake, even to me. "I had a lot of Diet Coke this morning."

"Well, maybe cut back a little," she suggested. "Oh, and your father will be here soon. He's taking me out to dinner. Do you want to come?"

Out to dinner with my parents exchanging lovey looks? I could think of a million other things I'd rather do. "No, thanks, Mom. I'm going to work on a paper. It's due on Wednesday."

"You sure?"

"Yes. Thanks, though."

"Okay, then." She kissed my head, and then closed the door as she left.

I listened as Mom walked back down the hall. Then, feeling stupid talking to an empty room, I said, "You can come back now."

"She's gone?"

Ula once again sat cross-legged at the end of my bed. She smiled at me apologetically. "I didn't mean to scare you."

"I just wasn't expecting it," I said, referring to her ability to appear and disappear on a whim. "David can do that, too. Will I be able to?" It'd be kind of cool to pop in on my friends. Or Evan. Definitely would save on gas and time.

"Probably." Ula shrugged. "It's a family talent."

"Family?" I just learned Ula was my aunt. Were there more? "Are there more of you?"

Ula tilted her head and studied my face. "I'm not sure what you're asking. There are many of our kind, but I have one sister and five brothers."

My mouth fell open. "Have I met anyone else?"

"Not that I know of. The only other one here with us is Brigid." She made a face that I couldn't read. "You'll probably meet her eventually."

I tried to wrap my mind around that. David had a family. A large family. "Does David have other children?"

Ula shook her head. "Just you. Some of my brothers are married though, and I do have other nieces and nephews..." Ula trailed off. She looked close to tears. "I'm sorry for deceiving you. I wanted to help. I didn't know how else to get close to you."

A surge of emotion swept through me. I took a deep breath before responding. "Why didn't you just enroll in my high school like a normal teenager?"

Ula shuddered. "I hate school. I've never been good at it." She gave me a crooked smile. "Besides, I'm not a teenager."

I leaned close and studied Ula's face. She looked bemused, so apparently she didn't mind. Not a wrinkle or a gray hair. Her face was so young and innocent; I assumed she was either my age or a year or two younger. She acted older, though, and it would explain her love of vintage clothing. I was sure it was rude, but I asked anyway. "How old are you?"

Her reply was instant. "Older than you think."

"Forty?"

"I was born in 1912."

I laughed, but Ula didn't even break a smile. She continued to watch me, her expression neutral. I stopped laughing when I realized she wasn't joking.

"You're over one hundred years old? That's ancient!" The words came out, and I slapped my hand over my mouth. That was so rude! "I'm sorry! I'm so sorry!"

It was Ula's turn to laugh. "I'm not offended, Meara."

"And David is older?"

"He's the oldest in the family, next to Uncle Angus," she said. "But Angus is ancient. Over five hundred years old."

I fell back against the headboard. Was this another of her stories? "How do you look so young?"

"We're not human." Ula shrugged. "We don't age as fast."

We sat quiet for a few minutes. I think she was letting me digest the news. Ula gestured to the books spread in front of me. "I see you've been reading. Find anything interesting?"

I sighed and flipped through a few pages. "Not so much, unless I'm the daughter of a merman or swamp monster."

Ula giggled. "Um, no. Swamp monsters don't exist."

"How do I know that? I just recently found out I'm half human, half something else. For all I know, vampires and werewolves exist. It's a whole new world."

Ula grew serious. "Truthfully, I don't know about those creatures. We typically don't spend much time amongst humans. We stick with our own kind, the ocean, and the other beings that we share it with."

I couldn't take it any longer. "What are you?"

"What do you think I am? Do you have any ideas?"

I looked down at the books in front of me. "What you are...it's in one of these books?"

"Yes."

I shivered. "I'm not sure I want to know. Most of the creatures in these books seem evil."

Ula studied my face. "And humans are not? Humans kill each other. They kill animals and pollute the land and water. Is this not evil?"

"Not all humans are evil," I protested.

"Not all sea creatures are either." Ula reached for the book. "May I?"

I handed it to her silently and waited. She flipped through several chapters, found what she wanted, and turned the pages toward me.

"Selkies." I read the title and looked at the image of the furry brown animal. "You're a seal?"

Ula looked insulted. "No, I'm not a seal. Seals cannot change shape. Seals are seals."

"That picture looks like a seal."

"We are not seals. The best way I can describe us to you is that we are shape shifters. We can take the form of a human or a seal."

I wiggled my toes, which were safely tucked into my socks. I thought about the flippers on a seal. I thought about becoming a seal. Was it possible? What would it feel like?

"I'm one, too?" I couldn't help asking.

Ula grinned. "Oh yes! You'll be able to Change, too."

"When?" I didn't want to change in the middle of history class or something. Talk about embarrassing.

"It's not a 'When'. It's more of a 'Where'."

I frowned at her. "Okay, now you sound like David."

She leaned forward and patted my leg. "He's frustrating, isn't he? Try growing up with him, and five other older siblings who all had your best interests in mind." She made a face, and I laughed.

The doorbell rang. The sound of my mom's voice filled the house, followed by the deeper, rich tones of David's voice.

"David's here?" Ula paled. "I have to leave. Please, don't tell him that we talked."

"Will he be mad?" What would David do if he knew she told me?

"I don't know. I don't want to find out. He's protective of you, you know."

"I won't say anything," I promised. "I have more questions. We barely started talking."

Ula patted my leg again. It was an aunt-like gesture. "We'll talk again soon. For now, read the books. You won't find much that's useful, but there's some information there."

She waved at me, and then she was gone.

I closed the books and shoved them back into the plastic bookstore bag just before my door opened.

"Hey, princess." David poked his head in and smiled. He'd taken to calling me pet names—princess and sweetheart, among others. I wasn't sure how I felt about it, but I knew he was making Mom happy, so I let it slide.

"Hi."

He eyed the bag on my bed. "What's that?"

I hugged the bag to my chest, suddenly feeling protective of my secret. "It's Evan's Christmas present. I was just about to wrap it."

David nodded and let the subject drop. "So, you don't want to come to dinner with us?"

I tried to sound apologetic. "I appreciate the offer, but I'd rather just stay home and study for my tests this week."

David's eyebrow rose. "Your mom said you had a paper."

"Oh yeah. That, too. Busy week, you know, last couple of days before winter break."

"All right, then. We'll bring you back some dessert."

"Thanks. Have a great time!"

He blew me a kiss and closed the door. Mom must have stayed in the living room with my grandparents. I wasn't worried about dinner. Grandma Mary would have something delicious for us, even if it was just leftovers.

I listened until I heard the front door close and the low hum of David's car disappear into the distance, then I pulled the books back out of the bag. I scoured every bit of information I could find on Selkies. When I ran out in the books, and it didn't take long, I went online and searched some more. There wasn't much.

The most consistent information I could find was that Selkies lived in and near the ocean. The legend seemed to originate on the Orkney Islands, near Scotland. That explained the accent that David and Ula tried unsuccessfully to cover up. It also said that the Selkies shed their sealskin to take human form. What did they do with their skin? Store it somewhere? I guess David could leave his at his apartment. Would he trust it there? From what I read, if a Selkie lost its skin, it could no longer change form. It was stuck as a human forever.

Could Mom take David's skin? Would that keep him here? Legends spoke of fishermen who hid the skin of Selkie women to keep them as wives. That wasn't any different, was it? But, it wasn't right either. Keeping someone from their true nature, forcing them to stay with you, well, that wasn't love any more than abandoning your woman and newborn baby daughter was. What a crappy mess.

Once again, I thought about calling Evan, or even texting Kim, and telling them about what I learned. Something told me to keep it to myself. The more people who knew, the harder it would be to keep it from David, and I wanted to know more. If David found out, I was positive he would order Ula not to tell me more. I didn't know if she'd obey him, but I didn't want to take that chance. No, the secret was mine. For now.

Chapter 29

"Mom, are you awake?" I cracked open her bedroom door, praying she was alone. I didn't think David actually stayed over. I wasn't naïve enough to believe that nothing happened between them. The last thing I wanted was to find them in bed together. I shuddered at the thought.

I barely heard my mom's sleepy reply. "Meara?"

I fully opened the door and saw that she was alone. I breathed a sigh of relief before running over and crawling into bed next to her. She jumped when my cold feet brushed her leg.

"Merry Christmas, Mom," I whispered.

She kissed my nose, and then whispered back. "Merry Christmas, honey."

This Christmas morning ritual went back as far as I could remember. I would crawl into Mom's bed and lay next to her until she was fully awake, and then we would walk together into the living room to open the presents under the tree.

The smell of coffee infiltrated the room just before I heard the distinct sizzle of the frying pan, followed by the heady scent of bacon. It wasn't our habit to eat breakfast before opening gifts. Then again, it wasn't just our tradition any more. Now, my grandparents were a part of it.

"How are you feeling, Mom?"

"Cold," she said. "Your feet are ice cubes, Meara. Really, where are your socks?"

"I can't sleep with socks on," I said. "It bothers my feet."

"Well, go put a pair on now." She sat up and ran her fingers through her hair. "Your poor feet! I'll get my robe, and then we'll join your grandparents in the kitchen."

"Okay." I threw my arms around her and squeezed before I got up. Was I imagining things, or did she feel a little less bony? "I love you, Mom."

"I love you, too, sweetheart."

I ran to my room and put on some fuzzy Christmas socks that Mom gave me last year. When I walked back down the hall, she was waiting for me in her doorway. Her robe looked rattier than ever, and I couldn't wait for her to open her new one.

"Merry Christmas!" we called out simultaneously as we entered the kitchen.

Grandpa Jamie set down his paper, stood up, and gave us each a kiss on the cheek. "Merry Christmas, girls."

His voice sounded gruff. It was a surprisingly emotional display from him. I was touched. Grandma Mary was scrambling eggs, so we met her by the stove. I kissed her cheek, and Mom gave her a hug. Although my grandma laughed, there were tears in her eyes.

"Is something wrong, Grandma?" I asked. I had taken to calling them Grandpa and Grandma recently. I didn't feel right calling them by their first names anymore, not when they truly felt like my grandparents.

"No, child," she said. "I'm just so happy that we're all together. Do you how long it has been since we had a full house for the holidays?"

"Oh, Mom." Now it was my mom's turn to tear up. She gave my grandma another hug and kissed her cheek. I heard her whisper, "I'm so sorry."

Grandma Mary shook her head and waved us off. "I'm just happy to have you both here. That's all."

When I turned to go to the fridge and get my usual Diet Coke, Grandma stopped me. "Not this morning, Meara. I made you hot chocolate, and not from that awful powdered mix. There's whipped cream too." She poured me a mug of cocoa from the pan simmering on the stove. The canned whipped cream sat on the counter. I created a mountain on top of my drink. Yum.

I sat at the table across from Grandpa and next to my mom, savoring the rich, chocolate flavor. It was the best hot chocolate I had ever tasted. Mom eyed my mug. "Is there enough left for me?" she asked.

"Of course." Grandma Mary poured her a cup.

After we finished with the eggs, bacon, and toast, we headed into the living room to open presents, leaving the dishes for later.

My mom loved her robe, and my grandparents liked their gifts, too. Grandpa and Grandma gave me a lamp, a new book in a series that I was reading, and an electric blanket, which I couldn't wait to try out. My room was a bit drafty. Mom gave me two sweaters and a perfume that I had admired the last time we went shopping together. She also gave me a large box covered in a nursery-rhyme print. When I opened it, I realized that it was a memory box. It held items that I had no idea she saved—my baby shoes, report cards, artwork, and letters that I wrote to her over the years. We spent about an hour going through the mementos, laughing at memories and sharing it all with my grandparents.

"I have one more gift for you, Mom," I said when we were done. I reached behind the chair next to the tree and pulled out a flat, square package.

"What is this?" Mom asked as I handed it to her. I just shrugged and sat back to watch her open it.

She unwrapped the package, lifted the cover, and gasped, running her hand over the first page. "Oh, Meara."

I smiled. "It's a scrapbook of us, Mom."

She turned the pages slowly, commenting on each one. When she was done, she handed the album to Grandma, and then slid over to hug me.

"Do you like it?" I asked.

"It's beautiful, honey," she said. "I love it."

We cleaned up the wrappings. While my grandparents continued to look at the scrapbook and memory box, Mom and I went to our rooms to get dressed. After, I went to the kitchen and started washing dishes and cleaning up.

"You don't have to do that," Grandma said from the doorway.

"I want to," I said. "You shouldn't have to do it all. Besides, you're probably going to spend most of the day in here anyway."

Evan and his family were coming over for dinner. They would be here around four. David was coming about an hour before them.

"Do you need help cooking?" I asked, although I figured she'd tell me no, even if she did need help. The last time I cooked with her, I burnt the sauce she asked me to stir.

"No, honey," she said. "You can just relax with your mom and grandfather."

She insisted on taking over in the kitchen, so I went back to the living room. Grandpa put on an old movie, Going My Way, with Bing Crosby. "This is what we watched when I was a kid."

I curled up next to my mom to watch the movie. "You're wearing your robe," I said. "I thought you went to get dressed."

She winked and showed me that she wore a blouse and dress pants underneath. "I couldn't resist. It looked so comfortable."

She covered my legs with her blanket, and I leaned against the fluffy sleeve of her new robe.

When the movie ended, I stood and stretched. Mom stood, too.

"Should we see if your grandmother needs help?" she asked.

Grandma seemed to have it all under control in the kitchen. "Recruit your father to bring up the folding table. You girls can set it." She told us where she kept her holiday linens and sent us off.

Grandpa placed the folding table in the living room, since there was not enough room in the kitchen. There would be two sets of diners. At least we had an open doorway between us. When he was done, Mom declared, "Time to decorate!"

Grandpa mumbled something about needing to test the food, and disappeared into the kitchen. Mom and I barely noticed him leaving the room. We loved to decorate, so we had fun arranging the tablecloths, cloth napkins, and napkin rings. We scouted the house, finding candles and holiday decorations to place along the center. When we were done, it looked like something out of a magazine—festive and elegant.

The doorbell rang a few minutes before three, and Mom ran to get it. I refrained from rolling my eyes, but just barely. She acted like a teenager when my father was around. Although, I had to admit, when he walked into the room, he did look striking.

"It's snowing," he said, running his hand through his hair to remove the unmelted flakes. Under his leather jacket, he wore a dark green, cashmere sweater and black dress pants. Once he took off his well-worn coat, he looked like he just stepped off the set of a movie.

He kissed my cheek while placing a small package in my hand. "Merry Christmas, Meara."

"Merry Christmas," I replied brightly. I hoped he didn't notice that I purposefully left off his name. I wasn't ready to call him Dad, but David did not seem right today, either. The holidays were about family after all. I looked at the gift in my hand. It fit comfortably in my palm, and was beautifully wrapped in gold foil paper tied with a red velvet ribbon.

"Are you going to open it?" David asked.

"Can I? I wasn't sure if I have to wait for everyone to get here."

"Go ahead. I'd like to know what it is, too." Mom, at David's side, leaned forward with curiosity. I carefully unwrapped the package—it didn't seem right to tear such beautiful paper—and opened the box to find a gold bracelet inside. It was decorated with evenly spaced charms—a sand dollar to match my necklace, a starfish, a seahorse, a seal, and two pearls.

"It's lovely," I said. "Thank you." I didn't have much jewelry, and I loved the delicate beauty. The charms sparkled as I turned the bracelet in my hand.

"Do you want to put it on?" he asked. When I nodded, he encircled my wrist with the bracelet and closed the clasp. "Perfect fit."

I gave him a hug before I showed the bracelet to my mom. She turned my wrist to the sides to view all the charms. "It's beautiful, David."

"I have a gift for you, too." He reached into his pocket and pulled out a box slightly smaller than the one he gave me. Mom's was tied with green velvet that almost matched David's sweater.

Mom took the gift and unwrapped it with shaky hands. When she lifted the lid, she gasped and looked at him. David dropped to one knee. I swallowed painfully.

"Sharon," he said, and his voice was not steady. "I have not done well by you, but I know you are a generous person. I'm hoping you'll give me another chance. I love you and have loved you since I met you. Will you do me the honor of becoming my wife?"

"Oh, David!" Mom exclaimed. "Yes!"

Mom wiped the tears off her cheeks, as David took the box from her and placed the ring on her left hand. He bent his head, and she met him for a kiss. I was too stunned to be embarrassed. My parents were getting married?

"About time," Grandpa grumbled, although he looked pleased with David for once. I wondered how long they had been standing in the doorway of the kitchen. Grandma's cheeks were wet. When the kiss ended, she ran and hugged them both, taking my mom's hand to gush over the ring.

Mom gestured for me to join them, so I did. I had to admit, it was a gorgeous ring. Instead of a diamond solitaire, the ring featured a huge, creamy pearl encircled by alternating diamonds and sapphires. It fit Mom's finger perfectly. When I looked up, I realized that everyone was watching me, waiting for my response. I thought for a moment, trying to figure out how I was feeling and what I wanted to say. I was confused, surprised, and, I realized, happy for them, too. For us. We were going to be a family. A real family.

"Congratulations," I said, hugging Mom first and kissing her cheek. I hugged David next, and he whispered in my ear.

"I'm sorry," he said. "I should have asked you first. My mistake."

"It's okay," I whispered, and I meant it. "You gave my mom the best gift ever."

"Yes," he said, pulling back to look in my eyes. "You."

I blushed and lowered my head. David, realizing he had embarrassed me, took the opportunity to give presents to my grandparents—a box of spiced nuts for my grandfather, and two bottles of white wine for my grandmother.

"We'll serve these with dinner," Grandma said. "I'll just go and chill them."

The shock mostly wore off by the time the doorbell rang again, and Evan and his family came in. Evan crossed the room to me just before Mom ran over to show Lydia the ring. She screamed, and then they were hugging, crying, and laughing.

Evan raised his eyebrow at me.

"My parents are engaged," I said, much calmer than I felt.

"Wow," Evan said. "Are you okay with that?"

"I'm happy for her," I said. "For them."

Evan reached out and, touching my wrist, lifted the bracelet lightly. "From David?" he asked, and I nodded in reply. "Nice."

Katie came over and hugged me. "Merry Christmas! Sounds like it's been an exciting day here."

"You can say that again," I said, and they both laughed.

Plates of roast beef, roasted potatoes, asparagus, and rolls were passed around the table. Katie, Evan, and I ate at the small kitchen table. We joked about being at the kids' table while the adults ate in the other room. Talk of wedding plans drifted through the doorway. I was glad I didn't have to sit there with a goofy grin on my face. Just because I was happy for them didn't mean that I didn't need time to adjust.

I sipped the glass of wine I convinced Mom to give me. "All right," she said. "Just one."

When she wasn't looking, Evan refilled my glass. After I drained it, I felt slightly warm and relaxed.

Evan, Katie, and I cleaned the kitchen, while the adults relaxed in the other room. Over dinner, Mom had asked Lydia to be her Matron of Honor. She also asked Katie and me to stand up for her.

"Bridesmaids," Katie gushed. "I can't wait to go dress shopping!"

"Any excuse to shop." Evan smirked at me behind Katie's back. I laughed, and Katie hit him with the dishrag. He threw it back at her, hitting me in the process. Soon, we were all quite wet and laughing. The kitchen got more of a cleaning that we originally intended. We put the last of the clean dishes away, dried off the counters and floors, and returned to the living room.

"What happened to you three?" Grandma asked. I looked at Katie and Evan. Their sweaters were covered in wet spots, and their hair was standing up in strange spots. I held back a grin, knowing that I looked just as bad, if not worse.

"She started it!"

"He started it!"

Evan and Katie spoke at the same time, pointing fingers at each other. Lydia sighed, and Darren laughed, saying, "Good to know that some things never change."

"Meara, take Katie to your room and find her a dry shirt," Grandma said. "Evan, come with me. I'm sure Jamie has something you can wear."

I looked at my grandfather. He was at least double Evan's size.

What could he possibly have that Evan could wear?

"Mary," David said. "I've got a few things here. Evan can come with me, and I'll find something for him."

Grandpa glowered momentarily, but then he glanced at Mom's ring and his expression relaxed a bit. He didn't say anything. Wow, if that was all it took, David should have proposed weeks ago.

"C'mon, Katie," I said. "Let's see what I can give you."

When we got to my room, Katie dug through my dresser and pulled out a pale pink sweater. "Can I wear this?"

"You can have it." The sweater was pretty, but bubble gum pink was not my color. Mom's friend, Rebecca, gave it to me a couple of years ago for my birthday. I only wore it a couple of times to Sew Beautiful so she could see it.

"Really?" Katie took off her sweater, and pulled the pink one over her head. She ran her hand down the front. "I can keep it?"

"Yes," I said. "It looks better on you anyway."

I pulled out my favorite hoodie and held it up. "Would it be wrong to wear this?"

Katie shrugged. "Go ahead…day's almost over anyway."

I took off my wet sweater—the tank underneath was fine—and put on the hoodie, zipping it halfway. I'd rather be comfortable, and this was about as comfortable as I could get.

There was a knock at the door, and then Evan called, "You girls decent?"

"Yes," Katie and I said at the same time.

Evan opened the door and came in. He wore a dark gray sweater that I saw David wear often. It looked good and fit him well. "Mom wants to see you," he told Katie.

"She does?" Katie frowned at Evan. "Oh, right. Yeah, okay."

"What was that about?" I asked as Evan sat next to me on the bed with his hand behind his back.

"Merry Christmas, Meara." He brought out a package almost as small as the one David gave my mom. My heart skipped. Oh god, don't tell me that he's proposing too, I thought.

The gift was wrapped in pale blue paper and covered in silver snowflakes. A small, silver bow graced the top. Once again, I took my time unwrapping. I lifted the box lid and saw a pair of earrings inside. They were gold sand dollars that matched my necklace. They each held a dangling pearl.

"I noticed that you always wear your necklace," Evan said before I could say anything. "And I wanted you to have something to remind you of me, too."

"I love them." I leaned forward and kissed him. I meant for it to be quick, but he pulled me closer. When we parted, I was breathless. "Thank you."

He laughed. "Anytime."

I slapped his arm lightly. "For the earrings." I stood and walked over to my dresser. Glancing in the mirror, I took out my current pair and put in the new ones. I noticed that the pearls swung gently when I moved my head. Evan came and stood behind me.

"They look beautiful on you." He touched one with his finger, and I shivered when his fingers brushed my neck.

I turned, took his hand, and led him back to the bed. "Sit down. I'll get your gift." He gave me a wicked grin, and I laughed. "Is that all you think about?"

He shrugged. "Pretty much."

Kneeling, I pulled his present out from underneath the bed. I was glad that he gave me mine in my room. Now that I knew what David was, I didn't want him to see Evan open his presents. He would ask too many questions. I planned to bring Evan back here anyway.

"Merry Christmas." I handed him the packages and sat next to him on the bed. Unlike me, Evan had no qualms about opening his gifts fast. He tore the paper off the first book. He turned it over in his hands and looked at me quizzically.

"How did you know?"

"Katie told me," I said. "Open the next."

Evan seemed to hesitate, but then he did as I said. "Wow. Thank you."

"Why did you want them?" I tried to keep my voice casual. Was it my imagination, or did Evan blush a little?

"I have a few ideas about what David might be. I wanted to do some research."

"What do you think?" I asked.

"I'd rather not say yet," he said. "It's kind of crazy."

"Try me," I said.

He laughed and kissed me. "I tell you what. Let me read these first. I promise we'll talk as soon as I'm done."

"Okay." I knew I was pouting like a little kid, but I wanted to know what he thought. Was he close? Did he think David was a Selkie? Or did he think he was something else? Like one of those blue men?

"Thank you," he said, kissing me again. I wasn't sure if he was thanking me for the present or for not forcing the issue.

Chapter 30

On Christmas, when David and Mom announced their engagement, Lydia told us she could pull off a wedding in less than a month. I didn't believe her, and yet here we stood in a small room in the back of church—the one that was usually reserved for the minister to get ready for service. The only exception was for weddings, when it became the bridal chamber.

Mom kept patting her hair.

"You look beautiful," I told her, and I meant it. She wore a long, silk sheath in a blue so pale it was almost white. A sheer, iridescent layer floated over the top. It shimmered and created the illusion that the dress changed color. It reminded me of the inside of an oyster shell—all silvery whites, pale pinks, light blues, and lavenders.

"Is it time?" Katie opened the door and peered out into the chapel. "It looks like everyone is here."

"A few more minutes," Lydia said, looking at the clock. "Close the door so no one sees us." She fussed a bit with the back of Mom's dress, adjusting the sheer layer. Lydia's own gown was subdued next to Mom's, but elegant all the same. She wore a pale, beige, tea-length dress with a sheer jacket.

Katie and I also wore tea-length dresses, but ours had capped sleeves. Mine was a shimmery, light blue, and Katie's was silvery lavender. We held small bouquets of lilies of the valley. Their sweet fragrance filled the air. Mom's larger bouquet was accented with small purple and blue flowers that matched our dresses.

I heard the soft notes of the wedding march. Pachelbel's Canon in D Major. David specifically picked that song.

There was a brief, but loud, knock at the door, and then we heard

Grandpa's gruff voice. "Are you ready?"

"Come in," Mom said. She ran her hand once more down the length of her dress, took a deep breath, and smiled as my grandfather stepped into the room. He paused for a moment, his eyes widening.

"Dad?" Mom's voice sounded uncertain as his eyes watered. He ran his hand over them quickly, before stepping up and kissing my mom on the cheek.

"You look beautiful, honey." He turned to me. "You two better get out there. You're walking down the aisle first."

"Oh, right!" Katie and I quickly left the room. Lydia followed us out. Evan and Darren stood in front with David. I'd never seen Evan in a tux before. I stared until Katie elbowed me in the rib.

"Close your mouth," she teased. "You're drooling."

"Haha." I felt my cheeks burn even as I looked away.

While Katie walked down the aisle, I waited. I knew when she was about halfway down that it was my cue to go. The small chapel was full. I assumed both sides were for the bride, since David didn't seem to have a lot of friends. I recognized some of the people from town. Everyone smiled at me expectantly. Although I was nervous, I made a point to smile back.

Taking a deep breath, I began to walk and met Evan's eyes. He looked stunned at first, but then he smiled. A huge smile, which brought out his dimples. He mouthed, "You look great," and I blushed.

"You too," I mouthed back. He did look amazing in his tux.

Once I took my place at the altar, we all turned to the back of the church. The music swelled as Grandpa and Mom came toward us. A sigh rippled through the crowd, and I noticed Grandma going through several tissues, dabbing her eyes and wiping her nose. She beamed at them both.

Mom's eyes were for David only. When I followed her gaze, I inhaled slightly. He looked so intense. Even Grandpa cocked his head at David, as though trying to figure him out. Clearly, Mom and David were very much in love. I thought about all the years they lost being apart, and it made me sad. Why didn't they stay together?

Before I could dwell on that, they were at the front of the church. Mom kissed Grandpa on the cheek. He took her hand, placed it on

David's arm, and then he leaned in, whispering something to David. David nodded curtly and clamped him on the shoulder. I wondered what the exchange was about but, apparently, all was good. Grandpa, with a slight smile on his face, took his seat by my grandmother, and David turned to give his full attention to my mom, a dazzling smile on his face.

They exchanged vows, promising to care for each other in sickness and in health. I swallowed painfully at the "to death do us part" line, but my parents continued to smile at each other. They were alone in their love, and we were merely spectators.

Then the vows were over. They were officially husband and wife. When invited to do so, David tipped my mom back and kissed her passionately. I had to look away, and when I turned, I caught Katie's eyes. She grinned. I looked at Evan, and he smiled back.

Everyone clapped. Joining arms, David and my mom walked out of the church. Darren and Lydia went next, and Katie, Evan and I followed.

Evan leaned down and whispered, "You look amazing."

"You look pretty good yourself," I said.

At the back of the church, I was able to briefly hug and congratulate my parents before we formed a receiving line. I smiled and shook hands with people I knew and people I didn't. I accepted their compliments with a gracious nod and, in between greetings, I rubbed my hands up and down my arms. Every time the door opening, a freezing blast of artic air filled the small space.

A warm blanket covered my shoulders. Well, that was what it felt like, but I realized it was Evan's coat. "Is that better?"

"Yes, thank you." I looked at his long-sleeved dress shirt and vest. "Won't you be cold now?"

"I'll be okay," he said. "You're clearly freezing."

The warmth of Evan's jacket relaxed my muscles. I leaned forward to see around my parents. How much longer was the line? Coppery curls caught my eye, and I gasped. Surely, Ula didn't come. My mom knew that I had a friend named Ula, who I met at the clinic. It wasn't like Ula was a common name, like Becky or Amy. I'd never heard it before I met her. How was she going to explain that she was my aunt and her mom was already dead?

"You okay?" Evan looked at me closely. He must have heard me gasp.

I grimaced at him. "Fine. Just tired of standing in line."

He nodded. "It's almost to the end."

I couldn't see the other end of the receiving line where Katie stood next to her parents, but I could see that it was Ula standing there. I knew Katie would remember her, since they'd met several times, but I wondered if Evan would. He'd only met her once, and it was brief. I didn't hear Katie shout anything, so it couldn't have been too bad.

Ula stopped in front of David. She exchanged a look with him, and then hugged him tightly. By his response, I gathered he was expecting her. A tall woman with exotic features stood behind her. She wore a long, clingy dress of deep purple with bell sleeves. A silver belt of Celtic knots rested on her hips. Her long, straight hair was black and glossy, and her eyes were a bright, clear violet. She was breathtaking, but her expression was cold as if she surveyed the wedding party with disdain. She nodded at David. To my surprise, he pulled her into a hug. She stiffened at first, and then hugged him back. Who was she?

Mom looked as bewildered as I felt. When David released the woman, he tugged at his collar before taking Mom's hand. He leaned forward and looked at me, addressing us both. "Sharon, Meara, I want you to meet my sisters, Ula and Brigid."

Mom's brows wrinkled as if trying to remember something, but then they smoothed over and she smiled. "Pleased to me you both. I had no idea David had sisters. He never said anything."

The reproach was clear in her voice. David had the decency to look sheepish. Ula squeezed Mom's arm. "No doubt you had more important things to discuss than us."

"Doubtful," Brigid said with a frown. "We are, after all, his only sisters."

Once again, David squirmed. Ula seemed to take pity on him. "C'mon Brigid, we're holding up the line."

Ula rolled her eyes at me and stuck out her tongue when her back was to Brigid. I bit my own. I didn't think I should laugh as my new aunt approached. She looked much too severe.

"Hi Meara. Evan." Ula's tone was chipper, almost unnaturally so. Maybe she was trying to make up for Brigid's frown.

Evan's brows knitted. "You're David's sister?"

"I am." Ula looked sheepish. "It wasn't nice of me to keep it from Meara."

Evan gave me a pointed we'll-talk-later look, then said, "Good to see you again."

"You too." She squeezed his hand. It must have been her signature gesture—the squeeze.

"You must be Meara." Brigid's eyes pierced my own. Her cold gaze made me shudder. "Merry Meet, niece."

I didn't know what that meant. I assumed it was a friendly greeting. "A pleasure to meet you, Aunt Brigid." I extended my hand. She stared at it for a moment before taking it in her own. Her slim hand was cool and dry.

"Brigid. Just Brigid." Her accent was much more pronounced than Ula's was.

"Will you be going to the reception?" I asked, trying to address both of my aunts. It was difficult, since Brigid was scanning the room, her eyes on alert.

Ula frowned before answering. "Unfortunately, no."

Brigid's eerie eyes snapped back to my face. I tried not to flinch. "We have a previous engagement. Fare thee well, niece."

"It's Meara," I said weakly as she stalked away.

Ula hugged me and whispered in my ear. "Don't worry about Brigid. She's always like that." She pulled back and winked. "I'm your fun aunt."

"What—?" I started. She shook her head.

"I'll talk to you later, okay?" She turned and quickly followed Brigid. I watched as they left through the side door of the chapel. What kind of engagement could they have that would keep them from celebrating their brother's marriage?

Several long minutes later, the last guest was greeted and we were free to leave. I gave Evan back his coat and went to get mine from the room where we got ready. It was a new faux-fur cloak that matched my dress, completely impractical since I had no idea when I would use it again, but warm and lovely. David paid, so I didn't worry about it. I did wonder how much money he had, and where he got it from. I couldn't bring myself to ask.

The reception dinner was in Halifax at one of the nicer seafood restaurants, The Shores. David rented a private room in the back. He also arranged for a limousine bus for the entire bridal party.

"Have you ever been on one of these?" I asked Evan as we waited to board.

He shrugged. "A bunch of us took a limo to prom, but it was smaller than this."

The bus was elegantly decorated in dark grays and black. Plush couches lined the walls, broken only by two minibars. Champagne cooled in buckets.

We sat, and champagne was passed around. Katie and I grinned at each other, raising our glasses in mock solute.

"A toast," David said, holding up his glass. We all followed suit. "To my beautiful bride, Sharon, to my lovely daughter, Meara, and to all our friends and family who celebrate with us, may the happiness of today be with you always, and the happiness of tomorrow come your way."

We clinked our glasses. I sipped the champagne and fell in love. The bubbles teased my tongue as the sweet flavor exploded in my mouth. I took a slightly bigger sip, and before I knew it, the glass was empty.

"Can I have some more?" I asked Evan, who was sitting next to the bottle. He refilled my glass.

"You like it?" he asked as he handed it back to me.

"Mmmmmmm," I said, taking a sip and smacking my lips. "Yum!"

He laughed and put his arm around my shoulder. "Just don't drink too much. That stuff can give you a nasty headache."

I tried to sip slower, but it was hard. I looked back where David and Mom sat. They were talking softly, his arm around her shoulder and hers around his waist. She laughed at something he said, and he bent to kiss the tip of her nose. They were cute together, but it was a bit weird to think of my parents as married. My whole life I had wondered about my father, and now he was here, married to my mom. I should be elated, but it just felt weird.

I finished the rest of the champagne and held my glass out to Evan.

"You sure?" He frowned at my empty glass. "Maybe you should wait a bit."

I shook my head. "This is my last one."

"Okay," he agreed, even though it sounded like he thought the opposite. He refilled my glass and handed it to me. Then, he placed his arm around my shoulder again, and I snuggled into his warm side.

Katie pouted at me from across the aisle. She was next to Lydia, and Darren was closest to the champagne. They cut her off at one glass, and she clearly wanted more. "No fair," she mouthed to me.

When we stopped in front of the restaurant, I stood to get off. I swayed a little before Evan caught my arm. "Easy," he murmured.

"Maybe I should have stopped at two." I giggled, and then frowned. I didn't giggle, did I?

"You think?" He rolled his eyes, but held tightly to my arm, helping me off the bus. Once we had more room, he slid his arm around my waist, which was more comfortable and supportive anyway.

I leaned into him. He was so warm, so cute. I hugged him and then hiccupped, right before I tripped over the uneven pavement.

Evan snorted. I gave him the evil eye, which made him laugh out loud. "Let's get you some food."

The party room was at the back of the restaurant in a private wing with its own bathrooms and a concierge to take our coats. Classical music played softly, and the air smelled sweetly floral from the garland draped along the entranceway and the cascading bouquets on the tables. Serving staff circulated trays of appetizers as guests mingled. As we walked around, I nodded and smiled at everyone. Evan filled a plate and handed it to me.

"Eat up. You'll feel better."

"I feel great!" I grinned at him, but he took a stuffed mushroom cap off the plate and held it to my mouth.

"You won't for long unless you eat," he insisted, so I took it and ate it. It was delicious. So was everything else on the plate. Soon, it was gone.

"Oops," I said. "I hope you didn't want to share."

Evan laughed. "No, you needed it more than me. Did you even eat today?"

"No," I said. "I was too nervous."

"Do you feel better?"

"I guess." I didn't know if the word I was looking for was "better", but I did feel more like myself. That lovely, fuzzy head feeling was almost gone.

"Do you want something to drink?" When my eyes lit up, Evan laughed. "I meant, like a Coke or something, Meara."

"Oh," I said, trying not to sound disappointed. "Diet Coke it is."

I followed Evan through the crowd to the bar in the corner.

"Do you have another drink?" Katie asked. I turned to see her glaring at us, her hand on her hip.

I raised my glass. "Diet Coke."

"Hmmmpf," she said. "Well, okay then. I was going to insist you get me some too if it was more of that delicious bubbly."

"I know, right?" I said. I looked around for Katie's boyfriend. "Where's Brian?"

"On his way, I guess." Katie shrugged. "He's coming right after work."

I bounced a little on my feet. "I can't wait for the dancing."

"Me, too!"

The head server announced dinner, and everyone began to move to their assigned seats. Katie, Evan, and I were at the head table. Lydia, Darren, and Katie sat on Mom's right. I sat on David's left, and Evan sat on the other side of me.

David squeezed my hand. "How are you doing, kiddo?"

"I'm good," I said. "You?"

He laughed. "Never been better."

Our server set the plates in front of us—lobster tails, filet mignon, scallop potatoes, and asparagus.

"Oh wow." I didn't have seafood often. It was a luxury Mom and I rarely splurged on.

"Do you like seafood?" David asked.

"I love it," I said.

"What's your favorite?"

I thought for a moment. How to pick a favorite? "Probably crab legs. They are so sweet."

"I like oysters best myself," David said. "But crab's delicious, too."

I managed to eat about half of my dinner before it was time for speeches. David greeted everyone and thanked them for coming. Mom went next and said more or less the same thing. Then Lydia gave a speech as Matron of Honor. I listened to her tell funny stories about my mom from their childhood, relieved that I didn't have to give a speech. I wondered what she would say about David, but she didn't say much. When she finished, she hugged my mom and then David.

I was almost done eating when David led Mom to the floor for their first dance. The lights dimmed, and the song began. I recognized it right away, Unforgettable by Nat King Cole. It was one of my mom's favorite songs. David held her close, one hand on her lower back, the other clasping hers. They spun slowly around the room, and Mom's dress floated out around them. Conversations faltered as the room fell under their spell. When the song ended, everyone clapped.

The next dance was the wedding party dance. Evan offered me his hand, and I took it. When we reached the dance floor, he pulled me into his arms. We moved slowly with the music, and I relaxed against his chest.

"Are you having fun?" he asked. I looked up at him and nodded. He kissed me lightly. "Good."

The song ended, and everyone was invited to dance. The music switched from slow and romantic to a pulsing beat. Katie joined us on the dance floor. Evan didn't have the best rhythm, but he tried. After a couple of songs, though, he told me that he wanted to grab a Coke and get some fresh air.

"No more than ten minutes," he promised.

We kept dancing, and my skin grew hot. I was about to suggest that we grab a drink, too, when Brian came up behind Katie. He ran his hands down her side and kissed her neck. Unlike Evan, he was a great dancer. The three of us danced to the next couple of songs, until a slow song began. Brian wrapped his arms around Katie and led her away in a dance. I looked around the room for Evan, but he was gone.

Mom and Lydia sat sipping wine at the head table. They were flushed and a little sweaty from dancing. I imagined that I looked the same. I couldn't wait to get a drink of something cold.

"Have you seen Evan?"

"No," Mom said. I noticed dark shadows under her eyes. "Maybe he's with David."

"Where's David?"

"He went outside to get some air."

I got a ginger ale, nodding at Darren and Grandpa, who were drinking beers by the bar. I pushed open the door to the private outside patio.

The patio was deserted, which wasn't surprising since it was the middle of January and pretty damn cold. I welcomed the frigid air against my hot skin. All that dancing worked up quite a sweat. I stood, sipping my drink. As my ears adjusted from the loud music to the outdoor silence, I heard hushed male voices.

"...it was you. I know...admit it."

"So what...me? You need to...out...Evan."

I heard Evan's name, and my heart jumped. Who was he talking to? I strained to discern the voices, but they were too quiet. Distinctly male, but it could be any guy in the room. I couldn't tell if the voices belonged to David or Evan. I didn't know if someone was addressing Evan or just saying his name. I longed to peek around the corner and find out, but I wasn't sure how far away they were standing. While I stood trying to decide, the door opened behind me.

"There you are, Meara!" Katie said. "What are you doing out here?"

"Oh, I just came out to cool off." I made my voice sound carefree, in case they were listening, whoever they were.

"Where's Evan?"

"I don't know," I said. "Maybe he's inside looking for us?"

She frowned. "I didn't see him, but I guess we can look again."

It was another ten minutes before Evan found me. He wrapped his arms around me and kissed me. I jumped a bit. "You're cold!" I protested.

He laughed. "Sorry, I guess I stayed out a little longer than I should have."

I took a chance. "I went out on the patio about ten minutes ago, and I didn't see you."

"I took a short walk," he said. "C'mon, let's dance some more."

"Did you walk by yourself?" I asked as I wrapped my arms around his neck, which was cool to the touch.

He raised an eyebrow at me. "Who else would I walk with?"

I was disappointed. Was he one of the voices I heard? It would make sense since he was outside, but why hide it from me?

David tapped Evan on the shoulder. Did I imagine it, or did a look of irritation flash across Evan's face.

"May I cut in?" David asked.

"Of course." Evan stepped back, turned, and walked off the dance floor. If I didn't know better, I'd think he was angry.

David placed his hand on my waist and took my other hand in his. He smiled down at me. "You don't know how happy I am, Meara. I'm so glad that we can be a family now."

"Why now?" I asked. "After all these years?"

"I tried earlier," David said. "I couldn't find you."

"Couldn't find us?" I asked. "Did you try? Did you ask my grandparents?"

David's laughter was bitter. "You saw how Jamie treated me when I first came back. How do you think he would have reacted if I approached him without your mother there?"

"Ah," I hesitated. He had a point there. He was not one of Grandpa's favorite people. I tried a different approach. "Why did you leave in the first place?"

David sighed. "I had to."

"Had to," I repeated. "What does that mean?"

"I will explain," David said. "Soon."

"When?" I demanded.

"Not tonight," he said. "I know you want answers, Meara, but tonight is not the night. Tonight we are celebrating, yes?"

"Yes," I said. I wanted so desperately to tell him that I already knew what he was, what I was, that I didn't have to be pawn in his game. Instead, I dropped my head to his chest.

"Thank you," he whispered, pulling me into a hug as the song ended. I stiffened at first at the unexpectedness, but then I relaxed. I found myself hugging him back.

I blinked as the lights went up. Chair scraped against the floor as the guests stood to give their final wishes and leave. David squeezed my hand. "I should find your mother."

They were going to Niagara Falls for their honeymoon. I was staying with my grandparents while they were gone, and then Mom and I were moving into David's condo. On one hand, it made me nervous, and I was sad that I wouldn't see my grandparents as often. On the other hand, I was going to be much closer to Evan.

I followed David, since I wanted to say goodbye.

"Meara!" Mom pulled me into a hug and kissed my cheek. I held onto her tightly. When we pulled apart, my vision blurred with unshed tears.

"Have fun, Mom," I said. "I'll miss you."

Mom wiped a bit of her lipstick from my cheek and smiled at me. "I'll miss you, too, sweetheart, but I'll see you soon."

My grandparents started to say goodbye, so I moved to the side. Evan came up next to me. "You okay?"

"Sure." I sniffed a little. "It's just, you know, not every day that your parents get married."

Chapter 31

"It's so like you, Brigid." David's laugh was bitter. He stared at my aunt, his face full of scorn. She was beautiful with her long, dark hair blowing wildly in the wind, swirling around her pale face. Her beauty was only marred by her fury.

"She's a Halfling." Brigid's eyes flashed, and her fingers pulled at the choker around her neck.

"Nonetheless, she is my daughter." David spoke with authority, his voice full of contempt. "I'll have you show her nothing but respect."

"Respect," Brigid spat. "She doesn't even know who she is."

"She will," David said. "Very soon."

"Then take her and go." How quickly Brigid turned from angry to pleading. "Before it's too late."

I woke with a start. The sun, a sliver on the horizon, tinted the cloudless sky a deep purple. I studied the patterns of frost on the windows. What woke me up? My breath came out as a visible mist. As much as I loved having a converted porch for a bedroom, it wasn't too ideal in the winter. My nose was absolutely freezing. The rest of me, however, was toasty warm, thanks to the electric blanket my grandparents gave me for Christmas. At least I didn't have much longer to deal with it. My parents were coming home from their honeymoon today. Tomorrow, we would be moving to David's apartment.

A light tapping at the window made me jump. Who was out in this bitter cold?

I sat up, and saw Evan's face pressed against the glass. I laughed. He looked like a little kid, grinning from ear to ear. Well, he certainly had a way of waking a girl on her birthday.

I cracked the window open just enough so we could talk. The frigid air raised goose bumps across my arms. Grabbing the throw from the end of my bed, I pulled it around me.

"What are you doing here at this hour?" I yawned the last couple of words.

"I have to show you something." He was annoying when he was so awake and energetic. He didn't even seem cold. "Quick, get dressed and meet me out front."

I looked at the clock. "Evan, it's six am."

"Meara, hurry up before they're gone."

"Before who's gone?"

"You'll see." He started to turn away, and then turned back, giving me a lopsided grin. "Oh, and Meara? Happy birthday!"

I closed and locked the window. Grabbing the first sweater and pair of jeans I could find, I ran to the bathroom to get ready. I tiptoed to the front hall so I wouldn't wake my grandparents, bundled up, and ran out to meet him.

When I opened the car door, the warm air welcomed me. Once I was situated and buckled in, Evan handed me a Diet Coke. I smiled gratefully.

"Okay. I'm curious," I said. "What gives?"

He didn't answer right away. Instead, he concentrated on backing out of the driveway. When he kicked it into drive and didn't answer me, I persisted. "Where are we going?"

"The lighthouse." He kept his eyes on the road.

"You know, I like the lighthouse as much as the next girl," I said. "But, why are we going there at this hour?"

"I'd rather show you than explain."

"Taking lessons from David now?" I teased. He just glanced at me with his eyebrow raised. I gave up and looked out the window. A dreamy orange joined the vibrant pink in the early morning sky.

When we got within a few blocks of the lighthouse, Evan pulled over and parked.

"What are you doing?" I asked.

"We're walking the rest of the way."

"Isn't it a bit cold for a stroll?"

"I don't want to scare them."

"Scare who?" Who hangs out at the lighthouse, first thing in the morning, in the middle of February? Was there some kind of weird cult in Peggy's Cove?

"Meara." Evan took my gloved hand in his and pulled me along. "Come on!"

He broke into a light jog, and I struggled to keep up. What was he so eager to show me? He slowed to a creep as we neared the lighthouse—going into a crouch and placing his finger on his lips to warn me. I nodded and followed his movements. We approached a grouping of rocks, and that was when I heard it—the barks and the wails. My eyes filled; the cries were sad and beautiful all at once.

We passed the grouping and continued to draw nearer to the sound. When we'd walked a few minutes more, Evan stopped beside another rock formation.

"Do you see them?" He raised his arm in my line of vision and pointed toward the rocks about ten feet ahead. As I stared off the point of his finger, my jaw dropped. A group of seals crowded on the rocks, surrounding the largest, who was magnificent in size. Clearly the leader, his voice was the loudest. The others showed him deference and harmonized with his call.

"Why are they here?" I asked.

Evan shrugged, dropped to his knees, and sat back on his heels. Watching him, I realized this was not the first time he witnessed this scene.

"They appear every year on the same day." He didn't take his eyes off the seals. "Soon, they'll dive in the sea."

"How long have you been coming here?"

He shrugged and kept his eyes on the seals. "I was about fourteen when I first saw them. I was riding my bike past the lighthouse, delivering papers, when I heard their strange call. I sat and watched them until they left. I rode by here every morning, but it wasn't until February 9th of the following year that they returned."

"Are you sure?" My chest started to feel heavy. I wondered if Evan could sense my growing dread. Was this my family? Was David among them? Did Evan know?

226

Evan nodded. "I had that paper route until I graduated from high school this past June. Every year, they were here on February 9th."

"My birthday."

"As I got more into oceanography and began to study the habits of the local fauna, I learned how unusual this behavior is. Seals do not hold rituals on rocks for one morning, on the same day, every year."

I swallowed the lump in my throat and looked at the seals. I noticed the largest one was staring at me. Did his expression look human?

Evan touched my arm. "Meara, are you okay?"

"Sure...why?" I couldn't take my eyes off the seal.

"You seem quiet. Is something wrong?"

I shook my head. It couldn't be. He couldn't be. Was it possible?

"Meara, talk to me," Evan persisted.

I sighed. "You wouldn't understand."

"Why don't you try me?" Evan turned and put his arm around my shoulder. He lifted my chin and kissed me. His lips were cold, but his nose was colder.

I could tell him. I could trust him. He came out in the cold to show me this. I only hoped he wouldn't get upset that I didn't tell him sooner. I hung my head and whispered, so quietly he had to lean closer to hear me. "I know who I am, Evan. I know what I am."

"And," he said patiently, as if talking to a child. "What are you?"

I pointed at the group, singling out the leader. With an edge of desperation in my voice, I choked out. "Evan, that's David."

In the center of the pack, where the largest seal had been, stood my father, wearing an anxious expression. His leather jacket hung open to reveal a blue chambray shirt and blue jeans. On his feet were worn work boots. Where did he get clothes?

He nodded at Evan. Evan nodded back. I looked between Evan and David. What was going on?

"You knew?" I couldn't disguise the surprise from my voice. Evan blushed.

"I had a hunch," Evan admitted. "But I didn't have proof."

I thought back to Christmas, when I gave him the books. He'd promised to tell me what he thought when he had more information.

"When were you going to tell me?"

"Today." He looked uncomfortable. "That's why I brought you here."

I stared at him. I didn't know what to say. Then again, I hadn't been completely honest with him either. Evan cleared his throat. "Do you think David will give you answers now?"

We both looked back at the seals. They were sitting on the rock, watching us. David walked toward us. He approached with caution, as if he was afraid we might bolt. That was wise. I would flee if that were an option, if it made any difference.

"I think," I said to Evan, not taking my eyes off my father. "That we're best off asking David."

Once David reached us, he pulled me into a bear hug. His jacket was soft, and his shirt damp. His skin was sweetly scented with brine. I breathed deeply and felt the sudden urge to dive into the ocean. But that was crazy. It had to be freezing cold. I'd probably die within minutes.

David kissed my cheek. "We just got home a few hours ago."

"Where's Mom?"

"Asleep, I imagine."

Were they staying at my grandparents' house? "I thought Mom's room was empty when I went by."

"It is." David paused. "Your mom's at our apartment in Halifax."

"Oh." I didn't know what to ask or say. I stared at my shoes, then glanced between Evan and David.

David held out his hand to Evan. "Evan."

"David." Evan shook David's hand firmly.

My father turned back to me. His eyes crinkled at the corners as his words lilted. Could he control his accent? "I suppose you want some answers?"

When I nodded, he said, "Then, you'll get them, but first, let's go warm up. I could use a mug of coffee."

I looked back at the other seals. They watched us cautiously. "What about them?"

David turned and nodded to the group. One by one, they dove into the sea. "They'll be fine. This weather doesn't bother us."

"But you just said…"

"Warming up is for your sake. You're turning blue, you know, and the coffee, well, that's a weakness of mine."

"Oh."

"Evan," David said. "Can you drop us off at the house?"

"Uh, sure." Evan sounded disappointed. I was sure he thought that David would let him listen in too. I was relieved. I was going to learn more about who, or what, I was and, as much as I loved Evan, I wasn't ready to share that.

Evan dropped us off in front of my grandparents' house. David got out and went to stand on the porch. To give us privacy, I think.

"Thank you for taking me," I said. I suddenly felt shy, like I was doing something wrong, but I wasn't, was I? Was it wrong to want to discover what I was alone?

"Will you call me later?"

"Of course," I said. At least he didn't make me promise to tell him everything. Katie would have.

"I love you." His lips lingered on mine briefly before he opened my car door, and the cold bit my skin.

"I love you, too." I closed the door but didn't look back at him. Running up the stairs, I let David into the house. I smelled the coffee brewing before I even saw the lights on in the kitchen.

"They're awake," I whispered to David. I hung my coat, and he closed the door behind us.

"It's okay," he said. "We can talk in your room."

My grandmother ran into the hallway, looking worried. "Where were you, Meara? I was so worried..." She broke off as she noticed David. She took a step back. "David! Where's Sharon? Is everything okay?"

"It's fine, Mary. Everything is fine. When I left Sharon, she was sleeping. I thought it would be nice to surprise Meara on her birthday." He smiled down at me. "I plan to take her back to the apartment to see her mother."

"But where have you been?" My grandmother glanced at me. Her voice was weak, and she looked confused.

"She's been here, of course, sleeping." David's voice deepened. I hadn't noticed its musical quality before. I blinked and shook my head.

"Oh...of course." Grandma's brow smoothed, and her eyes lit up. "What a lovely idea to surprise Sharon! And this will be the first birthday Meara spends with both parents. How wonderful!"

She clapped her hands together and ushered us into the kitchen. "Come have some hot chocolate and coffee before you head out."

I followed my grandmother into the kitchen, but the last thing I wanted was to sit and visit. I wanted answers, and I wanted them before David changed his mind.

I looked back at David. "We won't stay long," he mouthed. "Don't worry."

I was surprised that the table was empty. "Where's Grandpa?"

Grandma made a noise. "Oh, he's not feeling well this morning. Poor dear. I think he's got a touch of the flu."

"I hope he feels better," I said lamely, not knowing what else to say.

My grandmother patted my hand as she set my hot chocolate in front of me. "That's sweet of you to say. I'm sure rest is all he needs."

The chocolate burned my tongue, but I drank it fast anyway. David smirked over his coffee mug.

Grandma Mary brought her own mug over and sat down. "How was your trip?"

"Lovely." David smiled at her. "But we're happy to be home."

"How's Sharon feeling?"

David reached across and squeezed my grandmother's hand. "Good. I think her doctors will be pleased."

"Should I grab my things then?" I didn't want to interrupt the moment they were having, but then again, I was ready to leave. Speaking of leaving, how were we going to get to Halifax? Where was David's car?

"Just a few things, Meara." David didn't take his eyes off Grandma. "We'll come back to get the rest later."

In my room, I pulled my suitcase out from under my bed. I packed about a week's worth of clothes, my makeup, and a hairbrush. On impulse, I added a few books and the picture of Mom.

"I'm ready." I crossed to the table and hugged my grandmother. "Bye Grandma."

"See you soon, dear." She smiled at me. "Happy Birthday, too."

David hugged my grandmother as well. "Give our best to Jamie, Mary."

David took my suitcase from me. "Ready, Meara?"

"As I'll ever be." I heard him chuckle as he walked toward the front door. I bundled up, while he waited. He hadn't taken his coat off. "How are we getting there?"

"My car, of course."

"But, where is it?"

He opened the front door. His car was idling in front of the house.

"How did it get here?" I asked, once we were outside. The door closed behind us.

"Your aunt dropped it off."

I squinted at the car as we approached it. "There's no one in there."

"I imagine not. Brigid is not one for socializing."

"Where'd she go?"

He set the suitcase down and opened my door for me. "Don't worry about Brigid. She takes care of herself."

I heard him open the trunk and put my suitcase in before going around to his side. He adjusted the mirrors, and then looked at me.

"Are you ready?"

My eyes widened. "For what?"

He laughed. "To go to your new home, of course."

"I thought we were going to talk," I mumbled, sliding down in my seat.

"We can talk as we drive," he said. He backed down the driveway and out onto the road. Then, he spoke again. "Tell me what you're thinking."

"You're a Selkie."

"Yes."

"What does that make me?" I asked.

"Half-Selkie?" His lips twitched, but he didn't take his eyes off the road.

"This isn't funny, David." Could he ever give me a straight answer? "I'm serious. What does this all mean?"

He sighed. "To be honest, I'm not exactly sure what it will mean to you. I can tell you what it's like to be a Selkie, but Halflings, such as yourself, well, you each experience things a bit differently."

"There are more like me?"

"Yes, although it's not as common as it used to be." He looked at me briefly before turning back to the road. "There are less of us who are pure of blood. As time goes on, many have turned against mingling with humans, attempting to preserve the purity of our species."

"What about your family?" I asked.

He looked at me pointedly. "Obviously, I am of a different opinion."

I felt my cheeks burn. "Oh, yeah."

"When I met your mother, it didn't matter to me that she wasn't Selkie. I only knew that I loved her. That was all that mattered then, and it's all that matters now."

I knew how much David loved my mom. I didn't doubt his sincerity at all. I thought about the seals that surrounded him this morning. "Who were the other seals? Were my aunts there?"

"Your aunts were there, and some others from our clan."

"Clan?" Like a tribe? Was that how Selkies lived?

"Yes. Our family."

It was like pulling teeth to get him to talk, even when he was willing to give me answers. "Why'd you come here?"

"For you and your mom, of course."

"So, I'm a Selkie?" I just wanted to hear him say it.

"You're not a Selkie yet," David said. "You haven't Changed."

There it was again. The big C word.

"How does that happen?" I asked.

He answered my question with one of his own. "Have you felt the pull of the sea?"

I thought about the voices calling to me, the swell of the waves, and the salty deliciousness. Just this morning, I wanted to jump in after smelling him. "Y-yes."

"If you follow it, if you jump in," he said gravely, "you will Change. You will become Selkie."

"B-but, I've been in lakes before, and nothing has ever happened."

"A lake is not the sea, Meara. Freshwater does not affect us."

"If I change, will I be able to be human again?" I thought of all the times that I almost gave into the temptation to jump in.

"You may take human form," David said, and I felt myself relax before he added, "But you'll never be human again, unless you destroy your seal skin."

"What?"

"If you're Selkie, Meara, the rules apply to you. If Selkies live amongst humans for more than one year, we lose our ways, our power."

"So I can live with humans for a few months at a time?" I knew my voice sounded whiny, but I didn't care.

"Of course," he conceded. "For short periods of time."

"You mentioned there was good news?" I crossed my arms and slumped against the seat again.

David laughed. He seemed relieved to get the worst of it out in the open. "I did, indeed." He looked at me speculatively. "Although this is the part where I can't say how you will be affected."

"So the bad definitely applies to me, but the good you're not sure," I muttered. "Figures."

"Oh, plenty of the good applies to you. You'll be able to swim fast. You'll never worry about drowning or freezing in the ocean."

"So, you're telling me I can compete in the Olympics?" I tried to make a joke of it, but David just frowned at me. "I'm kidding, of course."

He didn't say anything. I thought that maybe I confused him. When I realized he wasn't going to say anything until I did, I asked, "Is that it? Super-swimming power?"

"Of course not." Now he sounded impatient. "Selkies are known for the power of seduction. Almost all of us can influence human emotion. Some can control the weather, others can heal the sick or wounded..."

"Is that what you're doing?" I interrupted. I thought of Mom and how much better she seemed lately. Was David healing her?

"No, Meara," David said, his voice soft. "I know what you're thinking. I can heal a wound, not a plague like cancer."

"Oh," I said. We lapsed into silence. David's eyes remained on the road. I thought about how Mom acted when David was around. She had more energy, her movements fluid and not stiff. "You're taking away her pain."

"Some of it," David admitted. "I can't erase it, but I can transfer it. Take it on as my own. If I could cure her, I would. Since I can't...well, I can at least make her comfortable."

"Thank you." I reached across and covered his hand with my own. For the first time, I was grateful that David was in our lives.

Chapter 32

"David, is that you?" Mom came from the back of the house, a slight frown on her face. "Where were you? You know we're having everyone over tonight for..." She broke off, and her eyes widened in surprise. "Meara! You're here."

"David came and got me." My mom exchanged a look with my father. Did she know already? Did she know what David was? What I was? Before I could read her expression, she pulled me into her arms.

"Happy Birthday, honey." She kissed my cheek. She smelled like garlic and onions.

Wrinkling my nose, I waved my hand in front of my face. "Mom, what did you eat for breakfast?"

"Breakfast? I..." She looked confused for a moment, and then she laughed. "I'm making your birthday dinner. You okay with lasagna?"

"One of my favorites." My mom made the best pasta sauce. Kim always tried to swindle an invitation for dinner on Italian night. Thinking of her brought a slight pain to my chest. I missed her. I wanted to call and tell her everything, but I couldn't. This kind of news had to be shared in person. When she texted to wish me happy birthday, I just thanked her in reply.

"I've invited your grandparents and the Mitchells over for dinner." Mom smiled at me. Was I imagining things, or did it look fake? "Do you want to help me get things ready?"

I didn't. If I helped her, I'd have no choice but to confront her. How much did she know? I wasn't sure I wanted to find out.

"I'll go pick up the cake." David gave my mom a kiss on the cheek and whispered something in her ear. He kissed my forehead on his way out.

"Be kind," he whispered, so only I could hear him. I raised my eyebrow in reply. What did that even mean? When he realized I wasn't going to say anything, he patted my shoulder and stepped past me, calling back to both of us, "I'll be back in about an hour."

Mom wiped her hands on the towel, which was tucked into the waistband of her jeans. "Are you hungry?"

"Not really," I said.

"Okay." She stepped back and turned toward the kitchen. "Well, let's go grab a drink in the kitchen, and we'll talk."

I barely noticed my surroundings as I followed my mom. While she poured herself some coffee, I pulled out the chair closest to me and sat down. She set her mug on the table across from me, then turned back to the fridge and pulled out a Diet Coke. She slid the can across the table and then sat down.

"David told you?" Her voice was so quiet that I barely heard what she said. So there would be no pretenses here.

"You knew?" I blinked several times. Then, the dam broke, and I was bawling. Mom pushed the napkin holder closer, and I took a handful. "Why, Mom? Why?" My voice broke on a sob. I stared at the table, not trusting myself to look at her. The hurt was too great.

"I was young, Meara, and I was scared," she said. "I know that sounds like a pretty lame excuse, but it's true."

She stood and walked across the kitchen. Like our house in Wisconsin, this one had a window over the sink. She placed her hands on the edge of the basin and stared out, her back to me. She often took the same pose at our old house when she was thinking.

"I didn't know what David was when I fell in love with him. He told me he was in town dealing antiques. He said he wouldn't stay, but I assumed for normal reasons. He lived in another country or he was just here on business...I didn't know that he literally, physically, could not stay with me because of what he was."

A pain stabbed my chest. "What do you know about Selkies?"

She flinched when I said the word. "I know some." I stared at her back, willing her to look at me so I could see what she was feeling. "I know about the 'living as human' limitations. David told you this morning, right?"

Ignoring her question, I asked, "When did he tell you what he was?"

She turned then, her face wet with tears. "When I told him I was pregnant with you. He told me he couldn't stay, wouldn't stay, because he was Selkie. We fought for weeks. I was scared, carrying a baby that was only half human. I had no one to talk to."

"What about Lydia? Or Grandma?"

She laughed, but the sound was bitter. "Do you think they would have believed me? That anyone would have believed me? Selkies were myths concocted by sailors and their wives, an excuse for a liaison. They weren't real."

"But obviously they are," I insisted. "If you told someone, would David have supported you? Shown them who he was?"

She looked at me thoughtfully, a small frown on her face. "No, I don't think so. Not out of cruelness, but his first instinct would be to protect his kind. Imagine what would happen to Selkies if the world learned they were real. They would be hunted, gathered, and studied. Their lives would be ruined."

"There are Selkies everywhere?"

"I don't know, Meara." She sounded tired. "But I would guess wherever you find seals, you'll find Selkies."

"Why did you leave with me? Why didn't you stay with your parents?" I wasn't sure what hurt more, that Mom knew what I was, had known what I was my whole life, or that she purposely took me away from the only other family that we had.

She came back to the table and sat, taking my hands between hers and pleading with her eyes. "When David left, I didn't know what to do. I didn't know if he'd come back for you. Would he steal you in the night and take you away? The only thing I could think to do was move inland, somewhere that Selkies could not find you. I was so lonely, Meara, and confused. I had no money, no one to confide in. Nothing."

"Then how did you get the money to move?" As I asked the question, I realized I knew the answer—Phil Dunlop, my mom's first husband.

"Phil came along when you were a few months old. He was overseeing the restoration of the lighthouse. He asked me out, and I accepted. Before the project was done, we were engaged. And when he left, we went with him."

"Did you marry Phil to get away from David?" I wiped away the last of my tears. My eyes felt puffy and dry. Who was this stranger sitting in front of me?

Mom cringed. "It sounds cold and calculating when you say it."

"Mom!" I said, exasperated. "It was. It was cold and calculating. You didn't love him. He was your ticket out of here."

"I did it for you."

"Whatever you need to think to feel better about it," I mumbled under my breath. If she heard me, she chose to ignore it. "Why didn't you tell me about David? I asked you about him so many times when I was little."

She sighed. "I didn't know what to tell you, so I didn't say anything. I didn't think it would be an issue. I didn't think we'd ever come back here."

"You didn't think..." I repeated her phrase. "And what, you didn't think I'd ever want to take a trip to the ocean? Ever hear of Spring Break, Mom? What did you think would happen when I dived in?"

"I..." Her voice trailed off. She watched me warily.

How could a mother keep so much from her child?

"When you decided we were coming back, why didn't you tell me then?" I thought about our first few months here and added, "Or, when I told you that I dreamed of David?"

"I don't know, Meara! I don't know!" Mom raked her fingers through her hair. Her arm trembled. "I screwed up. I was trying to protect you, and instead I hurt you. I'm so sorry, baby, so sorry."

"I need to get some air." I stood. "I'm going for a walk."

Mom's eyes pleaded with me, but all she said was, "Be careful."

"I always am."

David didn't live far from the clinic, and without thinking, I found myself standing on the cliff that Ula first showed me. Was there anyone that hadn't deceived me? Lied to me?

The cold bit my nose and made my eyes water. The sun, high in the sky, did little to warm the brittle February air.

"So you know." A cold voice came from behind. I turned to face my aunt, Brigid. She studied me with sharp, clear eyes. "Humans are spiteful creatures. They destroy more than they create. That is why I do not associate with them."

She didn't move closer, but continued to assess me. I felt like a bug under a microscope.

"I'm human," I said, when it was clear she was waiting for me to say something.

"You are not." Her voice was clipped. "You are...more."

"Why were you and David fighting this morning?"

She raised her eyebrow, a look of surprise on her face. "He told you?"

"No."

"Then how did you know?"

"I saw it in my dreams," I said. "And you didn't answer my question."

She cocked her head to the side and stared at me. I felt exposed, as if she was peering into my soul.

"You are stronger than I thought." She ignored my question again. She looked like she was about to walk toward me, but her eyes flicked to something over my right shoulder.

"I must go," she muttered before her strange, violet eyes locked on mine. "I will see you again, niece." Her image wavered and, seconds later, a seal sat before me. It turned and dived into the sea.

"Are you okay?" It was David. How did he find me? I turned to look at him, but he was glaring at the point where my aunt disappeared. "Brigid was not supposed to be here."

"Why not?"

"Do not trust your aunt," David said.

"What do you mean?" She wasn't friendly like Ula, but she didn't scare me either.

David pulled me into his arms, resting his chin on my head. My arms hung at my side. I didn't move from his embrace, but I didn't hug him either.

"I fear she does not currently have your best interests at heart," he said after a moment.

Who does? I thought.

Chapter 33

"Is it weird?" Katie asked.

"What?" We were on our way to study hall, weaving through the students around us. Besides lunch, it was the only time we saw each other this semester.

"Living with your parents?"

"It's okay." I shrugged. "I mean, David was practically at my grandparents' house all the time anyway before they got married."

"And your mom's okay?"

"She seems better," I said. "She'll find out more next week."

I was glad that I didn't tell Katie what I was. I hadn't even told Evan much more, but he wasn't pressuring me. After my birthday dinner, once my grandparents left, I asked my mom if they knew. Mom assured me they didn't.

"Do you want to go out Friday night?" Katie asked. "I know you usually hang out with Evan, but I'm planning a girls' night. There's a new dance club in Halifax, and I've been dying to check it out."

"What club?" I didn't know any of the dance clubs, but it felt like an acceptable question to ask.

"Mirage," she said. "Heard of it?"

"Yeah." I actually had overheard a couple of classmates talking about it in English last week. It opened about a month ago and was supposed to be the place to go. They played the latest music, and teens from all over Nova Scotia went there to hang out.

"I'm in." I grinned. A night out with the girls sounded exactly like what I needed.

Katie smiled back. "It's gonna be epic!"

Mom dropped me off at Katie's house. After I said goodbye to her, I swallowed the lump in my throat. There was a distance between us now, and I wasn't sure what to do about it. I hurt too much, so the best I could manage was polite indifference. She was trying, but it was going to take more than a few kind words to heal my pain.

I hitched the duffle bag strap higher on my shoulder and started up the steps. I was spending the night, and so were Jen and Valerie, or Val as she kept insisting I call her. We were meeting here, and Katie was going to drive to the club.

The last time I had a sleepover was when Kim visited. I missed her, but I also realized, sadly, that we were growing apart. I hadn't talked to her in weeks, just exchanged a few brief texts. I knew she had a new boyfriend now, but that was about it.

When I knocked, Evan answered the door. He smiled uncertainly at me. We hadn't spoken much this week. It was hard keeping so much from him, but I wasn't ready to share. It made me feel uncomfortable. I was sure he felt it, too.

"You look great," he said.

I looked down at my puffy coat, the same one I'd worn all winter. "You can tell how I look through my coat?"

"You always look great."

I laughed. "And, you're trying to butter me up."

"Is it working?" He leaned in and wiggled his eyebrows suggestively.

"No." I tried unsuccessfully to keep a straight face.

He stepped back to let me in. "They're all upstairs in Katie's room."

When I set down my bag to take off my coat, Evan eyed it with interest. "You're staying over, too?"

"Katie asked me, so yes." I frowned at him, catching the wicked gleam in his eyes. "Don't get any ideas. This is a girls' night, remember?"

He held up his hands and gave me an innocent look. "Who me? Never. I'll just be in my room all night, studying and watching reruns with my friends."

"Friends?" Who was he having over?

"Yes." He paused. "Ebb and Flow."

Hearing their names, the two dogs ran over, bodies wiggling with excitement. I crouched and scratched them each behind an ear.

"How could I forget?" Straightening, I grabbed my bag.

Evan crouched and took over petting the dogs. "Have fun!"

When I reached Katie's room, I stopped in the doorway. Jen sat at Katie's desk, painting her nails. Katie was on the bed, and Val was on the floor in front of her, wincing as Katie tugged on her hair.

"Katie!" she cried. "That hurts!"

"Sorry," Katie said. "But it hurts to be beautiful." She bit her cheek to keep from laughing.

Val sulked. "I think my hair looked fine before."

"Well, it will look better now," Katie replied.

"Hi girls," I said, entering the room and setting my bag next to the bed. I sat on the floor in front of Val. "What's the plan?"

Katie glanced at the clock. "We'll leave in about an hour. We don't want to get there too early. I heard the place doesn't get going until about ten."

"Okay," I said. "So what will we do for the next hour?"

"Hang out?" Katie suggested. She twisted the last few strands of Val's hair and pinned them. The finished style was sophisticated and sexy. Val, free of Katie's hands, rummaged in her duffle and pulled out a bottle of red liquid.

"Drink?" she asked. She opened the bottle, took a long swig, and handed it to me, smacking her lips. "Yum."

I took the bottle and sniffed at the opening. It smelled like a cherry Jolly Rancher. I wasn't big on community drinking, but we were all friends here. I took a sip, then a longer drink. "This is good," I said.

Val laughed. "Right? Like liquid candy."

"Let me try!" Jen reached for the bottle. I handed it to her and she took it awkwardly to avoid smudging her nails. Taking a small sip, she shook her head and puckered her mouth. "Ewww. I don't like that." She set the bottle on the desk and pointed to her bag across the room. "Val, be a doll and get the bottle out of my bag?"

Valerie rummaged around and pulled out a small bottle with an old-fashioned picture on the front. Jen smiled at me. "I prefer mint."

Val took her bottle back and offered it to Katie. Katie shook her head. "I'm driving," she said.

"Not even a sip?" Val asked.

"I don't want to risk it," Katie said. "I'm good. You go ahead."

Val gave me a wicked grin. "More for you and me then, Meara."

Katie stood up and closed her door. "My parents aren't home right now, but you never know," she said. "And, Evan is here."

"Would he bust you?" I asked, surprised.

"Nah," she said. She looked at me pointedly as I took another drink from the bottle. "But he wouldn't like to see his girlfriend drinking and going out without him."

"True enough," I said.

She crossed behind me to her dresser and turned on some music. The heady beat made me want to dance. "This is what they play at the club," Katie said. She started to move, and we joined her, dancing around her room. Valerie and I continued to pass the bottle between us. Jen carried her own, singing into it like a microphone between sips.

I giggled. For the first time in weeks, I felt good. I threw one arm around Katie and the other around Val. "I love you guys."

They both hugged me back, and Jen came over and wrapped her arms around all of us. "Group hug!" she cried.

Katie disentangled herself first. "Easy on the refreshments, ladies. We have a long night ahead of us."

Val waved her arm in reply, and I said, "We'll sober up on the drive over."

Only we didn't sober up on the drive over. I tripped a bit as I got out of the car, and Val banged her head. "Ow!" Rubbing her head, she frowned. I wrapped my arm around her waist, and she put hers around mine. We supported each other to the club entrance. I looked back at Katie. Her arm was around Jen's shoulders. Jen swayed and hiccupped.

"Sober my ass," Katie murmured. I didn't think she meant for any of us to hear, but I heard anyway. I didn't care. I was having fun.

Once inside, it was impossible to hear anyone without shouting. The club was dark, pulsing with colored lights and a deep bass rhythm.

Heady perfume and sweat mingled in the thick, warm air. Bodies packed the dance floor, hands up and heads bobbing to the music. Katie grabbed my arm and shouted in my ear, "Let's see if we can find a table."

We found one in the corner and threw our jackets over the chair backs, eager to dance. I bounced to the music, not caring how I looked. Val pulled my hand, and I struggled to balance.

"Let's dance!" she shouted. The three of us followed her. We broke through the crowd only to be swallowed by it. It felt as though we moved as one. I let the music take me, losing myself in the beat.

It wasn't long before a group of guys discovered us. I looked up and saw one behind each of my friends. They looked like models—perfect hair, chiseled features, and thick, dark lashes. My friends' eyes widened in awareness as they realized someone was behind them. At the same time, I felt hands light on my hips and warm breath on my neck. A deep voice rumbled near my ear, "I haven't seen you before. Do you come here often?"

Do you come here often? Wasn't that, like, the oldest pick-up line in the book? I covered my mouth with my hand to hide the giggle that I couldn't hold back. I shook my head, but didn't turn around.

"What's your name?" he persisted. His hands touched me, my skin tingling where his fingers brushed. Did I tell him the truth?

"It's Meara!" Val shouted, winking at me.

Great, thanks for the help, I thought sarcastically.

"Meara." His pronunciation of my name sounded exotic, a roll to the r. "I like that."

The voice, the touch...I shouldn't be attracted, but my body told me differently. Guilt, hot and heavy, coursed through my veins. I should have walked away, but I couldn't help myself. I turned to look at him. I was eye level with his chest, showcased in a tight, black t-shirt. It was made of a shiny, slinky material that might look feminine on some men, but not him. It clung to his muscles and his flat abs. I swallowed and looked up, up, up, into dark, slightly upturned eyes. My breath caught. He didn't look like he was from here. He didn't look like he was from anywhere I'd ever been. His spiky, blond hair bordered on white, and his skin was buttery toffee. He smiled down at me, straight teeth gleaming in the club lights.

"I'm Kieran." His voice was melodic.

"Do I know you?" I frowned. Even with his unusual looks, I swore I'd seen him before. I tried to remember, but my foggy brain refused to help.

"We haven't met." He winked. "You would have remembered."

All that and arrogance, too, I thought as Kieran's hands gripped my hips tighter. He moved with me. "You're not from here, are you, Meara?"

I shook my head, and he nodded. "I didn't think so."

"What about you?"

"No, I'm not from here." He didn't elaborate. His hands felt good on my waist. I fought the urge to run my hand down his arm, to feel the strength. He must live at the gym to have muscles like that, I thought. My cheeks burned. I shouldn't be doing this. I shouldn't be having these thoughts. Evan was my boyfriend. I loved him. Yet, even as I chanted this mantra, my eyes were glued to the man in front of me. Unlike Evan, Kieran had moves.

The song ended and another began. He dropped his hands from my side and took my hand in his. "Can I get you a drink?"

"I think I've had enough." I wasn't trying to be funny, but he laughed. He had a beautiful laugh. It fluttered inside me and shivered down my spine.

"I meant a Coke or water or..." His dark eyes held mine.

"Diet Coke is great." I turned to see if my friends wanted anything, but they were gone. I quickly glanced around the area, but I didn't see them in the crowd. "Where is everyone?"

Kieran nodded toward the back of the dance floor, and I followed his gaze. Katie, Val, and Jen were all dancing close with the other guys. They were just as built and beautiful as Kieran. I looked at him and raised my eyebrow. "Friends of yours?"

"Friends." He seemed to mull it over. "Yes, I suppose you could say that."

I tilted my head and studied him. He was so different from other guys. Was he older? He seemed like it. Maybe early twenties. Mom would be furious. Before I could think about it more, he pulled me with him to the bar. He paid for the drinks and handed one to me, tilting his glass toward mine as if to toast. With a half-smile, he put it to his lips.

I drank greedily. I hadn't realized how thirsty I was. When the glass was empty, he took it from me and placed it on the bar. He ran his finger down my forearm. I shivered, but didn't pull away. Even as my body responded to his touch, I felt another burst of guilt.

"I have a boyfriend," I blurted.

Kieran laughed his delicious laugh again. "Oh, I know."

I stepped back, an alarm sounding in my head. "What do you mean, 'you know'?"

He gestured to me. "A beautiful girl like you is never free."

I felt my face grow hot when he called me beautiful. Stay focused. I closed my eyes to clear my head. "If you know I'm not free, why are you here?"

He grinned, and his teeth gleamed in the dark. He looked dangerous. "I could ask you the same thing."

My pulse quickened. He had a point. I knew it was wrong. I knew Evan would be hurt, but I felt flushed and reckless. I needed to go before I did something I'd regret. "I need to get back to my friends."

"They are fine." Kieran's expression softened, which made him look younger. Almost boyish. He took my hand in his again. "Please, stay."

Sadness filled my heart. I tried to shake it off. I wasn't sad, was I? The music slowed, and bodies coupled together on the dance floor. Kieran lifted my hand in his. "Will you dance?"

I considered him. A dance was not cheating, right? I placed my hand in his, and he led me to the floor. He pulled me close against him. He was so tall that my head rested on his chest, just below his heart. Its steady beat matched our steps. Why did he seem so familiar? I couldn't clear my head. It was like trying to wake from a dream. I took a deep breath and sighed. He smelled like spring rain.

Kieran didn't speak. He held me tight, his arms strong and comforting. When the song ended, he stepped back and looked down at me. He frowned.

"I must go," he said. "Can I see you again?"

I shook my head. "I don't think that's such a good idea."

He looked resigned. "I thought you'd say that."

He bent his head and I watched him, transfixed. When his lips touched mine, they were warm and inviting. I didn't mean to kiss him back, but my eyes fluttered closed and I did. He tasted like spring rain, too.

When he broke the kiss and I opened my eyes, I realized that I gripped the front of his shirt in my fists. I let go and jumped back, my hand flying to my lips. What had I done?

"It was a pleasure to meet you, Meara Quinn." He backed away slowly, his eyes never leaving mine.

It took a moment for his words to sink through the layers of guilt. "How do you know my last name?" I called, but he was already swallowed up by the crowd.

"Who was that?"

I turned to see Jen staring at the spot where Kieran last stood. "He said his name was Kieran." I touched my lips again. They tingled from his kiss.

"Oh my God, Meara!" Katie shoved my shoulder. "You kissed him."

"He kissed me," I corrected, although my cheeks burned. My friends saw us? I thought they were too busy dancing with their own hotties.

"Whatever." Katie frowned at me. "You shared a kiss."

I didn't say anything. All three of them stared at me, envy and disbelief clearly written on their faces. "What?" I crossed my arms and a looked behind them. "Where are the guys you were dancing with?"

"What guys?" Val asked. Her lower lip pouted in confusion.

"Are you serious?" I asked. What kind of joke were they playing? "I saw you dancing with them. They looked like models. I asked Kieran, and he said that they were his friends." I looked from one to the other. No one seemed to know what I was talking about.

Frustrated, I pointed at Jen. "You laughed at something he said to you. He was tall, blond, and tan. How can you not remember?"

Jen shook her head and looked at me sympathetically. "How much did you have to drink, Meara? Seriously, we all went on to the dance floor, and then you were gone. We've spent the entire time looking for you."

"Is this a joke?" I looked at Katie. She pursed her lips and drew her eyebrows together. I tried again. "I've been here the whole time."

"With Kieran," Katie stated, a cold edge to her voice.

"Y...yes," I stammered. Why were they acting like this? I knew what I saw. Katie, Jen, and Val, surrounded by guys, dancing with them. I thought they even kissed them, which made me all the more irritated by Katie's response. I mean, she was with Brian. It wasn't not like she didn't just cheat, too.

Katie shook her head at me. Jen and Val looked worried. Why didn't they remember anything? Unless...damn it! Unless Kieran and his friends were Selkies. His exotic looks, those dark, hypnotizing eyes—it was the only explanation that made sense. Had he used his powers on me? I remembered him perfectly; I wouldn't have trouble describing him. But did he influence me? Was that why I kissed him?

"You have to tell Evan," Katie said. She sounded angry, bordering on furious. "If you don't, I will."

"I was planning to." As guilty as I felt, I wouldn't be able to keep it a secret anyway.

"Tonight," she insisted.

"Back off, Katie," I snapped. "It's not your concern."

"He's my brother, Meara," she snapped back. "So I would argue that it is."

"Girls, let's not fight." Jen couldn't stand fighting. She was always trying to calm Katie down. It was a thankless job. At any rate, it was too late. I glared at Katie, frustrated that my friends couldn't remember, and bewildered by what happened. Katie scowled at me, her arms crossed in front of her.

"Let's get out of here," she said finally, spinning on her heel and stalking to the exit. She shouted above the music. "Going out tonight was a horrible idea."

I sighed and hurried to follow them, my mind elsewhere. How I was going to explain what happened to Evan? No matter what angle I took, I kissed another guy. The worst part, and the part I wouldn't tell him, was that I liked it. Even now, I felt a thrill as I thought about being in Kieran's arms.

Katie threw open the club door, and cold air blasted me in the face. My head cleared, and I remembered. I remembered Ula fighting with Kieran at the hockey game. I remembered Kieran standing on campus when I went to visit Evan. I didn't know it then, but in my memory, I saw his white hair, his unusual coloring. He was Selkie. I felt certain, and Ula knew him. I wished I could go home instead of Katie's house. I wanted to contact Ula. I wanted answers.

I couldn't believe that I didn't see it. I didn't even consider it. I knew other Selkies existed. Ula and David told me as much. I could blame my slowness on the alcohol, but by the time we left the club, I was sober. I didn't recognize what he was, and I couldn't think of anything that would have made me aware that he was Selkie. That, more than anything, worried me.

How many more Selkies would I meet? How could I better prepare myself for the next one?

Chapter 34

The car ride back to Katie's was icy torture. I felt like I already paid for my sins by the time we arrived at her house. She ignored me, the whole time, and she wouldn't let anyone else talk to me either. She pulled into the garage and shut off the engine.

"Jen, Val, let's go upstairs." She gave me a pointed look that clearly said, "You're not welcome." Jen and Val both glanced at me, but followed Katie into the house without a word. I sat alone in the back of the car. My stomach clenched as I thought about telling Evan, seeing the hurt expression on his face. Much as I'd like to, I couldn't sit in the car all night. The garage was bound to get cold.

With a sigh, I got out and trudged into the house and up the stairs. I glanced down the hall to Katie's room. My bag was lying on its side against the wall. I rolled my eyes. No one went to major B-mode quicker than Katie did. Kim would never react like this.

I knocked on Evan's door as quietly as possible in case he was asleep. When he opened it, my heart thumped painfully in my chest. He looked so cute in his faded Save the Whales t-shirt and black track pants, a dimple showing when he grinned at me.

"Change your mind about a sleepover?" He leaned against the doorframe.

I didn't return his smile. "I need to talk to you."

He frowned a bit, but he stepped back and gestured into his room. "Okay," he said. "Come in."

Ebb and Flow were on the bed, happy smiles on their faces, stubby tails wagging like mad. I gave them each a quick ear scratch before I crossed the room to sit on the desk chair.

Evan sat on the edge of the bed closest to me and rested his hands on his knees. He waited, but I couldn't loosen my tongue to say anything. As the silence grew, he looked concerned. "Meara, what is it?"

"I..." I started to tell him, but I choked on tears. I focused the shelf above his desk. The one that held his hockey trophies. I blinked to clear my vision. I was not going to cry. I tried again. "I...met someone tonight. We danced and then..."

"Meara, don't..." Evan looked alarmed, but I couldn't stop and the words poured out.

"He kissed me," I finished, my eyes leaving the trophies to study the pattern in the throw rug by the bed. Evan was silent. I counted to pass the time. One, two, three, four...

"Someone kissed you?" I could almost taste the hurt in his words. I didn't trust myself to speak, so I nodded. More time ticked by. "How could you let that happen?"

I looked at him. His hair stood up where he raked his fingers through it. A vein pulsed in his neck. I wanted to hug him, to kiss the pain away. But how could I kiss away the pain when I was the one who put it there?

"I...I don't know," I said. "We were dancing, casually talking, and then he kissed me."

Evan ran his fingers through his hair again. "Did you kiss him back?" I winced. "I'll take that as a yes."

We warily studied each other. I wanted to sink into the floor and disappear. This was one moment when Selkie powers would be useful.

"You like him?"

"I barely know him," I said.

"You didn't say no." Evan's voice filled with accusation. I wasn't sure if he was referring to the kiss or to the question he just asked me. In either case, the same answer would apply. I didn't say no. I didn't want to. When it came to Kieran, I didn't know what was real.

"Can I tell you about it?" I asked tentatively, and he blanched.

"You want to rub it in? Isn't this enough?"

"Please, Evan," I said. "I think it would help if I explain."

"Then explain."

It was as though he slapped me. His voice was so cold. He'd never used that tone with me before. He slid back on the bed until he reached the headboard. I didn't know if he wanted to get more comfortable or if he was putting distance between us. Ebb and Flow moved close to him, and Evan rubbed their ears. When I didn't say anything, he gestured for me to begin. I cleared my throat and told him everything that happened. I ended with Katie, Val, and Jen and their strange reactions.

"They didn't remember any of it?" he asked.

"Only seeing Kieran kiss me." He flinched when I said kiss.

"And you're sure of what you saw?"

"Positive."

He shook his head. "You know how strange that sounds, Meara."

"I know," I said. "But no stranger than a human turning into a seal."

Evan's brows shot up. "You think he's Selkie, don't you?"

"It's the only thing that makes sense," I said. "If it weren't for Katie, Jen, and Val not remembering anything, I would have chalked it up to being drunk, but it's just too weird that they don't remember the guys they were...uh, dancing with." I paused and took a breath. "I know what I saw, Evan."

"Well, they were buzzed too, right?"

"Jen and Val, yes, but not Katie. She had a Coke. That's it."

Evan continued to stroke the dogs' heads. He didn't seem angry anymore, more contemplative. Finally, he looked at me. "Do you think he, this Kieran, cast some kind of spell on you?" His voice lost its edge; he sounded genuinely curious.

I moved off the chair and sat on the edge of the bed, near his feet. "I don't know, Evan, but I can't pass all the blame. Regardless of what he did or did not do, I kissed him back."

Betrayal flashed across Evan's face, but I had to be honest with him and myself. I loved Evan, but I couldn't deny that I felt something with Kieran.

"Did you give him your number?"

"Of course not." When he didn't say anything, I added, "I told him I couldn't see him again."

He nodded and looked down at Ebb, who now had his head in Evan's lap. "I think you better go now, Meara." His voice was so quiet I barely heard him, and he wouldn't look at me.

A sharp pain pierced my chest. "Are you breaking up with me?"

His head whipped up, alarm clear in his eyes. "What? No!"

"Oh." I didn't know what else to say.

"I just need some time..." His voice trailed off.

I stood and moved to sit next to Flow, running my hand down the length of his coat. He gave me a goofy doggy grin. If only all love was this unconditional. "Are we going to be okay?"

"I don't know," he said. He swallowed hard and looked away.

"Do you still love me?" My heart broke to ask it.

He reached across and took my hand. Raising it to his lips, he kissed my palm. "I don't think I could stop loving you if I tried."

His words undid the careful net I had on my emotions. My eyes welled and tears overflowed. "I'm so sorry, Evan."

He squeezed my hand before he released it. "I know."

Chapter 35

I didn't want to stay at the Mitchells', but I had nowhere else to go. It was almost two in the morning. If I called my parents, I'd have to give them an explanation, and I couldn't.

Evan suggested that I use the room at the bottom of the stairs. "It's Dad's office," he said. "There's a couch in there." He made me take the blanket lying at the end of his bed and his extra pillow. It was torture. The spicy scent of his cologne enveloped me. I wanted nothing more than to crawl back and beg for his forgiveness, but he asked for space and I would give it to him.

The leather couch was surprisingly comfortable, but I couldn't fall asleep. My mind kept playing through the night's events. I had to know more.

"Ula," I hissed in the moonlit room. "If you can hear me, I need to talk to you."

She appeared in the desk chair, wearing bell-bottom jammies. Her curly hair was tied back in a scarf. "At this hour?" she asked through a yawn.

"Oh thank God!" I let out a breath I didn't realize I was holding. "Who is Kieran?"

She guarded her expression and sat upright in the chair. "Why do you ask?"

"I met him tonight at a club. His friends seduced my friends, and...and...he kissed me." I blurted it out in a rush.

"What?" Her green eyes widened in disbelief. "You let him kiss you?"

"Did I have a choice?" I wasn't being facetious. I wondered. Was I under his control or did I have free will?

"Of course you did. Well, at least...I think so." Her words faded into mumbles, and she frowned.

"Sorry, I didn't get any of that." Her non-answer left me even more confused.

Ula studied me, twirling a copper curl around her finger. She bit her lip and mumbled a bit.

"Ula?" I was getting worried.

She tapped her chin with one finger. With her face highlighted by the moon, I noticed that she bit her nails. "You are still human..." she mused. She got off the chair and crossed to me, holding out her hand. I took it and stood.

"Are you willing to try an experiment?" she asked. I eyed her skeptically, and she added, "It won't hurt."

"Okay." I wondered what she was going to do, but I trusted her.

"Don't be afraid," she said. Before she finished speaking, the room darkened to pitch black. I gasped. Just as quickly, orbs of all shapes and sizes flared to light around me. I smelled the sea. Each globe held a tiny ocean, churning wave upon wave. Though small, their light was brilliant. When my eyes adjusted, I looked around. Ula was no longer there, but I heard her voice.

"What do you see?" she asked.

"Glowing globes. So many of them. Beyond that, nothing."

The image blinked out and once again, I was in the office. Ula held my hand, and she gave it a squeeze before giving me an apologetic smile. "You are susceptible. Until you Change, Selkie magic can influence you."

I swallowed the panic rising in my throat. "Did he use magic on me?" I thought of Kieran's warm hands, his dark eyes, and my reaction to him. Was it real?

Ula's eyes were sympathetic. "I don't know. Tell me everything that happened."

We sat on the couch, and I repeated the night's events. It was a little easier this time, though guilt cut through me when I got to the part where we kissed. When I finished, she was scowling.

"Why make your friends forget and not you? What game is he playing?" She stood and started to pace.

Watching her made me dizzy. She held herself in the same rigid manner that she had at the hockey game. I thought of her fight with Kieran before the game. Before I knew who he was. Would she tell me why they were fighting?

"You were fighting with him," I said. "That night at the stadium."

She stopped pacing and stared at me. "How do you know that?"

"I remembered," I told her.

"You weren't supposed to see him," she said.

"Why not?"

"I didn't want you to. I don't trust him."

She didn't trust Kieran. My dad warned me about Brigid. Were any Selkies trustworthy? Or safe? Was Ula? I pulled me knees up to my chest. Might as well get it all out. "I also saw him one other time," I admitted.

Now she looked alarmed. "Where?"

"On campus, when I was with Evan. He didn't approach me."

"But tonight he did." She started pacing and muttering again. Finally, she stopped and knelt in front of me, resting her hand on my knee. "I'm not trying to scare you, Meara, but I'm worried about you."

"Can I protect myself from Selkie magic?"

Ula shook her head. Her curls bounced. "I'm not sure how. Tell David. He can help you."

"Why were you fighting with Kieran?" I asked again.

Ula sat back on her heels with a sigh. Her shoulders sagged. "I was warning him to stay away from you."

"From me? Why?" I didn't even know him.

She hesitated before she said, "He wants you."

My nerves flared, and I swallowed fear. What did that mean? "He doesn't even know me."

Ula laughed. The sound was bitter. "It's doesn't matter. It's your power he wants. You are David's daughter. David is very powerful."

"How does he know I'll be powerful? And, you're one of David's sisters, aren't you powerful?"

"Not powerful enough." She turned her head away, but not before I saw the sadness in her eyes.

"Ula?" I leaned forward and touched her shoulder.

She turned back and gave me a small smile. "Kieran and I? We were once betrothed." She stood and kissed my cheek. "Talk to David. He'll know what to do."

Her eyes filling with tears, Ula disappeared.

David picked me up from the Mitchells' house. I was happy to see him, but my automatic response was, "Where's Mom? Is she okay?"

"She's fine, just tired." David glanced over at me. "Buckle up."

His eyes were shadowed by black circles, and something glinted at his temples. I reached out and touched his hair. "Graying already?"

I meant to tease, but he looked worried. He didn't say anything and turned his attention back to the road.

"I'm sorry," I said. "I didn't realize you were so sensitive about your looks."

He smirked. "It's not that." He took a deep breath. "It's my power. It's draining."

"Why?"

"It's taking a lot, Meara."

His voice was so quiet that I leaned in closer and whispered, "What is?"

"Keeping your mother comfortable." He stole a glance at me.

"She's getting worse?" I hated the whine in my voice. She looked so healthy lately.

"Every day," David said. "It's taking more of my power to keep her comfortable."

I stared at him, swallowing the lump in my throat. "What are you saying?"

His eyes filled with tears. "I'm doing the best that I can."

"I know you are." I wanted to comfort him, but I didn't know how. I'd never seen my father cry.

"It's not enough," he continued. "Soon, I won't be able to help her."

My tears fell as his words sunk in. Mom was dying. Really dying. "Does Mom know?"

"No," he said. "If I told her, she would tell me to stop. I don't want to worry her; she already worries about you."

"Can I help?" If I Changed, could I combine my powers with David's?

"There is nothing you can do. I'm sorry, Meara," he whispered. He reached for my hand and squeezed it. I squeezed back.

I cried a little, but felt helpless. I needed to ask David about Kieran, but it was hard to think about that with the knowledge that Mom was dying. I didn't want my mind taken over by a power-hungry Selkie. I cleared my throat and shifted to the side.

"Dad?" David's lip quirked at the name. He liked it when I called him Dad instead of David.

"Yes?"

"How can I protect myself against Selkies?"

David looked at me and frowned. "Why are you asking?"

"I, uh, met a Selkie at the dance club yesterday. I'm not sure if he influenced me, but I want to make sure he can't."

"Did you get his name?"

"Kieran."

David sucked in his breath before hissing. "Kieran. I should have known." He reached across the seat toward me. "Give me your bracelet."

I took it off and handed it to him. He closed it in his fist and murmured under his breath. I couldn't make out the words, but they sounded foreign. A green glow seeped from his closed fist. His hand shook when he gave me back the bracelet.

"Keep that on at all times. It will protect you."

He breathed shallow and fast. He looked pale, too. "Dad? Are you okay?"

"Just tired, Meara," he said. "I will survive."

"You shouldn't have used your power on me. You're already helping Mom."

He laughed, although it sounded more like a wheeze. "And what would she say if something happened to you because of my kind?" In a quieter voice, he added, "What would I do if something happened to you?"

My wrist felt warm where the bracelet lay. My father gave his

259

energy to protect us.

"I'd sooner die," he added after a moment, "than lose either of you."

Humbled, I could only say, "Thanks, Dad."

Chapter 36

Monday when Mom dropped me off at school, I hurried inside. Despite her assurance that we had plenty of time, I knew I only had five minutes before first period. I needed to get my book out of my locker.

When I got there, I found Katie, Val, and Jen waiting for me.

"You've got to see this," Val said, thrusting her phone in my face. I stepped back so I could actually see what she was showing me. It was a picture of Katie and Jen from the club the other night. Behind them, I recognized two of Kieran's friends.

"I don't remember taking this," Val said, frowning. "But clearly, we did dance with the guys you saw."

"And we don't remember them," Jen added. "Even after seeing the picture."

They looked scared, and I didn't know what to tell them. There was no way I was bringing up Selkies.

"Do you think they drugged us?" Katie asked.

Drugs—a plausible explanation. "I don't know," I said. "Maybe?"

"I did feel weird the next day," Jen said.

"You drank half a bottle of peppermint schnapps!" Katie said. That set them off, and they started arguing about who drank what and how much. I didn't have time for this.

"Ladies," I interrupted. "Can we discuss this at lunch? We've got about a minute before class starts, and Jen, you're standing in front of my locker."

"Oops! Sorry." Jen jumped to the side.

"We'll see you at lunch then," Katie said with a pout. "Come on, girls, let's go."

Katie caught my eye and mouthed, "Sorry" before turning back around. It wasn't much of an apology, but it was something. I regretted my impatience. I didn't mean to be abrupt with them this morning, but seriously, I didn't need to get in trouble while they bickered. Frankly, I was getting tired of petty fights. There were usually at least one or two every week. I grabbed my book and headed off to class, so not looking forward to lunch.

I wanted to ask David more about Selkie powers, but he managed to evade me all week. Either Mom would be in the room, or I'd look for him once she went to bed and he'd be gone. I thought for sure that I could catch him on Saturday.

"Where's David?" I asked my mom. She was sitting on the couch with a magazine in her lap. Her coffee cup steamed beside her on the table.

"Your dad," she said, stressing the word 'dad,' "had a business trip. He'll be back tomorrow night."

She was getting tired of me calling him by his first name. I was trying to get comfortable with saying dad. Sometimes it felt okay, other times, just weird.

"Oh." I tried to cover my disappointment that I lost another opportunity to talk to him. Was he gone on Selkie business?

I flopped down next to her and asked, "What are we doing today?" It had been a while since we had hung out alone.

"Your grandparents invited us over for dinner," Mom said.

"Really?" I hadn't see Grandma and Grandpa since my birthday. After living with them for over half a year, I missed them. I missed my grandmother's cooking, too.

"We'll head over around four," Mom said. "I'm just going to do some housework and laundry in the meantime."

"Do you need help?"

"No. I'm fine, honey."

"Mom, are you sure? I can help." She looked pale. Had she started losing weight again?

She sighed. "Okay, Meara. Can you take care of the kitchen and bathroom? I'll start the laundry."

I kissed her cheek. "Sure, Mom. No problem."

It took about an hour to finish my chores. When I found my mom, she was folding towels. "Anything else?" I asked.

She shook her head. "I can finish this. Thanks for your help."

"Okay, then I'll get my homework done, I guess," I didn't want to do it, but it was better to get it out of the way.

"How's Evan doing?" Mom frowned at me. "You haven't said much about him lately."

"He's good. He's been, uh, busy. Big project," I lied. I hadn't told my parents about our fight. The truth was that I barely spoke to Evan all week. I texted him after lunch on Monday and told him that Katie thought it was drugs. I forwarded Val's picture to him, too. His replies were curt, but at least he replied. I was trying to give him space, but I was getting worried.

I hugged Mom before I went to my room, pulled out my backpack, and threw it on my bed, spreading the contents. I had a paper due on Wednesday and a Calculus test on Thursday. Neither prospect interested me, but I decided to tackle the paper first. I threw on some music, fired up my laptop, and started writing.

My stomach rumbled, and I was surprised to see that it was after three. Why didn't Mom come and get me? I saved my file, pleased that I only had the summary left to write. Walking down the hall, I heard the drying running, but the rest of the house was quiet.

"Mom?" I checked her bedroom first. The light was on, but she wasn't in it. I walked through the living room and peeked in the kitchen. Nope. Empty.

The basement door was ajar. She had to be folding clothes downstairs. I called down the steps, but she didn't answer. Maybe she couldn't hear me over the tumbling of the dryer. It was kind of loud. I started down the steps. When I got halfway, I could see my mom's feet. That wasn't right. Why was she laying on the basement floor?

"Mom!" I took the rest of the steps as quick as I could. She was ghostly pale. I shook her shoulder gently, calling her name. She didn't respond. Frightened, I lifted her wrist and felt for a pulse. Thank God, it was there. Weak, but there.

I grabbed my phone out of my back pocket and called 911.

I wiped at my tears, and my hands shook. Could I move her? I didn't like that she was lying on the cold cement. The basket of folded towels sat nearby. I grabbed a few and covered her. I left her head alone. If she was injured, I didn't want to make it worse. I couldn't see blood, but she was freezing to the touch. Who knew how long she was on the basement floor before I found her?

I sat next to her and held her hand while I called my grandparents. My grandma answered, and the words tumbled out. I couldn't disguise how frantic I was.

"Do you need us to come and get you?" she asked.

I shook my head before I realized she couldn't see me. "No, I'll ride in the ambulance."

"We'll meet you at the hospital." The line disconnected. I texted Evan and asked him to tell his parents. That left my father, and I had no way to reach him. He didn't have a cell phone, and I had no idea where he went.

"Ula," I said, "if you can hear me, tell David my mom's unconscious. We're going to the hospital."

Her voice came back, clear but faint. "I'll tell him. Take care of her."

"Thank you," I whispered. I didn't know why I had a connection with Ula, and not David, but I was grateful for it.

I rocked a bit as I sat by Mom's side, listening for the siren. Please be okay. Please be okay. The chant rattled through my head. When I finally heard the siren, I raced up the stairs to let them in and lead them down to Mom. They prepped her, checked her vitals, and loaded her onto the stretcher.

I went to find her purse, then decided to grab my purse and both our coats as well. She wouldn't need hers now, but she'd need it once she was released.

I sat in the back corner of the ambulance, trying to stay out of everyone's way. Mom's breathing was shallow and irregular. Her pulse, I learned, was super low. They were worried about a concussion. From what they could tell, she fell from a standing position and hit her head on the cement. The dryer was running, so she couldn't have been there too long before I found her. Thank God I found her when I did.

When we got to the hospital, they took her back right away. I knew from the last time that I couldn't go with her. I went to Admissions in the emergency room. The woman behind the desk raised kind eyes to me. Her nametag read Nancy. I explained that my mother had just been admitted by ambulance. She asked for my mom's identification and insurance information. On the ride over, I had already found it all in Mom's purse. I gave it to Nancy. Once she had all the information she needed, I walked over to the waiting area and sunk into a chair.

Grandpa must have floored his truck, because ten minutes later, my grandparents bustled into the lobby. I stood up, and Grandma pulled me into one of her big hugs. Her shirt was slightly damp, but she was warm and soft. I hugged her back, putting my head on her shoulder. She patted my back gently, and then stepped back, holding out a package.

"I brought you something to eat," she said. "I'm sure that you are famished, and this hospital food is just horrendous."

"It's not that bad, Mary," Grandpa said. He hugged me next. Not quite as exuberant as Grandma's hug, but it was nice. "How are you holding up, kiddo?"

"I'm okay," I said. "It was just such a shock. I mean, Mom's been doing much better, but she did look pale this morning..."

I trailed off as my voice cracked. "If I hadn't been so focused on my paper, maybe I would have known something was up sooner. I just can't get over seeing my mom lying cold and pale on the basement floor."

"Shhh..." Grandma soothed. "Don't blame yourself. You did everything you could, and she's in the best of hands now." She patted my knee and nudged the container closer to me. "Eat. You'll feel better."

I opened the lid. It was chicken and dumplings, the dish she made the first night we were here. My throat constricted again. So much had changed, and yet, Mom was still sick.

"Jamie," Grandma said, "why don't you get Meara something to drink."

"I'm okay," I said.

"Nonsense!" Grandma waved her hand at me. "You can't eat

without something to wash it down with. Maybe they even have milk in that god-awful cafeteria."

"You want me to walk over to the cafeteria?" Grandpa asked. Grandma gave him a look. His shoulders slumped, but he walked off without another word.

I tried to eat slowly, but I was starving. I finished before my grandfather returned. I hated milk, but I resigned myself to drinking whatever it was he brought me. The cafeteria was on the other side of the hospital. I was touched that he went there to get me something, even if my grandmother strong-armed him into it.

She brushed a few hairs off my forehead. "Do you feel better now?"

"Yes, thank you," I said. "It was good."

She smiled at me before picking up a magazine off the side table and flipping through it. Apparently, it didn't interest her, because she snapped it closed and offered it to me.

"No thanks, Grandma." It was Reader's Digest. I hated that magazine. Why couldn't they have teen magazines in hospitals? I didn't think to bring along a book, either.

The minutes turned into hours. There was no news on Mom, and it was after nine. I knew my grandparents were tired and worried. So was I. David hadn't arrived yet either. Lydia called, but I had nothing to tell her. I promised to call when we knew something.

"Meara!" Evan crossed the lobby and pulled me into his arms. I buried my face in his neck. He wrapped his arms around my waist and held me close. "I'm so sorry," he murmured into my hair. "Did you hear anything yet?"

"No," I said. "Nothing."

"I came as soon as I could." He looked around the waiting area. "Where are your grandparents?"

"They went to get some coffee," I said. "Did you go by the apartment?"

"Yeah." Evan shook his head. "It was dark. He's not home yet. I left a note on the door to call when he got back."

"Okay," I said. "I guess that's all we can do. I don't know why he doesn't have a cell phone."

Evan was about to respond, but I grabbed his forearm and he stopped. Dr. Riley had just walked into the waiting area and was heading our way.

"Meara." Dr. Riley stopped in front of me. I was impressed that he remembered my name. He looked tired, and although he tried to smile, it came off as more of a grimace.

"How's my mom?" I asked. Dr. Riley looked at Evan, so I added, "This is my boyfriend, Evan Mitchell." When he hesitated, I said. "It's okay to talk in front of him."

"Is anyone else here with you?" Dr. Riley asked, and I felt my stomach tighten. If everything were okay, he would have said so.

"My grandparents are here," I said slowly. "They're in the cafeteria right now."

"And your father?" Dr. Riley asked.

"He's on a business trip," I said. "We haven't been able to reach him. Please, Dr. Riley, how is my mom?"

Dr. Riley sighed. "She's resting right now. I'd prefer to speak to all of you together. Would you like to go and get your grandparents, or would you like me to have them paged?"

Evan squeezed my hand. "I'll go. You can stay here."

I watched Evan walk away, and I didn't know what to do. Something was wrong. Doctors didn't wait to give you good news.

Dr. Riley cleared his throat. "I'm going to check on your mom, and I'll be back in about ten minutes."

I nodded before sinking into the chair. Where the hell was my dad? How was I going to find him? Silently, I pleaded, Please, Dad, if you can hear me, come to the hospital. Please. Hurry. If Ula hadn't reached him, I didn't think he would get my message, but I didn't know what else to do.

I swallowed the lump in my throat and stared at the poster that gave disease prevention tips. When I heard David's voice, I turned around to see him crossing the room to me.

"Meara, what's going on? Where's your mom?"

"Well," I started. That was as far as I got before the dam broke and the worry, guilt, and sadness came pouring out. I tried to continue through my tears, "S-she collapsed...and...the a-ambulance...and..."

David pulled me into his arms and patted my back. "Calm down, Meara," he crooned. "I can't understand you, honey."

I tried to stop crying, but I only cried harder. Luckily, Evan returned with my grandparents, and the three of them took turns filling David in on what happened.

As promised, Dr. Riley returned within ten minutes. "Are you Mr. Quinn?" he asked.

"Yes, but you can call me David."

"David." Dr. Riley shook my dad's hand before he motioned to all of us. "Please come to my office."

We followed him through the side doors and down the hallway. His office was bright and organized. Besides his diplomas and certifications, the walls were covered with beautiful nature scenes. A brown leather couch ran the length of one wall, and two cushioned chairs faced his desk.

"Please have a seat," he said. David took one of the chairs near the desk, and I sat next to him. Evan sat with my grandparents on the couch. Dr. Riley waited for us all to be settled before he began. "Sharon is stable, but she suffered an internal hemorrhage. We've stopped the bleeding."

"So, she's okay." Relief flooded through me, until I noticed Dr. Riley was frowning.

"She lost a lot of blood and needed a transfusion."

"Is she in pain?" My father looked ready to bolt to find her.

Dr. Riley shook his head. "We gave her a sedative. She's resting peacefully now."

David relaxed back into the chair, but Dr. Riley leaned forward. "The cancer has spread throughout her abdomen. Although we stopped the bleeding, there's a good chance it will start again. The prognosis does not look good."

"What does that mean?" I asked.

Dr. Riley looked at me. I shrank back from the concern in his eyes. I didn't want his sympathy.

"Your mother needs hospice," he said. "We can ensure that she is comfortable, and that her pain is manageable."

"Hospice care?" I asked. "I don't understand." Wasn't hospice care for the elderly and terminally ill? My grandmother sobbed behind me. Hands rested on my shoulders, and I looked up into Evan's eyes. I reached for one of his hands, and he covered mine with his.

"Can she come home?" my dad asked. His voice broke when he said home. He reached over and squeezed my other hand, but continued to look at Dr. Riley.

"We can certainly arrange for care in your home," Dr. Riley said. "It will take a few days, of course, for equipment and staffing."

Equipment? Staffing? "When will she get better?"

Dr. Riley frowned, and this time I clearly saw pity in his eyes. "She won't," he said, not unkindly. "The cancer has progressed too far. We've done all we can do. Our goal now is to make her comfortable."

No! I screamed in my head, as my dad asked, "How long does she have?"

Dr. Riley shook his head. "I can't say. It's different with each patient."

"An estimate, then," he insisted.

Dr. Riley took his glasses off and rubbed the bridge of his nose. Finally, he said, "Anywhere from two weeks to six months, I would guess."

Chapter 37

I stood inside the doorway, watching the rhythmic rising and falling of her chest. The medical equipment arrived the previous week. Next to her bed, machines beeped and whirred, their sounds foreign to me. They tracked her heartbeat and breathing. At irregular intervals, she gasped in pain and the machines spiked in response. I cringed, my nails biting into the flesh of my palms. How could I endure watching my mother, the person who gave me life, fight a losing battle to keep hers?

Her eyes moved restlessly under bruised eyelids, though she never opened them. What did she dream about? I wondered. When would she wake up? I tried not to worry that she wouldn't. Her alertness was fading away. When she was conscious, she made little sense. The painkillers had a hallucinogen effect. She saw angels in the corner of the room, David, when he wasn't there, and occasionally, she mistook me for my grandmother or Lydia.

Those lapses were scarier than watching her struggle in her sleep. She was my mother, but in those moments, she was a stranger—easily angered, confused, and demanding. The stranger surfaced more frequently during Mom's conscious hours. My hope crumbled. I knew our time together was limited to days, maybe hours, rather than months or years.

I heard a throat clear and looked up, startled. David sat against the headboard, holding Mom's hand. His eyes were filled with pain and sorrow, but he searched my face and asked, "How are you holding up, Meara?"

I shrugged, not wanting to answer. I was tired of everyone's concern for me. I wasn't the one who was dying, at least, not physically.

"Maybe I should ask you the same thing," I said. "You look like hell. You should get some sleep."

"Do I?" He looked down at Mom's fingers. "I feel like hell, too."

"Sorry," I mumbled. "That sounded kind of jerky." I wasn't trying to be mean, but he was a mess. His eyes were bloodshot, his face lined and whiskered. He must have aged five years in the last two weeks. His clothes were wrinkled, like he slept in them all week, which he just might have done.

He rubbed his eyes roughly and pinched the bridge of his nose. "Don't worry about it, Meara. It's a tense time for all of us."

I glanced down at my mom. Over the past couple of days, her skin had turned a yellowish hue, the onset of jaundice. That meant the cancer was in her liver, and it wouldn't be long now.

"She's not doing well," I observed. It wasn't a question, but David answered me anyway.

"No." He lifted her hand to his lips and kissed it. He laid it back alongside her and stood to stretch, rubbing his temples. When he bowed his head, his shoulders shook. He looked up, his eyes full of tears. "I would trade with her, Meara, if I could. If it was in my power, I would do anything to keep her alive and here with you."

In that moment, I saw the man my mother loved – kind and generous. I hugged him to comfort us both. I'm so selfish, I thought. I never considered my father's feelings. Of course, he was in pain. Of course, he would grieve Mom's loss when the time came. He loved her.

"I'm sorry," I said. "That you're in so much pain."

"Don't apologize," he said. "I love your mother more than I've ever loved another, but you love her, too." He reached out and squeezed my hand.

The tears I held back, in a useless attempt to be strong, poured out. I cried for my mom, for my dad, and for what could have been. If Mom had stayed in Peggy's Cove all those years ago, would we have become a family sooner? Could we have made it work in some strange way?

"Your mom asked me to look after you once she's gone," he said quietly. "I'd like you to come with me."

I shook my head. "I don't know. I'm not sure..."

"Remember, you are half-Selkie, so you'll have the ability to transform."

"It's not that," I said quickly, "but Evan, my grandparents…" I looked at him and sighed. My shoulders sagged. "I don't want to leave them all."

"You could appear as human for brief periods, like your aunts do." He studied me. "It's your choice, of course. I can't pretend you're a child and make decisions for you. But could you live, truly live, without ever knowing that other part of yourself?"

Could I? I would probably wonder what I missed, but life without Evan? A day here or there would not be enough. Could I just leave him, as David left my mother? Would he be willing to have me just a few days a year? Would I want him to?

David moved close to me and lifted my chin to look into my eyes. "You don't have to make your decision today, Meara. I'm not planning on leaving your mother's side until she's at peace. And…after…I will give you time."

"If I go," I considered, "can I come back? I mean, will I be able to come back to my human form, my human life, if I want to?" The question I left unasked—Will I want to?—was what worried me most.

"If you so choose, you may return to being human." Then, as though he read my mind, he answered my unasked question. "Will you want to? I can't answer that. Since you are only half-Selkie, the pull may not be as strong. What I can tell you is that it's not possible to live a dual life. At some point, you must choose—Selkie or human."

I nodded. I didn't expect it to be easy—not really. Nothing ever was. "If Mom wasn't sick, would you choose human?"

He met my eyes. "I didn't before, but this time? Yes. I already made the choice. If I hadn't, I wouldn't be living with you day in and day out like this."

Tears filled my eyes, and I blinked to clear them. I looked down at Mom; she relaxed and smiled in her sleep. "Looks like the morphine is working. Why don't you get cleaned up? I'll stay with Mom." When he hesitated, I added, "Dad, you're no good to her if you don't take care of yourself."

"Thanks, Meara." He smiled slightly when I said 'Dad'. It was amazing that such a small word pleased him so much. He kissed my forehead before heading out the door.

Once he was gone, I sat on the edge of the bed and looked around the room. The only light came from a small lamp in the corner, and the green glow of the machines. I listened to Mom's rhythmic breathing, taking her pale, bony hand in my own. The skin felt fragile, and her hand was cool. I leaned over and brushed a few strands of hair off her forehead. Her pillowcase was a cheery floral, but the bright, colorful pattern only accentuated her paleness. I shuddered and bent to kiss her paper-thin cheek.

"Mom," I whispered near her ear. "Can you hear me?" Her lips lifted in the hint of a smile. There was no other change in her expression. I felt a desperate need to talk to her, to confess my fears. I might never have another chance.

"I'm so scared, Mom. I'm so scared of losing you, but I want you to know that it's okay. When—" I broke off with a sob, blinking furiously. To calm myself, I stroked her arm and leaned in to kiss her cheek again. I wiped my tears from her cheek, sniffed, and started again. "When you're ready, when it's time, don't hold back because of me. I'm going to be okay."

I curled up next to her on the bed, propping my head on my hand so I could look down at her. I took deep, calming breaths and watched her for a while. When I felt I could go on, I continued. "I'm not sure what I'm going to do yet. Dav...uh, Dad, wants me to go with him, to become Selkie. And, well, I can't deny that part of me wants to try, you know? I mean, a magical creature? Me? It's so wild! But...then there's Evan. I know I'm only eighteen, but I think when you find the person who you're going to love forever..."

I looked down to see if she was hearing any of this. She looked the same, but I could hope. "How do I choose what life I want to live? If I go, I'll learn a lot about the other side of myself, but what will it cost me? I can't ask Evan to wait, to put his life on hold. I can't believe I'm even considering it. What about my life here?"

I brushed the back of her hand with my fingertips, resting my cheek on the top of her head. I thought I heard her sigh. "Whatever happens, I'll figure it out, Mom. You've done a great job of raising me, and I'm an adult now." I choked the last words out. "I love you, Mom. I'll never forget you, and I'm ready to let you go, if that's what you need."

Mom gasped, and her eyes flew open. She grasped my hand tightly. "Meara?"

"I'm here, Mom," I said calmly, touching her forehead. "I'm right here."

"David?" She scanned the room.

"Right here, Sharon." David stood in the doorway, his hair damp. He came to Mom's other side, taking her hand in his. How long he had been standing there? He gave no indication whether he'd been listening before Mom woke up.

His eyes met mine briefly. "Get your grandparents."

I ran to the living room and announced, "She's awake."

They rose and followed me. They spent hours every day at our apartment, staying in the living room to give us time with her, but asking to be notified when she was alert.

When we returned to the room, David sat at the headboard on Mom's right side once again. She swallowed with some difficulty and closed her eyes. I thought maybe she was going to go back to sleep, but she opened them slowly. This time, she seemed more herself, more alert. I realized that David was probably helping her fight the effects of the drugs.

"I'm glad you're all here." She spoke with calmness, turning her head to acknowledge each of us. "I love you all so much."

Her lips trembled, and tears pooled in her eyes and overflowed. David gently wiped them from her cheek, and she smiled up at him gratefully, seeming to regain her composure. "I don't have much more time. The pain is crushing and, frankly, I don't want to fight it anymore." When Grandma opened her mouth to object, Mom just shook her head to silence her.

Mom looked at me. "Thank you, Meara. Although I may not have looked like it, I heard every word you said. I have no doubt that you will choose the right path for yourself. I am so proud of you, honey. I love you."

She kissed me and stroked my hair like old times. I hugged her and rested my head on her shoulder.

"David." Her voice shook with her emotions. "You will never know what it has meant to me that you came back. I'm at peace knowing that you are now part of Meara's life. I'm so sorry for taking her away." She frowned, and David leaned down to kiss her.

"You have nothing to be sorry for," he said.

"I'm sorry," she repeated as though he hadn't spoken. "And I love you so much."

"I love you, too, Sharon."

Then Mom looked up at my grandparents, who were standing at the foot of the bed. Grandma hugged herself, her eyes bloodshot. Grandpa's arm was around her shoulder.

"Mom, Dad." She smiled up at them. "Thank you for taking us back into your lives and into your home."

"Oh, Sharon." Grandma was openly crying now. "Of course you were welcome home at any time. We love you."

"I know, Mom," she said. "Thank you, nonetheless."

Mom sat up and gestured for my grandparents to come forward. I stood and moved back so that they could get close and hug her. When they stepped away, Mom was smiling, but her face was pale. It seemed that this last round of exchanges wore her out. I watched her warily, but she just patted my hand.

"I'm just tired, Meara. I'm not going to die on you this second."

"Mom!"

She chuckled then, although it sounded a bit raspy. "Sorry, honey, but it's true." Mom's eyes settled on my grandma. "Mom, would you mind getting me some tea?"

Grandma left to fix Mom's tea. My grandfather wrung his hands. "I'll be in the living room," he said, turning quickly to leave.

Mom sighed, but her eyes lit with humor. "Emotional displays make him nervous."

David and I resumed our positions on either side of the bed. Grandma came back with the tea, and then left us alone. The three of us talked about everything and nothing as Mom drank her tea. She finished it, eventually settling back to sleep.

Once I knew she was out, her breathing deep and regular, I

looked at David. "Will she make it through the night?" I asked.

"I don't know." He frowned down at her. "She might, but I don't think she has more than a few days left. I'm having little impact on her now."

I nodded, biting my lip to keep the tears from starting again.

"That was a brave thing you did, Meara," David said.

"What?" I asked.

"Letting your mom go."

Chapter 38

What teenager ever imagines she would attend her mother's funeral? I certainly didn't. Although Mom joked that she wasn't going to die right away, she didn't make it through the night.

She woke one more time and asked for more tea, but she fell asleep before the second cup grew cold. As she slept, we listened as her breathing grew raspy and irregular. The night nurse kept an eye on her vitals and administered morphine, but otherwise sat discreetly in the corner of the room. Around two, my mom stopped breathing. Her face, relaxed in sleep, looked peaceful. I gave her one last kiss on the cheek before I collapsed on the floor.

I didn't remember much after that. I woke the next morning in my room, and the days that followed were a blur of funeral planning. My father and grandparents handled most of the details. I only spoke when someone asked me something.

Evan was by my side whenever he could slip away from school. I worried about him falling behind, but he told me not to. The awkwardness between us faded. I knew he had forgiven me, although he never said as much.

I reread the card Kim sent that arrived the day before. She apologized that she couldn't be there, but she provided just the right words of comfort. I missed her. I set the card back on my nightstand and rose to draw back the curtains. How appropriate that the sky was thick with angry clouds. A bitter wind blew, and thunder rumbled in the distance. I felt the electrical charge in the air—the barely contained fury. I wondered absently if my father was behind it—if the pending storm was a manifestation of his grief.

I dressed methodically, slipping into the black dress I bought the day before. I brushed my hair, but skipped the makeup. I would only cry it off anyway.

Evan waited in the living room. I was grateful he was here. He looked handsome in his dark suit.

"Thanks for waiting," I said. He crossed the room and held me close. I relaxed into him. He was so warm, and I was so cold.

He slid his hands down my arms as he stepped back, grasping my hands in his. "Are you all set?" I was glad he didn't say "ready". How could anyone be ready for this?

The drive to the chapel went too fast. I wanted to run, to hide, to go anywhere but inside, where I would face the inevitability of my mother in a coffin. The finality of it all.

It was a fruitless wish. Nothing changed the fact that she was gone forever.

My grandparents stood next to David in the front. Mourners continued to arrive for the visitation. I felt obligated to stand near them, although I stayed as far away from the open casket as I could. I didn't need or want the closure of seeing her lifeless body. I had all the closure I could handle for the moment.

Evan stood beside me and held my hand. The line of visitors grew—it seemed everyone one in town and the surrounding area had come—people I didn't even know and never saw before. The strong perfume of flowers cloyed the air, and it was difficult to breathe. My throat started to close, and I collapsed against Evan. He caught me, his movements so subtle that I doubt anyone else noticed. He leaned over and whispered something to my grandfather, who looked at me and nodded briskly.

Next thing I knew, Evan was leading me out of the chapel and down an empty corridor. He sat me in a chair and pushed my head toward my knees. "Breathe, Meara," he instructed firmly. "You're about to pass out."

I breathed slowly, deeply, closing my eyes and concentrating on the movement—in, out, in, out. With a barely audible sigh, I sat up. I felt a fraction better, one step back from the edge. I focused on my surroundings, the creamy brick walls, the dark blue linoleum tiles, and the long row of fluorescent lights. One flickered at the end of the hall. Evan crouched in front of me, his hand resting lightly on my knee. His eyes were shadowed in concern. I attempted a smile, but grimaced instead.

"I'm better. Thanks," I said.

Evan ignored me. "When was the last time you ate something?"

I tried to remember. Was it yesterday? The day before?

"I thought so," he said when I didn't answer. "Stay here."

He didn't have to tell me twice. I was more than happy to avoid prying eyes and stay in the hall.

"There you are!" I looked up and saw Ula hurrying toward me. I almost didn't recognize her. She swapped her vintage hippie chick for subdued black dress pants and a black, silk blouse. Her hair was a riot of curls. "I've been looking all over for you," she continued. "Thank goodness I ran into Evan."

She hugged me before sitting on the floor next to my chair. She rummaged through her worn leather backpack until she pulled out something wrapped in brown paper.

"For you," she said with a flourish. "Evan said you were hungry."

I unwrapped it and discovered in was a salt bagel, my favorite kind. It felt a little warm. I took a huge bite. It was chewy and delicious.

"Thank you," I said.

"I have water, too." She handed me a metal water bottle.

"Are you always this prepared?" I joked. "What else do you have in that magical pack?"

"You never know what you'll need." Her mouth curved up briefly before she frowned. She moved from sitting to crouching in front of me, placing her hand on my knee and searching my eyes. "How are you?"

"Better now," I said after I swallowed a bite.

"Well enough to go back out there?"

I grimaced. "I'd rather not."

She patted my knee. "I don't blame you. I've never understood human customs surrounding death. Placing the body out to be viewed. Burying the remains in the ground." She shuddered.

"What do Selkies do?" I asked with curiosity.

"We send the body out to the sea, of course," Ula said. She recited,

"From whence we are born, we return."

I wondered if that was their mantra or something. "Isn't that like a funeral?"

"It is not an event," she explained. "We do not wait for a time that is convenient for the survivors; we do not invite others. Whoever is there performs the blessing, and the sea takes the body away. It's much simpler."

I thought of the lines of people waiting to offer their condolences and the ceremony to follow, orchestrated by a minister who didn't even know my mom. "Sounds nice," I said.

Ula nodded and smiled. "You'll like being a Selkie, Meara. I promise."

"I'm not sure..." I looked down the hall, hoping that Evan would come back. I didn't want to talk about this at my mom's funeral.

"But of course, today is not the day to discuss this," she said. She stood, brushed off her pants, and offered me her hand. I took it and stood. "I'll stay by you for the service, if you like."

I squeezed her hand. "Thank you."

We walked back into the parlor. The pallbearers stood in the front of the room with the caretaker. They were preparing to close the casket. I'd been gone long enough that the ceremony was about to begin. Evan stood with his family, but when he saw me, he came over and took my other hand.

"Feeling better?" he asked. He kissed my cheek. "At least you have a little color now."

"Where's my dad?" I scanned the room, but didn't see him.

Evan gestured to the door. "He stepped out."

"Is he coming back?" I asked. Now that I understood Selkie custom, I realized how much harder this day was for him.

"I think so," Evan said. "He didn't say."

"How much time until the service?" I asked.

Evan looked at his phone. "About five minutes. Are you going to look for him?" I nodded. "Do you want me to come?"

I gave them both an apologetic smile. "I'd rather go alone."

"Hurry back," Ula said.

I found my dad around the corner, sitting in his car. His head was in his hands. He was so still that I wondered if he was asleep. I opened the passenger door and slipped in.

"Dad?" I touched his arm. "Are you coming in for the service?"

He rubbed his face before looking at me. His eyes were bloodshot. I could tell he'd been crying. He cleared his throat before he gruffly said, "I don't think so."

"I understand," I said. "Ula told me your customs."

When he gave me a sharp look, my face grew hot. I probably shouldn't have said that. I may have just gotten her in trouble.

"What customs?" he asked.

"Regarding death," I said. "Sending the body to sea."

He nodded curtly before he reached inside of his suit coat and pulled out a sealed envelope. "Your mother asked me to give this to you once the funeral was over. I imagine this is as good a time as any."

"Thanks." I took the envelope, tucking it into my purse so I could read it later in private.

"I'm going away for the night." He frowned at the sky. It was quickly changing from gray to black. "I don't trust myself right now."

Was he creating this storm? What was he going to do? "Are you going to Change?"

He looked at me a moment before answering. "Yes, but I will be back. Will you be okay for a night?"

"I'm not a child," I said, and then softer. "I'll be fine, Dad." I pointed at the blackening sky. "Are you doing this?"

He looked a bit sheepish. "I imagine so. I'm struggling for control. Spending time as my true self will help."

As he turned to leave the car, I felt the strangest impulse not to let him go. "Dad?"

"Yes?" He turned back, his eyes filled with pain.

I threw my arms around him. "I love you." It was the first time I said it, and I realized I meant it. Somehow, in the past few months, he became my father.

He hugged me tight, resting his cheek against my hair. When he pulled back, his eyes were full of tears. "Thank you, Meara. I love you, too."

I watched him walk away, and then hurried back inside. I was probably late for the service, but I didn't care. Mom was already gone, now my dad was too, if just for the evening. For the first time, I wished I could have gone with him.

Chapter 39

I managed to survive both the service and the short prayer at Mom's gravesite. I swayed a bit on my feet, feeling so tired. Most of the mourners had already left the graveyard. Evan went over to speak to his family and my grandparents. I stood next to Ula, who rubbed my back.

"Give me your bracelet," she whispered.

"Why?" I asked. I knew it protected me, and I was reluctant to take it off, although the only Selkie I saw here was her.

"Trust me, Meara." Her green eyes were solemn. I took it off and gave it to her. She closed her eyes and murmured. I couldn't catch the words, but it was lyrical like a song or poem. She handed it back. "Put it on."

When I reclasped the bracelet, I felt a surge of energy. It was like waking from a power nap without the bed head. "What did you do?" I asked.

She shrugged. "Shared a bit of my energy with you." When I stared at her in awe, she laughed and hugged me. "You looked like you needed it."

"I feel wonderful," I admitted.

"Good." Her eyes sparkled.

"Are you going to find my dad?" I asked.

She looked off in the distance. We couldn't see the ocean from where we stood, but we could hear it, smell it, and taste it. My heart raced with longing. She turned back to me suddenly.

"You feel it, don't you?" she asked. "The pull."

"Yes."

"I don't want to leave you alone . . ." She looked off again as her

283

words faded.

"You won't be," I said. "I have my grandparents and Evan." I touched her shoulder, and she turned back to me. "Go to him, Ula. He needs you. I don't want him to be alone."

She kissed my cheek. "I'll see you again soon." She started to leave, but turned back one last time. "You make him proud, you know."

"Everyone's leaving for the Inn," Evan said as he returned to my side. He watched Ula walk away. "Where's she going?"

"To be with my dad."

"As in...?" His eyebrow rose in question. I knew he was wondering if they were going to Change. When I nodded, he didn't say anything else.

"What do you want to do now?" he asked. "Do you want to meet up with everyone at the Inn?" Evan's parents were hosting a luncheon.

"Can we go back to my place?" I asked. My voice was barely a whisper. I did not want to see another sympathetic face. "I...I just want to be alone...with you."

"Sure," he said. "Whatever you want."

We walked silently to his car. He started it and put the radio on low. I stared out the window, grateful that he understood I wasn't up for talking. I watched everything and nothing pass us by as he drove. The sky wasn't clearing, but it hadn't broke. The threat of rain hung in the air. Where would my dad and Ula go? What would they do? My thoughts slowed. The warm air from the heater sapped my energy, and my eyes grew heavy.

I woke to Evan touching my knee. "We're back."

I yawned and stretched. "Sorry I'm not much company."

"Don't apologize," he said.

We got out of the car, and I let us into the house. I headed straight to my room, kicked off my heels, and pulled the pins out of my hair. I was numb, but at least here, when it was just Evan, I could breathe. He followed me back and sat on my bed, watching me but not saying anything. I sat down in his lap and wound my arms around his neck. At first, I just rested my head on his shoulder, grateful for his strength and support. After a while, I lifted my head and kissed him, lightly, but with growing need. I lifted one trembling hand and started to unbutton his shirt. He covered my hand with his and held it.

"Meara, I don't think this is a good idea."

I stood up and began to pace, my fragile nerves already stretched too far, frayed. I felt the sting of his rejection. "Why not?"

"You're not yourself for starters. For Christ's sake, you almost passed out a few hours ago. And, we're not prepared, well, I'm not prepared with, you know..." He trailed off.

"You don't have to worry about that," I said. "My mom took me to the clinic a few months ago and got me the pill."

He looked up at me, surprised. "She what?"

"She knew we were serious. I told her we hadn't done anything, but she convinced me, 'just in case'."

Evan studied me with a slight crease between his eyes. Was he weighing my mood and wondering how much I would regret after? I wished he wouldn't. I was sure of myself, sure of us. In this, I was absolutely certain. We had waited long enough. I needed sensation to fill the emptiness in my heart. I closed my eyes. I knew I would be begging, but I didn't care. I was desperate to feel again, to be human and alive.

"Please, Evan? I can't handle the numbness any longer."

With my eyes closed, I leaned against the wall and let my head fall back. I waited, silent. Eventually I sensed, rather than heard, him move toward me. He stopped in front of me. He radiated warmth, and my fingers itched to touch him. I willed myself to stand still. The move was his. He bent his head and kissed one of my closed eyes, and then the other, trailing his fingers over my tear-dampened cheeks.

"Okay." His voice was soft and firm. "Okay, Meara. If this is what you want."

I opened my eyes to ask, "Don't you?"

He laughed and pulled me into his arms. "More than you know, but I was respecting your decision to wait." He moved back slightly and looked in my eyes. "I'm not convinced that this is the best timing."

"I don't want to wait anymore," I whispered as I held his gaze. His eyes were dark with emotions that I couldn't place, as deep and fathomless as the sea. "I'm not going to regret this."

He stared at me. I must have looked convincing, because he

sighed once before he leaned down and kissed me.

The desire and need I so carefully locked away broke free and overwhelmed me. I tangled my fingers in his hair, crushed his lips to mine, and pressed my body against his. My sudden, bold moves made him shudder in response.

I stopped thinking. I stopped hurting. I could only feel. Evan consumed my senses, and I couldn't get enough of his lips, the feel of his skin, the urgent, yet gentle way his hands caressed my body. He stepped back toward the bed and fell with me in his arms. I lost track of everything that wasn't him.

Rain pelted the windows. Glad to be inside, we sat at the kitchen table eating leftover pizza. I felt a slight twinge of guilt that I hadn't gone to the luncheon. I hoped my grandparents weren't mad. That they would understand why I couldn't possibly face everyone after the funeral and try to smile. It would have been torture.

I wore a t-shirt and yoga pants. Evan put his dress pants and shirt back on. I offered him one of my dad's t-shirts, but he refused. He looked unbelievably sexy sitting there with his sleeves rolled up and his hair slightly rumpled. His bare feet were propped on the chair next to me. My heart skipped. I loved him so much. I couldn't believe I ever doubted it.

"What are you thinking about?" he asked me, a small smile playing on his lips.

I felt my face grow warm. "You."

"Good thoughts, I hope?" he teased. He twirled a strand of my hair on his finger and leaned in to kiss my nose. My eyes welled, and he noticed as he sat back.

"What's wrong?" he asked. "Are you regretting it?"

I shook my head, unable to speak. How could I have tears left to cry? I grabbed a napkin and dried my eyes before I gave him weak smile. "I love you."

He pulled me into his arms, resting his chin on my head. I listened to his heartbeat and smelled the spicy scent that was him. "I love you, too."

We sat in silence for a while. Eventually, Evan stood and threw out our plates and empty soda cans. When he was done, he pulled me up and into his arms again. "It'll work out, Meara."

"I know," I whispered. "I just wish it didn't hurt so bad."

The phone rang, and Evan looked at me. "Do you want me to answer?"

"No, I will." I grabbed the phone off the counter. "Hello?"

"Meara! Thank goodness." Grandma sounded upset. I mentally slapped myself for not calling her. "We got worried when you didn't come to the Inn."

"Sorry, Grandma." Guilt tore through me, and my full stomach protested. "I should have called you."

"Where's your father?" she asked.

"He has a migraine. He's sleeping," I lied. I didn't want her to worry or, worse, drive here. I assured her that I was okay, and that Evan and I just ate dinner. She seemed relieved and assured me that she wasn't angry. She promised to let Lydia know that Evan was okay, too.

After the call, Evan and I moved to the living room. We sat on the couch and watched TV. I didn't care what was on. It was comforting to rest my head on Evan's chest and listen to his heart. It grew dark, and the storm ceased.

"You better get going," I said. "It's getting late."

"I don't want to leave you alone tonight," he said.

"You want to stay?" I lifted my head and looked at him.

He leaned forward and kissed me. "Always."

I gave Evan a pair of my dad's sweatpants and a t-shirt. While he changed, I brushed my teeth and washed my face. He was already in bed when I returned, so I crawled in next to him.

"Goodnight," I whispered.

He leaned forward and kissed me lightly. "Goodnight, Meara."

I rolled over onto my side with my back to him. It was the only position I could fall asleep in. He pulled me back against him chest. His warmth penetrated my body and relaxed me. My eyes grew heavy and soon closed.

I woke several hours later. The house was dark. Evan's hand

rested on my stomach, and his breathing was deep and rhythmic. He was sound asleep.

I thought about the letter my dad gave me from my mom. Untucking myself from Evan's arm, I slipped out of bed. I went to the bathroom and splashed water on my face, before padding down the hall to the front entranceway where my purse hung to get the letter.

I shivered at the slight chill in the air. Wrapping the throw from the back of the sofa around me, I turned on the end table lamp. Snuggling into the corner of the couch, I opened the letter and began to read.

Dearest Meara,

As you are reading this letter, I can safely assume that I'm no longer with you. Please know that I held on as long as I could but I am, after all, only human.

You know how very proud I am of you, but I wanted to tell you one more time so that you would never forget. You have become the young woman that I always hoped you would be. You are smart, loving, and kind. I am so proud to call you my daughter.

I have talked extensively with your father. He gave you this letter, and I know he has told you that he wants to take you with him to meet the rest of your Selkie family. I think you should go.

I know, I know, it's convenient for me to say this now that I am gone, and I'd like to think that if this hadn't happened, if I was healthy and still with you, I would eventually have said the same thing. I guess we'll never know if that's true or not.

It's obvious how much you love Evan, and he loves you. I know that makes your decision harder. As your mother, I'll advise you that true love waits. As a woman who has loved, lost, and loved again, I tell you to follow your heart. Only you know if your relationship can survive this.

You are half-Selkie. It's a side of yourself that you've never known. I don't want you to live your life afraid of what might or might not have been. Learn your lesson from me. I am not proud of keeping you from your father, nor proud of the fact that I was too weak to bear losing you. In the end, fear cost me much. I now realize my mistake. In denying David you, I also denied myself.

Know that, whatever your decision, you have my support and blessing.

With all my love,
Mom

Tears blurred my vision, running down my cheeks in fine little rivers to splash on the paper. I hastily wiped my eyes and placed the letter on the table to dry. I wasn't about to ruin the last thing that my mother ever gave to me.

After folding the blanket and turning off the light, I walked down the hall and slipped back into bed. Evan stirred and rolled over, his back to me. I snuggled up behind him and wrapped my arm around him. He covered my hand with his own.

I tried to fall back asleep, but lay awake for several hours, my mind spinning. Should I move in with my grandparents and go to college? No. I loved my grandma and grandpa, but the idea of living with them without my mom there was not appealing. What about my dad and Ula? I didn't understand the Selkie world, but it would be exciting to see new lands and meet family. A large family, Ula promised. I might even feel like I belonged.

Evan's body rose and fell with each breath. He slept so peacefully. How could I leave him? If I went with my dad, would I ever see Evan again? Would he wait for me? A wave of hysteria bubbled up in my throat, and I choked on it. I buried my head in my pillow and cried myself to sleep.

Chapter 40

"Meara, are you in?"

I looked up and found Jen, Val, and Katie all staring at me, expectant looks on their faces. What did they ask me? My mind was somewhere else entirely, certainly not on the conversation in the lunchroom. "Sorry. What?"

"Cancun?" Katie waved her phone in front of me. A picture of a beach at sunset. "We've been talking about it for weeks."

"My parents said I could go as my graduation present." Val grinned at me.

"I'm in, too," Jen added.

I shook my head, knowing that they'd be disappointed. "I...uh, I can't. Sorry."

Katie leaned closer. "Why not?"

"My dad wants me to go home with him this summer. Meet the rest of the family."

Katie knew this already. In the weeks after my mom's funeral, we talked about it often. I hadn't said anything to Val or Jen. Apparently, neither did Katie.

"Where's home?" Val tilted her head to the side and wrinkled her nose. She reminded me of a curious puppy. I stifled a laugh. Val always wrinkled her nose when she was confused. "I thought you lived with him here."

"I do." How little could I tell them? The more information I gave, the more questions they'd ask. "He moved here to marry my mom, but he's from Scotland."

"Scotland!" Val rested her chin on her hands. "How exotic!"

Katie snorted. "Cancun is exotic, Val. Hot temperatures and

hotter men. What does Scotland have? Kilts?"

"Katie." Jen's warning got a reaction out of Katie. For once, she actually seemed to regret her words.

"Sorry, Meara," Katie apologized. "I'm sure Scotland is lovely."

My friends resumed their graduation trip planning, and I resumed playing with my food. I wasn't hungry these days. Maybe it was nerves. I pulled out my phone and texted Evan, "Come over tonight?"

He replied immediately. "Sure."

The weeks following the funeral, my dad wasn't much company. He looked better. The Change helped him to recover his youthful appearance, but his mood was poor. He slouched on the couch in front of the TV or slept late into the day. His five o'clock shadow was now a beard, and I needed to remind him to shower at least a couple times a week. While school kept me busy, his days were long and empty.

"Go become a seal or whatever while I'm gone. Relax, go for a swim." I told him one morning, but he said the temptation to stay that way was too great. He was waiting for me to make my decision, and he'd wait as a human. A human martyr, I thought.

"Meara?" Jen stood behind me, her eyebrow raised in question.

I realized I was in the lunchroom. I had to stop daydreaming. "Yeah?"

"Bell rang. You ready for class?" She gave me a sympathetic look and waited while I stood. Jen's dad died when she was in second grade. More than any of my friends, she understood what I was going through.

"Sorry I wasn't much company at lunch." I fell into step beside her.

"It's okay." She touched my arm. "I understand."

We walked in silence the rest of the way to class. Once we took our seats, Jen turned to me. "Are you going to go with your dad then? To Scotland?"

I'd asked myself the same question countless times, weighing the pros and cons. I thought I was undecided, but I realized I'd made up my mind. Slowly, I nodded. "I think I am."

When Evan came over that night, my dad excused himself. My heart dropped. I knew that he avoided people now, but I hoped Evan was an exception. While Dad walked down the hall toward his room, Evan stared after him.

"He's not getting better, is he?" he asked low enough that only I could hear.

"He's worse." I waited until my dad closed his bedroom door. Turning back to Evan, I forced a smile. "Are you hungry?"

"I'm okay. You?"

My stomach twisted in knots. I couldn't eat if I wanted to. "I'm fine."

He sat on the couch and patted the spot next to him. I cuddled close and rested my head on his shoulder, delaying the inevitable. Now that I'd made up my mind, I needed to tell him. He lifted my chin, and his lips met mine. We kissed, and I lost track of time. My stupid brain wouldn't leave me alone. Tell him, tell him, tell him, chanted through my head. I broke away and stood up to pace.

"What's wrong?" Evan looked worried. At least he had stopped asking me if I regretted taking our relationship to the next level. It had been over a month. I had no regrets.

I didn't want to worry him, but he needed to know what I decided. I stopped pacing and sat back down. "Evan, we need to talk."

He studied me for a moment. "You've made your decision."

I'd been weighing the pros and cons with him for weeks. He even asked Professor Nolan what he knew about Selkies. It hadn't amounted to much, certainly nothing I didn't already know. When I didn't speak, Evan prompted, "Well?"

I tugged at the hem of my shirt, delaying for a few more seconds before I met his eyes again. "I'm going with my dad."

He looked resigned, as if he was expecting it. "When?"

"After graduation."

"That day?" He looked shocked, and I couldn't blame him. It was only a month away. We were running out of time.

"Maybe that evening or the next day. I don't know." I took his hands, wanting to touch him. He gripped mine in return. Despair wound its deadly vine around my heart. "Evan, you're the only thing that makes this difficult. I can't breathe when I think of leaving you."

"But not enough that I can convince you to stay." I barely heard him, and he wouldn't meet my eyes.

"I'm sorry," I whispered. "I have to know what I am."

"I know what you are, and I love you. Isn't that enough?" He searched my face.

"I wish it was." My eyes filled with tears. Why was this so hard? Why couldn't he understand?

He let go of my hand so I could wipe my eyes. "Where will you be going?"

"A small island near Scotland, I think."

"Can I visit you?"

"I'm not sure." I wasn't clear on how often I could be around humans while I lived as a Selkie. My dad needed to explain it to me.

"Will you come back?"

I studied our hands joined together. I loved him so much, but the best thing I could do was let him go—let him meet someone else. A day here or there would not be fair to either of us.

"Meara?" His voice sounded strained.

"I'll come back." I couldn't let him go. I was too selfish. "If I can."

He brushed a strand of my hair out of my face before resting his hand on my shoulder. "Why couldn't you?"

I sniffed and thought about what he said. Why couldn't I? Dad never said I couldn't come back here. He told me I could appear as human for small amounts of time. I could come back to see Evan, at least once after the Change. Would I feel the same?

"I'll come back on my birthday." I said the words as I finalized my decision. "My dad has come here on that day for years. I'm sure I can convince him to bring me."

"Next year on your birthday." He seemed to mull it over. It wasn't much, but it was all I could promise. "It's a date," he said finally.

"A date," I repeated. We sealed our promise with a kiss.

Chapter 41

"Quinn, Meara."

I stood as my name was called, moving forward in the sea of students. I couldn't see my family, but I knew they were out there. My dad sat with my grandparents. They hadn't quite forgiven him for leaving Mom's funeral, but they weren't being rude either. At least he shaved and cleaned himself up. They would have had a conniption if they saw him a week ago. I searched the crowd and found Evan sitting with his parents. He waved.

My face grew hot as I thought of the previous day. We'd spent it together. It had been wonderful and bittersweet. It was a day I'd never forget.

Evan whistled as I crossed the stage. I accepted my diploma, shook hands with the principal, and smiled at the photographer. My moment was over, and I crossed to the other side where I could descend the steps back to my seat. That's it, I thought. One chapter closed, and another about to begin.

My grandparents and David found me after the ceremony, standing with Katie, Jen, and Val. We were thrilled, riding the high of our symbolic entry into adulthood.

Evan and his parents came up next. Evan had a camera and took several pictures of all of us, and more of just me. I smiled brilliantly. I wanted to leave him with nothing but happy images.

"Ready?" Dad placed his hand on the small of my back. For a moment, I panicked. His eyebrow shot up. "For dinner, Meara."

"Of course." I gave him a shaky smile. Maybe I was a little nervous. I hugged Evan and kissed his cheek. "See you there?"

"We'll be right behind you."

We headed into downtown Halifax. Katie and I agreed that we couldn't possibly go anywhere else but our favorite Italian restaurant. I had looked forward to this all week. Who knew when I would eat garlic bread and tiramisu again?

The Mitchells arrived when we did, and the hostess ushered us to a long table in the back. I sat next to Evan, and he held my hand under the table. This last week, we found ourselves touching as much as possible. I smiled at him to keep things light. He returned the smile, though his eyes were sad.

The atmosphere around the rest of the table, however, was one of celebration. Evan and I were not allowed to sulk. Katie chatted about her upcoming trip to Cancun and her plans for the fall. She decided to study Journalism.

"Meara, you're rather quiet," Lydia observed, turning everyone's attention to me. "What about you? What are your plans for the fall?"

"I'm going to take a little time off." I met Grandma's eye, and she gave me a shaky smile. I'd announced my plans to my grandparents the week before. They weren't happy about me leaving, but they were supportive. "I'm moving to Scotland with my dad for a while."

"Oh…" Lydia looked nervously at my father. He gave her a charming smile.

"I discussed it with Sharon naturally," he said to the table at large. "She felt it was important for Meara to meet her relatives on my side of the family."

"What's Scotland like?" Katie's blue eyes were wide and innocent. She pretended to be interested, but I knew she was just digging for information. She wasn't going to get much. Even Kim got modified information when I called her earlier this week. She was happy for me and jealous that I was going to Europe before she could. If only she knew.

"Beautiful," David said. "My family comes from the northern end of Scotland. The winters can be harsh, but the rest of the year, it is a lush green."

"Do you have a large family?" Grandma asked.

"I do." David nodded. "Two sisters and four brothers."

"Of course. Your sisters were at the wedding, but not your

brothers?" She phrased it like a question. My grandma seemed surprised to learn he had such a large family.

"My brothers were unable to travel."

"And your parents?" Grandma persisted.

"They are gone." My dad was back to his abridged answers. I knew about his mom, but not his dad. If Selkies lived so long, I wondered what happened to them.

"I'm sorry to hear that," Grandma murmured. Thankfully, the food arrived, and the topic was dropped while we were served. Smaller conversations broke out around the table, and I busied myself eating. No one would question me if I had a mouthful of food.

After dinner, Lydia and Darren invited us back to the Inn for coffee and dessert. I thought it was rude to decline, but I didn't want to go. There were only so many hours left in the day, and I wanted time alone with Evan. He squeezed my hand under the table. When I looked at him, he mouthed, "We'll get away." Then, he winked at me. I felt better. If anyone could maneuver his way out of a situation with parents and guardians, politely and without raising any questions, it was Evan.

We had the whole evening together. It wasn't like I needed to pack. My dad laughed when I asked him. "No, Meara. What are you going to do? Push your suitcase across the ocean with your nose?" More kindly, he explained that material items weren't necessary for Selkies. Whatever I needed, I would be able to get once we were on the island.

"But what if I want to bring things with me?" I thought of my mom's picture, my necklace from Evan, and my charm bracelet.

"Put together what you must have," he relented. "I will make sure it arrives safely." Yesterday, I'd gathered those few items into a small box and given it to him. Leaving most of my possessions was freeing and nerve-wracking at the same time. I was trying to wrap my mind around it. At least I could bring the things that mattered most.

We gathered in the Mitchells' living room. Lydia asked Evan to help her in the kitchen. She came out with a beautiful cake for Katie and me. Evan followed her with coffee service. I was touched that she went to the trouble of making the cake. Katie and I posed for more pictures before it was sliced and served.

I barely finished my last bite when Evan took the plate out of my hands. "If you don't mind," he said, "Meara and I are going to go out." He pulled me off the couch. My dad frowned slightly, and I wondered if he worried that I was bailing on him.

I kissed my grandparents on the cheek as I held back tears. This could be the last time I saw them. I kissed my dad's cheek as well and whispered, "We'll see you at the lighthouse later." He nodded and visibly relaxed. Taking Evan's hand and feeling like a fraud, I smiled brightly at everyone one last time. "See you later!"

Once outside, I broke apart. Tears streamed down my cheeks. Evan handed me a tissue. "I'm sorry," I said between sobs. "I've got to pull it together. This is our last night, after all."

Evan smiled sadly and touched my cheek. "All the more reason to cry, right?"

We got in his car. I wasn't sure where we were going. He'd been pretty secretive about our final evening together, but I trusted him. I sat back and looked out the window, not paying attention until we stopped.

"I used to come here a lot." Evan stared ahead. "When I wanted to think or just be alone."

"Where are we?" I asked as I opened my door. Though the ocean roared nearby, trees and tall grasses obscured the view.

He grinned at me suddenly. "Let's check it out."

He got out and pulled a couple of blankets from his car's trunk, along with a picnic basket. I stood next to the car and watched. He shut the truck and grabbed my hand with his free one.

"Evan." I eyed the basket warily. "I am so full I couldn't possibly eat anything else."

He laughed. "That's good, then. I don't have food in here."

We walked through the tall grasses to a small beach area surrounded by large rocks. The waves lapped lightly on the shore, calm tonight. The moon turned the water black and the sand silver. "It's beautiful," I said.

Evan found the perfect space to set down the basket and lay out one of the blankets. He patted a spot for me to sit, and I did. Then he opened the basket and took out a bottle of champagne. "I thought we should celebrate."

"Oh." I was surprised and touched. He handed me two glasses to hold while he opened the bottle. I laughed when the cork flew off into the grass. He poured the champagne, placed the bottle back in the basket, and then took one of the glasses from me.

He lifted his glass to mine. "Here's to new beginnings and new adventures. May you find everything you're looking for."

I lowered my glass. "That's sounds so sad," I complained. "So final."

"I'm sorry," he said. "I didn't mean for it to sound that way. I guess I don't know what to say."

"Let me try." I raised my glass. "I'll keep it short and sweet. Here's to us."

I touched my glass to his, then raised it to my lips and drank slowly. The bubbles tickled my throat. Evan slammed his, twirling the empty glass in his fingers.

"What is it?" The more he fidgeted, the more I knew he wanted to tell me something.

"What if I can see you before next February?" He watched me carefully.

I lowered my glass and held his gaze. "What do you mean?"

"Professor Nolan offered me an internship this summer."

"That's great!" I hugged him before sitting back down. "I don't know what this has to do with—"

"It's in Scotland," he interrupted. "Aberdeen."

My heart leapt. I didn't know where Aberdeen was, but Scotland wasn't that big. He'd be close—close enough that I could see him. I whooped and threw my arms around his neck. Knocking him off balance, he fell back with me lying across his chest.

"I take it you're okay with it?" He gave me a lopsided grin.

I kissed him and laughed. "I'm more than okay with it. I'll be able to see you!" I would, wouldn't I? I let the thought slide away as quickly as it came. Of course I would. We'd find a way. Dad didn't say I couldn't leave the island. I lowered my head until I was just a fraction away from his mouth.

"I don't deserve you," I whispered. "But I love you."

Our lips met. The kiss was slow and tender. I wanted to remember our last time together when I was just a girl. A human girl. He wrapped his arms around me and brought me closer. I sighed, savoring the feel of his lips on mine, his arms secure around my waist. The champagne was forgotten, left to go flat.

Much later, our skin cooled in the evening air as we lay on the blanket. Evan covered us with the other throw and pulled me close. I'll always love you, I promised him silently. In my heart, I knew it was true. No matter what happened.

He stroked his hand through my hair and down my back. Neither of us spoke. What words could we say in these few, final moments? Evan sighed and kissed my head. "I better get you to the lighthouse, Meara. Your dad's waiting."

We dressed quickly and gathered the blankets and basket. His eyes were devastatingly sad, but I held onto the hope that we'd see each other soon.

"When does your internship begin?" I asked as he started the car.

"July. I'll be there for five weeks." He smiled at me, reaching for my hand across the seat. I tried to look as optimistic, but I failed. I didn't let go of his hand.

We arrived at the lighthouse in record time. How did we get here so fast? I thought shakily. I couldn't bring myself to open the door. Evan came around the car and opened it for me. I didn't move.

"Are you okay?" He crouched down to my eye level.

"Okay? Okay?" I heard the hysteria in my voice. I didn't care. I started to breathe rapidly—quick, shallow bursts.

"Slow, Meara," Evan commanded quietly. "Take a deep breath." Just as he had at Mom's funeral, he gently pushed my head down.

I found my breath, but I couldn't swallow. How was I going to do this? What was about to happen to me? Relax, I told myself. "All right," I said to Evan. "I'm okay now."

He straightened and backed up, offering me his hand. I took it and stood. The lighthouse cast a glow on the surrounding area. I didn't see my dad. Evan held my hand and walked with me. As we approached the lighthouse, he asked, "Where's David?"

"I'm here." My dad stepped out of the shadows. One look at my face made him ask, "Are you nervous?" I swallowed hard and nodded. He looked sympathetic. "Don't be. You'll be fine. I'll take care of you."

"Will it hurt?" I asked in a small voice.

"No. It doesn't hurt at all." He looked off in the distance. "Sometimes, at least for me, it's harder to take a human form." He smiled apologetically at Evan. "Sorry, but it's true."

Evan nodded curtly. He hadn't released my hand. I turned, placing my other hand on his cheek. My father walked toward the rocks, giving us some privacy.

"See you soon?" I whispered, meeting his eyes.

"Not soon enough," he said before he bent his head and kissed me breathless. When our kiss ended, he hugged me fiercely. "I love you."

"I love you, too."

My dad cleared his throat. It was time. No amount of goodbyes would be long enough anyway. I stepped back. "I have to go."

Evan nodded, but didn't say anything. I walked to the large, flat boulder on the water's edge where my father stood. Together, we watched the waves break rhythmically against the rocks. The air, though cool, was calm.

I looked at my dad. "I just jump?"

He nodded with encouragement. "I'll be right behind you."

I didn't turn back to look at Evan, but I felt his eyes on me. For a moment, I was torn, but then I breathed deeply and closed my eyes. The sea air cleared my head. There was only one option.

I dove in.

The End

Acknowledgements

To John, Dori and Nate, I love you with all my heart. To my friends at Allwriters' Workplace and Workshop, especially Michael and the Thursday night group, your support and feedback helped make Meara's story into something better than I could imagine alone. To my wonderful publisher and fellow authors, I haven't just found a place for my book, I've found a home. Thank you for everything! And last, to my friends and family who believed in me all these years and knew it was just a matter of time until I published a book. The time is now, and I hope you enjoy the story.

About the Author

*K*elly Risser knew at a young age what she wanted to be when she grew up. Unfortunately, Fairytale Princess was not a lucrative career. Leaving the castle and wand behind, she entered the world of creative business writing where she worked in advertising, marketing, and training at various companies.

She's often found lamenting, "It's hard to write when there's so many good books to read!" So, when she's not immersed in the middle of someone else's fantasy world, she's busy creating one of her own. This world is introduced in her first novel, Never Forgotten. Never Forgotten, a YA/NA Fantasy, will be released by Clean Teen Publishing in the Summer of 2014.

Kelly lives in Wisconsin with her husband and two children. They share their home with Clyde the Whoodle and a school of fish.

CPSIA information can be obtained at www.ICGtesting.com
Printed in the USA
LVOW06s1517131115

462403LV00001B/2/P